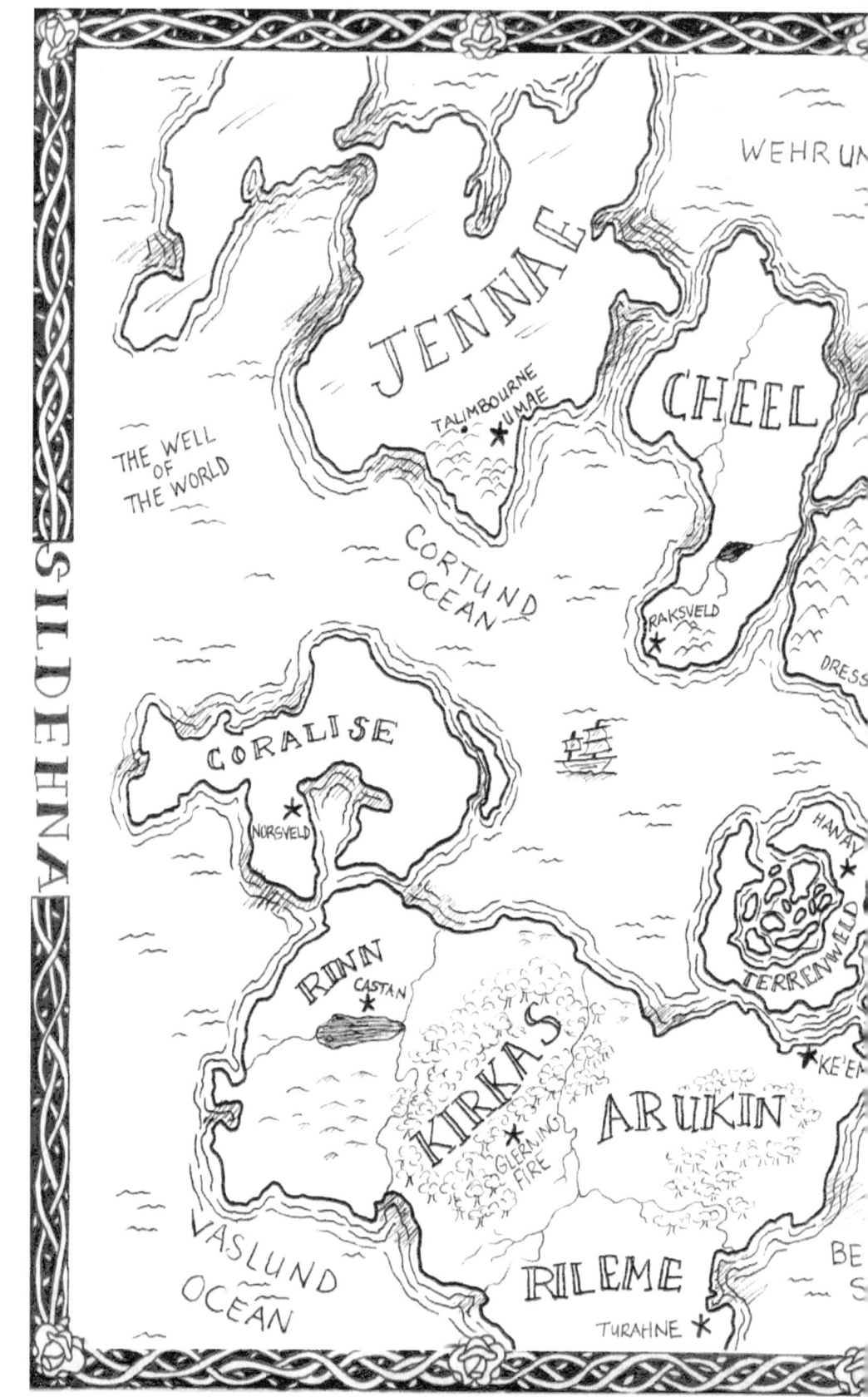

OUTCAST

KIM VANDERVORT

HADLEY
RILLE
BOOKS

ISBN-13   978-0-9892631-1-5

Edited by Terri-Lynne DeFino

Published by
Hadley Rille Books
Eric T. Reynolds, Publisher
PO Box 25466
Overland Park, KS 66225
USA
www.hadleyrillebooks.com
contact@hadleyrillebooks.com

For Brandon and Justin Gould

Acknowledgments

I am blessed with a vast and talented support network, all of whom have contributed in some way to the creation and publication of this novel.

To my readers: thank you for reading, for recommending my books to your friends, for waiting patiently for my other novels. It means everything to me that there are people out there in the world who enjoy my stories. First and foremost, I write for you.

To my publisher, Eric T. Reynolds: You were the first to believe in my work. Thank you for continuing to enthusiastically support my writing and publish my books, and for your friendship. May our partnership continue on for many years to come!

To my editor, Terri-Lynne DeFino: thank you for always challenging me to write my best. More importantly, thank you for all of your love, support and friendship over the years. You believed in me, and in this book, and I could not have published this without you.

To the professional writers and editors who have critiqued this novel over the years—Patrick Nielsen-Hayden, Teresa Nielsen-Hayden, Cory Doctorow, Steve Gould, Laura Anne Gilman, Margaret Ronald, Terri-Lynne DeFino, Eric Griffith, Julia Dvorin, Heather McDougal, Rosamund Hodge: know that every bit of your feedback has positively impacted this story. Thank you for the reads, the re-reads, and the invaluable advice!

To the other instructors and fellow students of Viable Paradise XI, my "Elevensies": to work with so many talented people at one time still stands as one of the most inspirational and motivational experiences of my life. Thank you for your criticism, your motivation, and your friendship. I love my VPeeps!

To the Second Breakfasts, Marta, Jean, Rose, Pam, Julia, Eric and Heather: thanks for devoting so much of your time and effort to making this a better novel. I hope you see a little of yourselves in these pages. I look forward to seeing ALL of your novels in print someday as well!

To the ladies of Lumosliterati, Ginger, Ginger, Mari-Lynne, Marilyn and Candy: without our writing group, I never would have finished a word of my first novel, never mind this one. I am eternally grateful for your love and support, and for always believing in me, even when I don't believe in myself.

To all of my friends and family: thank you so much for giving me time and space to write, for pushing me, for praising me, for reading my books and for forcing all of your other friends and family members to buy them, too. You hold me up when I want to quit, motivate me, and inspire me in more ways than you will ever know.

Chapter One: The Body

Skerth shouldered through the crowd to see the body. No easy feat, given the sheer number of gutterscuts and orphans who'd turned out to gawk. They packed together into such a tight circle that if they'd had a pocket to pick between them, Skerth could've eaten for a week, with none of them the wiser.

"Back off, scat!" growled a tall, lanky kid as he made to elbow Skerth in the gut.

Skerth raised his arm to block the blow and wedged himself past before the kid finished cursing. He couldn't get into a fight. Not now. Not here. He just had to see, to *know*—

A few hard shoves, another near miss—this time a cuffed ear on one side, a trip on the other—and he broke free into the center of the circle, where one glance told him what he needed to know.

He exhaled, his shoulders sagging with relief. *Not Kiri.*

The dead boy looked about his own age—fourteen or so, give or take a street year. Lice-ridden, gutter-blond hair fell lank and matted from a blue-white face. Dried blood caked the grisly gash across the boy's neck and crusted his clothes, while filmy brown eyes, the whites shot with red, stared sightlessly up at the blazing sea-summer sun.

"Get his boots!" someone shouted.

"He don't have none," the boy next to Skerth called back before kneeling to paw at the boy's pockets. "Nothin' here, either."

"Too late in the day," muttered another boy. "Scats already picked him clean."

"He's still got his clothes," offered another.

"You want 'em, take 'em," said the first boy as he rose, wiping filthy hands on the front of his breeches. "They're a ruin. Not even worth the thieving."

Skerth agreed. The shirt was frayed, blood-stained, with too many knife slashes to count, the breeches tattered and soiled beyond color.

"Who cut him, you think?" someone muttered.

"The Staves, no question. He nabbed one too many purses and they laid him out for the birds."

"Nah, the Staves take hands for thieving and give beatings for sport, or drag you off to the mines. They don't kill. Least, not like this."

"Maybe it was the Fury what got 'im," breathed another, his voice trembling with fear and awe. Even though most of the Lower City scats had never seen the giant of a man who served as Captain of the Blades, all of them knew him by reputation: fierce, merciless, brutal. Rumor told that he'd killed twenty-seven rebels during the Purge without even raising his sword; that he had stood over the body of the dead king at the center of the burning Palace until the last rebel fell; that for his loyalty, the Caretakers had appointed him Captain—

". . .was probably one of those scats down by the Wedge. The whole lot of 'em stink. And that leader of theirs is the worst. Trades the young ones straight to the slavers, he does, and takes the biggest share of anything the others bring in—"

Time to go, Skerth decided. He'd lingered too long. If they found out who he was. . . . He spared one last glance at the unfortunate boy and shoved back into the crowd, but he didn't make it past the first circle of shoulders before a hard blow to the side of the head caught him up short. Swaying, he blinked clear the sight of a tall, dark-skinned boy towering over him, ringed fingers clenched into fists at his hips, lips curled into a familiar sneer.

Fear knotted Skerth's stomach. "Malyn."

The press of street boys, scenting the first stirrings of a fight, shifted their attention from the carcass with new interest. The net of bodies surrounding Skerth and Malyn tightened, closing off any hope of escape.

Skerth swallowed hard. "Who's the kid?" He gestured toward the dead boy. "One of yours?"

Malyn shrugged. "Yeah. Once."

"This your work, then? Family spat?" He watched Malyn struggle with the truth, wanting—and not wanting—to take credit.

"No," he admitted at last. "My scats didn't do this."

"Who did?"

Malyn shrugged. "Not my fuss. What I want to know—" he stepped forward, his eyes menacing—"is why there is a sudden stink of *filth* in my quarter." He grinned, showing yellowed incisors filed to fangs.

Anticipation shuddered through the mob. *Was one dead street kid not enough?* Skerth's stomach twisted again. "I was looking for one of mine."

"Who, the silver-haired scat?" Malyn's lips tightened into a thin white line. "You better hope I don't find him."

Skerth fought the sudden urge to laugh. Kiri had made a fool out of Malyn the last time they crossed, a fact he wasn't likely to forget. The few scattered coughs and sniggers of the crowd suggested no one else had forgotten, either.

"I'll be sure to give him your best," Skerth assured him, backing toward the corpse.

Malyn brandished a fist, shoved it in front of Skerth's face. "Remember this?" he said, taunting him with the sight of a large ring capped with a smooth black stone. Skerth knew it well; he had surrendered the ring many years earlier in exchange for the privilege of running streets with Malyn's successor, Jax. Since then, the large black stone had taught him a painful lesson or two.

"Yeah, I remember."

"This is going to give you my best," Malyn said, and lunged.

Skerth dodged, stumbling as his bare heel brushed against the cold, rubbery flesh of a dead limb. His skin prickled; he fought aside a wave of nausea and ducked as his opponent swung wide. The next fist didn't miss, slamming hard into his gut. Gasping, Skerth darted out of reach and sank into a defensive crouch, dimly aware of the jeering crowd.

The combatants circled. Malyn stood at least a head taller, but what he gained in bulk was lost in strategy; brute strength and reputation won his battles, not his wits. But caught in the midst of a bloodthirsty mob of boys with only his greatest enemy and a dead street kid for company, Skerth wasn't exactly sure his own wits served as much of an advantage.

Malyn's next fist caught Skerth on the side of the head. He swore and lunged, managing to land a double punch to Malyn's stomach before dancing out of reach. Malyn hissed and shifted into a half-crouch, settling in to the fight. Skerth narrowed his focus, releasing control to instinct honed by a decade of living on the streets. Nearly tripping over the body a second time, he worked

13

Malyn farther away, closer to the crowd, but not close enough to give those nearest the fight the opportunity to help their leader along. Most knew better than to interfere in Malyn's sport, but there were always a few who couldn't leave well enough alone, who were too new or too bold to mind the tenuous order he imposed on the streets. Even here, far out of mind of the Caretakers and the Quarterstaves who carried out their masters' justice with staffs of hard wood and cold steel, there were rules.

Skerth dove forward and hooked an arm around Malyn's neck while lashing out with a swift kick. The combination would have brought a lighter opponent to the ground, but Malyn was an older veteran of the streets, tall and hard-muscled. Still, Skerth managed to knock him off-balance, making enough of an opening to bring the heel of his hand hard against his opponent's nose. The circle of boys gasped, some even voicing their admiration. Malyn staggered back, blood streaming, eyes glittering hate. Steel flashed into his palm.

"Malyn's going to kill him," someone murmured.

Fighting panic, Skerth scanned the circle for a breach, found none. Street kids packed the alley; any passerby stupid enough to try and scatter the fight couldn't get through if they wanted to. It'd been a long time since Malyn's scats had cornered one of Skerth's, and here they had the leader himself, ripe and ready for the plucking. Reluctantly, Skerth drew his dagger.

Malyn sneered, raised his knife—

"Malyn! Cut it off, you dreg-sucker!"

Skerth's heart leapt at the familiar call. Malyn turned just in time to dodge the broken brick that shattered harmlessly behind him. Skerth glanced up and caught a glimpse of silver-white hair. Then—

"Staves!" came a shout from the rear of the crowd. "Staves, Staves, Staves! Scatter!"

Skerth bolted into the crowd as a sea of bodies surged in every direction. Arms and legs kicked and clawed as he passed, all of the boys in a panic to scramble out of the closely-packed alley ahead of the Caretakers' Quarterstaves.

The shouts of men joined the cacophony of chaos. "Scatter! By word of the Caretakers! Scat!"

14

A handful of soldiers garbed in boiled leather and cerulean short cloaks burst into the alley, wielding the blade-tipped quarterstaves of their office. One grabbed at a smallish kid dashing past and threw him to the ground. Another worried the fringes of the crowd with his staff, while the largest of them, a broad-chested giant, used his quarterstaff to sweep kids out of his path like gutter rats from a stoop.

The mob broke. Some boys flew toward the Staves with a battle cry. Others fled. Enough stayed to trouble Skerth's escape, but he elbowed and kicked his way through until at last he broke into the open alley. Dodging past a Stave struggling to haul a boy up by his neck, Skerth ran like the sea winds chased him, relying upon his old knowledge of the dark corners and narrow passes of the Old Quarter to get him as far away from Malyn's territory as possible.

He raced down an alley, sprang over the crumbling stone wall that barricaded another, and dropped down into a full sprint on the other side. Only then did he risk a glance behind him. Fueled by adrenaline and the promise of sport, a scatter of pursuers still gave chase. Skerth aimed for the docks, hoping that risking unwanted attention in the more regulated parts of the city would deter his remaining followers.

Skerth blinked as he lunged from the shadowed alley into full sunlight.

"Watch it, scat!" A stocky sailor cursed colorfully as Skerth flew by, narrowly dodging the load of crates swinging past. Skerth winced at the sound of a meaty crunch, followed by a loud yelp and another bout of the sailor's curses. He slowed, wondering at the boy's fate, then changed his mind when shouts of "There he is!" and "You're dead, Scat!" overcame the wails and curses left behind on the dock. There would be no mercy from Malyn's scats.

Skerth negotiated the slippery planks and salt-pitted shipping crates with practiced ease, breathing deep the reek of fish, sweat, and rotting refuse until he reached the end of the docks, where the cobbled public thoroughfare led straight from the Fishermen's Haul to the marketplace.

The thoroughfare became more crowded the closer he drew to the more populated hub of the Lower Wedge, but most of the passersby either shifted aside as he flew past or pointedly ignored him. The sun was setting in earnest; mothers with children in tow, merchants, and those dealing in the more dubious trades rushed to finish their business before dark. None of them had a glance to spare for a few battered, filthy orphans on the chase; this wasn't their fight.

"You there! Halt!" The call came from a couple of Staves stationed, predictably, near a cart offering cinnamon and sugar puff pastries. The handful of seconds they took to shove the rest of their pastries in their mouths and toss coins to the hawker saved Skerth; he elbowed through a patch of women gathered around a fabric cart and veered well out of reach before the men had swallowed.

His pursuers weren't as lucky. One turned tail and rain, a Stave in close pursuit; then a loud crash and screaming as the other scat toppled the fabric cart.

"Got you!" bellowed a triumphant Stave.

Any other pursuers scattered; tracking Skerth wasn't worth getting caught and entering into service in the Caretakers' "charities"— more commonly known as the workhouses and the mines. He spared a moment of pity for the captured boys, then doubled his own pace.

He ran until he'd left the marketplace proper and turned into the warren of streets that characterized the Lower Wedge. Only then did he stop, sagging against a nearby wall and clutching the stitch in his side. The hunt was over, but he still had a long, uphill walk ahead. Exhaustion settled in, weighting his aching limbs, slowing his pace to a near-crawl. No doubt Malyn's scats could easily catch him now—if they dared cross over the boundary separating Malyn's run from his. He wasn't sure what they would do if they did catch him and wasn't certain he even cared. He didn't think he could run anymore if he wanted to. Instead, he kept his head down and slid from shadow to shadow.

It wasn't until he rounded the corner into a familiar alley walled by crumbling brick and patterned with wash hung out to dry that his tension eased. *Home.*

Skerth knew every loose cobblestone and soft spot in the road, even in the gathering dark. He avoided them easily, eager to reach the abandoned building he shared with the few other young tenants who had chosen to ally themselves with him. It wasn't much, but he'd be grateful enough to see it.

The skitter of a cobblestone startled Skerth to attention. He halted and pressed deeper into the shadows, dagger in hand. Waiting.

A figure vaulted over the wall and dropped into the alley ahead. Skerth tensed, grip tight on his dagger, until he glimpsed the shock of silver-blonde, short-cropped hair framing a round, pale face.

"Evenin', Skerth!" Kiri said cheerfully. "Where've you been?"

Skerth struggled between relief at seeing Kiri alive and the overwhelming desire to throttle his friend. After all he'd been through that day—the week, for that matter—Skerth's feelings were less than charitable.

"Where've *you* been? I thought for sure when I heard about the dead scat—"

Kiri snorted and waved aside his concern. "You've no faith in me. I've more important things to do than get myself gutted on Malyn's streets."

Skerth's eyes narrowed. "Like?"

Kiri grinned and tossed a burlap sack at his feet. Skerth didn't need much light to see that it was full nearly to bursting. His mouth instantly began to water. Good things often traveled in Kiri's sack. *Really* good things.

He swallowed hard, trying to keep his mind on the matter at hand.

"Three boys have turned up dead in the last seven nights, all about our age, all fair-haired—"

"What, you thought I was one of them?" Kiri laughed and pulled an eba fruit and a small loaf of bread out of the sack. She tossed the bread to Skerth. "You should know better than that."

He flushed. "As far as I know, I'm the only one knows you're a girl. Unless someone tugs down your breeches, you look just like all the rest of us."

Kiri's eyes flashed. "True enough." She bit into the eba and let the red juice drip down her chin. "Good thing I showed today, and with the Staves on my heels. Looks like you wouldn't have fared much better than that dead kid."

"I had the jump on Malyn."

"Right. I could tell."

"I didn't need your help," Skerth snapped. "And you shouldn't scuff Malyn like that. If he catches you—"

"He won't."

"Kiri—"

"He won't!"

Her denial settled between them; they both knew what Malyn would do if he ever managed to lay hands on her. Especially if he discovered it was a girl who'd gotten the best of him.

Skerth broke the silence first. "So are you going to tell me where you've been?"

"No. But I will tell you to stay clear of your warehouse for a bit. The Staves didn't take well to your little scuffle. They're raiding tonight. Caretakers' orders—or so they say."

His shoulders tensed. "What about the others?"

"I warned them off already. The smart and healthy ones have cleared out. A few others stayed on to carry out the sick."

"How'd you find out so fast?"

"I hear things now and then." She shrugged and offered him the sack. "There's much more than bread and ebas in here. You're hungry, right?"

"Fine. Keep your secrets." He snatched the sack and dumped it. As usual, her haul did not disappoint; in addition to another loaf of fresh-baked bread still warm from the oven, the sack held dried meats, several eba fruits, and even a pouch of chocolates, all of which Kiri shared. They ate until their stomachs ached, and still they did not finish everything. When they could eat no more, they sagged side-by-side against the alley wall, legs outstretched.

"So," she began, rubbing her belly with a sigh of contentment, "I've found us a new street."

Skerth studied her with a mix of dread and anticipation. Sure, there was nothing better than discovering a fresh street full of unpicked pockets and unwary merchants. But finding such streets was rare, and often involved long, risky trips into the more respectable city districts, where someone was bound to notice two kids who didn't belong. She was none too cautious, either. Still, Kiri was a master of finding good marks and knowing where to run first, before the other kids moved in, too. And the spoils were often well-worth the trouble.

"Tell me," he said at last.

"Better. I'll take you. Tomorrow." She stood, gathered the sack. "Come on, let's find a safe place to bed down for the night."

Tomorrow. Something to look forward to, for once. With the dead boys momentarily forgotten and the memory of bread and chocolate still pure on his tongue, Skerth followed her back over the wall.

Chapter Two: The Royal Thief

They left just after sunrise and kept to the rooftops, Kiri's preferred method of travel. This time she led him a long way from the Lower City, so far that he stopped paying attention to where they were headed and narrowed his focus to stepping where she stepped, gripping the spaces her fingers abandoned. He concentrated only on keeping his footing, one rooftop at a time, never thinking about all the others that lay ahead, or those that lay behind.

By the time they stopped, he was well out of the bounds of everything familiar. Even the rooftops had changed. In sharp contrast to the crumbling brick, rotted wood and old thatch that capped the buildings of his world, they stood on a blue tile roof in good repair lost in a sea of others, all in shades of cobalt, scarlet or russet, separated by patches of carefully tended gardens and the orderly red-brown and grey ribbons of cobblestone roads. The air smelled fresh, without its usual tang of human filth and rotting garbage. Below, the streets were quiet and tidy; no shouting, no brawling, no cries of "murder!" or "thief!" to break the day. Only the occasional passing cart, horse whinny, or muted conversation reached Skerth's ears.

Somehow, impossibly, they had crossed, without challenge or even a noticeable degree of difficulty, into the one sector of the city their kind dared not go: Upwedge. The Royal Quarter.

"How—" Skerth broke off, staring back the way they had come, seeing nothing but rooftops. Up here, high above the walls and guards, there was nothing to mark the boundary between his world and this. Even the Wedge—the cliff border that turned inland from the coast to knife between the Royal Quarter and the rest of the city—had lost its prominence somewhere between the brightly-colored rooftops and the dull. To the people of the Lower Wedge, the great Wedge towered high and impenetrable, a visual reminder to all below of their inconsequence. But here it was only a rock wall, not much taller or more imposing than a battlement, and as effortlessly overcome from the rooftops as a garden gate. Given how easily they had circumvented it, Skerth realized that the Wedge served as more of a visual than an actual deterrent. Then again, those toiling to keep the Royal Quarter free of undesirables probably hadn't looked to the rooftops.

Skerth faced the Royal Quarter to admire the city he had never seen. Off to his left, the city swept to the edge of the cliffs; far below, where the shipping tunnels met the sea, sails billowed in brilliant hues of scarlet, violet, gold, and blue. Farther out to sea, two more ships dotted the horizon; whether coming or going, Skerth could not tell.

To his right, the city fanned out for a good distance, to the Western Gate and beyond, to where the land divided into a scatter of ramshackle houses and neat squares of farmland. Far to the horizon, he could just make out the coastline where the Quistand Ocean met the Berune Sea. Directly ahead, butted up against the jagged range of volcanic rock that formed the southernmost tip of the world, rose the Palace--a pure white jewel in the crown that was the Royal Quarter of Endelas Ortanos, capitol city of Erados, the last great southern city before the uncharted waters of the Unknown World.

Stark white in the morning light, the marbled stone glowed. Tall, thick walls ringed the grounds. The fortress itself, built in layers over time, was not so much one significant architectural piece as a commune of buildings, some short and wide, others tall and arched; square towers slit with narrow windows loomed high above, while rounded turrets and wide windows paned with colored glass capped some of the smaller buildings. Climbing vines, fruit trees and spots of bright color hinted at lush gardens covering the grounds—a rumored paradise of climbing vines, fruit trees and lush gardens Skerth had often conjured in his mind in his rare quiet moments. The image of neat, graveled pathways lined with roses came to mind, and he wondered—fleetingly—how he could imagine such a thing he had never seen.

He realized he had been staring, slack-jawed, when Kiri grinned.

"How did you ever find your way here and back again?" he marveled.

She shrugged. "I just kept coming. I'd go a little farther out each time until I knew my way."

He studied her through narrowed eyes, wondering just how much more she knew, how far she'd traveled from the relative safety of the Lower City. Never mind Malyn—if the Caretakers learned of Kiri's unique talent for drifting unseen through the upper city, she'd have more than the wrath of a bully street boy to fear.

Kiri shifted foot to foot and met his gaze warily. "Skerth?"

He shook off his worries and looked to the street below. "Was this the street you wanted to work? I'm sure the take will be worth the risk, but I'd feel better in more of a crowd."

"No. It's close, though. Come on."

A short time later, Skerth wiped sweaty palms on his breeches and squinted into the sunlight.

"What do you think?" Kiri whispered, squatting beside him.

Skerth shook his head, speechless. Spread out on the avenue before them was nothing but opportunity. They had ventured an uncomfortable distance into the Royal Quarter, too near the Caretakers' influence for Skerth's liking, but the prize was well worth the journey. Cobbled walks and shops with glittering glass windows lined this wide, gracious avenue. Gone were the muddy, refuse-laden streets crowded with makeshift carts and peddlars, the tumbledown abandoned warehouse buildings infested with dock rats, gutterbugs, whores and orphans. Young, neatly-dressed hawkers called the attention of passersby in pleasant voices that lacked the strident desperation of their counterparts in the lower city.

Throughout the scene, brightly-colored flocks of noble men and women moved as though they had nothing of import to do; no fish to clean, mending to manage, wares to sell, or starving families to feed. Even the servants, riders, and carriages that expertly navigated the crowd moved leisurely. Here there was nothing to fear. And certainly no one seemed concerned in the least for the fates of the full pouches that swung visibly from sword-belts or ladies' wrists. Skerth didn't need to venture a step out of the alley they crouched in to recognize that this one street could provide so much coin that he wouldn't have to thieve again until Auberdale Eve. Maybe even after.

With a heavy sigh, he rose and turned away.

"What are you doing?" Kiri whispered, grabbing his arm.

"Leaving." He shrugged out of her grasp and retreated farther into the shadows, already eyeing a way back up to the rooftops.

She rose and followed. "What? Why?"

"It's too fine. The Caretakers' Blades will call us out long before we near a good mark—"

"They're *all* good marks," she pointed out.

"—and we'll spend the rest of our lives in the mines or pressed into a merchant crew. Or worse." He'd learned a long time ago that there were many ways to use an errant street orphan, or make one disappear. An image of the dead boy rose to mind, and Skerth swallowed hard before renewing his efforts at escape.

"So that's it? After coming all this way, we just . . . run away?"

Skerth tensed, but said nothing.

Kiri took a step closer and crossed her arms over her chest, her mismatched blue and brown eyes narrowed to a glare. "What, are you *afraid*?"

Hot anger coiled in his stomach and curled his hands into fists. "If I were afraid, would I have followed you Upwedge without papers or permission, knowing just crossing out of the Lower City could get us both killed?"

"Then why come all this way just to turn tail? There's a ripe street here, Skerth! A few flicks of the knife and it's all worthwhile."

"One wrong flick and we're property of the Caretakers. I'm out."

Her eyes flashed. "I thought you had more spine."

"I've spine and sense enough to keep my skin on my back, which is more than I can say for you. I thieve to survive, Kiri. Sometimes I think you do it for fun." He turned and started back down the alley, his face hot and his stomach roiling. "There's nothing here worth dying over. Besides, Auberdale Eve is less than a fortnight away. There'll be so many revelers out in the streets that every thief in the city will eat well for weeks."

"So what'll you do until then? Starve?" she called after him.

"I'll take my chances picking pirates and fishermen back in our quarter." He reached for the wall. If he stretched, he could just reach the brick that jutted out over his head—

"Skerth—"

"No!" he shouted, rounding on her. "Don't you remember the last time we picked a street like this in stark daylight?"

Kiri rolled her eyes. "But we escaped! And that old pirate witch fixed your arm like new! You don't even have a scar."

"We wasted our entire take on that witch."

Her expression darkened. "Fine." She backed away, drawing her dagger. "Do what you want."

"Kiri—" He reached to pull her back, but she had already slipped out of reach and ducked into the wake of a passing crowd. Skerth cursed her in every way he knew and took his own dagger in hand. He could leave her to her own fate, and she'd deserve it. But the truth of the matter was, even if he could haul himself back to the rooftops, he had no idea how to make his way back. He'd either have to bide his time in the alley until she returned, or take a chance and cut a few purses.

While he debated his next move, he scanned the crowd for any glimpse of Kiri, any sign that she might need his aid. Instead, a wealthy female merchant and her entourage caught his eye. He recognized the merchant immediately as Sereia Benvedora, a bit of a legend in the city, as famous for her aggressive independence as the wines she brought in from the far North. True to rumor, she was a peculiar mix of masculine and feminine. She wore dark velvet breeches and a fine scarlet vest embroidered in gold that looked well against her copper skin and dark eyes. Her curly black hair fell unbound to her waist. An elegant sword hung at her hip, and Skerth counted no less than three visible daggers at her back, hip and boot. Rings glittered on every finger, and she walked with an aggressive confidence that impressed both men and women alike.

At first sight of her companion, instinct pressed Skerth back into the shadows. The Caretaker was tall, thin, and angular, and clad in the sweeping, unadorned grey silk robes of the Inner Circle. He held his hands folded inside his wide sleeves, and his pinched features looked as though he smelled something foul. His youth surprised Skerth the most; he had always imagined that the Caretakers were very old, but this man's hair swept away from his high brow in thick, dark waves and no wrinkles marred his smooth, clean-shaven skin.

On either side of Benvedora and the Caretaker walked a half dozen of the Caretakers' Blades. Cousin to their counterparts of the

Lower Wedge, the ruthless Quarterstaves, the Blades were the elite Guard of the Caretakers, the finest warriors chosen from across Erados. Their skill with blade and bow made the Staves look like thick, ham-handed bullies. Unlike the Staves, whose uniforms were often ill-fitting and plain, the Blades wore shining mail beneath silver-grey silk tunics marked with the Caretakers' sigil: the eye of wisdom centered between two halves of a broken crown. Silver-grey velvet shortcloaks draped over their right shoulders, and plumed helms concealed their faces.

Skerth's pulse quickened. Kiri was out in that crowd somewhere. Despite the Caretakers' public show of charity and peaceful values, those bound Downwedge knew better. It hadn't taken more than a few months of the Caretakers' regime for the city dregs to develop a healthy mistrust of those who governed the city, a mistrust supported by whispers of abductions, transportation, abandoned bodies. And Skerth wasn't too young to remember when the Caretakers had turned the full force of the Blades' fury on the Lower City in an attempt to eradicate the city's lucrative pirate trade. He had no desire to find out what would happen to a ragged street thief caught right beneath their notice.

Skerth gripped his dagger and studied the crowd, awaiting an opportunity to slip into action. But he no sooner found his chance than a telltale ripple fanned outward from the head of the crowd.

"'Ware!" someone cried.

"Thief!" called another.

The Caretaker turned sharply, his heavy brows knit into a frown.

Skerth hesitated, took a deep breath, and dove into the fray.

Two of Benvedora's personal guard pushed forward, struggling to clear enough space in the surging crowd to draw swords. A group of ladies drew back, loudly declaring their fear to one another and pressing trembling gloved hands to their fine silk purses.

A curious new crowd of passersby had also gathered, flirting with the chaotic edges of the entourage. Off to Skerth's right a woman screamed; more cries of "thief!" and "catch him!" rang out, followed by a ripple of motion. Benvedora cursed loudly and drew her sword, stirring up a flurry of activity near the front that jerked Skerth into action. He wove through the press of bodies, slicing the occasional purse-cord almost as an afterthought, his attention

25

focused on catching a glimpse of Kiri. Thieving was almost too easy with so many inattentive people packed close, a fact that Kiri no doubt depended upon. He knew from experience that she merely toyed with them, an alley cat to their collective mouse, using their panic and noise against them. He also knew that stirring up the crowd would make her even harder to find—and would increase the chances that there would be little left of her if they found her first.

"Greetings, little thief." A strong hand snapped tightly around Skerth's wrist. He tried to jerk away and looked up into the face of a man, not yet thirty, light brown hair curling to the neck of his threadbare travel-cloak.

Skerth struggled, but the stranger held fast, his free hand hovering near the hilt of his sword. Angling his dagger, Skerth stabbed for anything he could reach, but the stranger twisted his wrist. Hard. Skerth's dagger clattered to the ground.

"Let me go," Skerth growled.

The man ignored him and bent to retrieve the weapon. He rose, brow furrowed, flipping the dagger in his palm and rubbing away the years of layered grime to examine the hilt. His thumb found a design etched into the base of the hilt and paused; the stranger looked up sharply and studied Skerth with new interest.

"Where did you get this?"

Confused, Skerth only stared.

The stranger gave him a hard shake. "Boy! Where did you come by this weapon?"

Skerth shook his head to clear it. "It's mine. I've always had it, since—" His fingers, caught in the stranger's grip, had numbed; he glanced at the crowd for help, but those nearest were already backing away to either flee or turn and cry for help. Fear pitched Skerth's voice higher, louder, more insistent. "Let me go!"

But the man no longer heard. He fingered a lock of Skerth's hair, ignoring the way he cringed at his touch. Then, the stranger gripped Skerth's chin and gave him a long look. "Weyth," he breathed.

The word summoned strange images—a young boy's smiling face, crumpled rose petals coated in ash. A blue ball. The reek of old sweat, the feel of paper-thin, wrinkled skin—and caught Skerth with an unsourced terror. He clawed at the man's grip, scratching, pulling, prying at the stranger's fingers to release him. Tears burned in Skerth's eyes. "Please," he croaked.

"What goes there?" called the Caretaker. Skerth's capture had caused a stir to rival Kiri's. The crowd shifted to make way as the Caretaker turned, his eyes shrewd and searching, the Blades at his heels.

"Please!" Skerth cried, desperate. "My lord!"

Skerth's captor stiffened at the word, snapping to attention. He glanced to the crowd, alarmed and more than a little surprised, as though he had only just noticed them. He caught sight of the Caretaker and pressed his lips into a thin white line. Then he gave Skerth a long look—

And eased his hold.

Skerth didn't pause to wonder. He bolted, forgetting his dagger in his haste to escape.

He heard rather than saw the man dive after him. But Skerth had already disappeared into a crowd too stunned to catch him. He did not stop running until he was well away, until he clambered to the rooftops and somehow managed to find himself safe across the Wedge and in the Lower City.

Only then did he remember Kiri and hope she had escaped. Only then did he think of the word—*Weyth*—and question why a remark with no obvious meaning inspired such terror and called to mind the smell of ash and roses.

Chapter Three: Rot

The next morning, Skerth woke to a hard shake and a jab in the ribs. He cracked an eye open, then rolled over, anger tightening his chest.

"Go away, Kiri."

"Skerth!" she said with a shove.

He swatted at her arm, caught air as she dodged. "Leave me alone."

"You nearly ruined everything!"

He sat up and rubbed the sleep from his eyes. "What are you going on about?"

It was still early—not quite dawn—but enough light had filtered through the building cracks and high, unshuttered windows that he could see the fear behind Kiri's anger. In fact, she looked awful, as though she hadn't slept all night. Shadows underscored her eyes and added to an uncommon pallor. A livid bruise fanned across her right cheek.

Burgeoning rage shook off the last vestiges of sleep. "*I* ruined everything? You abandoned me in the Royal Quarter! Then I almost got caught trying to warn you about the Caretakers. And I lost my dagger. I spent the rest of the day and night trying to find my way Downwedge and wondering what'd happened to you." He paused. "Looks like you didn't fare too well, either."

She shrugged and averted her eyes. "I got away."

At what cost? he wondered. But Kiri didn't seem inclined to elaborate and he knew better than to push. She would tell him in her own time, and not a minute sooner.

"What did he say to you?" she asked.

"What? Who?"

Kiri sighed, irritated. "The man who grabbed you. What did he say?"

Skerth ran a hand through his hair. "He called me a thief, and. . . ." He recalled the stranger's irritation fading to surprise, to interest. *Weyth*, he had said. The word tugged at Skerth's memory, but he couldn't imagine why.

"And?" Kiri prompted, leaning closer.

He saw the stranger again, turning the dagger over in his hands as he looked Skerth over for—for what? *He let me go*, Skerth realized. *Why?*

"We didn't have much of a conversation."

She frowned. "Honest? I thought—"

"He caught me, I got away, I ran. What about you?" He motioned toward the bruise coloring her cheek. "Where did you get that?"

"Later." She waved away his concern like she would a persistent eba fly. "Here." She tossed a dagger between them. "You'll need this."

It wasn't his, but it looked familiar. The wood hilt was worn to a polish, stained with sweat and blood. He picked it up, ran a finger across the dull edge of the blade. The weapon was poor quality, but serviceable. Skerth scowled, regretting the loss of the dagger he'd carried for as long as he could remember.

He sheathed the knife. "Where did you get it?"

"Rot."

Skerth's eyebrows shot up in surprise. "How? Doesn't he need--"

"He's dead. I found him early this morning. In Malyn's run."

"Rot," he murmured, his mind reeling. Kids died or disappeared all the time, but this felt different. He and Rot had helped each other out of a scrape or two, shared the occasional take. "Are you sure?"

She nodded.

"How?"

"Beaten. Pretty bad, by the looks of him. And his throat was cut."

Just like the others. "Take me to him."

Kiri rocked back on her heels, her expression guarded. "Why?"

"I need to see him."

She shook her head. "Too late, Skerth. It's almost light, and we'd have to go deep into Malyn's run."

Skerth stood. "We'll just have to be careful. You can show me the way. After all—" Skerth tapped the hilt of Rot's dagger—

"you've already gone and come again today, with none of Malyn's scats the wiser."

"What's the use? I already took everything Rot had of any worth, which wasn't much." She sighed. "Poor Rot."

"I need to see him, Kiri." To her questioning look he replied, "I owe him one last look."

She tilted her head to the side, looking thoroughly unconvinced. Then she rose. "All right, but we need to be quick. It won't be long before Malyn gets to him. I'd hate to see him catch you near a dead body in his slum twice in one week."

"Or you," Skerth retorted.

"Oh, he won't catch me." She flashed a smile as she ducked through the crumbling door frame of the ruined building Skerth called home.

He grunted a reply, his mind already focused on more pressing matters. Who was knifing scats in Malyn's run? And why? They were thieves, beggars and nuisances at worst, orphans trying to survive on the fringe of society. They were hardly worth notice, let alone killing.

The sun hadn't crested the highest buildings of Malyn's run when Skerth and Kiri lay flat on their bellies overlooking the lonely alley where Rot rested. The Staves still had a sharp eye out for street scats, so they took what at first seemed to Skerth a mad weaver's thread through the streets, heading up and through buildings, doubling back over rooftops, and crossing narrow alleys by jumping windows, but in the end they arrived without a soul seeing them and in half the time. Skerth could see why Kiri felt so confident taunting Malyn in his own territory.

Rot's body lay sprawled in the alley filth below. Dried blood spattered his skin, which was peppered with cuts and bruises in various shades of severity. Even from their vantage point, Skerth could tell Rot's throat had been slit. And the raw meat of his fingers provided evidence that Kiri had not been Rot's only visitor that morning. Skerth swallowed against a wave of nausea and closed his eyes. No matter that he well-knew the fate of those unlucky enough to die on the streets; the reality that he could have been that body— that one day he, too would lie an unmourned feast for the oversized dock rats that nested all throughout the Lower City—always unsettled him.

Once the knot in his stomach eased, Skerth risked another look at the body. Something felt wrong. He shifted closer to the edge. As he moved, a healthy chunk of the roof beneath his palms broke off and smashed to the ground at Rot's feet.

Kiri grabbed at his flailing arms to steady him. "Careful!"

"Thanks." Breathing out his fear, he pushed himself a safe distance from the edge and rose to his feet.

She snatched at his hand to pull him back. "Someone will see you!"

"I'm going down there," he replied, but dropped into a crouch all the same.

"What for? I already told you, all he had was the dagger. I was thorough."

The unwelcome image of Kiri picking over Rot's body in the dark of the early morning flipped his stomach. She did many things that were decidedly un-girlish, and she accomplished them with a detachment that he found both admirable and repulsive.

Skerth forced this line of thinking aside. She'd done what had to be done, and he himself was one dagger the richer for her efforts.

"I need to get closer," he said. "Something isn't right."

She snorted. "Yeah. Rot's dead in Malyn's run and none of his boys have come to pay their respects." She shifted nervously and glanced at the sun. "Speaking of. . . ."

Skerth ignored her. He had spied a way down using the windows that faced the alley. The sills were crumbling, dusted with sediment, but if he was careful. . . .

"Fine," Kiri muttered, standing. "Since you're clearly going, no matter what I say, I suppose I'd better keep you from following Rot to the Sea Gods' Haven. Malyn might get upset if he's got two bodies to puzzle over, even if one of them's yours."

"Thanks," he drawled.

She sighed dramatically and lowered herself over the edge. "Just watch. And if anything happens, don't run. Go *up*. I'll take care of you from there."

He grinned. "Sometimes you're almost worth the trouble of knowing you."

"Sometimes," she muttered.

31

Soon they were down and at Rot's side. Kiri wrinkled her nose. "Guess he hadn't been to the bath houses in a while."

Skerth rolled his eyes. The girl in Kiri manifested herself at the strangest times. But she had a point. The bath houses were a luxury most street filth could afford only when the stink hindered their ability to slide into crowds unnoticed. Most times a quick dip in the sea sufficed for bath and laundry. But Rot reeked even by street standards. His clothes, more grime than cloth, crawled with lice and were layered with dried blood. A thick, black dirt, like soot, smudged his skin. His hair hung in greasy, blood-caked tangles.

"When was the last time you saw him?"

Kiri cocked her head. "Two weeks ago, at least, down by the market. He and I nearly got into a scrap because he tried for my mark. Why?"

"I haven't seen him around, either." Not that it meant anything, necessarily. Rot didn't run with anyone else very often—mostly kept to himself—but he had been one of Skerth's, and Skerth took care of his own.

"Do you think the Staves got him?"

Skerth shook his head. "The beating maybe, but we're worth more alive."

Something about the body still nagged at him. He bent closer.

Beside him, Kiri shifted nervously. "Look, Skerth. Now that you mention, the Staves ought to be round anytime now—"

"Hush."

Rot's eyes were open and clouded, the fear in them frozen. A familiar slash split his throat—clean, swift, a master stroke that would have spilled all of Rot's blood in a matter of minutes.

Skerth froze.

"Blood," he whispered.

That was it. Rot was covered in dried blood. By all rights, blood should have been everywhere, pooled beneath the body, coating the alley floor. He had seen enough of death in his lifetime to know he and Kiri should be slipping in it, not standing in an alley blanketed in nothing worse than the customary slime of feces, grime, and standing water.

He flashed back to another morning, another body. He and Malyn had fought close enough to the dead boy that his bare foot had nudged the rubbery arm. No blood then, either.

"No blood," he said aloud. "The boys aren't being killed here. They're being dumped."

Kiri's eyes met his. "If not here . . . then where?"

Skerth backed slowly away, suddenly remembering the stranger's tight grip on his wrist, the caress of his fingers on his hair. What had he said? *Weyth*.

"Skerth?"

He opened his mouth to reply, but stopped short at the sound of voices, the casual chatter of morning scheming rounding the corner into Rot's alley.

Malyn's scats.

Skerth and Kiri darted for their window-ladder to the rooftops and skimmed out of sight. As they made their way back to the warehouse district in silence, the same thoughts drummed a pattern in Skerth's mind: three dead boys left in Malyn's quarter, the stranger, the word. Were they somehow connected? Anger surging, Skerth thought of Rot, dead in the alley-filth, and vowed to find out.

Chapter Four: The Tunnel

Eager to avoid another confrontation with Malyn, Skerth spent the rest of that morning in the ruined warehouse he—and a crowd of other street orphans—called home. After a brief altercation with Patter, who had stolen and resold Skerth's tattered bedroll to a new kid for the third time in a fortnight, Skerth tracked down his possessions, sent the new kid to market, coin in hand, to get his own blanket, and settled down to rest in an open space near the back wall.

Thinking of Rot and the other dead boy, Skerth rolled onto his back and stared up into the gloom where the high ceiling disappeared into a riot of cobwebs and dusty air. The last rays of afternoon sunlight filtered through tall, narrow windows cut into the walls, most of which had lost their shutters long ago. The rotted wood that still remained hung by only one or two hinges at most. Battered wood shipping crates scattered across the dirt floor, commissioned as shelters by those who were either willing to fight for the privilege of ownership or lived under the protection of someone who would. Tattered blankets, sacks, and trash littered the rest of the room. And throughout, at all hours of the day and night, children of all ages and size came and went.

Skerth and Kiri were two of the oldest--nearly fifteen, as best they could reckon--which afforded them more respect. Anyone older tended to move on; some to make their luck outside the city, others to apprentice in more lucrative street professions: assassin, slaver, pirate, whore. Most of the children who squatted in Skerth's warehouse were under a decade, and scarcely streetwise enough to do more than pick the occasional pocket or raid the food merchants' carts now and again. He helped them out when he could—taught them a trick or two about thieving, warned them to stay clear of the Thumpers who lured the smaller ones away with promises of food and warmth only to turn and sell them to the skin traders or slavers. He told them about the Briskers and the Pouchers, too, but every day another face disappeared from the warehouse to end up thieving for others' gain or becoming lures themselves to bring more unwary children into the service of those who clung to the darker corners of the Lower City. And so many ended up like Rot, eventually—some sooner than others.

Thinking of the dead boys made Skerth restless, and holding onto the coin he'd culled Upwedge made him uneasy. He flipped to his side and closed his eyes, but their images taunted him. Finally he gave up. With a heavy sigh he rose and, after leaving his bed roll in the care of Yric—who was far more trustworthy than most and could hold his own against Patter's tricks—Skerth headed outside, where he nearly stumbled over two little girls on the stoop, who stopped playing with their raggedy makeshift dolls to stare at him.

"What?" he snapped, instantly regretting his harsh retort. They were small, no more than seven summers, if a day. One, a pretty girl with smooth dark skin and bright amber eyes, he recognized as Jemmy; Kiri had taken an interest in her, and had worked hard of late to convince her to trade her ragged dress for boy's clothes and cut short her waist-length black hair. When Jemmy's companion, a gangly redhead, looked up, tears shone in her eyes.

Skerth squatted down beside them. They shuffled backwards, maintaining a cautious distance, and studied Skerth through wide, suspicious eyes.

"Are you new here?" he asked the redhead.

"I'm Jemmy," her companion volunteered.

Skerth smiled. "I know." Jemmy beamed. He turned back to the other girl. "But I don't know you."

The girl studied him. Then, after glancing to Jemmy for support, she reluctantly offered, "Minah."

"I'm Skerth." He rose and gave them a sweeping bow worthy of a royal court. The girls giggled.

"Jemmy, Minah, when did you last eat?"

A long silence followed. Finally, Jemmy shrugged. "Some crusts this morning."

After a moment's hesitation, Skerth pulled two coins from his purse. The girls leaned forward, forgetting their dolls. He dropped a coin into each of their outstretched hands, trying not to think about how big the coins looked against their tiny palms. "The market's still open."

35

They squealed and threw themselves at him, all spindly arms and legs clinging to whichever of his body parts they could reach. Their gratitude embarrassed him. "Get. Be quick. And mind who you talk to."

He watched them scatter off, both reveling in and regretting his charity. He ducked his head to avoid the accusing stares of so many others he could not afford to help and headed out into the evening.

He didn't look up again until he was well away from the warehouse, and only then to scan the alleys for trouble. The hour was late; he would have to move fast if he hoped to make his errand and get back before full night. He caught himself wondering if the girls had made it to the market, then shook his head, angry with himself for falling prey to the most destructive sort of mercy. He could ill afford to support a warehouse full of street orphans, which is what his charity would come to if word got around. In no time he'd have an army of sullen brats as dependents, all wide eyes and hungry stares by day, knives in his back at night. Or worse, they might vent their jealousy on one another, brawling over the few coins his pity dropped their way.

No, he had made a critical mistake. They were better off learning the harsh lessons of the streets themselves, early and well; they'd have to make their own way, and fast, if they hoped to survive. Forcing aside thoughts of the little girls, he resolved not to waver so easily again.

Voices up ahead—the streets demanded his attention. He slowed, took his bearings, scanning automatically for hiding places, escape routes, weapons. A broken-down upturned crate. A half-boarded window. A side alley. He moved closer to the wall and waited.

Shadows paused at the alley mouth. One bent close to the other, murmured something to his companion. A woman's seductive laughter rang false in the alley, a place ill-suited for mirth and courting. Even so, the man leaned in for a kiss.

Annoyed at having to wait his task on a lover's tryst, Skerth shifted from foot to foot and considered his options. They presented no threat to him. Judging by their apparent lack of concern for the outside world, he could slip past unnoticed. Still, the man was large, and might not appreciate Skerth's interruption. Decided, Skerth gripped the hilt of his dagger and surged forward.

The couple paid him no heed. Nevertheless, he did not relax until he was well away and certain that they—or anyone else who might have watched, unseen, from the shadows—had not followed. Releasing his hold on the dagger, Skerth quickened his step.

As he moved closer to the sea, the landscape of the city changed. Short brick buildings crowded close and butted up against narrow muddy streets intersected by alleys no larger than crawlspaces that forced Skerth to turn sideways to slip through. Accidental gardens of weeds and wild grass lined rutted roads. Faded wooden signs bearing a variety of symbols—dragons, oxen, rutting pigs, and flagons, among a few too foul to name—swung from rusted iron poles to ply all the trades most attractive to sailors and vagabonds. Outside, the whores had begun to gather, smoothing their tattered skirts and calling out to those few men who had already started their night's quest for a tankard and companionship. A handful of Quarterstaves made their presence known, voices booming and chests puffed in a show of authority; one swept aside a mangy mongrel with one blow of his staff, sending it yelping to the shadows. His companions laughed, and the whores and passersby shrank into the shadows, eyes averted as the Caretakers' muscle passed.

A door slammed open and a body landed at Skerth's feet with a heavy thud and a pitiful groan.

"Stay out, you filthy cur, until you've got the coin to settle your debt," hollered the burly man who'd dumped him.

The bundle of rags in the street swayed to his feet. "I've coin," he slurred. "Plenty coin, now my luck's turned—"

"You can't turn luck you haven't got, old fool. Now get, before the Staves take your hand for the thief you are."

The Stave who'd beat the stray glanced up; his companions slowed. Skerth quickened his pace. This tale would end like all the rest: if the Staves let him pass unmolested, the ragged man would stagger off to find another alehouse that would let him in long enough to run up a debt he hadn't a hope of paying, then toss him out to become another tavern-master's problem, and so on, until one day he'd land in the street and not get up again.

Skerth moved on, past the rows of taverns and brothels, the broken-down inns, the shops where no signs advertised their wares, but merchants traded all the same—stolen goods, dark services, even people were bought and sold in such places. He stepped carefully in this part of the city; there were far worse ways to end his days than as a pathetic, drunken sot.

Skerth did not slow until he reached the southern edge of the city, where the last of the Lower City's aged and battered buildings shoved up against the Wedge that sheared high into the sky, settling them all in shadow. Here, away from the main thoroughfare, a scatter of tumbledown houses huddled between buildings that had once housed respectable trades before the city had widened and spread inland, then shifted up and around to the other side of the cliffs.

There, just beyond the Wedge, lay the Royal Quarter, where the nobles and merchants lived as effectively cut off from the low-lives and scum as if they did not exist at all. There the magnificent merchant ships and royal fleet docked, far from the rank grime of the wharves Downwedge, where the fishermen and less savory tradesmen still brought in their goods. There, beyond the wall of rock, lay the merchant and artisan Guildhalls, the nobles, the gardens and fountains, the Palace itself. There, far from the crumbling red brick, rotting wood, and old stone city was a world of gleaming white dotted with color: green gardens, silk House banners in every shade, vibrant clothing in rich textures.

He saw none of this when he looked at his city. This broken-down strip of land, this tattered stronghold of desperate lives, was home. And this ugly street, butted up against a world full of more to offer than these residents would ever hope for, was the source of Skerth's earliest memories.

He'd spent his early years here, in a makeshift shack that had crumbled to dust long ago. He had few memories of that time—he guessed he hadn't been much older than four or five then, and he hadn't stayed long. A woman had found him in an alley and cared for him—not his mother, he knew; he had no memories of a mother at all. But this woman had been kind and pretty. He'd liked to rub her soft hair between his fingers. And she'd smelled of jasmine.

Later, a man had lived there, too—not tall, but strong, thick-armed and foul-tempered. He hadn't minded Skerth at first, muttering that the boy was "little more than a dock rat." He'd pronounced him "Little Skerth." For lack of a better, the name had taken.

As time passed, the man's patience for women and children waned. The woman tried to protect Skerth from his fists, but her courage faltered with every beating. When the man put Skerth out, declaring times too hard to feed a brat that wasn't his get, she no longer had the will to protest. She had cried a little, but in the end, she had held the door fast against his pleas and pounding. Finally, he gave up, and found a different sort of family in Jax's gang.

The memory of his brutal initiation—and the ring he'd paid in exchange for even that meager semblance of a family—jerked Skerth back to the present. His story was no different from any other street orphan's tale. Maybe his had fewer beatings, maybe he'd managed a little more food. He knew he'd carry the feel of that woman's silken hair for the rest of his life, but it changed nothing. He was Skerth. A rat. He was alive. And he had far more useful things to do than dwell on a past he couldn't change.

It was nearly dark by the time Skerth slid sideways into a slender alley wedged between a money-lender's run-down shack and a strip of three hovels full of wailing children and their short-tempered dams. He stumbled and nearly fell over a rotted pile of rags that might or might not have been a body, shooed away a pair of skeletal stray dogs, shuffled through slick rubbish, and felt his way along the brick until the thin slice of alley gave way to a corridor leading around the rear of the buildings, where they shoved up against the cliffs.

He paused, allowing his eyes to adjust to the darkness. Once his fingers brushed brick on his left and rock on his right, he walked slowly on. Now, he could afford patience. The street noises gradually fell away, leaving only the low rustlings of small, interrupted lives. Something screeched at his approach, skittered past. He tread carefully, well aware that this was no longer his territory. He had no wish to offend the residents here, who would, like any creature of instinct, defend their little world to the death.

After a time, the air thickened. Both hands brushed rock. Reaching overhead, Skerth found the borders of the arched cave entrance. He grinned, savoring his secret. How many of Malyn's gang or the gutter rats who shared the streets knew that buried behind the shabby borders of the Lower City was an old musty cave? For that matter, how many of the wealthy merchants and nobles—or even the Caretakers themselves—slept soundly at night, made confident by their comfortable distance from the sledge of the city, never knowing of this wormhole through the cliffs?

Skerth had never actually followed the cave all the way through, but he had traveled far enough to know that the tunnels forked too many times for one boy to map on his own. And he was not about to trade this secret away to anyone, not even to know how deep the warren of tunnels went into the Wedge, whether they joined the merchant tunnels or led out to the sea, or if they even led anywhere at all.

He reached the first fork and veered left, then left again at the next. Here he stopped, cocked an ear, listened.

There.

A trickle of water. Quiet, thin, unmistakable.

He reached out and dragged his finger across the rock until he crossed a thin indent of wet stone and traced the fissure down the wall, where he snagged loose rock. He worked to pull out the wedge of stone that concealed a small hollow just large enough to hold a good-sized pouch of coin and a few other treasures he had managed to squirrel away over the years. A street rat's fortune.

He counted a week's worth of coin into the pouch at his hip before carefully replacing the rock. Then he straightened, set his right hand against the wall, and turned back.

He had not gone far when the screech of bats gave him one breath's warning. No sooner had he hurled himself to the ground than a fury of wings swept overhead, drawing a draft of cold, stale air across Skerth's back. He threw his arms over his head, cowering against the onslaught of wings and noise. But neither the panicked bats, nor the darkness, nor the latent knowledge that he had temporarily lost his sense of direction tightened a hard knot of fear in Skerth's stomach.

No, nothing terrified him more than the murmur of disembodied voices.

Chapter Five: Dreiwend

Skerth cocked an ear and crouched against the wall, his mouth dry, heart hammering. He'd come to these tunnels at least four days of seven for most of his life and never heard so much as a hint of human company. *Why now?*

Curiosity and an inexplicable anxiety drove him to find out. With a deep, steady breath, he oriented himself in the dark and settled his left hand on the rock. He charted the tunnels in his head as he moved—here a left, there a right, a lean to the left, a low overhang to duck beneath—and in between, his hand memorized the feel of deep fissures and slight outcroppings, the pocked stone and broken shards of a world that had existed long before Skerth and would far outlast him. Always he moved toward the voices, apprehension settling deeper into his core at every step. It wasn't the darkness he feared, or the musty closeness of the air, or even getting lost. He feared the small tug of memory that stirred deep within, triggering warnings that he didn't understand.

As he moved through the darkness, the voices, at first no more than a low, hollow hum, crystallized into patterns of sounds and pauses. He continued toward them, using his heightened sense of hearing as a guide, until he halted not more than a hundred paces from where warm torchlight spilled, flickering, from an arm intersecting Skerth's tunnel.

Skerth spread his fingers and held them out. While the light filtered far enough that he could make out the edges of his fingertips, the darkness still proved an effective cover—unless the strangers chose to turn his way. He shifted into a half-crouch and made ready to run.

"I believe . . . far enough," a man wheezed.

"That is for me to decide, Dreiwend, not you," drawled another voice; refined, authoritative. Here was a man used to giving orders, not taking them. The torch flared to the brink of Skerth's tunnel—and stopped.

"Please, Excellency," panted Dreiwend. "Where does this way lead?"

"This path here"—flames flickered into view at the mouth of Skerth's tunnel, forcing him to duck—"will take you to the outer reaches of the Lower City. Behind the pleasure district, I believe. I think you know where the other path terminates."

"My man does." Dreiwend took a deep breath. "All right. I understand the problem. What would you have me do, Lord Harrudrynn?"

Lord Harrudrynn. One of the most prominent—and most feared—Caretakers.

"Have your man chart the tunnels, but be discreet. No one else must know of them—or where they lead."

"Done. I will send word at first light." Dreiwend hesitated. "About the Great Council's directive—"

"Have you disposed of every possible candidate?"

A long silence ensued. At last, Dreiwend replied with a heavy "No. There are more than we ever anticipated." He paused. "Perhaps so many that the people would never believe—"

"They must not have the opportunity to choose to believe or disbelieve anything." Skerth could almost feel Harrudrynn's displeasure. "Every boy of age must be destroyed."

Every boy of age. . . . Skerth's gut tightened. *Rot. The other dead boys. The Caretakers are killing them all.*

"Yes. Of course, Excellency. And we are close, very close." Dreiwend's words tumbled out in a rush. "The last boy we interrogated gave us more names, places to search. There is a warehouse—"

"Find them!" the Caretaker hissed. "And eliminate them all. We have little time left to us. If anyone comes forward on Auberdale Eve—"

"No one will come forward," Dreiwend interrupted, his voice carrying a clear, deadly certainty. "I will see it done. Rest assured, neither I, nor my men will sleep until all potential candidates are exterminated."

Gravel scuffled; the torch flickered. Dreiwend grunted as his flesh slammed into stone. As Skerth listened, the man's breath thinned to a rasp.

"Nearly eleven years ago I charged you with this task, and you have failed me at every turn. Know this, Dreiwend: if any worthy candidate steps forward on Auberdale Eve, I will have your lands, your wife, and your heirs turned over to me. Then I will have you drawn and quartered, and your head will stand at the palace gates as a testament to all who oppose the will of the Caretakers. Have I made myself clear at last?"

"Yes . . . Excellency," Dreiwend squeaked, then gasped. For a time, he coughed and retched, dragging in deep breaths of air. "You should know," he panted when he could speak again, "my man has sighted the Exile in the city."

"Lord Feirwyn?" the Caretaker snapped. A pause. Then, more calmly: "When?"

Dreiwend cleared his throat. "Nine days ago. My man spied him twice near the hub of the city: once at the blacksmith's, once in Merchant Square two days later. He's been pacing him ever since."

"Good." The Caretaker paused thoughtfully. "Watch him, but keep a clear distance. We may have use for him."

"Indeed, your Excellency. We are of the same mind."

"On this matter, at least. Come. We have been absent too long."

The torchlight retreated. Dreiwend grunted and their footsteps receded.

Darkness rushed in to reclaim the tunnels. Skerth remained still, thoughtful. He didn't understand most of what he'd heard. *Eleven years. Extermination. Candidates.* But one fact he knew for certain: if Dreiwend and his man succeeded, more corpses would soon litter the streets of the Lower City, all boys "of age." *His* age: nearly fifteen, or thereabouts. What he didn't understand was why. What did the Caretakers want with the street scats of the Lower City? Something to do with Auberdale Eve—but what?

Using the mental map he'd sketched, Skerth picked his way back to his hidden stash, then refilled his pouch and pockets with coin. His tunnels were no longer safe. Not only did the Caretakers know of them, they would be crawling with Dreiwend's scouts by mid-day. He would have to find someplace new to stash his take. What remained of his collection he left behind, concealed in his stone hollow. He would come for it again, when he could.

If he could.

His thoughts awhirl, he made his way out of the tunnels, out of the close, musty air and quiet dark to the sharp smells of rotted fish, ale, and refuse, back through the pleasure district crowded now with sailors, whores, and pirates and peppered with Staves and the occasional Blade come Downwedge for a night's sport. Skerth pushed through them, stepping over the bodies of the drunk and the beaten, evading the notice of the Caretakers' men. He took little notice of any but the most obvious distractions, and then only to perceive whether or not they posed a threat. His mind was fixed on what he had overheard back in the tunnels.

As he at last slipped away from all of the noise and activity and into the quieter, more familiar alleys that led back to the warehouse, he turned the words of the Caretaker and his companion over and over again in his mind, but none of it made sense. *Dead scats. Caretakers and hired men. Candidates. Eleven years. Auberdale Eve.* Something scratched at the back of Skerth's memory. What had happened eleven years earlier? He frowned, trying to work it out. Eleven years earlier he lived in a shack at the back end of the pleasure district, waiting upon the charity of others. He knew nothing of how the city was run then, nor did he know much more now. Eleven years . . . and what was the significance of Auberdale Eve? Granted, it was one of the biggest city festivals, and one of the most lucrative opportunities for petty thieves and pickpockets of the year. Everyone would be out in the streets celebrating or attending the main ceremony in the Palace courtyard. But why such urgency about this particular festival?

Over and over Skerth turned these and other pieces of the overheard conversation in his mind, until he almost believed he had imagined it. By the time he had stashed his extra coin in his second best hiding place, returned to the warehouse, and rolled into his ratty nest of blankets, his mind was so busy that he lay awake, staring blind into the dark while the kids who shared his warehouse snored and murmured softly in their sleep, innocent of dead boys, secret tunnels and Caretakers.

Skerth was stretched out on the roof just before dawn when Kiri found him. She didn't say anything, just settled beside him to watch the sun rise over the ocean, barely visible beyond the network of dirty rooftops that tilted toward the sea. Orange slowly bled onto the horizon, pushing back the blue-black of night, leeching the shadows and dusting everything in a soft gold. Gilded thus, his city seemed less rank and desperate.

Like all illusions, this, too soon faded, shading the Lower City in its more familiar hues of brown and gray.

He was glad to see Kiri. Even though he didn't fully understand why, he knew for certain that they needed to act on the information he had overheard. The street scats had to be warned. All of them, from his kids in the warehouse to all they could reach of the loose gangs spread throughout the Lower City. And Malyn had to know, too. This point Skerth had debated the most. On the one hand, Malyn was more than capable of taking care of his own. But to the best of Skerth's knowledge, even he couldn't face down a cunning murderer.

A murderer who acted upon the will of a Caretaker.

No, Malyn had to know the truth, even if Skerth had to risk his own neck trying to convince him that this threat affected them all. But how? He couldn't just walk into Malyn's run on any given day and announce that he needed to see him. More likely than not, any scat Skerth approached to send him a message would knock him senseless before he could get a word out. He was too well-known to get anywhere near Malyn using the streets. And he couldn't do it alone.

He needed the rooftops.

For that, he needed Kiri.

He took a deep breath, filling his lungs with the courage to speak the truth aloud. "Someone is trying to kill us."

She looked up, mismatched eyes wide and wondering.

"All of us," he added.

"The dead boys," she replied, nodding. "I thought as much." She was alert, listening. "What have you heard?"

Skerth told her everything, and despite his fears and uncertainties, the telling felt good. The burden he had carried all night slowly eased. The fear clenching his chest relaxed its hold. He could breathe; he could think.

He watched as she took it all in. She chewed at her bottom lip, furrowed her brow. Then: "Malyn needs to know. Everybody needs to know."

He nodded. "More than that, though." He took a deep breath. "We need to find this man of Dreiwend's before he can kill any more of us. We need to find him, and we need to fight."

She nodded her agreement; he felt the tension slide from his shoulders.

The sun eased higher as they worried the problem in silence.

"So," she replied, "where do we start?"

"No idea. Why would anyone want to kill a bunch of scats and orphans? What're we worth to any of them?"

Kiri's eyes widened. "A kingdom."

"What?"

She turned toward him, recognition dawning. "The Caretakers are looking for the missing heir."

It took him a moment, but Skerth caught on. "They never found the littlest son of the king after the Purge. How old was he?"

"Four. He'd be just about our age, now. And they never found all of the royal decoys, either."

"Decoys?" Everyone knew of the citizens' uprising and the Purge, when the rebels murdered the king, his family, and every member of his household he could find. The Caretakers had created Auberdale Eve to mourn the lost and decry the slaughter, so that none would forget the benevolent king and his last days. Skerth knew all of this, but he knew nothing of decoys.

"It's an old, secretive tradition among the old families of Erados—"

He bumped her shoulder with his. "If it's so secret, what do you know of it?"

"Shut it and listen," she snapped, shoving him back. "To keep the young heirs safe from assassins, particularly when the family could only breed one child, the nobles would raise up a handful of look-alikes alongside the heir. They lived close as kin, so no one would know the true identity of the heir. If they used decoys, which they probably did, only the king and queen, the Caretakers, and the Royal Steward ever knew the real prince."

Skerth suddenly understood. "So if any of these decoys survived—"

Kiri nodded her assent. "Any one of them could step forward and claim to be the heir of Erados."

"Candidates. For the throne."

"Yeah."

"No wonder the Caretakers want them dead." It made sense. In the years since the Purge, the Caretakers had made little secret of the fact that they liked power. They wanted to keep it.

"Dreiwend said he's been searching for eleven years. In all my time on the streets, I don't remember so many boys murdered. Why the sudden urgency?"

Kiri sighed. "That, I don't know."

"It has something to do with Auberdale Eve."

But what, neither of them knew. They fell silent, each searching for answers that would not come.

Kiri looked at Skerth. "Do you think any of those decoys—or the heir himself—could have survived all these years on the streets, never knowing he could be King of Erados?"

He shrugged. "We survived."

"Yeah, but we're made of different stuff, you and I."

True enough, Skerth thought. He looked back over all his years, remembering the lives that had come and gone in that time. He had done better than most. But a noble-born boy, bearing no knowledge of anything other than a soft life? Not likely he had survived. Not likely at all.

Chapter Six: Malyn

The day quickly turned hot and sticky, despite the breeze that swept inland from the Quistand Ocean. Skerth and Kiri clambered down from the rooftops and headed for the marketplace, where they traded some of their hard-won coin to gorge themselves on meat pies and hot bread. By mid-day, the air became uncomfortably still and stifling, thick with the familiar odors of rot and fish. Skerth scratched at a flea bite behind his ear and contemplated a swim; instead they retreated to the warehouse to wait out the sun. Those they passed either languished in whatever shade they could steal or moved as slowly as Skerth and Kiri, who felt no need to rush in the oppressive heat.

"You shouldn't just give them coin, you know," Kiri remarked amiably, pulling a ripe eba fruit from her market sack.

Skerth suppressed a groan, nearly sick from overeating. He wondered how a person so slight could possibly eat so much. "Who?"

She gave him an exasperated look. "The young ones. Jemmy. Minah."

"Oh." He recalled the wide-eyed Jemmy and her friend Minah's wild nest of red hair and felt instantly defensive. "How'd you know?"

She shrugged. "I know a lot of things. This was no secret, though. Jemmy and Minah have been singing your praises like birds to the sea gods."

Skerth silently cursed the weakness in him that was going to get them all killed one day. To Kiri he said, "It does no harm in giving them a bit to start. They're new, and can hardly take care of themselves."

"Well, that's the point, isn't it?" Kiri took a healthy bite of her eba fruit. "I've worked hard to convince them that they ought to think up better disguises, learn at least how to thieve properly rather than beg, but they won't listen any more, now that Father Skerth's taking care of them."

Skerth flushed. "I'll talk to them."

"No."

He glanced at her, surprised, but she was in no hurry to elaborate. She took another bite, her expression thoughtful.

"No. Give them the coin, but make them work."

This made even less sense to Skerth. "How—"

"We need information, right? And we need to find a way to tell Malyn. Neither of us can set foot on Malyn's streets without all sorts of trouble, but one of the other kids could. If we could get even one of them into Malyn's gang—"

"No." Skerth shivered, remembering the price he had paid to get into Jax's gang—and out of it. "I won't put any of our kids through that."

"Fine, then. Not in Malyn's gang. But this could work, see?"

He did see, and caught some of her enthusiasm. "No one would suspect the little kids of anything."

"And between us, we've got enough coin for an army of spies, telling us anything we need to know."

They spent the rest of the conversation working through the logistics: how they would present their idea to the little ones, what they expected to gain, how they could even—if they played their hand well—use them to get word to Malyn. At the very least, the little ones would make excellent sentries and scouts; small enough to slip here and there unnoticed, innocent enough to avert suspicion, and younger than those the Caretakers sought to kill, they could prove very helpful.

"Let's do it," Skerth said at last. "Right away."

"As soon as we get back to the warehouse." She offered him another fruit. He declined with a wave, and she stashed it in her sack.

They walked on, discussing which kids would be better, where to send them. Engrossed in their conversation, they turned down a narrow alley permanently shadowed by the two buildings that towered to either side. A quarter of the way in, Skerth suddenly halted.

Something wasn't right.

The alley looked the same as always, flanked with broken-down crates, crumbled brick, and piles of refuse. Nothing moved.

And that, Skerth realized, was the problem. No rats. No carrion birds. No roaches scuttling in the shadows. The alley was too quiet.

Skerth started backing out the way they had come. "Kiri—"

Too late. The shadows lunged, leveling heavy blows at Skerth's head, stomach and legs, all at once. Pain burst in his left eye; his right knee popped as his legs were swept from underneath him. He hit the ground hard, knocking the breath out of him.

"Kiri," he groaned, struggling to see her, but she was a blur of motion and noise, laboring against two attackers of her own. He felt rather than saw another figure drop from the wall behind him. Skerth fumbled for his dagger, but it was too late; the other boy was already upon him, gouging his elbow into Skerth's throat. Skerth thrashed and kicked, then gasped as the boy jabbed harder, nearly cutting off his air. Skerth stilled.

"Get his dagger and pouch," the boy told the others. Rough hands searched Skerth, snapping away his pouch and taking his weapon. Skerth struggled, but they only laughed and pinned his arms to the ground.

Nearby, Kiri's scuffle continued. And from what Skerth could hear, she had gained the upper hand. The boys who had attacked her cursed and shouted, and a clear ring of steel on steel told him she had found time to draw her knife. One cried out in pain; briefly the hands on Skerth relaxed. He renewed his struggle, and nearly succeeded in wriggling out of their grasp.

"No!" shouted the boy who had mastered him. "Let the other one go. Malyn don't need him anyway. It's this one he wants."

Skerth rolled his head to the side, squinting with his good eye to glimpse what he could of Kiri's fate. She faced two of Malyn's boys, dagger-hand outstretched, a rare fear in her eyes as she glanced from her attackers to Skerth.

"Go." He could manage little more than a painful rasp. "Run."

She hesitated.

Skerth mustered his voice and put everything he had left into one bellowed word: "Go!"

Malyn's boys lunged. Kiri dodged lightly aside, then turned and ran. The boys guffawed and jeered, but Skerth sighed his relief. At least he wouldn't have to worry about her.

Violent hands tangled in Skerth's hair and pulled him face to face with Dragon. Skerth suppressed a groan. One of Malyn's inner circle, Dragon was notoriously ruthless, and carried a grudge against Skerth that went back many years.

Dragon grinned, showing several blackened and chipped teeth. "Don't know what Malyn wants with you, but I don't suppose he'll mind if you're missing a few pieces when you get to him."

Skerth thought fast. "If he wants to kill me, he might not be too pleased if you do half the job for him."

Dragon shrugged. "He'll manage. Don't suppose he would've sent me if he wanted you too healthy."

This was probably true. Skerth thrashed his arms and legs to test his attackers' grip, but they held fast. "Where do you think you're going?" Dragon shouted, slamming Skerth's head against the street. His head exploded; he bit his tongue and tasted blood.

Dazed, he looked up into Dragon's eyes and saw nothing but hate. Dragon back-handed him hard, snapping his head to the side. Skerth moaned.

"Dragon—" one of the other boys warned.

"I'm just having a bit of fun, Barter. We go way back, me and Skerth, don't we?"

Skerth mumbled something he hoped would pass for a reply.

"We need to get out of here," another boy insisted, "before the other comes back. Or the Staves."

Skerth watched through his one good eye as Dragon grimaced, then nodded. "Fine."

The boys eased their hold and Dragon stood. A moment later, Skerth was hauled mercilessly to his feet. He bit back a cry; he would not give Dragon the satisfaction of knowing how much he hurt.

Skerth swayed on his feet as he glanced around the circle of boys. There were five altogether, and he knew them all: Dragon, Barter, Runner, Taleryn, Fael. At least Malyn had sent his five best. Skerth took it as a compliment.

"Come on," Dragon ordered, shouldering Skerth's pouch. He turned, expecting the others to follow. Runner and Taleryn flanked Skerth, each pulling one of his arms over their shoulders to help bear his weight when he staggered. Fael lagged behind.

"Look, mate," Taleryn whispered once Dragon had gone out of earshot. "We'll do what we can to keep Dragon off you. But when you get to Malyn, you're on your own."

"Understood," Skerth croaked, just before the ground lurched and everything went black.

The shock of cold water and agony wrenched Skerth into consciousness.

". . .told you I wanted to talk to him, not nurse him back to life." Malyn's voice. Disapproving. *Good*, Skerth thought, although the worse for him if Dragon ever again caught him alone.

"Again," Malyn snapped.

Another pail of cold, stinging seawater doused Skerth. He jerked upright, gasping. Then, he turned to the side and retched over the edge of his rickety wooden cot, spilling the contents of his stomach onto the earthen floor. Malyn, Dragon and Taleryn immediately jumped clear; some of the other boys weren't so lucky.

"Out!" Malyn roared. The room cleared.

Malyn slammed the door and leaned against the wall with his arms crossed over his chest while Skerth vomited until he had nothing left to give. Skerth leaned his throbbing head against the cool stone wall and closed his eyes, laboring painfully for breath. Then Malyn crossed the room, picked up a threadbare rag, and tossed it to Skerth.

"What do you want with me?" Skerth croaked. He wiped as much of the blood and bile from his face as he could, then dabbed cautiously at his swollen left eye before turning to peer suspiciously at Malyn out of his right.

"Certainly not this." He motioned toward Skerth's vomit with disgust. "Can you walk? I'd rather not talk here, now that you've fouled the place."

Skerth doubted he could walk, but did not say so. Instead, he got carefully to his feet, bracing against the wall for support. Once his head ceased spinning his legs worked well enough, although he suspected Dragon had broken something in his knee.

Malyn led him down a short hall and into another room, not far from the first. His lair had also served as a warehouse once; however, unlike Skerth's, which had been mainly used for storage, this divided into many rooms, all different according to their original purpose. The room Malyn led him into was the nicest, with a high windowed ceiling and thick stone walls. He had added a few comforts, too: a plush, stained rug in gaudy shades of scarlet and violet covered most of the earthen floor; a rickety table and three chairs huddled against the left wall; a decent straw bed and faded blue coverlet flanked the right. Skerth even spied a thin, threadbare pillow on the bed and a set of dice lying beside a chipped glass stein on the table. Malyn had done well for himself. Skerth wondered how the others in his gang fared.

He dragged out a chair and motioned for Skerth to sit. "Foul my private quarters and I'll kill you."

"Maybe next time you shouldn't send Dragon."

Malyn shrugged. "You're here." He pulled a chair to face Skerth and leaned back, crossing his legs at the ankles. His posture was relaxed, but his dark, shrewd eyes never left his guest.

"So. I'm here. What do you want?"

"I want information." He leaned forward abruptly, his eyes menacing. "I want to know why you're killing boys in my streets."

"What? I'm not—"

"Every time a body turns up in my run, one of my boys catches you standing nearby. First that dead kid in the alley, then that other one—what was his name—"

"Rot." He and Kiri hadn't fled quickly enough; Malyn's boys must have seen them.

Malyn's eyes flashed. "Yeah. Rot. One of yours, wasn't he?"

One of yours. . . .

Skerth had a flash of insight: Malyn saw him as a leader—a rival. He supposed he should feel flattered.

This changed the rules. Skerth needed to tread carefully.

"Yeah. One of mine. And I didn't kill him, but I want to find out who did."

"Why? If you didn't kill him, then what do you care? Scats die all the time out here. You know that. Best not to get involved, or you're next."

"Because whoever killed Rot is going to kill again, and again, until none of us are left." Skerth took a breath deep enough to make his battered ribs ache, then told his old leader and onetime friend everything he knew. Malyn listened, without question or argument, until the tale of the decoys and the heir was done.

53

"Do you think it's possible that this heir or one of those decoys still lives? Out here, somewhere on our streets?" Malyn leaned forward and studied Skerth, his expression thoughtful.

Skerth shrugged. "It's possible, I suppose. What's more important is that the Caretakers think they do."

"Because as long as they think any of us has a sailor's chance at the throne, they'll keep killing our scats."

Skerth nodded. "And anyone else who fits the age and description of this missing heir and the other decoys. Though I'd wager anyone with a real name and papers is safe enough."

Malyn swore softly and slammed his palm against the table. Despite his better instincts, Skerth was developing some respect for Malyn. As he watched him rise and pace, Skerth caught a glimpse of the raw intelligence and concern for his own that had driven so many to follow his lead. He tucked the information away.

Malyn stopped, hands at his hips, and stared down at Skerth, then backhanded him—hard. Skerth's head snapped to the side, his cheek and swollen eye bursting into agony.

"What was that for?" He swiped at the line of blood and drool that seeped from the corner of his mouth and stopped short of spitting on Malyn's floor. Now was not the time to test the limits of his hospitality.

Malyn crouched until they were eye to eye. "Look. I believe you. You're a rat, a thief, and a pinch in my side, but you're not a liar. And if what you say is true, I haven't got much choice. Now, I've got to bring the others in on this so we can figure out what to do. When they come in here, it can't look like I've let you off too easy. Understand?"

Skerth scowled, but he did understand. The fact that Malyn looked after his own didn't change the fact that he ruled the streets with his fists. And he was aging; if his gang sensed that he'd gone soft, the Caretakers would prove the least of his worries. Reluctantly, Skerth nodded.

Malyn rose. "Good." He crossed to the door, flung it open, and spoke briefly with someone stationed outside. Then he returned to his seat across from Skerth.

"What now?"

"Now, we work ourselves a plan."

*　　*　　*

The sun had long set by the time Taleryn and Barter deposited Skerth in an alley just over the mutually acknowledged border between Malyn's run and Skerth's. Skerth was thankful that Malyn had spared him Dragon's fists this time, although Barter, still disgusted that Skerth had splattered him with vomit earlier, had given him a couple of half-hearted punches before they left. For a long time Skerth lay where they had dropped him, content to lie still.

While he would have preferred almost any other method of approaching Malyn, he was relieved that he had found a way to warn him. In the end, persuading his scats of the danger had proved even less difficult than talking to Malyn himself. Only Dragon and Lark—a tall, copper-skinned older girl with long, dark hair and shrewd eyes—had questioned Skerth's motives. But Malyn had made clear to them all that he believed Skerth, and that had proved enough. In the end, Skerth and Malyn bartered a truce: for the duration of this threat, there would be no war between them. Instead, they made a pact to watch the streets closely and send word if anyone discovered anything amiss. With any luck, they could not only prevent more deaths, they could also uncover the identity of the Caretakers' assassin.

As much as Skerth looked forward to telling Kiri the news, he hurt too much to move. So he lay on the cool pavement, appreciating the night breeze and listening to the dock rats as they scampered through the day's refuse. He dozed, drifting in and out of consciousness, grateful for the respite from pain.

Suddenly he startled awake, every muscle tense and alert. He did not immediately recognize what had woken him, but all of his street instincts screamed danger. He forced himself to stay still, fighting the urge to run, listening.

Silence.

As they had before the earlier ambush, even the dock rats had fled, leaving Skerth completely alone.

Unfortunately, he recognized the danger too late. He dared not move, or even breathe. Alone in the dark, he strained to catch the slightest sound. For the space of many heartbeats, he heard nothing but the distant carousing of sailors, whores, and noblemen, underscored by the steady suck and spray of the sea against the rocky coast. He had almost relaxed his guard when he heard them at last: footsteps. Slow. Stealthy. The walk of one used to silence and secrecy. Had he not caught the faint creak of well-worn leather, Skerth might have missed the steps altogether. As he waited, they reached the alley mouth, turned. . . .

And headed straight for him.

Too late to run. Too late to hide. Skerth groped for his dagger and cursed himself for losing his second weapon in as many days. He held his breath, closed his eyes, and prayed to all the gods he knew that whoever walked that alley would take one look at his beaten, bloodied body and mistake him for dead.

Gradually the footsteps neared. Closer, closer, until, inches from Skerth's nose, they stopped. Heavy wool brushed Skerth's bruised arms as the figure knelt and pressed cool, strong fingers to his neck. Skerth felt the leap of his pulse betray him, but remained still. *Please*, he begged silently. *Please*.

The stranger withdrew. Skerth heard a rustle of cloth, then the unmistakable sound of a dagger drawn from its sheath. His heart raced. He knew he should run, should fight, should do something, but he lay frozen, unable to muster enough will to do more than hope.

Suddenly, the dagger clattered to the ground next to his ear, the sound deafening to Skerth's heightened sense of sound. His eyes flew open.

The stranger laughed. Skerth grabbed the dagger and staggered unsteadily to his feet, but the stranger did not attack. Instead, the cloaked man nodded toward the weapon. "Yours, I believe."

Reluctantly, Skerth glanced from the stranger to the dagger in his hand. Instantly he recognized the weight and markings of the weapon he'd carried for as long as he could remember, the weapon he'd lost in the marketplace. Incredulous, he looked back at the cloaked figure.

"Who are you?"

"My name is Feirwyn," said the man as he stepped forward into a slash of moonlight and pulled back his hood. "But the more important question is: who are you?"

Chapter Seven: The Stranger

Instinct shouted at Skerth to run, and fast. Curiosity rooted him to the spot.

"What is your name, boy?" The man spoke with a slight northern accent and the gentled speech of the nobility.

"What do you want?" Skerth asked. Gritting his teeth against the pain and effort of motion, he shifted his weight to the balls of his feet and leveled his dagger at the stranger.

Feirwyn chuckled and showed his hands, palms-up and empty. "Easy. If I had planned to harm you, I would have already done so."

Skerth didn't answer, and he didn't lower his weapon. Instead, he propped his back to the alley wall and squinted at Feirwyn through his one good eye. The stranger had the bearing and accent of a nobleman, yet his cloak was worn and travel-stained. He carried a sword, but had not drawn. On the contrary, he watched Skerth patiently, as relaxed in this foul part of the city as he had appeared strolling in the wealthy merchant's wake. And there was something else, something that itched at Skerth, just out of reach. Something about this stranger—Feirwyn—Skerth felt he ought to know.

"I am looking for someone," Feirwyn said. "I think you might be able to help me find him."

"I don't seek runaways for slavers, skin traders, or nobles missing their young. I keep to myself and mind my own flanks. Find someone else."

Skerth sidestepped toward the alley mouth and bit down on a cry of pain as fire sliced through his injured knee. His leg buckled, but he kept his footing.

Feirwyn moved toward him. "You are hurt. Come with me. I have rooms at the Blighted Swine. Food. Water. We will see to your wounds, and—"

"Stay where you are!" Skerth's gut twisted, bringing bile to his throat. "I don't know what kind of easy mark you take me for, but

I'm not hurt so bad that I'll follow a Thumper straight into the skin traders' pens."

Feirwyn halted, palms lifted in supplication. "Peace, boy. Peace. I offer mercy and seek information, nothing more."

Skerth's arm ached from holding the dagger out; his ribs throbbed. He wasn't sure how much longer he could remain standing, let alone hold his guard. Skerth wanted him to go away so he could get back to his warehouse, his bedroll, a pip of water to wash the blood from his face and rinse the taint from his mouth. At the same time, the man piqued his curiosity. Had he felt better, with Kiri at his side and a few others at his back, he might've indulged his interest and followed this tattered nobleman back to the Swine. But not alone. And not now.

"You work for them," Skerth tried, squeezing the hilt of his dagger. "The Caretakers."

Feirwyn's voice hardened. "No. I do not."

The tone and strength of his refusal left no room for doubt, but Skerth hadn't survived so long on his own by trusting easily.

"I can't help you." Skerth shoved away from the stranger and staggered backwards down the alley, careful to stay focused on Feirwyn and on holding his dagger steady. "Thanks for the dagger."

"Wait—" Feirwyn reached for Skerth.

"Don't," Skerth warned, waving the dagger. It was a lame attempt; they both knew Feirwyn could easily best him in a fight, even if Malyn's boys hadn't beaten him bloody. But Feirwyn stopped.

"Look, boy. I mean you no harm. Just answer me this and I'll leave you to your rats and alleys, and with a coin or two besides. How did you get that dagger?"

The question caught Skerth off-guard. "Why do you want to know?"

"That dagger is familiar to me. I'd like to find its owner, if he lives." When Skerth didn't reply, he added, "Tell me. How did that weapon come to you?"

"It's mine. I've had it for as long as I can recall."

"Surely you remember obtaining it somewhere," Feirwyn pressed. "Did you win it in a fight? Take it from the dead? Was it a gift?"

"I don't remember."

Feirwyn closed the distance between them and, before Skerth could react, had him by the shoulders. "Come, boy! The knife is rare. It is—surely you remember something!"

"I don't!" Skerth's insistence rang in the quiet alley. Panic rising, he backed away in earnest. "I can't help you!"

Feirwyn let him go to run a hand through his hair, brow furrowed in frustration. When he spoke, his voice was resigned. "You remember nothing, then."

"No." To his surprise, Skerth felt sorry for him. And guilty, as though he had disappointed this stranger in some important task.

Feirwyn sighed. "When I saw you in the marketplace, I thought—I had hoped—" He fell into a thoughtful silence. Then he gathered himself and said, "I am sorry to trouble you. Should you remember anything, you may find me at The Blighted Swine." Skerth glimpsed the flash of moonlight on metal as two coins arced toward him. He snatched them out of the air and closed them in his fist. "For your trouble."

Feirwyn brushed past Skerth toward the alley mouth. Skerth squeezed his grip, feeling the smooth coin and the rough edges of the token bite into his skin. His own lack of memory disappointed him: where *had* he obtained his dagger? Why didn't he know the answer to such a basic question? And what did this stranger know about his weapon that he did not?

Feirwyn reached the end of the alley.

"Wait!" Skerth called.

Feirwyn stopped, but did not turn.

"My name is Skerth."

At first the man said nothing. Then he nodded and half-turned back. "My thanks," he said, before stepping out of the alley to fade into the maze of the Lower City.

His mind heavy with questions he could not answer, Skerth waited until he could no longer hear the man's footsteps before gathering what remained of his strength and dragging himself out of the alley.

For the next few days Skerth stayed wrapped in his blankets, lying as still as possible to keep the pain at bay. The other kids left him alone, which gave him plenty of time to fret about his tentative truce with Malyn, his exchange with Feirwyn, and the Caretakers' plot. Kiri wandered in and out at irregular intervals, usually only staying long enough to pass him some food and a cup of water before taking off again on another of her mysterious jaunts. When he could catch her for more than a few minutes, there were usually too many kids around to trade more than a few scattered comments about the general word on the streets. He managed to tell her about the truce, but little more, and nothing of Feirwyn.

When he could no longer stand the sidelong, worried glances of the smaller kids and the constant company of his own thoughts, Skerth declared himself well enough to manage and edged back out onto the streets. Deliberately choosing a crowded thoroughfare far from his usual haunts, Skerth wove half-heartedly through the throng of fishmongers and lesser merchants, his mind worrying the same refrain he had fixed upon for the past few days.

In the late afternoon, he was nearly ready to call off a good day's work when he heard the shriek. Skerth darted for the nearest escape route, an alley just visible behind the back end of a cart heaped with over-ripe fruits and vegetables. Another quick glance informed him that the shriek had come from the mouth of a passage across and down the lane, where a small crowd had gathered around the screamer, a young girl rapidly working herself into hysterics.

"Girls," Skerth muttered. She'd probably been some sailor's love, and just found out she wasn't the only one. Not his problem. Satisfied that no one would notice the lone, tattered boy slipping away in the other direction, Skerth grabbed an eba fruit off the cart and turned away.

But the screaming didn't stop, and acquired a chorus of raised voices, male and female, youth and adult. Skerth paused. Listened.

". . .poor boy. . ."

"So young!"

"*Dead.* . . ."

No, Skerth thought with a chill.

He leaned out from behind the newly abandoned produce cart and watched the gathering crowd, drawn to the macabre like carrion-birds come to feast. The girl's screams had disintegrated into choked sobs; two matrons and a hopeful young man had come forward to guide her away from the distasteful scene. The crowd parted for them, then closed in more tightly around the center, eager to view the spectacle.

Skerth suppressed a wave of nausea. Trapped inside the circle lay one of Skerth's few friends, or enemies: proof that Dreiwend's man—the Caretakers' assassin—had struck again.

Pushing his way through the crowd would attract far too much attention, but he would soon know who lay at the center of that circle. Under normal circumstances, it might take days, or even weeks, to notice that a common runner of his streets had gone missing. But now that he and Malyn had agreed to keep a closer watch on their respective territories, Skerth guessed that they would know the boy's identity much sooner.

Skerth backed into the shadows, slipped into the alley—

—and immediately ran up against something—*someone*—immoveable.

"Well, well," the man drawled, catching Skerth by the shoulders in an unforgiving grip. "What has found me here?"

The alley was more of a large crawlspace, so closed in by the buildings to either side that even in the filtered sunlight of early evening deep shadows obscured the man's features. The man himself was darkness, so completely cloaked and hooded in a swath of dark wool that his eyes stood out all the more—the sharp, ice-grey eyes of a murderer, narrowed ominously on Skerth.

"Beg pardon, sir," Skerth said. "I meant no harm. If you could let me pass, I'll be on my way."

The man shifted his hold on Skerth to one iron hand, and with the other, gripped Skerth's jaw and jerked his face into a shaft of light. The eyes swept over Skerth, taking his measure. "Skinny. . . small . . . but that gold in your hair . . . how old are you, boy?"

Skerth hesitated. *Skinny. Small. Fair-haired.*

He had managed, in the worst way possible, to find the Caretakers' assassin.

"Boy!" the man snarled, giving Skerth a hard shake.

His mind raced. The heir and his decoys—if they were indeed his target, as he suspected—would be nearly fifteen. "Twelve," he gasped against the tightening grip on his chin.

"Twelve, you say?" The assassin eased his hold on Skerth's face, but kept a firm grip on his upper arm.

"And I'm not small," he added. "Mum says I'm tall for my age."

The assassin chuckled softly. The grip loosened still more. "Mayhap your mum is right."

"Please, sir." Skerth glanced pointedly over the assassin's shoulder. "I've got to get back. She'll worry—"

"Will she, now?" The eyes narrowed thoughtfully. His hand relaxed to rest loosely on Skerth's arm. "I suppose so, fine boy like you."

He flinched inwardly at the assassin's tone. Had he just talked the man out of murder only to end up auctioned off to the skin traders?

Abruptly, the assassin let him go. In a blur of motion, Skerth darted out of reach and drew his dagger.

"Curse you for a liar!" the assassin growled, lunging after him. Skerth slashed out blindly, but his dagger caught in the folds of the assassin's cloak and clattered to the ground. He couldn't waste time retrieving it. He burst out of the alley at a dead run, chancing the attention of the crowds and the Staves, not once pausing to find out whether or not the assassin followed.

"Murderer!" he called out as he ran past, pointing back toward the alley mouth. "Murderer! There!"

A few of the townspeople turned to watch as he flew past, their faces a blur. He didn't wait to see if they had heard, or would even heed his warning. Surely the assassin would not linger; surely he had moved on to some other patch of darkness, awaiting his next kill.

Skerth made for the rooftops, where he skittered from one building to the next, making his way nearly to the sea before he stopped to rest, breathless, exhausted, muscles screaming in protest, on the roof of a dilapidated stone-and-wood-rotted structure not far from the docks. Only then did he have time to consider the loss of the dagger. Only then did he realize that if Feirwyn had recognized the dagger, so too would Dreiwend's man. The Caretakers' assassin.

He would never be safe on his streets again.

Chapter Eight: An Uneasy Truce

Skerth woke shivering. He lay curled into a stiff ball, blinking in the dark and damp, until he remembered that he had fallen asleep there on the rooftops overlooking the sea.

He sat up and stretched the ache out of his shoulders. The night was black and moonless, and a thick fog had settled over the city. He felt for his dagger, remembered its loss, and muttered a string of the foulest curses he knew. Once again, he was without a weapon. How many years had he carried that dagger before this without incident? Now, in such a short span, he had lost it twice. And this time, he had lost it in the worst way imaginable.

Still, he had fared better than the first boy to run across the assassin that day. Skerth thought of Kiri. Was she safe? Would she have heard of the boy's murder and search for him? He hadn't gone back to the warehouse that night. Had she? His face warmed. Between his weakness around Jemmy and Minah and his obsessive worry for Kiri's safety, he was going to end up in a gutter grave before the year was out.

Once his eyes adjusted to the darkness, Skerth carefully picked his way to the ground and moved slowly through the city, keeping to the less-frequented paths, halting at every sound or hint of light, pressing himself into the walls, always mindful that he lacked a knife. He rounded the corner to his warehouse to find a body slouched across the doorstep, a drained jug of ale dangling from its hand. His throat constricting painfully, Skerth nudged the body with his toe. It didn't stir. Dreading what he might discover, Skerth leaned close enough to catch the stink of filth and ale coming off the boy and gagged. But the boy—Gor, Skerth realized—breathed. Skerth briefly considered thieving the boy's knife—he was so big, stupid and fond of ale that he probably wouldn't notice the loss for days—but kicked him hard in the ribs instead.

Gor grunted and tried to roll over. Skerth kicked him again, harder. This time he lurched upright. The jug hit the ground and shattered.

"Wha'd y' do that for?" Gor slurred, squinting.

"Did Kiri come this way?"

"Skerth?" Gor had trouble processing information under normal circumstances; drunk, he was impossible. "Why'd y' break my jug?"

"I didn't. How long have you been here?"

"Since . . . dunno. Light. Now's dark." He chuckled. "Dunno, Skerth. Why'd y' break—"

"Have you seen Kiri?"

The urgency of Skerth's tone managed to sober him somewhat. He blinked a few times and frowned in his best imitation of a thinking person. "No. Haven't seen 'im in . . . days, I guess. Why?"

"Never mind."

Skerth squeezed past the drink-sotted boy into the warehouse. He glanced around, but could see nothing more than blurred shapes of varying sizes scattered across the room. He considered heading back out, then quickly rejected the idea. It was too late, too dark, and he had no way to defend himself. As he re-stole his blankets and settled in, he tried not to hope that wherever Kiri was, she was safe.

Skerth loitered near the warehouse for the better part of the morning, waiting for Kiri to turn up. By noon, he couldn't leash his anxiety any longer and headed for the streets.

No more than a few strides down the mud-rutted lane that flanked his warehouse he ran into Jemmy, Minah, and a couple of new boys crouched around a game of twigs and small rocks. He tried to slip by unnoticed, but the girls looked up hopefully as he passed. He quickened his step, ducked his head and averted his eyes.

"Who's that?" one of the boys muttered, irritated that the girls had paused in the game.

"Skerth," Minah whispered. "He's nice."

"Skerth!" called Jemmy.

He sighed and turned. Both girls grinned and waved. Skerth reluctantly lifted a hand in greeting, hoping that would appease them, and started to turn away. The boys glared, no doubt wondering when he'd shove off so they could continue their game.

"Want to play, Skerth?" Minah called after him.

Walk on, he told himself, gritting his teeth. *Cut them off now, before they learn to expect kindness.*

An image of the sweet lady who'd taken him in, then turned him out with just as much ceremony flickered to mind. Her memory still stirred mixed feelings: was he better off for having known her kindness, for however short a time, or would his life be so much simpler if he hadn't? Another question for which he had no answers.

He turned back to face the huddle of children. "I've no time for games, girls," he told them, not unkindly. "I've got to. . ." He paused, remembering his and Kiri's plan for the little ones. He and Kiri could circle each other in the Lower City for weeks without finding one another; with the kids' help, he could cut that time in half, at least. And with new bodies turning up by the day, what was the harm in putting a few more eyes and ears on the streets? They could help him find Kiri and bring in some news of the assassin, too.

A few steps brought him back to stand beside the circle—to the girls' great delight and the boys' disgust. He squatted to their level and smiled. "Actually, I'm looking for a friend. Would you like to help?"

"Yes!" chorused the girls. At the same time, the boys replied with a vehement "no." But he could tell from the practiced disinterest of their expressions that he had at least caught their attention.

"Do you know my friend Kiri?"

"The white-haired boy who's always after me to cut my hair?" Jemmy looked so incensed that Skerth couldn't help but laugh.

"Yes, that's him all right."

"Seen him yesterday," one of the boys muttered. "Come through about mid-day, I guess, then went off again."

Mid-day. Skerth's chest tightened. The body had been discovered late afternoon the day before. That could have been her lying in the alley after all.

65

He shoved these thoughts aside. "I'm looking for him. He might be in danger. Can you help me search?" The children looked dubious; he pulled a few coins out of his pocket and gave one to each. Suddenly they were not only attentive, but eager. "If you see him, tell him to meet me here, at the warehouse. I'll give you another coin if you find him."

Their game forgotten, the children rose, all chattering questions about where they should go first.

"Hold off." He out held his hands until they quieted. "It doesn't matter where you go, but stay at least two together. Look out for one another, and pay attention to what's going on around you. If you see anything strange I want to know that, too."

"What d'you mean, strange?" the taller of the two boys asked.

Skerth hesitated. "Just anything—different. Anyone seems out of place. Particularly—" he hesitated once more, then finished in a rush, "Just stay clear of anyone seems shifty, or too interested in one of us. And if you see a man a little more than my height, cloaked and hooded in black, get away, fast as you can, and tell me straightaway. Understand?"

Wide-eyed, the children nodded.

"Off you go, then."

After securing their coins, the four scampered off in the direction of the marketplace. No doubt they'd get themselves a bit of bread first. Skerth didn't blame them, although he hoped they wouldn't forget their errand—or his warning—before too long.

He decided to head back to where the latest body had been discovered. The body and the assassin were long gone, but he might catch a bit of gossip or find another scat or two hanging around who might know something of use.

He had turned into the last stretch of alley leading to his destination when a wild shadow flew at him out of the abandoned building to his right. He only had a second to grope for his missing dagger before his assailant flung skinny arms around him and clung tightly—sobbing.

"Um—?" he managed, trying to detach from the crier enough to get a good look. All he could catch was a shock of cropped white hair, but that one, small detail was enough. Unexpected relief flooded his veins, leaving his insides warm and tingling. "Kiri!" he breathed into her hair. "What's wrong?"

It wasn't like her to cry. This wasn't an ordinary cry, either; her body shook and his shoulder was already damp. As he stood there, her small body pressed up against his, and tried to figure out where to put his hands, a strange, not unpleasant sensation overcame him. Instead of pushing her away, he tightened his arms and held her until long after the shaking had stopped and her choking sobs quieted to wet sniffles.

"What's with all the water?" he asked.

She leaned away to look at him, one blue eye and one brown fixing him with a wet, mysterious stare. He loosened his embrace, but didn't let her go. He sort of liked holding her there, and she wasn't complaining, either.

"I thought you were dead." The clear emotion in her voice unsettled Skerth. "The townspeople found a body here yesterday. You didn't come back to the warehouse, and I thought—"

"I did come back, but not until long after dark."

She blinked up at him, surprised. "You did? I must have left before—"

Skerth was suddenly, irrationally irritated. "Yes, I did. And if you'd ever stay more than a minute in one place, you might've seen me."

She stiffened, then pushed out of his arms. "I spent the night looking for you. Fortunately, I ran into Jemmy and Minah near the gates to the Royal Quarter. They saw the body, so I knew then it wasn't you, but you didn't come back, and—"

"Wait—the girls saw the body? Did they recognize him?"

She shook her head. "No, so he was probably one of Malyn's scats. Tall. Stocky. Pale hair and brown skin, like the merchants from the high country."

"Fael." He had been one of the most fervent supporters of working together to catch the assassin. What happened? Had he discovered the assassin and decided to follow him on his own? Had he come too close? Somehow, Skerth didn't think he had been killed by chance; his murder lacked the forethought of the others. His body had been discovered in the light of day, near a busy thoroughfare. The assassin barely had time to hide, let alone move the body, breaking his usual pattern. Was Fael's death a clumsy strike to silence the boy and cover the assassin's identity? Or were the Caretakers growing desperate?

"We need to tell Malyn," he said.

"I already did." She rolled his eyes at his look of surprise and added, "When I couldn't find you, I wasn't going to just sit around and do nothing. I sent one of our kids with word this morning."

Something didn't seem right. "So if you knew I was alive, why were you so upset?"

She was quiet a long time. "I don't know. I knew that body wasn't yours, but I still didn't know what had happened to you. You always come back to the warehouse. When you didn't—" she broke off with a shrug that did not fool him for a moment.

"Well, I'm here. For now, anyway." After glancing around to make sure that they were still alone, he told her about his encounter with Feirwyn, bumping into the assassin and losing his dagger—again. "So if that dagger brought Feirwyn to me, I imagine the assassin will be after me next."

She frowned thoughtfully. "How *did* you get that dagger, Skerth?"

"I don't remember."

She looked skeptical. "How can you not remember something like that?"

"I don't know. I've just always had it," he snapped. "Do you remember every detail of your years on the streets?"

"Almost everything," she said quietly, making him instantly regret the question.

Once again, the feeling that he was forgetting something very important nudged him. He brushed it aside. "Come on, Kiri," he said softly. "Let's go. We've work to do."

"Skerth—"

"Let's go!" He brushed past her toward the open street, not waiting for her to follow.

She caught up a moment later and walked silently at his side. He led them back to the street where the townspeople had found Fael's body. There were fewer crowds than usual, murder proving an excellent deterrent. Skerth almost felt sorry for the shopkeepers, who would find business a little slower for the next few days—weeks, if the assassin struck again anywhere near. He felt a little sorry for himself, too; this had been a good street to work, and he would have to find another.

Someone had disposed of the body, leaving only blood-stained cobbles in that narrow corner between the fish-monger and the butcher. The evidence confirmed what Skerth had guessed: the assassin had struck out of his usual pattern. But why the change?

Skerth and Kiri settled against the wall of the poulterer's shop to listen for news. They loitered as long as they could without looking suspicious, until the poulterer's wife finally emerged and whisked them away. In the end, as they headed home, they had learned little more than they already knew, aside from a few embroidered stories about how the body had been discovered and who the boy might have been. Fael would have felt honored to know that he'd been *a decent boy* whom all of the shopkeepers had helped a time or two by giving alms, clothes, and food. Too bad Fael had really been an insufferable bully who stole far more than anyone had ever given.

Far more interesting than eavesdropping outside the poulterer's was running into Taleryn and Lark deep inside Skerth's territory, locked in a heated embrace. Upon sight of Skerth and Kiri they pulled apart and reached for their daggers. Out of instinct, Skerth reached for his own, swore, then called out, "We're under truce."

"Right," Taleryn said. Visibly unsettled, he released his dagger and ran a hand through his hair.

Lark, who still leaned casually against the wall, merely smirked. Skerth flushed. He had a hard time keeping his wits around Lark. Aside from dressing in boy's clothes, she made no attempts to disguise herself as male; with her curves, Skerth doubted she could. She was older—about seventeen, as best Skerth could guess—and by her age, most girls had either gone on to honest work or found a place in the taverns and brothels. A girl who looked like Lark— long, silky black braid, full lips, and dark eyes that turned up just so at the corners--would soon have her choice of lesser nobles and wealthy merchants competing to make her their mistress. But for whatever reason she had stayed with Malyn's scats to eke out a street living alongside the rest of the orphans, misfits and dock rats.

"Aren't you Malyn's girl?" Kiri asked, her gaze shifting meaningfully from Lark to Taleryn.

Taleryn looked nervously to Lark, who replied with a lazy smile, "I don't see how it's any of your affair. But no. I'm not."

"Then why come deep into my boundaries just to have a go at one another?" asked Skerth, trying hard not to think about what kissing Lark might feel like. "Can't find a private place in yours?"

Taleryn started forward; Lark shoved away from the wall and laid a hand on his arm. And just like that, he stopped. The unspoken power Lark held over Taleryn, the control, both intrigued and appalled Skerth. It was almost embarrassing. Skerth vowed then and there never to let any girl manipulate him like that.

"We have a message," Lark snapped. "Trick is dead."

Taleryn recovered his self-control. "Runner and Lark found him not an hour ago. His throat was cut."

Skerth's mind reeled. Fael. Trick. The assassin was striking more quickly, and with less caution. "Was there much blood?"

"What? Why—"

Lark's wave silenced Taleryn's questions. "No. Not a drop. Aside from the gore on his neck, of course." She cocked her head to the side and studied Skerth with new interest. "Why do you ask?"

His skin warmed under her scrutiny. Irritated by his own involuntary response, Skerth straightened and lifted his chin. He wasn't sure how much he should share; his deal with Malyn didn't necessarily extend to his scats. Still, they had come all this way to bring him the news of Trick's death.

"Most of the bodies weren't killed across Malyn's boundaries, only dumped there. Otherwise there would've been blood all around them, like with Fael. If what you say is true, sounds like Trick was dumped, too."

"How do you know this?" Lark asked, dropping her veneer of casual unconcern. She was alert, turning her full attention to Skerth.

Skerth opened his mouth to speak, but Kiri answered first. "Never mind how. We figured it out. If you put as much effort into thinking as you spend time kissing Taleryn, you might have worked it out, too."

Lark's lips tightened into a thin white line and she reached for her dagger. This time, Taleryn put out a hand to restrain her.

"Truce, remember?" said Kiri, a little too sweetly.

70

Lark scowled, but dropped her hand. Kiri grinned. Skerth shot her a look of warning, but if Kiri noticed, she didn't respond.

"If you know something, you should tell," Taleryn said, finally getting more than a word into the conversation. "Until the assassin's caught, we're all in danger."

Skerth knew he was right. At the same time, he had a difficult time trusting anyone from Malyn's side of the boundary, truce or no. Still, of all Malyn's scats, Taleryn had given him the least amount of fuss over the years, had even looked the other way a time or two when he had strayed too far into Malyn's run. And what good did withholding information do?

Skerth took a deep breath and told them everything. He started with his initial foray across the boundaries to get a look at the first boy's body and finished by recounting the events of the day before, only leaving out the bits about his tunnel, the conversation he'd overheard between Dreiwend and the Caretaker, and Feirwyn. Ignoring Kiri's sharp elbow in his ribs and her hiss of disapproval, he detailed his encounter with the assassin, beginning with the woman's scream and ending with his own narrow escape.

"You left your dagger?" Lark asked when he had finished. "Your only weapon?"

Skerth thought it odd that this, more than any other detail, caught her attention. "What else was I supposed to do? I'm no match for a trained assassin."

"I would've done the same," Taleryn replied, nodding. Unlike Lark, who wore an unreadable expression, Taleryn looked mildly impressed. He pulled a concealed knife from his boot and tossed it to Skerth. "It's not much of a blade, but it's better than nothing."

Taleryn shrugged off his muttered "thanks" while Skerth turned the knife over in his hands, taking its measure. It was small, but sharp, and of decent quality. It would do.

"We need to head back," said Taleryn. "If we hear anything—"

"We'll let you know, too," Skerth finished. The moment turned awkward. This exchange had already extended far beyond the familiar, and all four of them were eager to be done.

Taleryn slung his arm over Lark's shoulders and guided her past Skerth and Kiri.

"Be careful," Lark murmured as she passed. For the first time, her concern felt genuine. Skerth took that as a compliment.

She and Taleryn had scarcely passed out of sight when Kiri rounded on Skerth, eyes narrowed into a venomous glare, arms crossed tight over her chest. "Why did you do that?"

"Do what?" He stared, bewildered at her rapid change.

"Tell them everything! They didn't need to know about your scrape with the assassin. *Malyn* doesn't need to know."

Skerth straightened, clenching his fists. "Yes, they did. They *all* do."

"No, they don't. Not everything. What good does knowing that you so *bravely* faced the assassin do them? Unless, of course, you wanted to play the hero for Lark." She almost spat the name.

Skerth flushed. "I don't care what Lark thinks."

Kiri raised her eyebrows. "Really? From what I can see, you care a great deal about what Lark thinks. You should see how you look at her. It's disgusting—"

"The only thing I care about is finding that assassin!" he shouted. His voice echoed in the alley, but he didn't care. "Don't you see, Kiri? We could *die*! All of us! He's going to keep killing until he's satisfied that the missing heir and all possible decoys are dead. None of us are safe. Not even you."

He turned his back. His hands shook, so he jammed them in his pockets. "I don't much like the idea either, but we need to work together. It's the only chance we have."

"Fine. Tell them what they need to know. But don't give them everything. You, more than any of us, should know better than to trust Malyn."

Her words stung.

"Maybe you should dress more like a girl," he shot back. "Then the decisions I make wouldn't matter to you. At least you'd be safe."

A long silence settled between them. When he turned, she had gone.

Angry at her, furious with himself, and frustrated with Lark and Taleryn and Malyn, the assassin, the very streets themselves, Skerth ducked his head and moved into the shadows. Where he belonged.

Chapter Nine: Flame and Ash

Skerth didn't return to the warehouse that night, or the next. Instead, he kept to some of the less frequented holes and hovels, where he was certain to remain undisturbed. He slept in the back corner of a long abandoned shop coated in dust and, therefore, fairly safe. He picked enough pockets to get by, careful to avoid crossing anyone he knew. He even visited his tunnel, hoping to overhear something more of the Caretakers' plans, but the thick air and even thicker silence lulled him into an uneasy doze. When he woke, terrified and disoriented from a strange nightmare full of panic and noise, he almost forgot the way out in his haste to escape.

He emerged to the acrid tang of a heavy smoke that thickened the air and stung his nose. The sky glowed an unearthly orange and grey, confusing day and night; and, incredibly, it was snowing. He held out his hand to catch the flakes. They were fragile, but warm, and they did not melt away at his touch. He stared into his palm, uncomprehending, until he realized that he held not snow, but ash.

The wind shifted, puffing smoke into the streets of the pleasure district. Skerth finally caught on to the raw urgency, the burgeoning hysteria of the people around him. His back to the wall of rock that divided the rich and the poor, Skerth could hear the roar of flames, but he couldn't see them. He squeezed from his narrow passage into a whirlwind of panic and noise. Sailors, brawlers, pirates and drunks alike rushed past carrying sloshing water buckets, possessions, and stolen goods. Mothers struggling with more crying children than they could manage cursed Skerth for standing in their path. Slaves dragging chains and broken collars fled on swift bare feet, while whores and serving girls traded their comely calls for shrieks of terror. A few sturdy souls had organized bucket brigades to keep the fire at bay, but the flames had too much fuel—too many rickety wooden buildings, too much refuse, too many people. Skerth saw them all, heard their blended chorus of fear and action, but did not heed them, so intent was he on glimpsing something through the haze of smoke and ash that would tell him where the fire burned.

As though the trickster gods who governed the sea had guessed his thoughts, a gust of wind fresh off the Quistand Ocean cleared a small patch of sky, and Skerth saw just enough to confirm his fears.

The entire Lower City burned.

Skerth tried every path he knew to get to his warehouse, desperate to find Kiri, the little ones, anyone he recognized, but every street was blocked. Smoke smothered those streets not yet overcome by flames, which overflowed with panicked people struggling to escape. Makeshift barricades, hastily piled out of crumbling stone, blocked alleys and closed off avenues in an attempt to stall the fire long enough to quit its spread. There was no way in to the heart of the Lower City. For those trapped inside, there was no way out.

All throughout that long, black night Skerth searched every accessible corner, every face, for Kiri's. He shouted the names of all he knew—Kiri, Jemmy, Minah, even Gor—until his throat burned from the smoke and the effort, but no one came. He helped, too, when he could; men whose purses he might have cut the day before thrust buckets into his able hands and worked alongside him to save what they could of the city that belonged to them all. In the dim light of dawn, Skerth swore he even glimpsed the Caretakers, escorted by the Fury himself and a handful of Blades, moving like tall grey ghosts among the crowds of frightened and dispossessed. But they disappeared so quickly that Skerth almost thought he had imagined them there, walking aloof and silent among the people they claimed to serve.

A blood red sun rose, but could not pierce the thick blanket of smoke smothering the burning city. Grim-faced men and women replaced those who had labored through the night, shuffling into the brigades with slumped shoulders and dead eyes. Wordlessly Skerth passed his bucket to a sailor whose haunted look told Skerth much more than he wanted to know. Free again to search for his own lost, Skerth took to the streets to scour the haunts and alleys he could not access the night before.

He did find a few of the little ones down by the sea, where many of the night's refugees had gathered. On the rocky beach, a bedraggled young woman clutched Jemmy and Minah as close as her own get. The little girls acknowledged Skerth as he passed, but did not join him; he didn't blame them, nor did he begrudge them their place in the woman's arms. He only hoped that once the imminent danger had passed the woman would not forget them or turn them out. He found some of the smaller boys as well, gathered near the water tossing rocks into the sea, impervious to the great tragedy that played out all around them. Skerth saw other faces, too, some whose names he knew, others he didn't, and even a few of Malyn's scats. But he saw no sign of Kiri.

And still the fire raged, choking the city in ash and sorrow.

Skerth walked all that day in a daze while the efforts to fight the blaze continued around him. Whether from lack of nourishment, exhaustion, or grief he didn't know, but something about the fire felt strangely familiar, as though he had entered a recurring nightmare he had never quite remembered clearly until now. He looked at the men and women fighting valiantly to save their city and saw other faces: finely dressed men and women brandishing swords against a similar backdrop of smoke and flame, shouting commands he could not hear; servants running; and two women—one an old hag, the other young and pretty. The hag took him into her arms; he cried out, but it was no use. "Go," the hag said to the girl, "Go—"

A hand fell on his shoulder, startling the present into focus. The great halls and fine clothes, the servants and swords disappeared; around him he saw only crowds of strangers huddled here and there, masked alike in grime and ash. And directly before Skerth stood a tall man cloaked and hooded, his face shadowed.

The assassin!

Skerth shouted and twisted out of the man's grasp; no sooner did he free himself than another hand closed on his wrist. Skerth thrashed, but every time he freed himself the man found another hold. Skerth glanced about for help; there were more than enough gathered, but none seemed particularly interested in the scuffle. Most gave his cries for help a look before returning to their own business. That was the way of it on the streets: don't look, don't react, don't get involved. Safer that way. Knowing the truth of it didn't alleviate Skerth's panic.

The man managed to wrestle both of his arms around Skerth and pulled him closer. "Wait! Sea Witch take you, boy—hold still!"

Skerth registered the words, the tone of voice, the clean diction of the higher classes an instant after he slammed his heel backward into his assailant's knee. The man grunted, but did not release his hold. As recognition of the stranger's identity gradually settled in, Skerth let the fight go out of him.

"Feirwyn," Skerth rasped. Between the ash, the long night and the tussle, his mouth and throat had gone raw.

"Yes. Feirwyn. If I release you, will you run? Or can I trust you to stay?"

"Depends. What do you want?" Skerth snapped. Now that the imminent danger had passed, his anger quickened hot and fast. Twice Feirwyn had managed to catch him off guard; twice he'd failed to break away. Either the man had a special talent for stalking street rats or Skerth was losing his skill.

"Information."

"Yeah? Well, I want some of that myself."

"Perhaps our goals are not so different. Perhaps we can help one another. Will you stay and hear me out?"

Skerth nodded. Feirwyn's hands dropped away. Skerth bounded out of reach, then turned to face him.

"That dagger of yours. You've lost it, haven't you." A statement, not a question.

Skerth frowned. "How did you know—"

Feirwyn cut him off with a dismissive wave. "I know a great many things about what has happened on these streets of late. My question for you is this: do you know what it is you lost?"

Skerth had only a street scat's education, but he was smart enough to know that Feirwyn was asking the same old question in a roundabout way.

"No. I already told you, I don't know how the dagger came to me."

"But you know who carries it now." There was no mistaking his tone: he knew about the assassin.

Skerth said nothing, glad for the darkness that cloaked his shame.

Feirwyn stepped close and lowered his voice. "You're in grave danger. They are coming for you, and they will not stop until your blood soaks the street. I can help, if you will trust me."

"Why should I trust you?"

"Because I can tell you who's hunting you, and why. I can tell you the importance of that dagger. You want information. I can give it to you."

He narrowed his eyes at Feirwyn. "And what do you want in return?"

Skerth could feel Feirwyn taking his measure from beneath the hood of his tattered cloak. Thinking. Deciding. At last his words were few and quietly spoken, but the weight of them struck Skerth to his very core.

"A king."

Chapter Ten: Feirwyn

Between the fire, the barricades, and the general chaos into which the blaze had thrown the inhabitants of the Lower City, the circuitous journey to The Blighted Swine seemed to take an eternity. All the long way, Skerth kept his knife palmed and a wary eye on his companion. He wasn't sure why he had agreed to accompany Feirwyn to his rooms at the Swine; he had no reason to trust that the man wouldn't truss him up and sell him to the skin traders or slavers at the first opportunity. But then, Feirwyn had twice let him go—once in the Royal Quarter, once in the alley—when he could easily have had Skerth either captured or killed. And Skerth stood to gain a great deal if he could learn anything more about the assassin. So he followed, wisdom, curiosity and intuition churning at every step.

The Blighted Swine squatted near the Upwedge Gates in a much more respectable part of the Lower City, where tumbledown dwellings and shabby warehouses of rotting wood and repurposed rubble gave way to well-kept, if aged, buildings of scrubbed stone and mortar. The fire had presented a real concern here in the better districts, but had never truly threatened; the Caretakers had seen to that. Here, full squadrons of Staves and citizenry worked in a much more organized and concentrated effort to keep the fires at bay, and with far more success than the desperate whores, pirates and children struggling to rescue what little they had. The flame of resentment always burning deep at Skerth's core flared at this new insult on the part of the Caretakers. Once more, the grey ghosts who ruled the city had made plain to all that most of those who dwelled Downwedge, whether by birth or circumstance, were not worthy of saving. They were less than. Other.

Outcast.

At the tavern door, Skerth checked his anger and concentrated on the matter at hand. He watched apprehensively as Feirwyn shoved open the heavy oak door, and for a breath or two, his muscles tensed to run, he decided that nothing—not curiosity, not the promise of knowledge, not his own two feet—could persuade him to cross that threshold in the company of a man he hardly knew and did not trust.

Feirwyn paused, his hand still pressed against the polished wood, a question in his blue eyes. Skerth squeezed the hilt of his knife until his knuckles ached. It wasn't too late. Not yet. But once he stepped through the door. . . .

Briefly he wondered what Kiri would do, and knew, before he'd finished the thought, that she would cross. Without hesitation. She was too curious, too daring, while he always chose the more conservative streets to work and the careless, more distracted marks.

Yet the assassin had *his* dagger, not Kiri's.

Skerth sucked in a deep breath and pushed past Feirwyn.

The delicate tingle of a tiny bell juxtaposed against the door's heavy creak drew all eyes to the two travelers framed in the door. The tavern keeper, a muscular, dark-skinned man with a clean-shaven head and a gold ring in his right ear, looked up from behind the bar and narrowed.

"Friend of yours?" he growled, nodding toward Skerth.

Feirwyn clapped a hand on Skerth's shoulder, then gave it a warning squeeze. "My young cousin. He disappeared a sevenday ago and my sister is frantic to find him."

The tavern keeper swept his eyes over Skerth from head to toe, then back again. "Cousin, you say?" His tone suggested otherwise. Skerth reddened, humiliated by the implication.

Feirwyn seemed none too pleased himself. "Yes," he said firmly, eyes boring into the keeper's. "My cousin."

The innkeeper grunted. He picked up a mug, peered inside, then made a show of wiping it out with the grimy towel slung over his shoulder. "The boy's not welcome downstairs. I don't like the look of him. He comes near my patrons and I'll toss him out on his ratty arse," he said without looking at Feirwyn.

Skerth opened his mouth to inform the tavern keeper that the men slumped here and there over their cups didn't look much better than he, but Feirwyn's hand pinching his shoulder forced him silent.

"Very well. Send up a hot meal. And ale."

The tavern keeper beckoned to a dark-haired serving girl who didn't look much older than Skerth. She rose from the lap of a patron, whooped as the man slapped her hard on the rump, then ducked behind the counter, her wide, curious eyes trained on Skerth.

"Come," Feirwyn said in a low voice, steering Skerth toward a narrow wooden stair at the back of the common room.

A handful of soot-covered men and women gathered around the tavern's long tables cast a bored glance at the newcomers as they passed; the rest didn't bother to look up from their tankards. They looked like Skerth felt: bone-weary and beaten down.

They stopped at the last door at the end of a shabby hallway. Instead of drawing out a key, Feirwyn rapped twice, paused, tapped three quick knocks, then thumped once, open-handed. Skerth shifted from foot to foot, picturing the hallway and the tavern layout in his mind, mapping his escape route.

Before he had the chance, the door swung open and a woman peered into the hall. A beautiful woman, Skerth decided. She wore her long, dark hair bound into a thick braid and had smooth olive skin and light grey eyes. At sight of Skerth her eyes briefly widened in surprise before she quickly masked her features into a neutral expression and held the door wide to usher them through.

The room was luxurious by Skerth's standards: dim, but cozy, with two faded armchairs set before the fire and a rickety table and two chairs shoved beneath the shuttered window. A faded, but serviceable grey wool blanket covered the bed. Scrolls and papers littered the surface of the table, piling up against and around a pitcher and two mugs. A cloak lay tossed over one of the armchairs, and a bundle of gear rested next to the bed. A thin layer of ash dusted everything, a vivid reminder that much of Skerth's city lay in ruins.

"You are late," the woman announced as she moved to the table and poured a thick honey-colored liquid into one of the mugs. She offered it to Skerth; his first impulse was to accept, but instinct reminded him that good folk never offered such treats to scats like him without their own motives. He declined.

"I was delayed." Feirwyn removed his cloak and laid it over the back of one of the chairs. He looked far less threatening in faded breeches and a well-worn linen shirt, his unkempt brown hair brushing his shoulders and flaking ash. In the light and well away from the darkened slums and alleys, he seemed much younger than

Skerth had thought—no more than twenty-five, if a day—though some great burden had begun to take its toll at the corners of his eyes and furrow his brow. His eyes were bloodshot and red-rimmed from smoke and fatigue; more than a day's growth shadowed his face. Still, when he managed a smile for the woman, there was a kindness in it that calmed Skerth's nerves. There was something familiar about him, too, something that nagged at him.

"I worried for you all night."

"And I am sorry for it. Truly." Feirwyn looked to Skerth. "But I did not search in vain."

The woman turned to study Skerth with such scrutiny that he flushed hot and tensed to flee. "The resemblance is uncanny," she said at last, her expression approving, "though it has been years since anyone has seen the boys."

"Years that will prove to our advantage," Feirwyn pointed out. "Yet even if memories have not faded, I believe he will still serve."

"Serve what?" Skerth blurted out, unable to contain his irritation any longer. "Quit speaking in riddles. You promised me answers. I followed you across the Lower City as you asked, and I'll have them now, if you please." He eyed her warily. "Starting with who she is."

"My apologies," Feirwyn said. "Allow me to present Nirue of Estalor Keep. Nirue, this is Skerth."

"Well met, Skerth." Nirue reached for Skerth's hand in greeting. He recoiled, embarrassed by his filth and lack of grace, but she would not allow him to pull his hand from hers. Her full lips curved into a warm smile, and he felt all the more shamed by her courtesy. She didn't need fine robes or jewels in her hair to define her station; her manners and bearing distinguished her as nobility just as clearly as Skerth's rough skin and hungry look marked him as a street scat.

A patterned knock came at the door, sparing him the humiliation of additional social graces. Nirue admitted the serving girl, who entered balancing a well-laden tray on her hip. The smell of hot stew and warm, fresh-baked bread overwhelmed the room. Skerth's stomach immediately growled; he hoped Nirue hadn't heard.

As soon as she dismissed the serving girl, Nirue ushered Skerth to the table. "Eat," she encouraged when he merely stared, wide-eyed, into the heaping trenchers set before him, a feast the likes of which he had never seen. A whole roasted chicken. A heaping bowl of steaming greens. Meat pies and rolls. One large bowl full of ebas, another heaping with small red berries he didn't recognize. His mouth watered. "You are our guest. Please."

Skerth found his last measure of resistance slip away. He hated himself for it; at the same time, if he were to die, damned if he wouldn't die full. Before he could change his mind, Skerth tore into the bread and stew with a haste borne of too many years fighting to keep what little he had.

Feirwyn settled in the chair across the table. "You have questions for me. Ask whatever you like. I will answer, if I can."

Skerth wiped stew from his mouth with the back of his hand and narrowed his eyes. "You say you know who's hunting us."

Feirwyn's expression hardened. "His name is Kalen, and the Caretakers own him, blade and soul."

Skerth stuffed a roll into his mouth. "What does that mean, exactly?"

"It means that he has no loyalties to anyone but his masters, no conscience, and no understanding of mercy." The nobleman pressed his lips tight; a muscle twitched in his cheek. Nirue laid a hand on his shoulder, and he covered it with his own. "His sworn profession is to carry out the Caretakers' darker orders in secret and in silence. Now that they have set him on this path, he will not leave it until he has exterminated every last possible heir or decoy in the Lower City. None of you are safe for as long as he hunts you."

"Cheery thought," Skerth said. "If what you say is true, we might as well slit our own throats now and be done."

A mirthless smile twitched at the corner of Feirwyn's mouth. "That is his hope, that through fear and intimidation he can accomplish as much as he can with cold steel and the cover of darkness. But he is not infallible. He bleeds, as any of us do, and he has his weaknesses."

"Such as?"

"Arrogance. Confidence. He does not expect you to fight back."

Skerth leaned back and studied his companion with new interest. "How do you know all this?"

Feirwyn's reply was clipped. "I know his work. We have—a history." His tone indicated that he would speak no more on that score.

"Then what do you suggest we do?"

"My guess is that he depends on you and your fellow *scats* to remain autonomous. Silent. Afraid. He does not expect you to work together and fight back. If you can put aside your differences and band together in this common cause, you may yet survive."

"Easier said than done," Skerth replied, thinking of Malyn, and of Kiri's strident disapproval of his willingness to communicate everything to Taleryn and Lark. "But we're trying."

"I will seek him out as well. We have old debts to settle."

Skerth had hoped for something more, like a detailed map to Kalen's secret lair; but Feirwyn seemed less than eager to volunteer anything further, and Skerth doubted that pressing him to speak would yield much more of use. He opted for changing the subject instead. "You're always asking after my dagger. You called it—" Skerth paused, searching for the word— "unique. Why?"

Feirwyn seemed to visibly relax at the turn of topic. "That dagger of yours is—was—a weapon of superior quality," he said, "and worth far more coin than you could steal over the course of a lifetime. But the etching betrays its true worth. The hilt of that dagger—" he pointed to the empty sheath at Skerth's hip—"bore the sigil of the last royal house of Erados."

"What—?" Skerth began, but Feirwyn held up his hand.

"None have seen that mark in many years. The Caretakers outlawed every sigil, crest and banner of the royal house and destroyed everything bearing them in the year following the institution of their government. To see it again—" Feirwyn paused; for a brief moment both sorrow and hope crossed his features.

The moment passed. "Most have given up hope that the heir of Erados still lives," Feirwyn continued. "But some of us—only a few now, but enough—will not end our search until the last hope fades." He leaned forward, resting his elbows on his knees. "Even if you remember nothing, Skerth, or cannot aid our search, your dagger reminds us that somewhere out there, in the worst conditions imaginable, our prince may yet live."

"Or his decoys."

Feirwyn nodded. "Or the decoys, as large a part of the royal family as the heir himself, nurtured to rule in his stead if something should befall the heir, each a potential king in his own right."

Skerth glanced from Feirwyn's hope to Nirue's encouraging gaze. He shrank from the weight of their full attention and took an interest in his hands, examining the torn, grimy nails, the cracked, filthy skin, the cuts and scars that marked his trials, his triumphs, his narrow escapes. For years these hands had unknowingly held a priceless dagger—and lost it to one of the few alive who knew its worth, and would hunt to ground the boy who had possessed it.

"Skerth," Nirue said quietly, "Where did you find that dagger?"

He curled his palms into fists. "I don't know," he said through gritted teeth. He was sick of that question. "I've always had it."

Feirwyn leaned forward. "Think, Skerth. You must remember something. Did you find it? Win it? Did someone give it to you?"

"I don't know!" he shouted. Why did Feirwyn and Nirue's questions anger him so? Was he more upset that they had asked, or that he didn't have any answers? "I don't know," he said again. "I don't remember much of my early days, and nothing at all before the streets. But I will tell you what I can."

"That is all I ask," replied Feirwyn.

Skerth abandoned the table to lean against the wall near the window and cross his arms over his chest. He felt better standing, less restless and awkward. More in control of his emotions, if nothing else.

"Tell us, Skerth," Nirue urged gently. "What is your earliest memory of owning the dagger?"

As before, Skerth felt a surge of fury and resentment at the question. But this time, he fought through the feeling and worked through layers of memory until he identified the earliest. "I was little. I had it with me when the lady took me in." He paused. A memory nagged, just out of reach. "I had something else, too—"

"What lady?" Feirwyn prompted.

Skerth shrugged. "I don't remember her name. She found me in an alley and cared for me for a little while. She had dark hair and a pretty smile, until her man knocked her teeth out."

Feirwyn rubbed his chin. "How old were you?"

"Don't know when I was born, so I never really marked the years that way. I know it was early, though. Four summers, maybe?

I don't remember much of the streets before her." Skerth paused thoughtfully. "Actually, I don't remember *anything* before her, except sensations: cold, dark, and—" He struggled to name the last of them, the worst, the one that lay deepest within. "Fear," he said finally, feeling a simultaneous rush of shame and relief at the admission. "And I remember being alone." He met Feirwyn's eyes. "But that's all, really. Nothing else."

"Four," Feirwyn repeated, studying Skerth.

"I'm not him," Skerth stated firmly. "Or one of his decoys."

"But you could be," said Nirue. "You are the right age, you have the dagger—"

"Had," Skerth corrected. "Besides, I would know. If I had lived at least the first four years of my life in a palace, with servants and a mother and father, a brother . . . or sisters . . . I would remember something." Wouldn't he? He recalled his strange waking dream of the fire—people running, the young woman, the old hag—and for the first time, wondered if he didn't remember something after all.

"Perhaps," Feirwyn replied. "Four is very young."

Nirue and Feirwyn both watched Skerth with matching expressions that made him uncomfortable. "Even if I was your prince—" the word caught in Skerth's throat— "who would believe you? I've lived all my life on the streets, I've lost the dagger, and if the assassin has his way, I'll be dead well before Auberdale Eve."

"You speak more truly than you realize. I would stake my future that this fire was no accident." Feirwyn gestured toward the window.

Skerth stiffened. "What? Why do you say that?"

"Unfortunately, I have had enough experience with the Caretakers to recognize their hand in this. They will stop at nothing to retain the throne they usurped and have ruled ever since through manipulation and fear. Even if it means the death of every man, woman and child in the Lower City. All the better, even, if everything Downwedge burns to the ground."

The thought sickened Skerth and made his fresh-fed stomach roil. Caretakers, indeed. Who did they care for aside from themselves?

"At least, in that, they failed," said Nirue.

"But their plan to eradicate all claims to the throne did not, as Skerth's presence here can attest. Certainly many more will die in the coming days."

"Not so many as you think. We're working hard to warn everyone, and we're all looking out for the assassin. All the scats know better than to travel anywhere alone—" Skerth broke off when the full impact of Feirwyn's statement dawned. "In the coming days. . . ."

"Auberdale Eve," Feirwyn said, and the meaning of the phrase Skerth had overheard in the tunnel finally clicked into place.

"But the city celebrates Auberdale Eve every year. What makes this year's festival worth killing for?" asked Skerth.

Feirwyn sighed. "This Auberdale Eve marks the fifteenth birthday of the missing heir, the day he would come of age, if he lives. The Caretakers have built their stewardship of the throne on the lie that if any member of the royal family—no matter how thin the blood or distant the line—would come forward before the prince's fifteenth year, they would abdicate in favor of the rightful heir. After the dawn of the prince's fifteenth year passes, the heir will be declared lost and their power sealed.

"In truth, they have secretly murdered every known relative in their quest to keep their stolen power. Your unfortunate friends are only the latest in a long list of bloodshed. If the Caretakers can prevent anyone—the true heir, or a decoy—from coming forward before this Auberdale Eve, their claim to the throne will remain permanently unchallenged."

Silence settled over the three. Skerth didn't know much about the city's affairs or how the Caretakers governed; he did know that unless he wanted to disappear permanently from the city he needed to stay far out of their way. To the poor and the forgotten, to those who lived below the great cliff barrier that separated the city, the Caretakers and their odd ways were to be feared and despised, obeyed in all things, but never loved.

Had the people loved the king and queen? Judging by the outpouring of tears and celebrations every Auberdale Eve, they had; but something had happened to sway public opinion so heavily against them that the people of Erados failed to rise up in their defense during the Purge. Or perhaps the people hadn't had time to react. Could it be true that the Caretakers had engineered everything, from the Purge to the decree that the Auberdale Eve marking the heir's fifteenth summer would prove the last opportunity to yield the throne to the rightful claimant? Had they diligently worked this slow and purposeful plan for the past eleven years, all to grasp the kingdom of Erados for their own? For the first time, Skerth wished he had paid more attention over the years to the whispers of passing adults, learned more about those who pumped the heart of the city so that he knew better whether or not Feirwyn spoke the truth. More than anything, Skerth wished he could remember something—anything—of his brief life before the Caretakers had taken control of the city. Not only for Feirwyn, but for himself and Kiri, for all of the boys who had died, and those yet in danger for a cause that didn't concern them.

And for the first time, Skerth allowed himself to wonder: what if he *were* the missing heir, or one of his palace-bred decoys? A mix of feelings washed over him—excitement, dread, a rush of power, the weight of responsibility—and above all, an overwhelming and paralyzing fear. He suddenly felt dizzy; without warning, the hag's face coalesced and took shape. Grey ash fluttered in the air like snow, settling into her tight silver bun, drifting onto her shoulders. Breathing hard, she set him down in the curve of an alley heaped with refuse under the bold, glittering gaze of dock rats. He inhaled, then retched from the stench of smoke and sea, fish and grease— too many smells to count, none of them mixing well. "Here is where I leave you, boy." She straightened, her rheumy eyes glittering in the dark. She spoke again, but Skerth could no longer hear. . . .

He shook his head, disoriented, and realized that another voice—Nirue—was speaking.

". . .if one brave soul should step forward to state his claim."

Skerth wasn't sure how much of the conversation he'd just missed, but they both watched him intently. He cleared his throat. "You're just talking about tales told at mothers' laps now, aren't you? The idea that the heir will swoop in and clear out the Caretakers on Auberdale Eve?"

"Perhaps," Feirwyn conceded. "But many of us still hold out hope. We will continue to believe, and search, until this Auberdale Eve passes and with it, all chance of removing the Caretakers from the throne without more bloodshed."

Skerth suddenly understood. "And if you don't find this heir or his decoys. . . ."

"The Caretakers must be stopped, but the people of this city—the people of Erados, for that matter—cannot withstand another bloody rebellion. Nor can they afford one. The Caretakers strangle the people's will, exact their due from every coin that changes hands. Our best hope for a peaceful transition of power is to find the missing heir."

"Or create your own."

Feirwyn nodded. "If we must."

Skerth didn't know a single boy his age who wouldn't give a leg to change his luck and trade his life in the muddy gutters for a kingdom, and he didn't doubt Feirwyn and Nirue could clean up any number of them well enough to pass him off. But none of them, in his mind, had any business ruling a street, let alone a kingdom. "So you take your pick of the scats on the streets, dress him up in fine clothes, and hand him a throne. What happens then? What if you end up far worse off than under the Caretakers' rule?"

Nirue and Feirwyn exchanged a look. At last Feirwyn said, "We have a council in place, ready to govern when the time comes. The young man who ascends the throne will rule only in name and voice."

"A puppet for your strings."

"If you choose to think of it thus, yes."

"What's to stop someone else from doing the same thing?"

Feirwyn sighed. "Unfortunately, there are factions within the city that already move to secure their own heir. But if any of those other groups succeed, Erados may suffer more than under the Caretakers' hand."

The image of varied groups, each coming forward on Auberdale Eve to present their own hopeful 'heir' forced Skerth to suppress a laugh. "How do any of them—or you—hope to prove your heir's claim?"

"If the Sea Gods grant us luck, we will find one of the tokens gifted to the heir and his decoys, or some other such sign," Nirue said.

"Like my dagger."

"Indeed." She nodded. "Though with time running short, that hope fades."

"We must find the dagger," Feirwyn said. "It is a true weapon of the last king's house, and none of its like have been found in years. Until yours."

Skerth's memory stirred, summoning a vision of ash dusting smooth grey hair, a dark alley, the tang of garbage beneath the overwhelming reek of smoke. Cold eyes, even crueler for their absence of both love and malice. Skerth blinked; the images disappeared.

"Assuming you can pull off this trick: what makes you so sure we won't suffer worse under this council of yours?"

Feirwyn's smile was grim. "We work only for the greater good of the realm. None of us want power. All of us have little to gain and everything to lose." He glanced at Nirue as he said this. She gave him a small, tight smile and slipped her hand into his.

Skerth found himself wanting to believe Feirwyn, wanting to trust him and Nirue. But one piece still didn't make sense. "If all this is true, why are the Caretakers wasting their time killing street boys when they could just pick one of us off the streets and rule from behind an heir of their own?"

"Fear," answered Nirue. "For nearly eleven years the people of Erados have tolerated the Caretakers' harsh governance while secretly praying for the heir's return. Putting forth their own candidate would only shift the people's allegiance and strengthen their resistance to the Caretakers' stranglehold on the country. Better for them to eliminate all possibilities and secure their position than to risk having their own plan turn against them."

Skerth turned to look out the window. Deep in the heart of the Lower City the fire still burned, albeit with less fervor. Thick grey clouds puffed through the city; ash fluttered like snowflakes to the earth. His heart squeezed painfully at the sight of the blackened skeletons of buildings thrusting into the air like broken spears, the shattered rooftops, the thick coat of soot darkening the city. This was *his* city, and the Caretakers had brought it to ruin. A bitter rage burst within him, along with a hate strong enough to taste. None of those who died had aspired to anything more than a meal and a place to sleep. Yet die they did, and badly. How much more would they all lose before this nightmare ended?

"I don't have time for old tales or false hope," Skerth said, hearing the bitterness in his own voice. "I don't care who rules the city—most likely whoever steps in won't care any more about me than the Caretakers do. *My* city's on fire; *my* scats are dying. Unless you can help us, I'd best get back."

"Where will you go?" Feirwyn asked. "The assassin has seen your face. He has your dagger."

"You are safe here," said Nirue. "Please. Stay."

Skerth turned to face them. Both faces looked up at him, expectant. Hopeful. Skerth suddenly realized why Feirwyn had enticed him to the Swine, told him their plans. "You mean to make me your false heir."

"With your consent, yes."

Skerth wasn't certain why Feirwyn's bold honesty surprised him. Was there some other motive behind those weary blue eyes? What did Feirwyn want, if not the power to sway a kingdom?

"Why me?"

"Why not you?" Feirwyn countered. "You are the proper age and you bear an uncanny resemblance to the old king."

For some reason, Skerth felt disappointed. What had he expected Feirwyn to say? That his mastery of petty theft and purse-cutting had prepared him well for the dubious task of reigning over a kingdom? That his knowledge of the streets and ability to escape made him an excellent leader? These thoughts shamed him. He was a street scat, orphaned, cast out, left to make his own way in the world or die. He was strong, and a survivor, but he was no king.

"These are my streets," he told Feirwyn and Nirue. "To run, and to defend. I won't abandon them now. Not even for a kingdom."

Feirwyn studied Skerth, his expression unreadable. Finally, he nodded. "If you change your mind—"

"I won't."

"Perhaps—" Nirue began, but Skerth had turned away, was already striding toward the door.

Neither of them barred his way, nor did they protest as he let himself out. For a moment he wished they would call him back, ask him again to stay, persuade him to change his mind. Then he thought of Kiri, of Malyn, of Rot and Fael, of Jemmy and Minah, of all the lost souls huddled together on the rotted floorboards of his warehouse, of all who had disappeared and all of those yet to come. For one moment he considered turning back to accept Feirwyn's offer so that he could save them all: give them food, shelter, perhaps even loved ones to hold them close and sing them to sleep.

The reality of what he could and couldn't do settled in. The moment passed. And Skerth, Scat King of the Lower City, slid silent into the thickened air of the street and determined to salvage what he could of the only home and family he would ever know.

Chapter Eleven: Old Friends and New

Grey days blurred in and out of focus. Skerth wandered the smoke-choked and blackened streets, searching the faces of every passerby for one he recognized. His warehouse had become little more than a charred stain blanketed thick with ash and rubble. Bone-thin scavengers clad in blackened rags picked through the detritus for anything worth salvaging, all of them strangers. He considered joining them, but turned his back and walked on. He tried to feel something for the loss of the most stable home he'd ever known, for the kids he'd shared it with, for his ratty blanket and handful of possessions, but he just felt hollow inside.

He left the remains of his warehouse for Market Street, and found nothing recognizable in the marketplace, either. Gone were the faded banners and makeshift awnings, the carts and barrel-voiced hawkers declaring their wares. Fire had swept through the square, chewing stalls into blistered and blackened remnants, scorching and melting the stone cobbles into a lumpy mess. Scavengers hovered where the street vendors had stood, pawing for forgotten coin or buried treasures the fire had left behind. A few hawkers, either brave or desperate, called their wares in thin, hoarse voices, their arms cradled protectively around baskets of fish, cloth, or in one case, a trove of soot-covered miscellany, hand-picked from the refuse.

Skerth bought a lump of stale bread from a tall, reedy young woman with wild dark hair who insisted he take more once she tested the worth of his coin. He was stuffing the spares into his pockets and the front of his shirt when he heard his name.

He paused to scan the square, but could not find anyone he recognized in the ragged figures scattered about.

"Skerth!" he heard again, and a skinny figure separated from the others to rush at him. Filthy as she was, he could never mistake that shock of cropped white hair. The numbness squeezing his soul lifted.

"Kiri!" He met her halfway and pulled her into a tight embrace. A sudden rush of emotions—fear, relief, anger, and others he couldn't name—frightened him with their intensity. "The fire—I thought I'd never see you again. I'm sorry—" His voice broke. Tears welled, and he made no move to wipe them away. He didn't care if she saw them, or if anyone else saw, either. Everything was ruined and broken, his warehouse gone, his kids scattered or dead, but she was alive. That was all that mattered.

"It's okay, Skerth," she managed, wriggling free. "Really. I'm sorry, too."

He set her at arm's length and took a good look at her. Dark shadows ringed her eyes, bloodshot from too much smoke and too little rest. Her face was scratched, her lips cracked and swollen. Tears had left pink tracks in the layer of ash on her cheeks before congealing into a line of sludge along the edges of her chin. She looked tired and vulnerable; at the same time, the stubborn line of her chin and strong set of her shoulders proved her strength. He squashed the sudden, overpowering urge to kiss her. His emotions a turmoil, he pulled her back into his arms instead.

"Look here!" called a voice off to Skerth's right, where a small group of kids had gathered to stare. "We've got ourselves a pair of unnaturals!" The group elbowed one another, guffawed, jeered. A couple of them started forward.

Flushing, Skerth immediately pushed Kiri to arm's length. "What are you peepin' at?" he shouted. "Get!"

The leader sauntered toward them, making a show of rolling up his tattered sleeves. "Yeah? I don't see a quarterstaff or a fancy cape giving you the right to tell me what to do. In fact—" he turned in a slow circle and exaggerated looking all around—"not a Stave in sight."

The boys behind him shifted forward. Skerth tensed at the sound of muttered threats and cracked knuckles.

"Come on." Kiri tugged at his sleeve. "We need to get away from here." She cast the boys a look of disdain, then turned and walked away.

"We've no quarrel with you," Skerth said. Then, despite the fact that his every instinct screamed against it, he slowly, deliberately turned his back on them and followed her.

Jeers chased them, but the boys did not. Still, Skerth took care to keep a space between them as Kiri led them out by the docks and around the fire, back toward the southernmost spread of the Lower City—the ruin of abandoned, tumbledown buildings most referred to as Rat Alley. Everyone else, including Malyn's scats, called it the Deadrun. He almost protested when they reached the boarded and rotting old alehouse that marked the border between his territory and Malyn's, but Taleryn and Dragon merely grunted and stood aside to let them pass.

"Kiri—"

"Hush," she whispered. "Follow me."

Unlike the better parts Downwedge, which tended to run in straight lines and intersected into neat corners, the Deadrun spiraled in upon itself, all streets leading inward to one central square that used to mark the center of a bustling Endelas Ortanos before a fierce series of hurricanes had leveled the old city and forced most of the merchants and royals—along with their households, their trades, and their coin—Upwedge. Malyn didn't keep his quarters in the center itself, preferring instead one of the larger warehouses that flanked the outlying streets; therefore, when Kiri aimed for the center square, Skerth felt both relief and a heightened sense of curiosity. Nothing good had ever come of his few forays this deep into Deadrun; at the same time, Dragon and Taleryn had not only let them pass unmolested, they'd all but welcomed them.

They arrived to a square teeming with bodies—Malyn's boys, Skerth's, and quite a few he had never seen before. They lounged against the walls, huddled on the ground, or clustered into small groups playing at dice or sticks. Malyn stood at the center, talking with Lark and a couple of the older boys, as at ease in this mixed company as he appeared in his own quarters. At sight of Skerth and Kiri, Malyn abandoned his conversation and strode to meet them.

"Where have you been?" Malyn demanded.

Skerth bristled. "Looking for my kids, mostly," he hedged. "I also helped put out the fires. Didn't see you there."

"I've been busy." He gestured grandly at the kids filling Deadrun's center square. "Someone had to set some order with most of my scats busy searching for you."

Skerth masked his surprise. "For me? Why? What'd you want me for?"

94

Malyn frowned. "Don't you know?" He glanced from Skerth to Kiri, who shook her head. "The fire started at your warehouse."

Skerth shook his head in disbelief. "No. That's not possible." *Or was it?* his mind whispered. A few days earlier he'd been safe in his tunnels, asleep when the fire had started.

"Not possible?" Malyn echoed, eyebrows raised. "Which part? Burning down a warehouse full of sleeping kids, or managing to disappear while it happened?"

A warehouse full of sleeping kids. . . . The fire had started in the night, and would have caught them all unawares. Skerth pictured the little ones and wanted to vomit.

Malyn must have guessed at Skerth's thoughts. "Kiri got everyone out, although most of them scattered once they broke outside. He couldn't find you, though, so he came looking for me."

"Why?" Skerth asked, turning to her. "You don't think I did this, do you?"

"Of course not," she replied with an impatient wave. "But someone did. The fire wasn't an accident. It was set."

"Who—?" Skerth looked back at Malyn, dreading the answer.

"The Quarterstaves," she said firmly.

"Why would they do that?" Skerth asked, dumbfounded.

"Why do you think?" Malyn replied. "They do the Caretakers' bidding."

"Yeah, but why would the Caretakers set fire to the Lower City?"

"I don't think they meant to," Kiri explained. "They're getting desperate, and wanted to eliminate a few 'candidates' in one scratch. But the fire spread faster than they planned."

Malyn narrowed his eyes at her. "What makes you so certain?"

"I saw them," Kiri said. "I couldn't sleep, so I took to the roof. I don't know how long I was up there when I heard voices coming down the way. I flattened and crawled to the edge. It was dark, but I could make out four men—three Staves and a man cloaked in black from head to heel. A few minutes later they scattered, which I thought odd—until I smelled the smoke. That's when I woke the kids."

If Kiri hadn't stayed awake—Skerth shuddered at the consequences. Raw fury coiled in the pit of his stomach. Already the Caretakers' murderous search had destroyed more than the lives of a few street kids and the only home he knew. More than half of the Lower City had burned, leaving countless innocent people without homes or livelihoods. He recalled the grim faces of the men he'd helped to stall the fire, the devastated women, the children wandering lost, and curled his hands into fists. How many more would suffer or die to satisfy the Caretakers' quest to find and destroy anyone who might lay claim to the throne and put an end to their vicious rule?

"There's more," Malyn added. "Barter, Runner, Mak and Lash are all dead."

Skerth's mind reeled. "In the fire?" he asked, knowing the answer even before Malyn shook his head.

"The assassin. Beaten, throats cut, just like the others."

Skerth squeezed his eyes shut, dragged a trembling hand through his hair. Four more dead. He wasn't sure how much of this he could take. *You don't have to stay*, whispered a thought at the back of his mind. *You could go to Feirwyn. . . .* He shook his head, clearing it to focus on the matter at hand.

Kiri set her hand on his shoulder. "That's why we were trying to find you, Skerth. Between their murders and the fire—"

"You thought I was dead." He opened his eyes and met Malyn's steady gaze. "What happens now?"

"We're gathering all the scats we can find—yours, mine, strays—and bringing them here, especially those around our age. We'll be safe here for now. And the more kids we can keep together, under our protection—"

"The more kids stay alive," Skerth finished.

Malyn nodded. "I've got four guards posted at every border—two clear, two shadows—and, on the advice of your friend here, I've put a handful up high. Apparently," he added with a sidelong glance at Kiri, "people can cross into Deadrun using the rooftops."

"Not anymore," Kiri said wistfully.

Skerth coughed to cover his own smile.

Malyn continued, "If the assassin comes near, we'll know. If anyone's helping him, we'll know that, too."

"Helping him?" Skerth frowned. "What do you mean?" Malyn and Kiri exchanged a look. Skerth tamped down a sudden surge of jealousy at the two sworn enemies' newfound closeness.

"We think someone's passing information to the assassin," Kiri explained.

"Why? How?"

Malyn glanced around, then lowered his voice. "The boys who died— I think there's an order to it, of sorts."

"Do you have any idea who's betraying us?"

"No, but I suspect the traitor is someone in my inner circle." His eyes shifted meaningfully to the crowds of scats and orphans in the square. "We can't talk here. Find me later and I'll explain."

"Come on," Kiri said, tugging at Skerth's sleeve. "Let's get out of this crowd and I'll tell you what I know."

"Go," Malyn agreed. "I need to hear the rest of Lark and Ern's report so they can get back to their watch, and I've left Cavor waiting, too."

They made their farewells and he strode away.

Kiri drew Skerth to a side alley in a less crowded corner of the square. "The Caretakers have your dagger. They're looking for you."

"How do you know?"

"I wasn't exactly truthful with Malyn. I wasn't on the roof when the fire started." She took a deep breath. "I followed them, Skerth. All the way from the Upwedge Gates. I wanted to get away from you, I was so angry—but then I saw them, and I wanted to know what they were up to."

"What were you thinking? You could have been killed—"

"I know." She waved away his concern. "But I did it. I wasn't close enough to catch their words, but I followed them until they stopped just outside the warehouse. They met someone there. I couldn't see who it was, but the man in black raised his voice to the person waiting and showed him the dagger. I couldn't see the designs on it, of course, but I knew it was yours right off when the person waiting waved toward the warehouse. The leader tossed him a pouch and he ran off. Not long after, the Staves brought out their torches. I didn't hear any more after that—I ran around through a back window and started waking the kids."

"Why didn't you tell all of this to Malyn?"

"The person they met at the warehouse—he was tall and lean. He wore a cloak and hood so I can't say for sure, but it makes sense that the informer was probably one of Malyn's boys, or even one of ours. Skerth—" she paused to gather her words and looked him straight in the eyes—"it might have even been Malyn."

"Then why would he help us now?"

Kiri raised her eyebrows. "Is he helping all that much, truly? If he's on our side, gathering everyone together like this makes sense. If he's against us—"

"Then he can pick us off, one by one."

"Or bring in the Caretakers' Staves and stage a massacre."

He sighed. "You're right, Kiri. We're no better off trusting Malyn than working on our own."

She laid her hand on his arm. "You trusted him once before, Skerth, and he nearly killed you. You can't afford to make that mistake again."

He didn't know if it was her gentle words or the feel of her hand on his arm, but a strange feeling stirred within him. *Something else he couldn't afford to think about*, he told himself, and forced his attention back to the matter at hand.

"There's more," Skerth said, and told her about his meeting with Feirwyn and Nirue. By the time he finished, the sun had dipped low beneath the wedge. Kiri sat back against the alley wall, her expression thoughtful.

"It's not a bad plan." She turned to study Skerth through narrowed eyes, fingered a lock of his hair. "You should do it. You could be a king."

Suddenly awkward, Skerth forced a laugh and batted her hand away. "What, and walk away from all of this?" He swept his arms wide. "I'm already a king, or didn't you notice?"

"I mean it, Skerth. You could escape. Get off the streets, get away from the assassin, the Caretakers—everything." There was a vehemence in her tone, an intensity in her mismatched eyes that made him uncomfortable.

"What do I know about being a king? My place is here."

She opened her mouth to argue, then snapped it shut and turned her face away. Her shoulders slumped and the fight slipped out of her, leaving her looking drained and small. "Maybe you're right."

"Look," he said, crouching beside her, "it's been a long few days. I can barely think I'm so tired. Maybe we should rest up and figure out what to do in the morning."

Kiri sighed and nodded. "I don't think I've slept in days."

"Not here, though." Skerth eyed the cluster of Malyn's scats entering the alley and nudged her onto her feet. "If we have to stay under Malyn's eye, let's at least find someplace a bit quieter."

They found a vacant room in a building long-abandoned by all but Malyn's growing collection of street orphans and a pack of stray dogs that had lost their own homes to the fire. The room was tiny, but offered more security than the streets and a great deal more privacy. Skerth and Kiri settled back to back for warmth. Almost immediately Kiri's breathing slowed into the rhythm of sleep, but Skerth lay awake a long while, blinking into the darkness, his mind whirling with thoughts of kings and Caretakers, assassins and allies.

Morning dawned upon a much clearer day. Although a heavy layer of smoke still smothered the city, the fire was nearly beaten and the wind had shifted, baring a patch of blue and admitting an occasional sea breeze. For the first time since the fire began, Skerth allowed himself to hope.

For once, Kiri had not disappeared before sunrise; she lay curled against his side, snoring softly. He studied her, discovering, as if for the first time, her soft, full lips, the way a lock of white hair curled against the curve of her cheek just so, the thick flutter of her lashes. Something stirred deep within him, something fierce and protective, and something else—

He rose and hastened around the corner, his heart thumping wildly. Just out of sight, he leaned against the wall to catch his breath and order his thoughts. What was wrong with him? He and Kiri had run the streets together off and on for summers. Even after he'd accidentally learned her secret, he'd never really thought of her as a girl. So what had changed?

He took another deep breath and closed his eyes. . . . Rather than dissipate, his feelings intensified. Despite his best efforts, his imagination conjured the dreaming Kiri. He leaned in, pressed his lips to hers—

His eyes snapped open. Swearing softly, he jammed sweaty hands into his pockets and started walking. Anger—at himself, at her—surged. He couldn't afford this kind of distraction, but he couldn't stop it, either. *Kiri is a boy*, he told himself. *A boy, like me. Like all the rest.*

And that was the problem. She didn't look like a boy anymore.

The realization stopped him mid-stride. Recent images of her bubbled to mind, one after the other. There was a softness to her now, a curve to her hip, a subtle rounding of her chest that only appeared when she turned just so. She had lost the fullness of face that had blunted her features; at some point, her nose had grown straight and delicate, and long, wispy lashes framed her unique eyes.

Had others noticed as well? He had to warn her, but what, if anything, could she do? If she could no longer protect her identity, where would she go?

Nowhere, he realized. Warning her would be no gift either, for she could, in truth, do nothing. This new revelation about his friend, along with his confusion of new feelings for her, he must keep to himself. But he vowed to guard her—and her secret—for as long as he could.

He rounded the corner and came face-to-face with a yawning Kiri.

"You slept late." His voice cracked; thankfully, she didn't notice.

"Tired." She briskly finger-combed her hair and stifled another yawn. "We're still alive."

"For now. Come on. Let's see if we can find Malyn."

They arrived in the square to find that most of the occupants had cleared out, leaving only a few huddled groups and the occasional sleeper still stretched out on the ground. No Malyn. His absence irritated Skerth; working together was one thing, but living in Malyn's Deadrun and waiting on him for information felt too much like the old days for his comfort.

Skerth scanned the clearing for those in Malyn's inner circle, hoping for some news. He spied a group of boys he recognized standing off to the side and nudged Kiri in their direction. Taleryn broke away and hurried to meet them, visibly upset.

"The assassin got Dragon last night," Taleryn told them. "He's in a bad way."

The news stunned Skerth. Dragon was the toughest boy he knew: strong, ruthless, and expert with a knife. Skerth's knee still ached every time he heard his name. "Dragon? Are you sure?"

Taleryn nodded. "We had the watch. I only left him for a few minutes—" he paused, flushing scarlet. Skerth had a clear idea of what had distracted Taleryn. "I heard a scuffle. By the time I got there, Dragon was down. Grey and Seryn were already in the fight. I came around behind, pulled off the attacker's hood, tried to get a good swipe. That's when he bolted. We tried to catch him—"

"He got away?" Kiri burst out. "Three of you cornered him and you let him go?"

Taleryn's flush deepened. "He was too fast. Besides, we had to see to Dragon—"

"I don't believe it!" Kiri shouted, sounding so much like a girl that Skerth flinched. "Three of you had the assassin. Three! Four, if you count Lark—"

Taleryn tensed. "Who said anything about Lark?"

"Well she was right there, wasn't she?" When Taleryn didn't reply, Kiri rolled her eyes. "I can't believe you let him go."

"We didn't have a choice! He was too fast!" Heads turned; Taleryn lowered his voice. "At least I managed a good look at his face. I know who we're up against now. And if I see him again. . . ." He drew a hand across his throat.

"What does he look like?" Skerth asked, cutting off Kiri's retort.

"Dark hair to his shoulders, brown skin—looked fairly plain, to tell the truth, only his eyes—" he broke off, remembering, then looked directly at Skerth. "His eyes had no color, like gull wings, or sea clouds." He shivered.

Skerth nodded. He remembered them, too. And they had looked upon Skerth completely without mercy, measuring his age, his life's worth, in less than a moment.

"You'd better stay close from now on," Skerth warned. "He knows you've seen him. He'll be back."

Taleryn's laugh was shaky. "I know."

"How's Dragon?"

"The assassin went for his throat. Dragon fought hard, but he's really cut up. Malyn sent a couple of scats to find a healer. But with the fires—" He shrugged.

Skerth and Kiri exchanged a look. If Malyn was willing to risk—and pay for—a healer, Dragon was in bad shape indeed.

"Let us know if anything changes," said Skerth. "We're headed for my streets to learn what we can. If we don't come back—"

"Just be careful." Taleryn clapped Skerth hard on the shoulder, gave Kiri a stiff nod. "Both of you."

"We always are," Kiri said.

The smoke kept them off the rooftops, so Skerth and Kiri took to the streets. As they traveled through the ruins, Skerth's rage swelled. *Caretakers.* Who or what did they care for, aside from power? In all of his years on the streets, Skerth had only seen the Caretakers in passing. They never lingered to drop alms in the hands of the poor, to care for the orphaned or the sick, to comfort the old and infirm. Indeed, they glided past in their long grey robes like proud wraiths, their noses high and their gazes fixed always ahead, never below, while their Staves carried out their brutal justice against the weak and the hungry.

And now they had ruined his streets. His city. *His* Endelas Ortanos. This, the only home he had ever known, they had stolen from him. And what if Feirwyn was right? What if they had taken more than he knew?

He stared out at the rubble and allowed himself to wonder. What if he were truly the heir of Erados or one of his noble decoys? Had his life changed on a bright, clear day like this, when the smoke from the burning palace would spread for miles? Or had they made their bid for glory under cloak of night?

He breathed deep the reek of ash and a simple image surfaced from the depths of memory: a blue ball, nestled tight between the thorny stems of two pink and yellow rosebushes. Petals dusted the sun-dappled ground. A chubby hand—his? Strained toward the ball, dimpled fingers spread impossibly wide, unable to reach.

There you are! cried a voice he almost recognized. . . .

". . .listening?" Kiri's voice. Annoyed.

The spell broke; the scene fled.

No, he thought with frustration, remembering the ball and the voice, but not what they might have meant to him. Never any answers; only more questions.

Chapter Twelve: The Warehouse

Skerth and Kiri spent most of the day feathering the burnt edges of the South Wedge hunting for scraps of news. A few kids who refused to shelter in Deadrun confessed that they might have seen someone who resembled the assassin, but they wanted more for the information than Skerth could pay. As the boys' honesty and willingness to help depended a little too heavily on how much coin Skerth and Kiri carried, they abandoned those leads without a second thought. If, after learning of the potential dangers, the boys still wouldn't help for free, Skerth wouldn't spend much time mourning their fate.

"Dragon's dead," Taleryn announced when they dragged back into Deadrun that evening.

"And Malyn wants to see you," added his companion, Grey, a scat as nondescript as his name. Skerth wasn't sure he'd ever seen him on the streets before, although Grey's quiet disposition and bland features no doubt ensured that nobody saw Grey unless he wanted them to. Skerth nodded and started off, Kiri at his heels, but Grey and Taleryn shifted to block their path.

"Alone," said Grey.

Skerth and Kiri exchanged a look. "Kiri's with me. We go together, or I don't go."

Taleryn looked uncertain, but his companion's stony expression didn't change. "Then you are not to cross into Deadrun," Grey said.

"Fine. We have plenty of places to hide. Let Malyn know that we'll be back in a few days to see how he fared against the assassin—if he's still around." Skerth grabbed Kiri's arm and turned to leave. They hadn't taken more than a few steps when—

"Wait!" Taleryn called.

Skerth turned, eyebrows raised in mock surprise. "Did Malyn change his mind?"

Taleryn whispered urgently in Grey's ear. The boy shook his head, growled something, then narrowed his eyes at Skerth. "Just come. Both of you." He grabbed a torch from the street sconce, motioned for Kiri and Skerth to follow, and started off.

"Why the escort?" Kiri asked.

"Malyn's orders," Grey replied in a tight voice that brooked no further discussion.

At the end of a long and unnecessarily circuitous route, Grey opened the door of Malyn's warehouse and beckoned them inside.

"Thanks," said Skerth.

But Grey had already grabbed the torch and ducked back outside. The door slammed shut, leaving Skerth and Kiri alone in the dark.

"Trap!" Skerth yelled.

They pulled at the knob. The door didn't budge.

They beat at the thick wood and tore at the handle, but only managed to rattle the outside bar.

"Kiri—"

Something—*someone*—came at them in a whoosh of air and blind motion. Skerth fell to the ground and Kiri screamed, struggling in the dark against an unseen assailant.

Skerth fumbled for his knife, choking back panic. "She's a girl!" he cried out, lurching to his feet and running at the silhouette of darker space standing between him and his friend. "She's a girl! It's me you want!" He stabbed blindly, but his knife merely tangled in the thick folds of their attacker's cloak and glanced off the leather beneath.

The assassin shook him off with a harsh laugh. "I will deal with you—"

Bone slammed into flesh. The assassin grunted and jerked forward. Skerth guessed where Kiri had kicked him, but didn't waste his sympathy. With all the force he could muster, he grabbed the assassin by the hair and slammed his head into the door. The assassin roared. Skerth hadn't managed to knock him unconscious, but he'd bought enough time to free themselves and sprint down the hall.

"What now?" Kiri panted.

"We find another way out."

They rushed down the narrow hallway in the near-total darkness, feeling for doors, daggers out and ready. Skerth found an opening and pulled Kiri inside, then pushed her against the wall behind him and crouched by the doorway, hoping the assassin would pass them by. His mind raced, considering their options. Not counting his most recent visit, he hadn't been inside Malyn's warehouse in a long time, and he'd never earned enough of Malyn's respect to have free run. But if he remembered correctly, there was at least one other exit, near the back. A couple of windows.

Kiri gripped his arm. They froze.

Then he heard it, too. Less a noise, really, than a subtle rearrangement of the silence in one of the rooms across the corridor. *But which room?*

Skerth remembered three doors on his side of the hall, and two—no, four—on the other. Dead-ends, all. Their only hope was to make it to the end of the hallway, where the corridor took a sharp left to run along the back of the warehouse. That path led to more rooms, most of which he had never seen. Somewhere in that warehouse was their only exit. They had to find it.

There was no soft displacement of the air or whisper of breath to hint at the assassin's whereabouts. Sweat trickled down Skerth's temple. He closed his eyes and struggled to keep his breath even and silent. His knife felt slick in his palm; he tightened his grip. Finally, when he could bear the tension no longer, he squeezed Kiri's hand and flowed soundlessly across the doorway.

Nothing.

A strange mix of relief and adrenaline coursed through his veins, made his head spin. They crept to the next door. This one presented more of a challenge, as it directly faced another opening across the hall. The assassin could strike, unseen, from either gap. *Better to be quick than careful this time.* Skerth tensed for the crossing, tethering Kiri's hand like a lifeline. Then, together, they slid past the open doors. Emboldened by their success, they kept moving, brushing past the third of the four doors to their left before they even realized they had done so. By the time they came up against the final door on the right, Skerth sagged against the wall, his legs shaking and his heart slamming.

As before, they held still, listening intently for any hint of the assassin. Twice they tensed: once when something scampered down the hall and over their feet, and again at the faint creak of wood issuing from somewhere deep inside the warehouse. Outside, the wind kicked up; where it found cracks in the warehouse the air wheezed and whistled, but not loud enough to mask a breath too gustily sighed. They analyzed every sound, large or small, until, satisfied at last that the assassin had not moved, they inched past the last door on the right—without event.

Only one door remained to pass. Skerth breathed easier. They could stay close to the wall, as far out of reach as possible. If the assassin wanted them, he'd have to come out into the hall. With luck, they'd hear him move, feel a rush of air, anything—and have enough warning to sprint for the rear corridor. If their luck didn't hold. . . .

They backed against the wall. The wood and old, hardened clay felt cool and solid; he leaned into it, borrowing its strength. He could do this. *They* could do this.

Kiri gave his hand an urgent squeeze. When he didn't respond, she poked him in the ribs and gave him a small shove forward. She wanted to move on.

Well, so did he. Only a few steps remained between them and a clear run to the end of the hall. Gathering his courage, Skerth took the first step. Then, the next. Another. Slow. Careful. Noiseless. He did not breathe and kept his movements spare. Sweat stung his eyes; he blinked to clear them.

No more stopping. This was it: four steps. Three. Two—

The assassin slammed into him, throwing them both to the ground. Skerth's knife clattered to the floor. While he gasped for breath, leather hands settled on his throat. He wanted to tell Kiri to run, to hide, but the assassin's hands pressed, tightened, and all Skerth could manage was a rough gurgle. He started to panic; not for himself, but for her. In a few minutes, his fight would end. But why wasn't she running? What was she waiting for? He thrashed and pulled at his attacker's hands. If he could just get a breath, he could tell her. Just one breath—

Then Kiri screamed—not a girly squeak, but a gusty scream that echoed from the walls.

"Shut it, filth!" the assassin growled.

Distracted, his grip eased; Skerth seized the opportunity and shoved hard. His attacker's weight shifted just enough for Skerth to wriggle free. He clenched his knife and rolled out of reach.

Skerth swayed to his feet. He gasped for air, hoping that the pinpricks of light dotting the edges of his vision would disappear so he could focus. Kiri continued to scream as she backed down the hallway the way they had come. Skerth had a clear sprint to the back corridor. If he were Malyn, Taleryn, Rot, one of many scats he knew, he would save himself. But he wasn't them. She hadn't left him, and he wouldn't leave her.

"Stop screaming!" the assassin bellowed. "Stop that noise!"

The scrape of boots. A whisper of drawn steel. Kiri's scream pitched to an uncertain note. Skerth shifted closer. He would have one slim chance to take the assassin by surprise and win Kiri enough time to break away.

"Got you!" the assassin shouted. Kiri's scream broke into a choked gurgle.

Skerth ran forward, slashing blindly. The assassin cried out. Skerth found Kiri's arm and pulled; together they sprinted for the back corridor.

"Which way?" Kiri whispered.

"Don't know. Just run."

Skerth's mind raced. Malyn wouldn't choose headquarters that didn't offer multiple escape routes. But where would he cut the doors, dig the secret passages? And how would he conceal them?

The heavy thud of the assassin's boots announced his pursuit—slow, determined. Skerth swore under his breath and reached for something—anything—to throw in the assassin's path, but could find nothing.

And the corridor terminated abruptly in a solid wood door.

"No, no, no—"

He ran his fingers across the wood, searching for a loop, a bar, anything. He ignored the splinters that sliced into his fingers and, fighting panic, threw himself against the door.

At the same time Kiri cried, "Got it!"

A latch clicked. The two burst into a large storage room and slammed the door behind them. High narrow windows filtered the glow of the moon, giving them enough light to discern shape from shadow. Several large wooden crates, probably used for seating, lined the walls in neat rows. Some smaller and broken crates lay scattered in between. Otherwise, the room was devoid of objects or furniture.

The room also lacked an obvious exit.

"The crates," Skerth said, already turning to one nearby. He shoved it forward to barricade the door while Kiri pushed a stack of smaller crates beside it. They hastened to add as many crates as they could to their makeshift barricade before the assassin's steps paused outside the door. Then they made for the walls, where they confirmed with desperate hands that they were trapped. The assassin teased the latch and pushed. He encountered resistance, but seemed in no rush to break through. *And why shouldn't he feel confident?* Skerth thought, his anger surging. Two street kids armed with one knife didn't stand a chance against the Caretakers' trained assassin.

Furious, Skerth hefted another large crate and shoved it behind the others. They might be done for, but he wouldn't go easy. Kiri caught on and tossed some of the lighter crates toward the pile, bursting into mirthless laughter when one shattered and showered the floor in a scatter of rotted wood. Spying a shard with a good, sharp point, Skerth grabbed it and set it aside, hoping the makeshift weapon would serve.

As the assassin battered against their shield—they had only seconds left—they looked to the remaining crates for shelter. The far corner, where two large crates made for a better wall than the others, seemed the best place to make their last stand. Skerth grabbed Kiri's hand and pulled her toward them.

They ducked behind the crates just as their barricade started to topple. Kiri tugged urgently at Skerth's sleeve, but he ignored her, watching fascinated as the smaller crates at the top tipped and fell. The assassin worked in earnest, throwing his full weight against the door to wedge it open. Skerth knew he ought to feel afraid, but he only felt a strange numbness mixed with a morbid desire to know how long, how well this last defense would hold.

Kiri poked him in the ribs—hard. He turned to demand what she wanted, but paused, mouth agape. Kiri had shoved one of the neighboring crates just far enough out of place to reveal the distinct outline of a trap door. Searching frantically, they found the handle at the same time and yanked so hard that they toppled backward when the door flew open. Skerth shoved Kiri through. And by the time the assassin shattered their barricade, they had disappeared into the earth.

Chapter Thirteen: Flight

Skerth slammed back-first onto the ground, gasping for breath, then snapped his mouth and closed his eyes against the old filth shaking loose from the ceiling. Once the shower subsided, he dragged himself upright. Judging from the total darkness, he had managed to pull the door shut after all. But the assassin wouldn't be far behind.

Kiri lay nearby, breathing too heavily in the thick quiet.

"Kiri. Come on. We've got to find the way out." *If there was a way out.* He made his way to the walls, feeling for a gap wide enough for a passageway, and jerked back with a shock. The walls were rough, uncut stone. Natural rock, like the cliffs that divided his city.

Like the walls of his tunnel.

"*I think you know where the other path terminates,*" the Caretaker had said. A chill shot down his spine as Skerth recalled Dreiwend's reply: "*My man does.*"

The memory jolted Skerth into action. He felt along the walls, searching for the opening he was now certain existed, struggling to control the anger that threatened to cloud his mind and slow his task. Malyn must have known about the tunnel—no doubt he chose this warehouse as his headquarters specifically because it provided him with an escape should he need one. Did he know about the assassin, too? Had he betrayed them all?

His hand pushed into open air. *A way out.*

"Kiri!"

She didn't respond. He tried again, a little louder. Nothing. Stomach churning, he felt his way to where she lay.

"Kiri?"

He shook her. She moaned.

"Hush," he whispered. "We need to keep moving."

"Can't," she breathed. "You go."

"I'm not leaving you. Come on!"

He took her arm and pulled her up. Her cry echoed in the silence. Skerth jerked away, his heart hammering.

"Kiri, please! Stand up!"

"Hurts."

"What hurts?"

"My side."

Skerth gently touched her arm, felt for her waist. She didn't react. He moved his hand to her ribs, then her stomach, to where she pressed her palm against the curve of her waist. Wet. Sticky. *Blood.*

The whisper of steel drawn in the dark. Kiri's scream. Her choked gasp. All this time she had been injured, and he hadn't known.

High above, the trap door rattled. Debris rained down, and torchlight flared into the room as the door flipped open. Skerth leapt to his feet and awkwardly scooped Kiri into his arms. After a bit of searching, he made his way to the tunnel mouth and ducked inside.

Stay ahead of the torchlight, he told himself, abandoning stealth for speed. The tunnel twisted left, then right; sloped down, then up again for no apparent reason. When the tunnel split his heart leapt—but which path to choose? The right seemed the better choice; he could feel it angling toward the city. If the sea gods were on his side, he would emerge in a crowd, then find his way to a safe place to see to Kiri's wounds. But if he was wrong, he could end up anywhere—perhaps in the hands of Dreiwend himself. Or worse, the Caretakers. On the other hand, the left veered toward the coast and a far less familiar terrain.

Light flickered against the walls at the edge of his vision; no more time for debate. Skerth shifted Kiri's weight in his arms, wincing as her soft moan echoed dully in the tunnel, and dodged to the left.

Skerth had spent so many years using his tunnel as a sanctuary that this passageway, though untried, felt familiar and safe. Despite the gradual return to darkness and the weight he carried that increased with every step, Skerth made excellent time. Soon the glow of the assassin's torch faded completely, leaving him blind, but relieved.

After traveling what he hoped was a safe enough distance from the assassin, Skerth stopped to rest. He carefully lowered Kiri to the ground and settled her against the curve of the wall, forcing aside a wave of panic at her cry of pain. He needed to get her to a healer, but even if he could find one, he wasn't sure he had enough coin.

Feirwyn. He would know what to do. He would help her, Skerth was sure of it. The soonest he could, he would take her to The Blighted Swine. To Feirwyn. And once she was on the mend he would settle his score with Malyn, once and for all.

Skerth rose and stretched the burning ache out of his back, shoulders and arms. He breathed deeply the thick, musty air of the tunnel and tried to order his thoughts. Fretting wouldn't help Kiri or challenge Malyn. He had to keep moving. Muscles screaming and heart pounding, Skerth gathered Kiri into his arms—this time positioning her over his shoulder—and pressed further into the unknown.

The air became dense and humid, the ground increasingly slick and uneven, hindering his progress. He held Kiri tight, ignoring her feeble protests and gasps of pain. Periodically he reached for the wall to orient himself in the dark; otherwise, he kept to a slow, steady pace. *One . . . two . . . three. . . .* The pounding of his steps echoed the beat of his heart, the slow slip of time as long minutes passed. How many had slipped away since Grey first locked them in the warehouse? How long had he traveled these tunnels? How much time did Kiri have left? Forcing these questions aside, he gritted his teeth against the burning pain in his shoulders and urged his trembling legs from one step to the next, distracting himself by counting steps or trying to identify by sound the creatures that shared his tunnel.

A few times, when he caught the flap of bat wings or a whiff of something foul and dank, Skerth experienced an almost dizzying sense of familiarity. Memory stirred. Images surfaced: pink and yellow roses. An old hag, skin like soft, crumbling parchment.

The sharp stab of fear caught him off guard. He stumbled.

"Skerth!" Kiri gasped.

He cringed and tightened his hold.

"Hush," he whispered. "I'll take care of you. We'll be safe soon. Hush."

Hush, echoed the crone. *Hush, or I'll have your tongue.*

The words released something buried deep within his core. Fragmented memories of another cavern, another time, surfaced— his arms clinging to a withered old neck, the acrid smell of sweat mingled with the mustiness of age. He had squeezed his eyes tight to shut out his surroundings, but the flutter and screech of bats and the old hag's constant muttering only intensified his fears.

"*Hush.*" The hag's grating growl seemed more ominous than comforting, especially away from home and lost in the dark. His heart fluttered. This wasn't safe. She wasn't safe. Safe was home, or the garden. He would have felt safer with Jearney—

Skerth fell to his knees. He stifled a cry as the rough stone stripped through threadbare cloth and skin and jarred his bones from knee to neck. He managed not to drop Kiri, but he could no longer hold her, either. He eased her to the ground. Blinking back tears of mingled pain and frustration, he set his back against the wall and drew his throbbing, bloodied knees into his chest.

He fought back wave after wave of fear and panic, though whether these were new feelings or old he could no longer tell. Part of him wanted the memory back, wanted to know who that hag was and why she inspired such fear. Another part of him just wanted to escape the dark and save his friend. And deep within him, a small part of his soul cried for giving up altogether, and whispered that if he had just let the assassin have his way, all of the pain, struggle and mystery would have ended there.

Skerth angrily swept away tears, disgusted by his own weakness. When did giving up become so attractive—so easy? Kiri wouldn't give up. She never had, not even when saving him had meant putting herself directly in his enemy's path. Maybe he could give up on himself, but he couldn't give up on her. For all of the times she had faced down the other street boys, Malyn, even the assassin, he owed her that much.

He forced himself to his feet, wincing, then glanced to where he'd left Kiri and realized with a shock that he could see her. Or, at least, the shape of her. But the source of light was too subtle to come from torch or lantern.

He walked a little further, his hands splayed before him; he watched as they first gained shape, then color. He increased his pace almost to a run until, just beyond the next bend, the crisp tang of fresh sea air greeted him. There, framed in the opening of one last, long tunnel, Skerth could just make out the light of the full moon reflected on the ocean. For a moment he watched the refracted moonlight dance off the tunnel walls, savored the damp and salty taste of freedom. Then he ran back for Kiri.

Chapter Fourteen: Captivity

Skerth emerged to a view as disheartening as it was breathtaking. The tunnel terminated on a narrow strip of land halfway up the cliff wall that marked the seaward edge of the Wedge. Behind him the Wedge rose in a sheer wall of rock for hundreds of feet; below, the sea battered jagged spikes of stone that flanked the coast. Ahead and curving away to either side of the Wedge was nothing but ocean and sky. On the ledge where Skerth stood, the salted wind whipped and tore at his hair and clothes, threatening to pull him to the rocks below. At first glance it seemed his only choices were to sit and appreciate the view while his friend slowly faded or throw himself upon the rocks. Feeling lost and defeated, he lay Kiri on the ground and sank down beside her.

Now that he had some light, he awkwardly untucked her blood-stained shirt and lifted it just enough to see her wound. He sucked in a breath at the sight of the angry red gash that slashed across her left side. The cut was at least four inches long; he couldn't tell how deep it ran, but the wound had let a great deal of blood and, now that he had removed the temporary seal of her shirt and the constant pressure of her body against his, blood welled afresh. He tore a strip of his shirt and pressed it against the wound.

As he crouched beside her, a chill night wind swept against the mingled sweat and blood that soaked his shirt. He shivered, but welcomed the change from the stale, musty air of the tunnel. The breeze revived Kiri as well. She moaned and tried to curl onto her side.

"Don't." His voice sounded rough, unused; his tongue felt thick and dry. He reached out and held her still. "Stay."

Her eyes fluttered open. She stared for a moment, uncomprehending. "The warehouse—" She looked past Skerth to the clear, starry sky and frowned. "How did we get out?" She tried to shift into a sitting position, but Skerth pressed her back down.

"I carried you." He smiled at her disbelief. "And you're heavy, too—for a girl."

Skerth became painfully aware of how close she was, how thin the scrap of bandage that separated his hand from her waist. His neck warmed in a flush of embarrassment.

"You were injured. I didn't—" He started to pull away, but she covered his hand with hers.

"I know," she said, her smile weak.

Her skin looked as pale as her hair, though from an effect of the moonlight or loss of blood he could not tell. She looked so fragile; the desire to hold her overwhelmed him.

He cleared his throat. "I need to find a way down." He slid his hand from hers and made sure she held the bandage tight, then stood. "I'll be back soon."

"I'll just sleep a little." Her eyes were already closing.

Skerth swallowed hard against the lump in his throat and resisted the urge to shake her awake. "Just a little." He whispered a silent plea that she hold on until he could get them out and find help. If he could. If not—

The ledge extended a good distance to the right and terminated in a narrow winding trail that led down to a thin strip of beach. He couldn't tell whether or not that beach in turn would provide them with a way back to the city, but at least the path would put them on the same side of the cliffs as the Lower City.

He hurried back to Kiri and gently shook her awake, trying not to think about how cold her skin felt or why she didn't immediately stir. When she opened her eyes, he sighed with relief. "Come on, Kiri. Let's go." He helped her to her feet, steadying her when she swayed. Using the cliff wall for support, he helped her onto his back and linked her arms around his neck.

He started down, walking as quickly as he could manage while the path was still wide, trying not to think about the wind that gusted against him, the screaming pain in his back and shoulders, or the way his arms and legs shook from cold and exertion. The path narrowed; he gripped Kiri's legs tight and focused on making sure that each step found solid purchase before he made the next. He ignored the long drop to his right, the anxious churning of the sea against the rocks below.

When at last he stepped onto soft white sand, he eased Kiri to the ground and managed only a few more steps before his legs gave way and he splayed face-down on the beach. Every muscle burned and quivered. He craved water like he never had before. He knew he should get to his feet, rouse Kiri, go on—but he couldn't gain control of his seizing muscles.

"I'm sorry, Kiri," he mumbled, his lips crusting with sand. "I'm sorry."

And with the thunder of the ocean in his ears, Skerth drifted into a deep, dreamless sleep.

He woke to absolute darkness, the creak of wood, and nausea as the world swayed beneath him. No, *around* him. He sat upright, head spinning and stomach clenching as he struggled to get his bearings.

Blinking and squinting didn't clarify anything—he didn't even have enough light to see his hands before him. He sat on a rough woolen blanket tossed on a hard wooden floor, the smell of salt, wood and wine thick in his nose. Somewhere beyond him, whether outside, upstairs, or both he couldn't yet tell, he could hear the shouts and laughter of a raucous gathering. All the while, the floor beneath him rocked and rolled to the suck and swell of the sea.

"Kiri," he whispered.

No answer. He felt his way around his cell, searching for her, but the only other occupants were several barrels of wine and a couple of rats. The effort, combined with another sharp swell of the floor, sickened him. He turned to his side and dry heaved, grateful for once for an empty stomach. As if to mock him, the voices outside his cell roared and guffawed.

"Give 'im another!" someone shouted.

"Seaward, yeah? See if he's really meant to sail!"

There was a scuffle and a great deal of pounding directly overhead, followed by a wail, a heavy splash, and more laughter.

"That'll teach th' rotting scum!" A woman's voice this time, high and strident.

Skerth lay back down on the blanket and squeezed his eyes shut, forcing back waves of fear and panic.

Kiri was gone, and he'd managed to land in a sea nest of filthy, stinking pirates.

He curled on the blanket, knees to chest, and focused on breathing in and out while his mind worked to pick out the latest tangle he had created.

"Get up, scat, or I'll take the whip to your back!"

Pain exploded in Skerth's side and abdomen. His eyes snapped open and he scuttled to the far corner of his cell, where he blinked clear the sight of a thin older boy clothed in rags, a dagger at his hip. He wore his dark, stringy hair pulled back into a long tail, and a gold hoop glimmered in his right ear. He caught Skerth's eye and, with a sneer, brandished his dagger.

"Don't just sit there gaping, you idiot! Captain Xor wants to see you, prompt. You're to follow me now or I'll have you tossed."

He feinted at Skerth, who immediately leapt to his feet, ignoring another wave of nausea.

"I'm coming," he managed, swallowing hard. If he was going to vomit, he refused to do it in front of this mangy seasucker. "Where's my friend?"

"You've no friends here," said the pirate, turning away.

Skerth followed him out of the wooden cell and into the belly of the ship. They wove around crates and barrels of goods, food and wine, among other, less savory or more forbidden items. He scanned the hold for other doors to other cells, hoping for a sign of Kiri, but found nothing.

The pirate smacked his shoulder. "Better shift your eyes, scat, unless you want to lose 'em."

"I've no interest in anything here."

The pirate halted and raised a hand to strike Skerth. "Did I hear you squeak, little rat?"

Skerth met his eyes and stared, but the pirate showed no sign of backing down. Skerth slowly shook his head.

"You hear nothin,' see nothin' unless we say so."

They climbed a ladder from the hold to the next level of the ship, and ducked through a low-ceilinged corridor flanked with doors. The pirate paused before the last door at the corridor's end and rapped a pattern.

"Enter," rumbled a deep voice within.

117

The pirate narrowed his eyes at Skerth. "Mind your manners, scat. The Captain isn't in any mood for street tricks. Saved your life, he has, and livin' always comes at a price. Remember that."

He opened the door and ushered Skerth inside.

The sound of wood scraping against wood greeted him as two men seated at a long, polished wood table rose at his entrance. They were an odd pair: the man nearest Skerth was young—maybe twenty at most—and wore the deep violet and grey of the merchant's guild. A gold insignia clasp pinned a crisp wool short-cloak to his shoulder. He carried a longsword at his hip, but looked as though he probably didn't know how to wield it. He caught Skerth watching him and quickly masked a scowl with a weak smile.

The other man was tall and broad-shouldered, his skin and hair as dark as his companion was fair. He wore a vibrant mix of colors and designs: a billowing yellow shirt under a stained orange surcoat, loose scarlet pants tucked into scuffed black boots. A wide black belt slung at his hips displayed an array of interesting weaponry—daggers, knives, a curved scimitar at one hip, a whip coiled at the other. His head was shaved clean, like a warrior of Terrenweld, and he wore three gold hoops in his right ear—one for each wife. He greeted Skerth with a wide grin.

"Well, Janewyn, looks like our guest is finally awake."

"So it would seem," the merchant—Janewyn—replied.

The pirate of Terrenweld walked around the table to stand, fists on his hips, in front of Skerth. He shrank under the pirate's gaze, the practiced eye of a skin trader, and his skin prickled with fear. "Tell me, boy. What ill-wind swept you onto my sandbar last night? You're lucky one my men found you and your friend, or you would've swept out to sea with the morning tide."

"I don't feel lucky," Skerth croaked, his tongue swollen, his mouth sandpaper. "Where is my friend?"

The pirate who'd brought him up from the hold smacked Skerth on the side of the head. "Manners, scat. That's Captain Xor you're addressin', not those insolent little whores' droppings you run the streets with."

"Patience, Gryff. That's my guest you're battering." There was no mistaking the warning in Xor's tone. Gryff's face darkened, but he held his tongue.

"You must be thirsty." Xor grabbed a flask from the table and tossed it to Skerth, who caught it automatically. "Water." When Skerth didn't budge to drink, he chuckled softly. "You're a smart boy. Isn't he Janewyn?" he didn't await a response. "Drink. That's my personal flask. I don't poison my own trough."

Skerth tossed it back to the pirate captain. "You first."

"Careful," Gryff growled under his breath, but Xor merely laughed, making a great show of opening the flask, tipping it back, and spilling the clear, clean water down his throat. Then he capped the flask and tossed it back, this time with a hard glint in his eye that belied his smile.

"Drink or go thirsty. I won't offer again."

Reluctantly, Skerth sipped. At first taste of the clean water, he tipped the flask back and drank greedily, heedless of the liquid running down his chin. After drinking his fill, he wiped his face and tossed the flask back.

"You didn't answer my question," Skerth said, keeping his voice bold and hard despite the fear quaking his stomach. Pirates preyed upon fear and weakness; he had to be strong. "Where's my friend?"

"In good time, boy, in good time." Xor looked to Gryff. "Leave us. Tell your mistress the boy's awake and have Emme set to work on a meal."

Gryff nodded and showed himself out, tugging the door shut behind him.

"Your companion rests. Someone cut him deep, but he'll mend," said Xor.

Him. He. At least Kiri's secret remained safe. *For now.* "I need to see him."

"Later. First, I have some questions—"

"Now!" Skerth's intensity surprised them both. Xor tensed. Skerth dropped his shoulders and his gaze in a submissive pose and hastened to add, "Please. Sir."

Xor and Janewyn exchanged a look.

"Let him in, Xor," called a woman from a small room just off to Skerth's left.

Xor grunted a reply. "You heard her. Go." He motioned Skerth toward the door, catching his arm at the last second. "Mind your tongue or I'll have it out."

Skerth swallowed and nodded. The pirate released him, and in three quick strides he was at the open door. Inside, Kiri slept on a raised wooden bed of fresh rushes, a blanket pulled to her neck. A woman sat at her side, a pile of mending in her lap. She looked up and smiled when he entered. Aside from a few crooked teeth, she was pretty, with olive skin, long dark hair worn loose, and startling green eyes.

"Come in." Her eyes flicked beyond him, to Xor. "Alone."

"Gem—"

"He'll be fine," she said briskly. "And so will I."

Xor bowed and retreated. The woman rose, ushered Skerth inside, and closed the door firmly behind him before settling back into her chair.

"I am Gem. What is your name?"

"Skerth," he replied, before he could stop himself. He nodded toward Kiri. "How is he?"

"Better, though a fever's come on. Whoever cut your friend had a touch of poison on the blade. I've cleaned it best I can, but the next few hours will tell." She laid the back of her hand on Kiri's forehead. "What's your friend's name?"

He hesitated, reaching for a name—any name—that sounded more masculine. "Fael."

"Fael," she murmured thoughtfully. "An interesting name—for a girl."

He paled. "What do you mean?" His hands twitched; he jammed them in his pockets.

"You know what I mean." She gave him a meaningful look. "Don't you." A statement, not a question.

She knew.

His shoulders sagged. He shifted closer and looked down at Kiri, who appeared less like a boy with each passing day. "Please—don't tell them."

She raised an eyebrow. "Do you know what you ask of me?" Her voice was not unkind, but her meaning was clear.

Skerth straightened and crossed his arms over his chest, trying to appear more brave and relaxed than he felt. "Yes. I'm asking you to lie. To pirates."

Gem burst into laughter. There was such joy in it that Skerth relaxed a little, and the corner of his mouth twitched. But he kept his stance firm, for Kiri's sake. Once her laughter subsided, Gem took a deep breath and narrowed thoughtful eyes at Skerth. "You're sharper than I expected."

He shrugged. "I've seen a pirate or two. I know enough to stay out of their way."

"That's not what I meant."

Skerth shifted uncomfortably under her steady gaze. After the pass of a few heartbeats she rose and quietly barred the door before returning to her chair. She motioned him close, then spoke so quietly he had to lean in to hear. "Xor runs a tight trade, mostly in expensive fabrics, jewels, wine, and occasionally, skin." She paused, allowing this to sink in. "He prides himself on two things: the quality of his merchandise and his ability to sell anything, to anyone, for its highest market value. And everything—every*one* has value."

She looked directly at Skerth. "Your survival—and hers—depends upon your value. You're both young. A bit thin, but strong. Resilient. You'd bring a decent price on the skin market, but your friend here's a fair one. Xor could sell her to a brothel Upwedge or sail up the coast to Sahtamor or Maghinis and collect a king's ransom. So tell me: why should I guard your friend's secret and stay Xor's hand? What can you offer in return?"

Skerth's heart sank. What value *did* he have? To her, or to anyone? "I can fight," he said, hesitant. "Run scrolls. Anything."

"Anything?" She cocked her head to the side, her expression calculating. "How old are you, Skerth?"

His spine bristled a warning; he strove to keep the tension out of his shoulders, his voice. "Twelve."

Something—anger, perhaps?—flashed across her expression, quickly masked behind a tight smile. "You do not trust me."

"I don't trust anyone."

"Perhaps that is wise. But tell me, Skerth. If you don't trust me with such a simple scrap of knowledge, how will you trust me with her life? With yours? Everything comes at a price. You must decide if you're willing to pay."

Everything comes at a price. What will she ask of me? Skerth looked down at Kiri, so pale without her mask of grime, so delicate. So *feminine*. And he knew. *Whatever the cost, I will pay.*

"What do you want of me?"

Her eyes flashed triumphant and he instantly knew she had caught him like an eba fly in a spider's glistening web. "Information. Honesty. Loyalty, without question. In truth, a small fee for the great gift of my silence."

He glanced to Kiri, and a new, unfamiliar feeling squeezed his chest. He wanted so desperately for her to open her eyes, to help him think through this new problem, to overcome Gem and the pirates and escape this mess once and for all. At the same time, he was angry—at Grey and Taleryn, Malyn, the assassin, the Caretakers, and even Kiri, but mostly at himself. He could hardly breathe. He should have insisted she stay behind, like Grey and Taleryn wanted. He should have retraced their steps through the tunnel, gotten her to Feirywn. He should have—

Kiri shifted in her sleep, scattering his thoughts. Her lips parted slightly; her breath escaped in a whisper. His heart contracted, exploded in a rush of feeling so powerful he felt dizzy.

I will get us out of this, he vowed. *I will keep you safe, no matter the cost.*

"Agreed," he said at last. "What do you want to know?"

"Everything. Beginning with your true age and ending with how you landed on my beach."

He sighed, resigned. "I'm fourteen," he forced out around the sudden lump in his throat. "Almost fifteen summers, now, as best I can guess." From there he sketched out a story about running away from a gang of Malyn's scats, getting caught up in a knife fight, ducking into the tunnels with Kiri and carrying her out in the night. Before the assassin started harrying the streets, his tale might have been true. He only hoped she would find it convincing.

"You're a brave one," Gem said when he finished. She leaned back, her smile genuine. "Perhaps Xor may find you of value after all." She rose and smoothed her skirt. "I will keep your friend's secret. For now, make yourself useful to Xor."

Skerth frowned. "How?"

"Do what he asks of you. Be obedient. Keep your mouth closed and your eyes and ears open wide. But never forget: your loyalty is mine. I purchased it with your friend's secret, and I intend to collect my price."

His stomach twisted. *What have I done?* One last look at Kiri steeled his resolve, and he nodded.

"Go," she told him, beckoning to the door. "She needs her rest."

After one last backward glance at Kiri he let himself out, wondering not if he'd made the right choice, but if he'd ever truly had a choice at all.

Chapter Fifteen: Negotiations

"**B**oy!" shouted Xor.

Skerth jumped and hastened to the pirate's side. "Captain?"

Skerth's swift, respectful attention paid off; the pirate looked pleased. "My guest requires more ale."

Disheveled and red-faced, Janewyn didn't look like he needed more ale, but Skerth didn't argue. He picked up the pewter pitcher and bowed, gritting his teeth against the indignity, before dashing into the galley.

Emme, the serving girl, looked up sharply at his entrance, then returned her attention to cleaning fish. "You startled me."

It hadn't taken Skerth more than a few minutes to discover that almost anything startled Emme—a dropped mug, a footstep, a word. She was a petite, wilted girl, not much older than he. Wispy brown curls strayed from her white mob cap, highlighting the pale, watery blue eyes beneath. She didn't look like she would last a day on the streets, and, judging from the way she spooked, her life in Xor's house probably wasn't pleasant, either.

"I'm sorry," he replied, keeping his voice low and even. "Xor wants more ale."

She sighed. "Right." She wiped her slimy hands on her apron and reached for the pitcher.

While she moved to the barrel, Skerth searched for something to say. "Have you served here long?"

"All my life," she replied without looking up.

"That's nice," he said awkwardly.

She closed the tap and handed him the pitcher. "Gem's my mother," she explained. "I hadn't much choice."

"Better than the streets," he offered.

She arched an eyebrow and he could see Gem's look in her. "Is it?"

He shrugged. "Meals, a bed. A mother—"

Her mirthless laugh startled him into silence. "You won't be here long enough, scat, to learn what it's like to live with pirates, serving the same crooked merchants, smugglers, thieves and skin traders you spend your days avoiding. On the streets you can run. Hide. Here—" she shrugged. Before his eyes her spirit seemed to collapse inward. She gathered her meekness about her, cloaking herself in insignificance.

"Boy!" Xor roared.

This time, they both startled.

Skerth backed toward the door. "Thanks," he told Emme. "For the ale."

The corner of her mouth quirked into a smile, and she nodded.

He turned to shove the door open, but paused at Emme's quiet "Skerth!" and glanced back over his shoulder. "Pay attention out there. Learn as much as you can. You never know when you'll discover something you can use."

He waited for something more, but she had already returned to her fish. Bracing himself, Skerth pushed open the door.

"There you are! You waste my time, boy." Xor waved him impatiently to the table.

"You should flog 'im," Janewyn slurred. Skerth stiffened at the gleam of malice in the merchant's eye, and glanced warily to Xor.

"Perhaps, when our business concludes." Xor held out his flagon; Skerth poured, taking care not to spill a drop of ale. He'd already made that mistake once, and his ear still stung from the cuffing Xor had given him. Besides, the floor was already so sticky that he almost preferred walking in the muck of the streets.

Janewyn frowned. "Thought we'd finished." He waved his flagon at Skerth, who immediately moved to attend him.

"We've yet to decide on a price."

While the men started haggling in earnest, Skerth soaked up whatever information he could—most of which wasn't much use, since he neither understood nor cared much for the politics of lesser merchants and their shady dealings with pirate lords. As late afternoon wore on into evening and still Skerth stood by, his legs stiffened and cramped. He tried shifting positions to ease the aching, but after Xor cuffed him for distracting Janewyn one time too many, Skerth decided that the leg cramps were less painful than beatings and strove to remain still.

Skerth tried to follow Emme's advice and pay attention, but after a while the combined effort of remaining upright and staying alert proved too much to handle. For a time Skerth occupied himself by replaying the prior night's events over and over in his mind, trying to determine what—if anything—he could have done to escape the assassin without landing in an even worse situation. He envisioned the tunnel system, trying to determine how far from the scrabbly strip of beach and docks that lined the Lower City they'd landed and whether or not they had a hope of getting back, should they manage to escape. Skerth even spent a good hour plotting revenge against Malyn. But mostly he worried about Kiri. Until her fever broke he couldn't risk escaping with her—and he wouldn't leave without her. Their only hope, as far as Skerth could tell, was to trust Gem and pray she didn't hope to exact her toll from him too soon.

". . .Auberdale Eve."

Janewyn's words immediately caught Skerth's attention.

Xor's congenial expression faded and the muscles that corded his neck and upper arms tensed. Beneath the table, his hand settled on the hilt of one of his many knives.

"Careful, merchant."

Janewyn was so well-dipped in drink that he missed the warning in Xor's tone and posture. Missed—or didn't care. There was a reckless glint to his eyes, and his lips twisted into a sardonic smile.

"Careful?" said Janewyn. "Why? Are you in league with—" he leaned in close and lowered his voice to a dramatic whisper—"the people?"

Xor narrowed his eyes at the merchant. "My men side with no one. This is not our fight."

Janewyn lifted his eyebrows in mock surprise. "No one?" He leaned back in his chair and studied Xor over the rim of his flagon. "I doubt that very much. Surely the captain and crew of *The Scarlet* purchased their right to dock and trade in these waters from someone."

Xor's rich, baritone laughter jarred against the quiet. "Come, merchant. You know, perhaps better than anyone, that trade rights and goods can always be negotiated. But our loyalty cannot be bought—or sold." The color drained from Janewyn's face. Xor drained his flagon and motioned for Skerth to refill it. "We and the Caretakers have a mutually beneficial arrangement, nothing more. Not that our affairs are any of your concern."

"Of course." Janewyn shifted uneasily in his chair and stared into his flagon as he swirled the dregs of his ale. "But there's a great deal of profit in it for those willing to take the risk."

"We do not interfere in politics," snapped Xor.

"For the right price—"

"Not for any price!" Xor slammed his flagon on the table. Janewyn and Skerth both jumped. A long, tense silence followed, during which Xor visibly struggled to control his anger. "We will not risk everything we have built to chase old tales."

Janewyn leaned forward. His eyes shone, though not with drink. "That's the wondrous part. Why chase the tales when you can take part in the telling?"

Xor considered his companion for a long time. "Explain."

"Boy." Janewyn waved to Skerth and held out his flagon. Skerth obediently moved to his side, but when he reached for the pitcher the merchant's hand shot out and grabbed Skerth's wrist. "The Caretakers' popularity wanes. The people don't want their promises and ceremonies any longer. They want an heir. Why not give them one?" Janewyn glanced meaningfully at Skerth. Xor didn't reply, so the merchant seized his chance. "Think of the opportunities available to the men who hold the strings of the puppet king. The trade, the gold . . . the power. . . ."

Skerth shrank from the sudden interest in Xor's eyes. "Give them an heir," he murmured thoughtfully. "How old are you, boy?"

"Fourteen summers." He tried to slip out of Janewyn's grasp, but the merchant held him tight.

"He's about the right age."

"And the right look," Janewyn agreed. "But if this one doesn't work, we can find another. Brats like these are easy to come by."

Xor shook his head. "The Caretakers know better than to allow just anyone to come forward and steal the throne they bought with spilled blood and hard coin." Xor glanced pointedly at Janewyn's hand, still clutching Skerth's wrist; when the merchant released him, Skerth scurried back to the wall, more comfortable in the shadows, away from Janewyn's greedy stare. "This is a dangerous game you propose. And without proof—"

"Proof can be manufactured," Janewyn interrupted with a derisive wave. "This scat of yours is a quick study. See how quickly he has learned to bow and scrape and hold his tongue? We can teach him a new name, a new history—enough details of the old family still exist that we can easily create a new identity out of old cloth. With all of the royal family either slain or exiled and so few of their closest courtiers and counselors left in the city, who will challenge his facts? The people who chafe under the Caretakers' rule and long for their precious heir's return? The Caretakers themselves, who have sworn to abide by the old codes and abdicate their stewardship of Erados should the true successor to the throne return to make his claim?"

"I confess, merchant, you make a keen argument. If what you say is true, a well-groomed pretender just might stand a chance." Xor leaned back in his chair and studied the merchant. "Who else knows of this plan of yours?"

"No one." Janewyn hesitated before adding, "Although—"

The pirate's snort of disgust cut him off. "I thought as much." He pushed back his chair to rise.

"Wait! Hear me out!" Janewyn's tone pitched to a note of desperation. The pirate remained poised to stand, though he did not rise. Even from his position against the wall nearer Janewyn's side, Skerth could clearly see Xor's hand firm on the hilt of his scimitar. The merchant noticed too, and swallowed hard. "I have discussed this plan of mine with no one, as I hoped we could strike a favorable—arrangement. But I have heard whispers that other, similar plots exist."

Feirwyn, Skerth thought with a jolt, wondering just how much Janewyn knew.

". . .must act quickly if we are to find the right candidate and groom him well by Auberdale Eve," Janewyn finished.

Xor considered this. "Too many candidates increase our risk and reduce our chances of success."

"The Caretakers themselves have already seen fit to exterminate any potential aspirants to the throne who might clamber out of the gutter, which makes finding our boy as soon as possible a high priority. There are a few other potential pretenders here and there who have managed to evade the Order's notice, but even if they succeed in coming forward on Auberdale Eve, I possess information that will significantly improve our odds."

Xor looked skeptical. "And what is that?"

Janewyn's lips curled in a satisfied smile. He leaned back and drained his flagon. "Shall we discuss the details of our partnership?"

"Not yet." Xor narrowed his eyes at the merchant. "How can I trust that you speak the truth? Where did you acquire information valuable enough to secure your false heir's claim and denounce all others?"

"I keep my secrets, pirate, just as you keep yours."

"Secrets poison sincere negotiations."

"Perhaps," Janewyn conceded. "All you need to know is that my informants are well-placed and well-paid. Their information is reliable." He flashed a smile. "And well-worth its weight in gold."

The two men's eyes locked and held. Skerth remained very still, hoping the men had forgotten him there. At last, Xor broke the silence. "Boy." Skerth's shoulders dropped in defeat. "More ale. And get Emme in here to stoke the coals. The merchant and I have much to resolve before the night is out."

Chapter Sixteen: Plans in Motion

That night, Skerth dreamed of soft pink roses tinged with the orange and gold of a summer sunset. He dreamed impressions and feelings: he felt safe, cherished. Wanted. But the dreams quickly turned to fire and ash, to armed men chasing him through the streets of Endelas Ortanos, to a woman's screaming and the ragged voice of an old crone. . . . Her screech became a load scraping, the raking of clawed fingernails against stone, and Skerth bolted awake, gasping, heart hammering in his chest.

Dizzy, disoriented from the dream-turned-nightmare, he blinked clear the sight of Emme dragging a metal washtub across the floor of his small room.

"Apologies," Emme huffed, red-faced, as she gave the tub a shove. "Captain wants you to wash, quick-like. He and the merchant have plans for you."

Skerth shook off the last lingering aftermath of his broken sleep and rose to help her push the tub through the door.

"Thanks."

His eyes flickered to the open door. Emme was slight. It would be so easy—

"Don't think about it," she warned. "You might make it abovedeck, if your luck holds. You probably don't want to know what they'd do to if you don't."

"I wouldn't—"

"Of course you would, if you had the chance." She gave him a rare half-smile. "I would, were I in your place. But what would happen to your friend?" She handed him the towel thrown over her shoulder and pulled a slip of soap from her apron pocket. "You'd best hurry. Xor isn't a patient man."

Before he could respond, she slipped out the door. A moment later, a key turned in the lock. *I'm a prisoner, not a guest*, he reminded himself. The tidy little room they'd given him next door to Kiri's might have convinced him otherwise. He slept in a wooden bed filled with fresh, clean rushes, covered by a warm wool blanket without a single fray or tear. A trunk shoved to the side might have held his belongings, had he any, and the early morning sun slanted through a small window near the ceiling. Only the lock and key reminded him of his place—prisoner to the pirates, powerless to their bidding, unwilling pawn in their ill-fated plan.

Nevertheless, he welcomed the prospect of a good wash. He tried to go to the public bath houses every so often when the keepers opened them for half-price or less at the end of the day. The lukewarm water had usually served quite a few customers by then and was good for little more than a quick rinse, although he could still soak off most of the city well enough to get by. But with the dead boys and the assassin to worry about of late, he hadn't managed a bath in a long time.

And his clothes—caked with the grime and sweat of daily street life and now layered with Kiri's blood—were a complete ruin. He eagerly stripped them away and stepped into the lukewarm water. He scrubbed everywhere, paying special attention to his bare feet, tough and blackened from too many years without shoes. He scrubbed until the dappled pattern of orange and gold on the floor had turned to long stripes of full sun and he could hear the first stirrings of the crew abovedeck.

He had no sooner dried and dressed in a more serviceable pair of breeches and shirt he'd found in the trunk when heavy bootsteps paused at his door and a key turned in the lock. The door swung open.

Xor grunted his approval at sight of Skerth. "You're hardly the same boy as yesterday. Just the right age, right build, I'd say. And that hair—" He fingered a lock of Skerth's hair and studied him thoughtfully. "Uncanny." He chuckled and slapped Skerth on the shoulder. "Come, Boy, we've got work to do. It's not every bit of street filth gets your luck. Today we're going to make you a prince."

Skerth forced a smile. True enough, so many of the kids he knew wouldn't blink at the opportunities Xor and Janewyn's scheme—and Feirwyn's too, for that matter—offered. A lifetime of good clothing, more food than he could ever eat, permanent shelter—and at the palace, besides—if their deception succeeded. A few months earlier, Skerth himself might have questioned what he would have to lose when he stood to gain everything. But now that he had seen the full force of the Caretakers' resolve to destroy any potential claimant to the throne, Skerth wasn't so sure he liked his chances. If he could return to his streets, he would gladly trade his present "luck" for a lifetime of uncertainty.

Outside in the common room, Xor shoved Skerth into a chair in front of Naz, the weathered old pirate given the dubious task of combing and cutting Skerth's hair. He walked stooped over and limped on his right leg, but his hands seemed steady enough.

"So full o' nits he's like to be better off if I shave it to the skin," Naz complained after a preliminary inspection.

"The hair stays," Xor said firmly. "You've got the whole morning to pick it clean and you can cut it short, but give him so much as one nick to the scalp and I'll take your ear."

Naz grumbled something under his breath, but took to the task of grooming Skerth with surprisingly deft hands. What felt like hours later, he set down his comb and knives and pronounced, "this scat's as clean as a Caretaker's whore!"

"Caretakers don't have women, Naz," pointed out Janewyn, who seemed to have taken up permanent residence in Xor's common room. He had already worked through two tankards of ale and motioned for Emme to fill a third. "They're celibate."

"That's my point, you stupid—"

"Enough," Xor said, rising. He set his tankard on the table and motioned Naz away. "Let's go, boy. Day's waning."

Skerth's heart skipped as he followed the pirate out of the common room. Go? Were they moving him so soon? He glanced to Kiri's door, which remained firmly closed; whether that was a good sign or bad he could not tell. He wanted to see her, make sure she was all right. He vowed to make a point to request a visit later.

At the stairs Xor tossed Skerth a worn, stained cloak that smelled of sea salt and rum before swinging a short cloak of fine black wool around his own broad shoulders. "Stay close and keep your eyes down. Don't speak. If anything looks interesting, best look away. My kin don't take chances when they think someone's got an eye on their business. And don't even think of running." He settled his right hand on the hilt of his curved sword. "Plenty of wharf dodgers out there to pass off as the prince if something happens to you."

Skerth nodded, but Xor had already started up the spiral stairs.

A crisp sea breeze greeted the pair as they stepped on deck. Despite his reservations, Skerth was glad to be outside in the fresh air, and the opportunity to see more of Xor's world had sparked his curiosity. He also hoped the trip would prove useful. He had always done a fair job of visualizing the layout of the streets and, more recently, the rooftops; if he could fix a decent map of the pirates' settlement in his mind, he and Kiri might be able to escape after all.

Xor's ship was anchored across the entrance of a small cove inaccessible by land and peppered with ships and stilted shacks, all connected by a maze of rickety wooden rope bridges and floating landings moored against the ships with tight sea knots. All of the ships flew Xor's standard—three gold rings on a field of black. The same cliffs that divided the city curved into a rough semi-circle that shadowed the cove and provided for a perfect pirate's nest. To the south, fine ships boasting brightly colored sails in shades of scarlet, gold, emerald and sapphire rocked gently against their moorings, laden with the fine goods of the world's merchants. Sturdy docks swept upward at a steep incline, showcasing the brightly-colored rooftops of shops, warehouses and homes that increased in opulence as they moved inland. Just to the north, the cliffs abruptly fell away to a narrow scrap of beach dotted with the fishing shanties and tumbledown docks of the Lower City. Positioned as they were between the two worlds, pirates would have no trouble thriving unseen, and at high tide their ships could make their way out to sea virtually unchallenged.

As he tried to keep pace with Xor's long stride without tumbling off the maze of bridges, Skerth took in as much as he could, from the lay of the wooden paths that passed for streets to the colorfully dressed men and women who bustled about on their own early morning business. Children dressed in well-kept clothes and shoes chased one another, laughing, across the bridges, careless of the sea to either side. A group of elderly men mending their nets glanced up and lifted their hands in greeting as Xor passed. Women carrying baskets full of washing and mending, men settled on landings to sharpen their blades, merchants and pirates conducting business of their own—all nodded respectfully to Xor, though their faces just as often shifted to scowls when they caught Skerth's eye. Always he looked quickly away. These weren't gentle folk who lived in the shadow of the city. Pirates traded on secrecy, double-dealing, and murder. They would give no quarter to a common pickpocket from the city who dared memorize their faces or purpose.

Their journey ended before a tidy houseboat trimmed in weathered blue. Beneath the windows, slender boxes full of wilted herbs struggled to thrive in the heavy sea air.

"Fae!" Xor called from the platform. He didn't wait for an answer before starting up the rope ladder. When Skerth hesitated, Xor gave him a glare that made his ears ache.

"Yes, yes, come in," a breathless matron said, bustling into view. She was stocky and short, with a broad bust and frizzy salt and pepper hair swept up into a messy bun. Unlike the others they had passed, she gave Skerth a warm smile. They followed her below deck into a tidy little room not unlike Xor's common room.

"So this is the boy," she said, her eyes sweeping Skerth from the top of his head to the heel of his borrowed boots. She began to circle him thoughtfully as she spoke, occasionally reaching out to tug a lock of hair or squeeze an arm. "Fair, like the old king. Sweet face. A little young, perhaps . . . small . . . but close enough." She paused, hands on her hips, and gave Xor a look of approval. "I think he'll do."

Xor gave Skerth a wicked grin. "Hear that, boy?" He thumped Skerth hard on the back, nearly knocking him off his feet. "Looks like you're going to be our prince."

Skerth doubted he'd live long enough to see the inside of the palace.

"But you can't go before the Caretakers on Auberdale Eve looking like the street scum you are. Fae here is going to see to that. She's the best Needle in all of Erados, I'd wager."

"That so?" she chuckled. "Then we'd best discuss what you're willing to pay the 'best Needle' before we get started on this little project of yours."

They settled into chairs across the table from one another and fell to haggling in earnest. Unsure if he should sit or not, Skerth remained standing just behind Xor and studied the room. Like Xor's common room, the centerpiece of Fae's was a wooden table and four chairs, though the surface of her table was worn and badly scratched. Blades, papers and scraps of fabric in a range of textures and colors littered the table, and more bolts of fabric lay in piles about the room. There were two doors: one led out, the other, presumably, led deeper into the ship. Skerth made note of both should he have the opportunity to escape.

"I'll not do for less than a hundred fifty gold, Xor," Fae said at last. Her tone shifted to that of a practiced negotiator, her eyes sharp and shrewd. "Remember, you're not just buying the work. You'll be wanting my silence, too."

Xor didn't look pleased, but he nodded. "Done. But she'll not be pleased when she hears you're gutting me like a fish."

The sound of Fae's laugh reminded Skerth of warm, sugared cream, of firelight dancing against polished stone walls, of a honey-haired smiling noblewoman. He felt loved, he felt safe, he felt . . . dizzy, disoriented. He reached out and clutched the back of Xor's chair for support.

"What's the matter, boy?" Xor growled.

Skerth managed to collect himself and step back before Xor moved to swat him away.

"Nothing, Captain. My apologies." He felt shaky inside, but his voice, to his relief, remained clear and strong.

"Have you fed him?" Fae rose, her eyebrows knit into a frown. "He looks half-starved."

"I'll leave that to you, for the price I'm paying." Xor tossed a pouch onto the table and stood. "You'll have the rest when you've delivered the goods." He glowered at Skerth. "You mind the lady, scat. Give her any trouble or try to run, I'll have your feet and your tongue, and I'll fly your head from my eagle's nest as a banner to all who cross me. Hear me?"

"Yes, Captain."

"I'll be back for him at sundown."

Xor no sooner left than Fae tucked Skerth into a chair and called for a serving girl to bring him meat and bread. While he ate, she bustled about the room sorting fabrics and piling papers, all the while chattering at him about how lucky he was to have such an opportunity, and how grateful he should be that Xor had scraped him off of that beach. After he finished his meal, she stood him on a stool and bent to work in earnest. She measured and held fabrics to his skin, all while keeping up a constant stream of chatter in which she questioned Skerth about everything from growing up on the streets to his exciting new future as the King of Erados. Before he knew it, Xor returned to make arrangements for delivery, and

Skerth was no closer to escaping than he had been when he boarded Fae's boat.

On the way back to Xor's ship, Skerth comforted himself with the knowledge that running from Fae's would have proved useless without a way to get across the bay. Besides, he would have had to leave Kiri behind. Still, he couldn't fight the despair that settled on his shoulders more heavily with every step. How many scats had died since Xor had captured him? How many more would kill for the opportunity that Skerth had fallen into by chance?

Skerth realized that he only half-heartedly resisted Xor's plan, that a soft bed, a bath and warm food had lulled him into obedience. He could have easily overpowered Fae, distracted her. Instead, he ate her food, stood patiently atop the stool until his legs ached, answered all of her questions, and failed to ask any of his own. And not once, in all that long day, had he given more than a passing thought for Kiri. He flushed with shame to think of her, sweating out a fever and fighting for her life, while he turned obediently on the pedestal so Fae could clothe him in the garb of a puppet prince.

By the time Xor ushered him across the network of water planks that led back to *The Scarlet*, Skerth's stomach churned at all of the opportunities he'd missed. *No more*, he vowed. Let the pirates find another scat to play the prince; Skerth would not live the rest of his life as their pampered slave. He would seize the very next chance for escape that crossed his path. And he would take Kiri, or die in the attempt. *I will not fail her again.*

·

Chapter Seventeen: Enemies and Allies

Skerth winced as Xor landed another meaty punch on the elderly fisherman's face. Blood and spittle sprayed across the table, the floor, and the two big men holding the old man upright between them.

"Please," the man panted, and spit one of his few remaining teeth onto the floor. "Give you . . . anything. Just . . . no coin yet. The fire—"

"Fire's got nothing to do with pulling fish from the sea and trading them at market. You owe me coin, fisherman, and it's coin I'll have." Xor raised his fist for another blow.

"I've a cow," the man squeaked, flinching as far from the fist as he could manage. "She's thin. Old . . . but yours if you'll have her. Until I get . . . coin."

Xor lowered his fist. "A cow, you offer me? What fool do you think me?"

"No fool . . . sir! No fool at all! Smart, to take both. Fire's made food scarce . . . the cow will feed you well. And the fish'll go as fast as I pull 'em from the sea, yes they will, and then you'll have your coin besides." The man's adam's apple bobbed nervously in his skinny neck. "Please, sir."

The fisherman shrank under Xor's gaze, his arms going limp. The man's legs quaked so hard he could barely stand; the pirates on either side braced him upright with a rough shake.

"Boy," Xor said at last, his eyes firm on the fisherman. "Towel."

Skerth obediently brought forward the silver tray that held a bowl of water, two neatly folded towels, and a goblet of wine. Xor dipped a towel in the water, then slowly, deliberately wiped the fisherman's blood from his hands.

"Throw him off the starboard bow. If he can swim ashore, he lives. And if you live, fisherman, you send me that cow, and I'll have your grandson to hostage, too, until you get me that coin."

The man's face paled beneath its mask of swollen cuts and bruises. "My grandson—but my lord—he's only a boy of five—"

"A good age to learn the importance of paying one's debts." Xor nodded and his men dragged their prisoner out. The fisherman's sobs and wails echoed long after they pulled him abovedeck, only ceasing when a heavy splash sealed his fate.

Skerth remained motionless as Xor dropped the towel onto the tray and tilted back the goblet. He downed the wine in a few swallows and returned the goblet to the tray.

"More," he growled.

Skerth headed for the kitchens.

"Is it over?" Emme asked, her attention fixed on the dough in her hands.

"Yes." He went to the decanter and poured Xor's wine. "Is it always like that around here?"

"Some days worse than others."

He wished he could read her expression and learn what she thought of the display outside that had soured his stomach. He felt a strange kinship with Emme, imprisoned in a life she did not choose and bound to make the best of it. He wondered if she felt the same.

She straightened and wiped her hands on her apron, turning to face him. "You won't have to suffer here much longer. They're moving you."

Skerth stiffened in alarm. "What? When?"

"Xor and Janewyn want to move you out and put you under guard in the Merchant's Guild."

"Merchant's Guild?" he echoed, trying to process this latest news.

"They've been arguing about it ever since they put you away that first night. Janewyn's convinced Xor they've got to get you away before the rest of our kin hear rumor of their plan to put you in for the heir. Otherwise they'll all want in, and there'll be blood to decide what happens then."

"What about my friend?"

"The girl?"

His chest tightened. "You know?"

Emme half-shrugged and tucked a wisp of hair behind her ear. "I have eyes and ears." She turned back to her dough. "I'm not sure what they'll do with her. Once you're gone, it won't matter much, will it? You'll be King of Erados." Her tone was bitter. "Kings don't care much for the fate of their subjects."

I would, Skerth swore, thinking of Kiri, the kids on his streets, the constant struggle of the people of the Lower City to eke out a living and fill the bellies of their children. He thought of the fisherman, forced to borrow money from pirates to survive, now either drowned or making his way to shore, where he'd give up his livestock and his grandson in exchange for his life. He thought of the Caretakers who drained the city and its people of resources in the name of peace and learning, and the Blades and Staves who exacted vengeance and brutality in the name of order. *I would care*, Skerth reaffirmed, and in that instant knew that he would do right by the city—and all of Erados—as its leader. But he would not claim the throne in the name of pirates. He had to find a way off that ship, fast.

"I do care," he told Emme. "I won't leave without Kiri."

"Gem might have some say in that."

He shook his head, confused. "She's protecting her. She—"

"—is a pirate, and makes her living like the rest of them." Emme turned and gave him a long, steady look. "She's making the girl well and holding her secret close—for now. Because it suits her. You've probably gone and made some stupid bargain with her, like that fisherman, or all the rest of them, and think she's going to keep her promises out of some sense of decency. But she's a *pirate*, Skerth. You ought to remember that, and be careful who you trust."

"Boy!" Xor bellowed, startling them both.

"You'd better go," Emme said, turning her back to him. "He's ripe for a cuffing."

Skerth stared at her back for a moment, then grabbed the tray and hurried away, his head reeling from all he'd just learned.

Emme's words frightened him more than he first realized, and nearly two days later, long after the common room fell silent, he lay wide awake in bed fretting about Kiri's fate. His mind had spun all sorts of possibilities, none favorable. Had she succumbed to fever, or had they already sold her to the skin traders? What would they do with her after they moved him? His need to see her bordered on obsession; his thoughts of escape sidetracked into plans to coerce or force his way into her room, just to get a look and make certain, with his own eyes, that she still lived.

But at every turn, the pirates' close attention frustrated these, along with any other plans, before he could set them in motion. If they intended to move him they had not done so, nor did Skerth see any sign of them transferring him to the Merchant Guild in the near future, despite the fact that Auberdale Eve loomed ever nearer. Instead, they kept him close at hand during the day and locked tight in his cabin at night. He served Xor, aided Emme in the kitchens, swabbed the floors and polished the table, stoked the fires and carried water from the cisterns. In truth he worked so hard during the day that it was all he could do to stay awake until Xor finally released him to fall senseless into bed at night.

But on this night, sleep would not come. In the distance, the roll and crash of the waves beat like the steady hearbeat of the sea. The rocking ship creaked and groaned, feet scuffled abovedeck, the crew called out to one another and sang sea shanties as they tended the masts and rigging. The heat in Skerth's cabin was wet and stifling; he longed for fresh air and moonlight, for the rooftops where he could lie flat on a hot summer night such as this and catch the cool sea breeze against his warm skin. He and Kiri could make for the beach and soak in the warm waters of the Quistand until their skin withered, then climb up onto the sand and study the stars until sleep took them or someone chased them off.

Eyes closed, he could picture her smile, a glint of mischief in her eyes, the shock of moonlight in her short-cropped hair. She threw back her head and laughed, the sound like music, and he leaned in close—

The slow scrape of the lock, no louder than the scratch of a rat, jolted him upright. A tiny click. Skerth instinctively reached for his missing dagger, swore softly at his vulnerability. The door handle turned, slow and steady. Quietly he rose and, matching his visitor's stealth, crept to the door. He pressed himself flat against the wall and tensed to spring.

The door inched open, concealing Skerth behind. Heart pounding, Skerth waited until his visitor stepped clear of the door and into view, waited for him to notice the empty bed. The shadow eased into view; Skerth pounced. He threw one arm around his attacker's shoulders and reached with the other to muffle the figure's screams, but something felt—wrong. His attacker was slight, soft. His hands brushed against something distinctly feminine. His captive bit his hand—hard.

He muffled a cry and let go. She staggered back until she ran up against the bed and half-fell, half-sat onto the edge. Thick dark curls tumbled over thin shoulders, wide eyes framed by a pale face. Even with only a slash of hazy moonlight to aid him, Skerth recognized her immediately.

"Emme?" he whispered, shaking his wounded hand.

She hastened to close the door before turning back to Skerth. "Sorry I bit you."

"It's all right. I didn't know. I thought. . . ." he fell silent, painfully aware that despite his tendency to think of her as an ally of sorts, separate from the others, she was still Gem's daughter. A pirate. One of *them*.

She shook her head. "You were right to be cautious." She glanced nervously at the door and shifted closer. "I haven't much time. They plan to move you tomorrow. I thought you'd like to see her before you go."

"Tomorrow?" the word caught in his throat. "When?"

"Late morning, when the tide is at its lowest, baring a clean path almost all the way around the cliffs. Folk here will be scrambling to get the ships loaded before the tide returns, so Xor and Janewyn stand a decent chance of passing you through the cove and into the Lower City unnoticed."

"What will they do with her?"

Emme looked sympathetic. "I don't know. I'm sorry. But I can take you to her now, to say your farewells."

Hot tears of frustration pricked behind Skerth's eyes. He willed them away. "Let's go."

He followed her out the door into the common room, stepping where she stepped to avoid creaking planks. Twice he considered bolting upstairs; only his memory of the fisherman and the thought of the pirates similarly punishing Kiri for his flight stopped him. He forced himself not to think of anything but her, to stay focused on Emme's feet, and the planks beneath him, and on maintaining the silence.

The key in the lock sounded abnormally loud; Skerth cringed, but when nobody came rushing in to stop them, he relaxed. Emme peeked inside, then motioned for him to follow. In another moment, he was at Kiri's side.

Her window angled to catch the moonlight, which offered enough light for him to see her face and the gentle rise and fall of her chest. She wore a clean shirt and someone had washed her face and hair. Thick lashes lay against pale cheeks; soft pink lips parted slightly with every breath. She looked frail, delicate, so when she snored he grinned with giddy relief. She wasn't a frail, perfect doll he didn't recognize; she was still Kiri.

"How is she?" he whispered.

"Well, for the most part. Her wound still needs attention, but she will heal."

He laid a hand against her cheek. She was hot as summer sand. He drew back his hand as though burned. "Her fever still rages."

"Effective, don't you think?"

He studied Emme, uncomprehending.

"Gem doses her daily with an herb that heats her skin and brings on the sweats."

"Why?"

Emme shrugged. "Stalling Xor's sale, keeping her quiet and still for the healing—who knows? Gem keeps her own counsel."

He turned back to Kiri. "So she doesn't suffer a fever?"

"No. The wound still pains her, but the herb helps with that, too. She takes food and water and has asked for you, but I can tell her nothing."

A hot flash of anger momentarily blinded Skerth. "So she is kept alone and afraid, believing I abandoned her?" He moved to shake her. "Kiri," he whispered urgently, "Wake up--"

With more strength than he thought she possessed, Emme grabbed his arm and pulled him back. "No!" she hissed. "Don't!"

He shook her off. "I need to talk to her."

"It's not safe! Gem will return any moment—"

The creak of footsteps on the stairs down the corridor silenced them both. They froze, scarcely daring to breathe. Emme still held Skerth's arm tight, her eyes widening in fear.

"Go!" she said at last. "Back to your room!"

Skerth debated for a heartbeat. He could wake Kiri. Together they could overpower Emme, take the newcomer by surprise. He knew they could make it abovedeck before anyone stopped them. But where to then? The thought stopped him cold.

"Hurry!" She tugged his arm toward the door.

Disappointment crushing his chest, he let her drag him away. After one last glance at Kiri through the closing door, he headed for his room. Emme hastened to the door, then ducked after him. She had scarcely turned the key in the lock of his door from the inside when the door to the common room squeaked opened, admitting not one, but two sets of footsteps. They crouched behind the door, willing themselves silent.

". . .heard noises," said Xor. His heavy bootsteps halted outside Kiri's door. He tested the knob, jiggled the lock.

"Best be cautious," Gem replied. "It wouldn't do for our young prince to go missing just days before his debut."

Skerth froze. *Our* prince? He glanced at Emme, but her attention remained focused on the door. She crouched tense and alert, poised to spring.

Xor's footsteps approached at an agonizing pace. One step . . . two . . . three, and he paused outside Skerth's door. A scrape of the lock, a jiggling of the handle. Skerth held his breath, preparing for Xor to open the door and find him crouched on the floor with Gem's daughter.

Instead, he pulled the key from the lock. His footsteps retreated. "Shut tight as I left him."

"Good. Then leave him again. I'm off to Miri's. There's gossip in the clan that another boy's been found dead in the Lower City. . ."

The common room door cut off the rest of Gem's words. Skerth and Emme remained as they were until they heard Xor and Gem's bootsteps make their way abovedeck. Only then did they breathe a sigh of relief.

"I shouldn't have come," Emme said, rising. "I took a great risk bringing you to her." Her hands shook as she fit the key into the lock.

Skerth reached out and stopped her. She looked up, a question in her eyes. "I'm glad you did. Even if I couldn't talk to her, it meant everything to see her, to know she's going to be all right. Thank you."

Emme lowered her eyes and nodded. "You care for her."

His throat tightened. "I do." Afraid of what that meant, he added, "She's my only friend."

She nodded again. "Then I'm glad I helped you."

He dropped his hand. With surer hands, she twisted the key and let herself out. "Peaceful dreams," she whispered as the door closed behind her.

"And you," he replied, his mind suddenly full of new possibilities and complications.

He lay awake for the rest of that long night, his mind consumed by thoughts of dead street boys, assassins and Caretakers, pirates and merchants and false kings. But amidst all of these worries, one important question surfaced to repeat over and again in a sickening refrain: once the pirates sealed his fate, what would become of Kiri?

Chapter Eighteen: The Pirate Lords

Gem stormed downstairs in the early morning, interrupting Xor's breakfast with Gryff, who took great pleasure in trotting Skerth back and forth to the kitchen on the most mundane of errands.

"Trouble," she said in greeting. "Somehow the lords have heard whisper of our plan."

Skerth tried not to stare at her transformation. She had traded her demure dress for boiled black leather breeches and a striking scarlet tunic embroidered in gold over a wide-sleeved silk shirt. Jeweled rings adorned every finger. In addition to the curved sword slung at her side, Skerth counted the outlines of at least three hidden blades strapped to her wrists and beneath her tunic. She wore her dark hair loose and she'd lined her bright green eyes with kohl, making them all the more intriguing.

"How?" Xor's voice went as cold and sharp as a blade.

Gem shook her head. "I heard some of the scuts at Miri's muttering over their ale last night and made them talk. All I got out of them was that the lords are unsettled we've worked a deal without their say, though I didn't hear clear if their masters know aught of the actual plan."

"Mutiny?"

"I don't think so. Not yet. But we've got mending to do." She started to say more, then paused, her eyes glancing meaningfully to Skerth.

Xor looked at Skerth as though he'd just remembered his presence there. "This is none of your affair, boy. To your room."

Gem caught Skerth's arm as he moved to comply. "No time, Xor. We're having guests tonight." To Skerth she said, "Into the galley with you. Emme needs your help." Skerth nodded and turned to go, but she held him fast. She caught his eye, her gaze shrewd. "Mind you don't take advantage of our inattention, else your friend might wear out *his* welcome."

More to hide the surge of anger that seethed beneath his skin than out of respect, Skerth bowed. "Yes, my lady."

She barked a laugh. "My lady. At least someone here recognizes the right order of things."

Xor thumped him hard on the back of the head. "You heard her, boy. You've work to do. Move."

Skerth ducked to avoid Xor's cuffing and, to the music of their laughter, raced for the safety of the galley.

Emme looked even more harried than usual, and the galley was a disaster, littered with all sorts of dishes in various stages of preparation. Vegetable peelings, animal blood, and bone littered every available surface and lay half-crushed into a sickening compost on the floor.

"I'm to help you—"

"Bring water, if you will," she said without stopping to give him so much as a glance.

Skerth set to work hauling water from the hold. The temptation to drop his buckets and jump ship was almost too difficult to resist, but concern for Kiri stopped him. He dipped his buckets into the cisterns with a savage splash and resolved to make the best of his lot until he could do something about it.

He returned to find Emme sagged against the wall, red-faced and sweating from exertion and the heat of the galley. She managed a thin smile as she wiped a greasy handkerchief across her brow.

"Why all the fuss?" he asked, setting down the buckets. "Who are these 'lords?'"

"Gem's captains and trusted men."

Skerth looked up, startled. "Gem's?"

"Aye." She looked puzzled. "Didn't you know?"

Skerth reddened and renewed his interest in the fire. "Know what?"

"Gem's in charge here, not Xor. She's mistress of the Eastern Seas from here all the way up the coast to Maghinis and across to Terrenweld. She'll have command of every splash of water in Sildehna by the end of her days, if she has her way."

Suddenly all of the scraps of conversation he'd gathered during his time on *The Scarlet* made sense. *She'll not be pleased*, Xor had told Fae. *Our plan*, Gem had said. *Our prince*. He tried to take this all in, wincing as he recalled how much he'd told Gem that first day, how fool he'd been to trust her, never guessing that she, not Xor, was the one he should have feared. "Then who's Xor?"

"Her right hand. Mostly he works as her negotiator, though he'll do murder if she asks it. She does the thinking and he keeps her safe and manages the trades—in her name, of course. That's why she's in a snit today. It's not Xor they blame for dealing behind their backs."

"How'd they find out?"

She shrugged a shoulder. "I was with you, remember?" She stowed her handkerchief in a pocket of her dress and returned to her task. "Looks like you're staying put for now. This new mess with the lords has bought you another day. But we'd best get on with our work or we'll bear the mark of Xor's temper for days to come."

Emme kept him busy until early evening, when Gem banged open the galley door. "Boy!" He looked up just in time to catch the bundle of clothing she tossed his way. "Wash, then put these on. You'll serve tonight." She looked Emme over slowly, her disapproval clear. "You look more like mountain filth than any lass of mine. Scrub up and change."

Emme curtsied. "Yes, my lady." Her cheeks aflame, she cast a sidelong glance at Skerth before scurrying past her mother.

Gem raised an eyebrow at Skerth. "You're still here?"

Startled into motion, he half-bowed and ducked out.

After the sticky heat of the day and the sweltering galley, Skerth didn't mind the cool water drawn from the hold. He scrubbed as best he could without soap or cloth, then traded his rags for the sturdy black breeches, crisp white shirt and scarlet tunic Gem had given him. They weren't new, but they fit decent and were far nicer than anything he'd ever worn.

By the time he finished, the sun had disappeared behind the cliffs and shadowed the cove in an early night. Already Skerth could hear new voices mingling with those that had become all too familiar of late. The gathering of Gem's pirate lords had begun. With a heart thumping half from excitement and half from dread, Skerth took a deep breath and left his room.

Lantern light flickered off of scarred faces and boiled leather. Twelve in all crowded around the table that night, together forming one of the most impressive gatherings of notorious men and corrupted nobles Skerth had ever witnessed. He knew a few of their faces—and all of their reputations. Five of the nine guests joining Gem, Xor and Janewyn for dinner were infamous pirates wanted for everything from petty theft to murder, though their long list of crimes didn't stop them from keeping a tight hold on their interests in the Lower City and on the seas.

Skerth recognized Dark Pieroth's greasy black hair, pitted teeth and signature scowl right off, having nearly lost a hand picking the pockets of his crew in the Pleasure District two summers earlier. He entered the common room alongside Captain Briand of Sahtamor, an old sea-dog whose salt-and-pepper hair belied a sharp eye and a quick, merciless way with a sword, and Kamor of Terrenweld, a strong, bare-chested black man who nodded to Xor as they entered. Skerth didn't know more than the names and reputations of Dak Sieger and Mistress Blay, but that was enough to encourage him to give the deceptively amiable looking man and absurdly tall, muscular redhead a wide berth.

The other four guests were city natives, two of them merchants of the highest class: Lady Ridah Viorre traded in fine wines and, rumor had it, skin; Lord Holwyn was a fat, balding noble from one of the oldest families in Erados, known for his exotic textiles and rare opiates. The other two guests made Skerth's skin crawl. Notorious throughout the Lower City for their brothels and ale-houses, Fa and Ma Algar owned more property—and people— than any other landlord in the city. Skerth had heard countless stories of families turned out of their homes by the Algars, only to buy their way back into the couple's good graces by selling off a child or two. He'd known more than a few who'd managed to escape that fate, too, and each time he heard a new story he thanked the luck that had kept him out of the hands of the skin traders.

Despite Skerth's best attempts to eavesdrop, Gem and her guests kept him too busy fetching ale or carrying and clearing dishes to pay close attention to their talk. What little he gleaned either didn't make sense to him, having mostly to do with the raiding of trade routes and general complaints about unseaworthy weather or the cheapening of textiles in the day's market, or didn't offer any information relevant to either his predicament or the Caretakers' careful eradication of all claimants to the throne. He had almost given up trying to follow the talk when Dak Sieger shoved his dishes aside, leaned back in his chair and said, "All of this is very well, Gem, but you know as well as I why we're all gathered here."

The table fell silent. All turned a nervous eye to the man who had spoken. Dak Sieger was tall and lanky even seated. He had strangely rosy cheeks, curling dark hair that brushed his shoulders, and a thick white scar that crossed his face from cheekbone to chin. He gave no outward acknowledgment of the increased tension in the room as he tapped a forefinger on the handle of his dagger.

"Of course, Sieger." Gem flashed a winsome smile that briefly reminded Skerth of Emme. She motioned for her daughter and Skerth to clear the table before rising. "I've a plan in the works that will secure our grip on the Eastern seas and expand our reach all along the Southern Coast. I'd like to bring the lot of you in, if you're willing."

Murmurs and whispered exchanges broke the quiet as Gem's crew shared their surprise or affirmations of her trustworthiness with their neighbors. She waited them out, hands firm against the table, until they quieted. Then she briefly outlined the plan: they would find a boy, educate him with the best details they could learn about the old royal family's history, and put him forth as the lost heir of Erados. She had a storyteller's voice, steady and sure, and in no time had the rapt attention of all as she spelled out the risks and profits of such a venture. She was persuasive, too. By the time she finished, even Skerth had to admit the plan had merit.

Sieger spoke first. "An excellent plan. Profitable, too. Even moreso when there are fewer chickens for the pecking." His casual manner had not changed, though he had shifted to flipping his dagger in lazy circles. When his eyes met Gem's, however, none could mistake the challenge in them.

Gem stiffened. "As with any venture, Sieger. But while only a few need directly risk the gallows-tree for this, we all stand to benefit."

"How?" growled Mistress Blay, leaning forward in her chair. "I'm at sea three parts of the year. What good's a pawn to me and my crew if I'm not here to play the pieces?"

"What good will it bring any of us who ain't got nothin' to do with the city?" Dark Pieroth added, scowling. "Leave the politickin' to them what know how to do it, I say. So long as the Caretakers're willin' to keep their cut and leave us to our own business, no reason to get involved in squabbles over what happens on land."

"Careful, Pieroth," murmured Lady Ridah. Her voice was as dark and rich as the wine she traded, her expression unreadable as she studied him through heavy-lidded eyes. "What happens on land is as much your business as it is ours. The Caretakers choose to overlook the less . . . *acceptable* business transacted within the boundaries of the city because the bribes they collect from the merchants—from *our* coffers, not yours—keep them in power."

Pieroth slammed his tankard onto the table. "Aye, and you make us pay, right well enough! Goods I sell you bring nearly double if I take 'em up the coast a bit."

"Isn't that Gem's point?" Janewyn said, his eyes shifting nervously from Pieroth's reddening face to Ridah's cool gaze. "If we take control of the city, we won't need the merchant bribes or the tolls we charge you to pay them."

The merchants and nobles tensed. Realizing his misstep, Janewyn paled.

"Well, that's interesting," said Sieger. He leaned back in his chair and laced his fingers over his chest. "You merchants bribe the Caretakers and pass the cost on to us, maybe even shave off a little for yourselves, and we're never the wiser."

"That's not how all of us trade." Fa Algar shot an accusing glance at Janewyn, who slid a little lower in his seat. "We skim the bribes off the customers, water a little ale, do what needs fixin' ourselves when the buildings rot. We know better than to double-deal on the goods what come from pirate trade."

"But the royal merchants don't know better." Kamor's quiet baritone cut through Algar's protests to silence the room. His hand slid to rest on the hilt of his sword. "Perhaps it's time to teach them what folk in the Lower City have already learned."

Skerth eased toward the wall as pirates, nobles, landlords and merchants all lunged for weapons. Across the room, Emme caught his eye, then glanced meaningfully toward the galley door.

"We're not here to discuss bribe taxes," Lord Holwyn said over the growing din of threats and drawn steel, "we're here to discover why Gem would involve herself in a brazen bid for the throne without cutting us all in."

The room quieted. Skerth and Emme froze. Captain Briand, looking more bored than irate, motioned Emme close, then handed her his empty tankard. "More ale, love." He glanced over the table, then added, "all around, I think. It's going to be a long night."

Emme caught at Skerth's arm on her way past and half-dragged him into the galley.

"What did you do that for?" He shrugged out of her grip and pushed the door open a crack to watch, but Emme hauled him back.

"Are you dull-witted?" she whispered. "Things are going to get rough in there. We'd best be ready."

"Rough?"

She thrust a full pitcher of ale into his hands. "Janewyn just blurted the merchant guild's best-kept secret. Once those fools do their adding, they'll realize how much the merchants have skimmed off of their profits and things will go hard for Gem."

"Did she know about the taxes?"

Emme rolled her eyes. "Course she knew. She got her share to stay quiet and keep the captains from asking too many questions. Problem is, it's out now."

"And the captains are already unhappy that she's kept her plans for the heir a secret."

Emme nodded.

The sound of raised voices, steel on steel reached them. Skerth ran to the door and peeked out. All five of the pirate captains and Xor were on their feet, swords drawn against the merchants and Gem. As he watched, Lady Ridah, Lord Holwyn and Fa Algar kicked back their chairs and drew, though he couldn't quite tell whose side Fa Algar had taken. With a malicious grin, plump Ma Algar drew a dagger from her bosom and rushed Xor while Janewyn backed quietly toward the shadows.

As the fray began in earnest Skerth glanced to Kiri's door, measuring the distance between her room, the fight, and the stairs.

"Do you have the key?"

Emme frowned. "What?"

"The key. To Kiri's door."

He watched her face as comprehension slowly dawned. She immediately set down the tankard and wiped her hands on the front of her dress. "Of course. But you can't—they'd kill you—"

"Now," he said firmly. "Where's that key?"

She fell to her knees and started emptying the cupboards nearest the door. Skerth cracked the door. The fight had turned into a brawl. Combatants had broken into dueling pairs—pirate against merchant, merchant against landlord, noble against pirate, pirate against pirate—Skerth wondered if any of them even knew whom they were fighting or why anymore. Pieroth confirmed this point when he grabbed a chair and, bellowing obscenities, brought it crashing over Sieger's head. "Ha!" he shouted when Sieger crumpled. Pieroth turned just in time to parry Ma Algar's attack from the side.

Emme returned to his side cloaked and hooded, a cloth bag slung over her shoulder. She held out the key. He reached for it, but at the last second, she tugged it out of reach.

"What are you doing?"

"I'm coming with you."

"You can't."

She tensed. "What do you mean?"

"I mean, you can't. Where will you go? It's not safe—"

"—for a girl?" she finished, her bitterness shocking him into silence. "It's not safe here, either. At least out there I could run. Hide. I wouldn't have to feel their filthy hands on me as I wait their table and bring their ale. And *she* wouldn't—" Emme broke off and took a deep breath. "Besides, your friend's a girl—"

"That's different."

Her expression darkened. "Is it?"

"Well—" He broke off, suddenly unsure. Was Emme all that different from Kiri, or any other number of girls who'd survived the streets?

A chair smashed into the galley door and splintered into pieces.

She took a step closer. "I can get you out. But you've got to take me. I hate this place—all of them—but more than that, when they see you and your friend have gone missing, they'll guess I had something to do with it."

Skerth's mind raced. He recalled Emme's admonition: *be careful who you trust*. He had been wrong to trust Gem. But could he trust Emme? Did he have a choice?

"All right," he said at last. "Come with me. I promise I'll do what I can to see that you last more than a day."

152

Her smile illuminated her face. In that moment, he knew he'd made the right decision. This time, she let him take the key.

"Go," he whispered. "I'll get Kiri and meet you on deck."

"Make way to the port side of the ship. I'll show you the way from there."

Skerth watched her slide through the room like a spectre; the combatants paid her no heed. He crouched at the crack in the door until long after she had gone, sweat beading on his brow. When his opportunity came he dashed out the door into the fray. Deftly he maneuvered through the brawl, only once catching a blow to the back before he made it to Kiri's door. Without pausing to look back he slid the key into the lock and burst inside.

Kiri bolted upright. "What—"

"Come on." He grabbed her arms and hauled her to her feet.

She didn't ask any more questions. He shoved her behind him and looked out. Briand and Lady Ridah were nearest the stairs, exchanging repartee as lightning fast as their swords. While Skerth briefly debated whether or not he and Kiri should just risk running past, Briand swiftly disarmed his opponent and, in one fluid motion, swept her into his arms and kissed her.

"Pirates," Skerth muttered. Seizing Kiri's hand, they sprinted for the stairs.

Chapter Nineteen: Escape

They had scarcely hit the deck when the distinct sound of a scuffle and a muffled scream stopped them short.

"Emme," Skerth breathed, and dashed to the ship's rail. Down below, two figures balanced on the bobbing platform, engaged in a struggle. The larger of the two held up his hands to shield his face against Emme's dagger slash; the blade found a mark and the man roared. With a broad slap, he knocked the weapon from her hands. Her dagger clattered across the platform to land on the edge, only inches from the sea. She shrieked and turned to run, but he seized her from behind and pinned her arms.

Skerth leapt over the side onto the platform below. As he struggled to maintain his balance, he barely registered Kiri making her way down the rope ladder behind him.

Emme struggled toward him.

The man's head snapped up in surprise.

Skerth stopped short. "Janewyn."

The merchant set a dagger to her throat. Emme ceased struggling and slackened in his grip.

"Don't!" Skerth called out. "Let her go."

"I don't take orders from Lower City scats."

"What do you want with her? She's nothing to you."

Janewyn laughed. "She's everything, boy. After that little bungle inside, she's my salvation. For as long as I've got Gem's lovely girl in my care, I live to see another dawn."

"But your quarrel's not with Gem," Emme panted. "It's the merchants you've angered tonight, and they don't even know who I am."

"No matter. I'm sure you'll fetch a fine price from one set of poxy scoundrels or the other. I'm taking you for my surety, either way." He looked up at Skerth. "I suggest you disappear before they settle up inside and start looking for their heir."

Skerth glanced back at the ship. Even this far from the common room he could still hear the fracas inside. The absence of

154

crew on deck told him that either Gem had reinforcements or someone had bribed her crew to look the other way. *Good*, he thought. They had some time.

He remembered Emme's dagger, still lying where she had dropped it. Skerth edged toward the weapon, his gaze fixed on the merchant. Kiri shifted to his other side, dividing Janewyn's attention in a familiar pattern they had used well over the years.

"She won't ransom me, if that's what you're thinking. Gem doesn't pay." Emme punctuated her words with a backwards kick to Janewyn's shin.

"Curse you and be still, stupid chit, or I'll bargain you to the skin traders." Janewyn shifted the blade closer to Emme's skin. "Hold off," he told Skerth and Kiri. "That's close enough."

Skerth brushed his toe against the blade of Emme's dagger, then glanced to Kiri.

"May as well let her go," Kiri said. "Whether you get yours from the pirates or your own kind, you're gutted either way. No one trusts a shifty coward like you once you've lost their back in a fight."

She had moved just out of Janewyn's field of vision so he could no longer keep an eye on both her and Skerth at the same time; a more experienced fighter would have seen through such a ploy, but the merchant was too soft and sheltered to know better. "Who are you?" he growled.

The heartbeat's inattention was enough. Skerth rushed Janewyn, scooping up the dagger and leveling it at the soft flesh of his waist.

Janewyn shifted Emme to shield himself. Skerth diverted his blow and darted aside, wheeling his arms to stay balanced on the rocking platform. Kiri fell in behind and kicked the merchant hard in the back. He loosened his hold on Emme just enough; she bit down on the hand holding the dagger to her throat. Skerth slashed at Janewyn's other arm, ripping through his sleeve to draw a thin line of blood. The merchant cried out his rage. Kiri brought her foot up between Janewyn's legs—hard. He buckled; Emme broke free.

"Bastard," Emme said, giving him a solid kick in the stomach for good measure. He tumbled into the sea with a heavy splash. She gathered her pack and adjusted her cloak. Kiri scooped Janewyn's dagger off of the platform, flipped it once, and wedged it into her belt. She and Skerth caught up with Emme, who had already started away on the floating catwalks; Janewyn, who clung spluttering to the edge of the platform, wisely let them be.

"How do we get back to the Lower City?" Skerth asked, falling into step beside Emme.

She chewed her lip thoughtfully. "We have to cross the bay. The tide's still a bit high, but it's our only chance--"

A loud crash and the sound of breaking glass came from Gem's ship. Up ahead, the whisper of drawn steel. Before the three could react, figures separated from the shadows and ran toward them from every direction.

"What now?" Kiri hissed.

"I don't know." Emme's voice trembled.

"I don't think they'll mind us," Skerth said. "Just keep walking. Try to look like we're supposed to be out on Gem's bidding."

Emme nodded while Kiri took the lead. True enough, the pirates ran past, swords high, more intent on joining the fray than on the three youth clinging to the bridge ropes. In the end, the biggest challenge they faced was holding on.

Emme led them across the web of bridges until they terminated at a stilted house near the cliffs.

"What next, Emme?" asked Skerth, eyeing the jagged mound of rocks that edged this side of the cove.

"Swim?" Kiri asked nervously.

"We should be able to stand, though the current's strong." She glanced over her shoulder, then quickened her step. "We'll do what we must. Just hurry."

Emme slid off the bridge into the waist-high water, careful to hold her sack high. Kiri and Skerth followed, more nervous about the water than either of them would like to admit. They made decent time despite the heavy drag of water and a swift current, and soon scrabbled out of the sea and onto a series of jagged black boulders. Skerth was glad for the boots, but Kiri had a harder time navigating the terrain in her bare feet, and Emme's dress kept snagging on the rocks. Despite the cover of night, Skerth felt exposed moving out in the open, and at such a crawl; however, once they crowned the line of boulders, it was only a few more feet to the beach on the other side. No sooner did their feet sink into the sand than they broke into a run.

They followed Emme all the way to the water's edge. For what seemed a long time she studied the thin finger of water that separated them from a strip of sandy beach on the other side. Skerth propped his shoulder against the cliff wall and waited, listening to the suck and swell of the ocean and fighting his fear that the pirates would catch up to them at any moment.

"What now?" Kiri asked Skerth, crossing her arms over her chest.

Emme answered. "If we stay close to the cliffs, we should be able to find our footing well enough to cross."

"Should?" Kiri echoed.

"Would you rather wait until tomorrow?" Emme snapped. "The tides will be lower, for certain, but you still won't be able to see where you're stepping—even if we aren't shut up tight in the ship by then."

"I don't like her," Kiri told Skerth under her breath. "Why is she leading?"

"Because she knows how to get us back home." He nudged Kiri toward the water. "Just go." She resisted. He tugged at her arm; she pulled away.

"What—"

"I can't swim!" she shouted.

Skerth stood stunned. "What about all those times we've dipped in the ocean?"

"In the shallows, you mean? Hardly the same, is it?" Her eyes flicked from Skerth to Emme.

For once, Skerth was at a loss. Now that he looked back, she never had gone beyond the calms, and had to be coaxed even then, often using her secret as an excuse to linger on the sand while he stripped off his shirt and dove in with the others.

"You can't swim," he repeated, still only half-believing the words.

Emme stepped forward and gently took her arm. "Then we'll walk."

"What if I fall?"

Following Emme's lead, Skerth grabbed Kiri's other hand and gave it a reassuring squeeze. "We won't let you."

Emme edged into the water until she was waist-deep, keeping her right hand on the cliff wall and feeling carefully with her foot before every step. Kiri came next, holding onto both of them like lifelines in a storm, trembling so violently that Skerth worried she would pull them all down. He could hardly believe that this terrified girl was the same one who scurried across rooftops and baited Malyn and his gang without a thought to the consequences. The idea frightened him a little; but he remembered how the fire had nearly unhinged him, kindling fears and conjuring images so old he could not remember why they terrified him. Everyone—even Kiri—feared something.

The crossing was difficult. The current was strong, but not strong enough to tow them off the sandbar and out to sea. At its deepest point the water only reached to his waist, though the girls sank a little deeper and had more trouble pushing through. Kiri relaxed a little when she did not immediately flush out to sea or drown. She eased her grip on Emme's hand and eventually let go of Skerth's too, though she clung close to the cliff wall. The sandbar gradually firmed to rocky ground. After what seemed an interminable passage of time, the three staggered out of the waves onto the shore where they collapsed, shivering with cold and legs trembling, onto the beach.

Somewhere beyond the nest of sheer rock that faced the sea lay the city. They kept moving through the night, keeping the ocean to their left and the pirate cove firmly at their backs. Now that Emme's familiarity with the terrain was no better or worse than theirs, she and Kiri fell a little behind, leaving Skerth to find the way. Although he searched for hand and foot holds in the rock or—thinking always of the tunnels—a way *through*, he had no luck. So he kept them to the beach, cursing the barren landscape that exposed them to any eye that knew where to look.

The moon had nearly set by the time they rounded an outcropping of rock and stopped in their tracks. Before them, the barrier of black rock gave way to a wide swath of beach pebbled with smooth round stones and black shale. Not too far in the distance, the darker silhouettes of rickety fishing boats and supply ships rocked gently with each new swell of the sea. Settled beneath the cliffs that bounded the city from the beach, the Lower City spread from the Wedge to the edge of the horizon in an unsteady tumble of houses, fishermen's shanties, market awnings and warehouses set at all different heights and angles, all faintly aglow with the warm glow of street lamps, torches, and tallow candles. When Skerth squinted closer at the cliffs, he could almost make out a path leading from their beach to the city.

The three exhausted fugitives tapped energy reserves they didn't know they had and broke into a run, until they reached a narrow path hewn from the surrounding stone that wound all the way from the beach to the outer reaches of the city. A little farther on they found an unlocked storehouse where they bedded down at last in soft heaps of fishing nets and old sails. While he had no complaints about the proper bed back on *The Scarlet*, Skerth slept better that night with a lump of hemp at his back and the stink of fish in his nose than he had slept in weeks.

Chapter Twenty: The Return to Danger

"What's this!" The irate fisherman's roar startled everyone awake. "Get, you filthy gutter scats, 'fore I truss you up an' feed you to the sea nattles!"

Skerth and Kiri, bolstered by a lifetime of practice, were halfway out the low window at the back of the storehouse before their unwilling landlord had finished his first word. Emme remained behind, frozen, as the fisherman stalked toward her. While a string of threats, curses, and general insults rang loud in the storehouse, Skerth leapt back to Emme's side, hauled her to her feet, and practically shoved her out the window before following her through.

"I left my bag!" she cried, fighting his hold to get back to the window. "It has everything—"

"You can't go back, Emme. It's gone. Come on—" He pulled her away, but she shook him off.

"No! I'm not leaving without it!"

Emme was working herself into a panic trying to get back inside.

"Is it worth dying for?" he asked.

The question made her pause. She stopped struggling and met his eye.

"Because he'll beat us for crossing onto his property if we go back. And if he doesn't, someone else will kill you trying to take whatever's in that bag once they find out what you risked to save it."

The fisherman's shouts retreated to a dull, blustery roar. The words "poxy" "coin-scutting" and "scum-crusted" drifted out the window.

He let go of her arm. "Come on, Emme. Let's get out of here."

She allowed him to lead her away, reluctantly at first, then with more confidence. The farther they got from the bag, the fisherman, and the filthy insults, the less she hesitated. Soon they were well away from the fisherman's village and nearing the city proper.

When they crossed into the outskirts of the Lower City, they instantly recognized that something had changed. It was mid-day and people bustled through the streets as usual. Fishermen mended their nets, women minded their market baskets, and men of all trades, ages, and purposes darted through the crowds, wary of thieves. But something felt amiss. Quieter. People glanced over their shoulders and kept a tighter grip on both their children and their purses. When Skerth finally caught their wisps of conversation, he understood.

Everyone whispered of murdered boys.

This worried Skerth. People—especially children—died all the time just the way they had lived: unknown, unwanted, forgotten. The only people who usually noted the passing of kids like Rot and Fael were other street kids, and only then because their deaths served as a caution. Townspeople and merchants never mourned the street dead. "One less thief to mind," they'd say, or "that's what a gutter scut deserves." They turned their backs without a moment's sympathy.

But now they whispered of dead boys with slashed throats and bruised bodies, broken limbs and stabbed hearts. So many deaths now that the townspeople had taken to locking their doors and shuttering the windows lest the murderers steal their own beloved children right out of their beds.

Who else had fallen to the Caretakers' knife? Did anyone suspect Malyn's treachery?

Skerth's anger seethed, fueled his hate, quickened his step. *Malyn* did this. *Malyn* allowed the assassin free passage through the tunnels under his warehouse. *There is an order to it, of sorts,* he had said. Did he choose the victims, too? How did he determine who would live and who would die? And for what? Surely the Caretakers had promised him something—was he betraying his kind, enemies and friends alike, for mere coin? Or had they offered something more? Whatever Malyn's reward, Skerth intended to ensure he didn't live long enough to enjoy it.

"Skerth?" Emme ran to keep up. "Where are you taking us? And at such a pace?"

He stopped and studied her. Her face was red and sweat trickled down her brow. Flakes of hemp and dried sea-salt flecked her tangled dark hair and crumpled dress. The sight of her calmed him, forced him to think. He couldn't face Malyn with Emme in tow.

And Kiri was in much poorer shape than she would admit. While Emme swore Kiri's fever had been induced by herbs and not infection, Kiri's face was nearly grey and her skin glistened with a sheen that had nothing to do with the sticky heat of the day. Fresh blood stained her shirt. She wouldn't last much longer without rest and a decent healer.

He started in a different direction. Kiri fell into step beside him while Emme dragged behind.

"Where are we going?" asked Kiri.

To the only place where you and Emme will be safe.

"To Feirwyn."

At first sight of the three tattered street kids, Nirue ushered them inside and hastened to lock the door.

"Thank the goddess you are alive." Her eyes widened a little when she spied Kiri, clutching her wound, and Emme beside her. "Who—"

"Kiri," she blurted, warning Nirue off with a look.

Nirue studied her thoughtfully, then inclined her head. "Kiri."

"I'm Emme, my lady," she said with a pretty curtsy.

"A pleasure to meet you both. I am Nirue."

Skerth shifted anxiously. "Where's Feirwyn?"

"Out. But he will want to see you. I will call for some food and drink—"

"No," he interrupted. "At least, not for me. I need to find . . . an old friend." He ignored Kiri's curious stare and continued in a rush, "But if Kiri and Emme could stay, I'd be grateful. Kiri's too hurt to go on—though she'd never admit—"

He broke off at Kiri's sharp hiss of breath. It took him a moment to realize his mistake; by then it was too late. Kiri glared, fists clenched at her side, while Nirue studied her with renewed interest.

"Kiri, I'm sorry. I didn't mean— I've never before slipped—" He reddened.

"Are you certain?" Kiri snapped. "Chances are if you're forgetting your tongue now you've lost it before."

"Yes! I mean—yes, I'm certain! I've never—I *would* never—at least, not on purpose. . . ." he faltered to a stop. "I'm sorry," he whispered.

"It doesn't matter now," she muttered, scowling.

"We do not have time for arguments," Nirue chided gently. She turned to Skerth. "Your friends are safe here, I give you my word. But tell me, where are you going?"

Skerth looked to Kiri. "The Deadrun."

"Not by yourself, you're not," she argued, shaking her head. I'm coming with you."

"No."

She crossed her arms over her chest. "Yes. It's too dangerous."

"Dangerous?" Nirue frowned. "Perhaps you should wait for Feirwyn—"

Skerth backed toward the door. "You know I have to find out if he betrayed us," he told Kiri, as though he hadn't heard Nirue. "And you're wounded—"

"You're not going alone! Especially after what happened at the warehouse! Have you forgotten the assassin?"

"What happened?" asked Nirue sharply, glancing from Skerth to Kiri. "Tell me!"

Skerth sighed. Reluctantly he told Nirue of Grey's betrayal, the assassin's attack, and their escape from the warehouse, though he wisely decided to leave out any mention of the tunnels. He told her very little about the pirates, taking extra care to avoid discussing anything even remotely connected to the pirates' plan. Better to save that until the information would benefit him most.

At the end of his tale, Nirue turned immediately to Emme, her voice and expression neutral. "So you are Captain Gem's daughter."

Emme lifted her chin proudly. "I am."

"They will want you back."

"Perhaps," Emme replied with a half-shrug.

"What will you do if they come for you?"

"Run, I suppose."

"Will you, then?" The corner of Nirue's mouth twitched. "You look like you just might succeed, too. Very well." She turned back to Skerth. "If you intend to risk the streets you ought to know what has happened in your absence. Your skirmish with the assassin has started a war. I do not know how many boys have died all told;

163

what I do know is that enough have been murdered now to spread word beyond the bounds of the Lower City.

"Worse, the son of a shopkeeper up Milliner's Market Street was found dead in an alley not far from his father's shop yesterday morning. He was of an age with your dead boys. The merchants and traders have banded together with the Quarterstaves to create a citizen's army—only they don't know of the assassin. They believe the boy was killed in a street brawl or fell victim to your kind. They have formed patrols to rout out the gangs, thieves, pickpockets—anyone worthy of blame."

"I'll be careful," Skerth vowed.

"Skerth—" Kiri pleaded.

"Don't!" he shouted. "Stay here. Care for your wound and keep safe. Let me handle Malyn."

For once, she didn't pursue the argument. He turned to Emme. "Make sure she rests, will you?"

Emme replied with a nod.

At last, he looked to Nirue. "I'll be back to see Feirwyn," he promised.

He hoped it wasn't a lie.

Between the aftermath of the fire and the murders, reaching Deadrun proved much harder than Skerth had anticipated. Fewer people braved the streets, and Nirue had given a timely warning; Skerth managed to spot and evade three heavily armed patrols—one made up of two beefy Quarterstaves spoiling for a fight—thanks to her advice. He hesitated to consider what might have happened had he run headlong and unsuspecting into the patrols, most of whom were out for blood and vengeance rather than order.

The fourth patrol forced Skerth to the rooftops. He much preferred trailing in the wake of Kiri's reckless confidence, but he did his best to find the better paths to Malyn's territory.

He knew he had neared the border between his and Malyn's territory when he caught sight of two of Malyn's guards perched awkwardly on the roof of one of the larger storehouses. Kiri had advised Malyn to post them there, but they didn't look either comfortable or useful, especially since one passed the time dicing while the other clutched at the crumbling tile beneath him, looking deliberately away from the ground.

Skerth crept closer to observe them. He doubted the terrified boy—Skerth thought his name was Pesh—would muster up enough courage to do anything more than get down off that roof, and past experience assured Skerth that he could easily overcome his distracted companion, Maggot, if necessary. Maggot was taller and fleshier than he, but he moved slowly and thought even slower. Skerth settled his hand on the hilt of his dagger and stepped into the sunlight.

Maggot didn't notice him until Pesh thumped him on the back hard enough to scatter his dice.

"What! You—" Maggot broke off immediately and scrabbled to his feet. He arched a hand to shade his face and narrowed his eyes, then muttered a curse and hauled his cowering companion to his feet. "Halt, you! This here's Malyn's turf, and you'll not cross without his leave."

Skerth faced Malyn's boys across the clear drop to the street below. "Shut it, Maggot. I'm here to see Malyn."

Maggot frowned. "Thought you were dead."

"Obviously not. You going to let me pass?"

Maggot chewed on his lower lip with an expression that almost passed for thoughtful. Pesh inched closer to his companion. "Maggot," he whispered. "Malyn said we were to—"

"I know what Malyn said." Maggot kept his eyes fixed on Skerth. "Right," he said at last. "Run ahead, Pesh. Let Malyn know he'll have a guest."

"Maggot " Pesh whined.

"Shut it."

Pesh took a deep, unsteady breath and started to pick his way down to the pavement.

"You'll follow me," Maggot told Skerth. "And I'll have your weapon."

Skerth had lost enough daggers. He wouldn't give this one up without a fight. "Last time I followed one of your gang to a meeting with Malyn I barely escaped alive. So I'll be keeping my knife. Just in case."

"It's his law—"

"I've no quarrel with you, Maggot. Not yet, anyway."

To Skerth's relief, Maggot backed down from the challenge. "Fine. But you best not draw any blood in Malyn's quarter. We've had enough spilled of late, and I, for one, am fair sick of seeing it."

Without looking to see if Skerth followed, Maggot started the climb down.

Skerth leapt the gap that separated them and scrambled after him. "Have more boys been killed?"

"More'n what?" Maggot grunted. "More'n usual? More'n there used to be?" He paused to ease across a window ledge, then felt with his toe for the next foothold. "All I know is more'n half of the boys I grew up running with are gone now. Fael. Trick. Runner. Tost, Skid, Grit—now Taleryn's done, too—"

Skerth slipped and nearly lost his hold. "Taleryn?"

"Yeah. Malyn found him with his throat cut just this morning, Lark screaming-hysterical at his side. Guess Lark and Taleryn were—"

"Malyn found him?"

Maggot fell silent as he thought this through. To Skerth's aggravation, it took him a while. "I guess Lark must've been there first. It was her screaming what brought Malyn running." He paused. "Never heard screamin' and cryin' like that in my life. Didn't much like Lark, but I feel sorry for her. Must've cared for him, the way she carried on." He crossed one last window, then dropped to the ground with a thud. "Kept yellin' about betrayal and vengeance, stuff like that. Didn't make much sense. Took Malyn and two others to drag her off Taleryn and back to the warehouse."

Betrayal. Did she know, then, that Malyn was involved in the attacks? If she spilled too many secrets, Malyn would ensure that she became the first girl to fall victim to the assassin.

Skerth hit the ground running.

"Wait! You can't go to Malyn without an escort!" Maggot panted, trying to keep up.

He gave up the chase long before Skerth shoved his way through the crowd of boys outside Malyn's warehouse and slammed open the door. Unlike his last experience there, scats lingered in the halls and doorways, diced and drank in the rooms, and waited on Malyn's call. None of them tried to stop Skerth as he made his way to Malyn's private quarters and paused outside the door. Muffled sobs told him that Lark was still alive; lowered voices warned that she wasn't alone. Skerth burst through the door and flung Malyn up against the wall with a dagger to his throat before anyone had time to react.

"Caretakers' Piss!" Malyn roared. He tried to throw Skerth off, but stopped short at the bite of metal on his skin. "What in the—Skerth?" Some of the color drained from Malyn's face and he stilled. "I thought you were dead."

"He can be!" Seryn reached out to pull Skerth away. Seryn was older and stronger, but Skerth was determined. He dug in both of his heels and tightened his grip on Malyn.

"Stop!" cried Malyn.

The glimmer of real fear in Malyn's eyes bolstered Skerth's courage. "Back off, or I'll cut a smile into his throat."

"Just get out," Malyn added, without his eyes leaving Skerth's. "I think our ghost wants to talk." Somewhere behind Skerth, Lark sniffled. He rolled his eyes and added, "Take her with you."

Seryn hesitated, then crossed the room to Lark. "Come on," he said. "Let's go find some food."

Skerth didn't release Malyn until the door closed and he heard Lark and Seryn's footsteps retreat down the hall. As soon as Skerth moved the knife away, Malyn gave him a hard shove.

"What do you think you're doing, pushing into my quarters and threatening me like that in front of my scats?" He advanced, curling his fingers into fists.

Skerth stood his ground. "That's not the worst that will happen to you once your scats find out you're having them killed!"

"What?"

"What did they offer you?" Skerth and Malyn circled one another, Skerth's dagger steady before him, Malyn's fists ready. "Coin? Do the Staves look the other way when they catch one of your boys thieving? What do the Caretakers pay you to betray us and give the assassin clear passage to our streets?"

Malyn dropped his fists to his sides. "What are you talking about?"

"Shut it, Malyn, I'm no fool. I know everything."

Malyn sighed and tugged out a chair at the worn table. "Sit down, Ghost. I have no idea what you know or how you know it. But I do think you need to drop that weapon and speak plain if we're going to find a way out of this massacre alive." He sank into a chair across from Skerth and leaned forward to pour two mugs of ale from the chipped pitcher. Skerth stood firm at first, then relented. He sat, but kept a firm hold on his dagger.

"So you think I am responsible for all of this murder," said Malyn.

"Yes."

"Why?" Malyn leaned closer. "Most of the dead have been part of my trusted inner circle for years—we've fought together, thieved together—" he broke off thoughtfully, staring into his mug as he turned it from side to side. Finally, he met Skerth's eyes. "These were my brothers." He slammed his fist on the table, nearly upsetting both of their mugs. "I should kill you for even thinking I would have any part of such a slaughter."

"Then explain why you ordered Grey to lure me and Kiri here to have us killed."

"What?" Malyn snapped. "I did no such thing. I haven't seen Grey since. . . ."

"Since the night the assassin tried to kill me in your warehouse?"

Malyn's eyes widened, comprehending. "Since the night he came and told me you were dead. I didn't order him to do anything," Malyn insisted. "I didn't know—"

"How could you not know?" Skerth shouted. He leapt to his feet, knocking the chair to the ground. "How could you not know the assassin uses the tunnel beneath your warehouse to slip in and out of the Lower City undetected?"

Malyn frowned and shook his head. "What tunnel? I have no idea what you're—"

"Are you telling me you know nothing of this?"

Malyn looked him in the eye. "I am."

A long silence settled between them. Skerth studied Malyn, searching for the lie, but couldn't find it.

"If you didn't help the assassin, who did? Grey?"

"Someone close enough to know of our truce."

Someone with enough power to empty the warehouse and lock it behind the assassin's next victims.

Malyn caught his gaze and held it. "I don't like you, scat. You're a lone runner and too smart for my taste. But I didn't try to kill you."

Instinct and experience warned him not to trust Malyn; but this time, Skerth believed he told the truth.

There was only one way to find out.

"Come with me," Skerth said, kicking back his chair.

"Where?"

"There's something you should see."

For once, Malyn didn't argue. Skerth opened the door, and two of Malyn's boys nearly toppled into the room.

"Want us to take care of him?" one asked, flushing as he straightened.

"Move," Skerth growled, pushing him off.

"Scatter," Malyn barked. Because the boys loitering in the hallway didn't immediately leap out of their way, he added, "Get!"

A path cleared, and Skerth made straight for the back of the warehouse. Their passage generated a great deal of interest. He didn't worry that the other kids would find out about the trap door and the tunnel; in fact, he wanted them to know. They would all sleep easier if that path was blocked or guarded. What irritated him were the boys' constant offers to catch him, toss him out, or beat him senseless.

Several crates had been strategically re-positioned to cover all evidence of the door since the night he and Kiri had used the tunnel to escape. Boys—and a few girls, Skerth noticed—lounged around the room and atop the crates, dicing, playing at sticks, trading stories, or eating. The realization that Malyn's warehouse was abnormally full for a sweltering sunny day finally dawned on Skerth. These kids should have been out earning their keep and filling Malyn's larder—and his pockets—not lazing around dicing and flirting.

"A lot has changed since I worked for you," Skerth commented.

"Yeah. My scats started dying." Malyn brushed past him to stand at the center of the room. The noise dropped to a murmur, but he didn't seem to notice. "So. You wanted me to see . . . what? That I'm not earning any more coin until we find this assassin?"

Skerth headed straight to the back wall, where a group of kids lounged on and around a pyramid of crates stacked a little higher and more neatly than all the rest. "Move," he told them.

Their conversation faltered. They looked from Skerth to Malyn.

"You heard him," Malyn said. "Scatter."

As soon as the last boy sauntered off, Skerth started moving crates. Malyn joined him. Soon they'd managed to attract the full attention of everyone in the room. The kids crowded closer, forming a circle of curiosity around Malyn, Skerth and the crates.

They scraped aside the last crate to reveal the trap door beneath, spawning a shocked murmur from the crowd. Skerth gave Malyn a triumphant look and pulled the handle.

The door wouldn't budge.

Skerth pulled again, harder. A nearby group of younger boys snickered; Skerth resisted the urge to punch them. He glanced up at Malyn, whose expression gradually shifted from intent curiosity to irritation.

Skerth tried the door again, to no avail: the passage was shut tight.

Malyn folded his arms over his chest. "What is this?"

Ignoring him, Skerth leaned close to inspect the door. It was made of solid wood, same as the flooring, and showed no signs of rot. The iron loop handle was rusted, yet sturdy. And there, at the center of the iron panel binding the two together, was a tiny keyhole.

The door was locked.

Which meant someone had a key.

Chapter Twenty-One: Lark

Malyn knelt beside Skerth. "I don't know what this is all about Ghost, but whatever you're trying to show me better be worth my trouble or I'll break every one of your fingers so badly you'll never cut another purse."

Skerth paused and studied Malyn's face. He took in the narrowed glare, the pointed yellow teeth—and realized, for the first time, that he wasn't afraid. "Just help me get this open, Malyn."

More whispers at this. Malyn glared at Skerth, clenched his fists, and then looked to his scats. "Shut your holes or shove off. There're still pockets to be dipped in this city if you're looking for sport." Then, with another hard look at Skerth, Malyn put his hands on the iron loop and pulled.

The door didn't budge. They jerked at the handle in tandem, pried at the edges, stood and braced themselves to provide more leverage. A few of Malyn's boys even stepped forward to lend their own muscle to the task. Despite their best efforts, they only managed to loosen the screws binding the iron plate to the wood door.

They stood back in a rough circle, panting and sweating, and studied the door.

Malyn motioned to a couple of boys. "Axe. Now."

Skerth admired the way they rushed off to do his bidding, though he suspected their own curiosity proved motivation enough. Moments later, they returned with the axe. As Malyn tested its weight in his hands and considered the door, Skerth felt the crowd of boys shift closer. Malyn raised the axe, aimed, swung—

"No!" The scream cut across the room. Malyn's blow glanced against the metal plate, ringing loud in the sudden quiet. All eyes turned to Lark, who stood pale and trembling in the doorway. "Don't."

Dread curled in the pit of Skerth's stomach as one by one the pieces of the puzzle shifted into place. Mostly Malyn's boys dead, not his. Tunnels beneath Malyn's warehouse. Taleryn and Grey on watch the night Grey locked him in the warehouse. Taleryn on watch the night Dragon was attacked. The fire. The figure who had led the Caretakers straight to Skerth's warehouse. Lark's interest in his dagger.

"Lark," Skerth breathed.

Malyn looked up sharply, eyes widening in sudden understanding. "No—"

The crowds parted and shifted away from Lark as she made straight for Malyn and Skerth. Tears had swollen and blotched her skin. Long strands of dark hair escaped her braid and lay limp and dull against her face and shoulders. She looked as though she hadn't slept in days. But her eyes were clear, and Skerth could not mistake the warning in them.

"Don't," she hissed. "You don't know what you're doing."

Skerth faced her. "'Course I do. We're cracking this door open to see what's inside."

She glared; he challenged her with an unflinching, unforgiving stare.

Lark looked away first.

"Suppose you tell us why we shouldn't splinter this door," Malyn said quietly.

She opened her mouth, then paused, glancing around at the crowd of kids as though seeing them for the first time. Her hands shook. "Not here," she whispered. "Just trust me—don't do this."

Her eyes shifted from Skerth to Malyn in a silent plea.

Malyn took Lark by the arm and led her out, leaving Skerth to trail in their wake. The crowd filled in the spaces they left behind, inspecting the trap door, tugging at the handle. Already he could hear them discussing what had just happened, what it all meant. Skerth hoped, for Lark's sake, that they wouldn't soon figure out the depth or extent of her involvement. Street vengeance was an ugly thing, and she had a lot to answer for.

The walk back to Malyn's quarters felt long, but Malyn didn't rush as he led Lark past the curious stares of his gang—all of whom seemed tucked into the warehouse at once. Alone at last with the door locked tight behind them, Lark sank into a chair and buried her face in her hands. Her shoulders shook with choked sobs.

"The door," Malyn said at last. "Talk."

She wiped her nose on her sleeve and took a deep, shuddering breath. "If you open that door, you'll grant him free passage. He'll be able to come and go whenever he pleases. He'll—" her voice dropped to a whisper and she had trouble meeting their eyes. "He'll kill everyone."

Skerth thought of all the boys who had died—twelve that he knew of, maybe more that he didn't. "Who?" Rage curled his hands into fists. He shoved them into his pockets, waiting for her to say the words, but she only pressed her lips together and bowed her head.

Malyn leaned forward. His words were calmly spoken, deliberate. "What have you done, Lark?"

Her lower lip trembled and she dissolved into sobs. Skerth muttered a curse and crossed to the shuttered window. The late afternoon sunlight slanted through the cracks, illuminating fragments of dust that hung suspended in the air. He focused on them rather than on Lark's hysteria or the macabre faces of the once-living that haunted him, or even his own rising fury. "Shut it, Lark," he growled, facing her. "Crying all night won't bring Taleryn back. Tell us what you know and save the rest of us."

Lark's head snapped up. She slashed at her tears with her fists and glared at Skerth. "What do I care about any of you?"

"Do you know where that door leads?" Skerth asked.

She hesitated, looked from Malyn to Skerth and back again. "Yes," she told Malyn, who nodded for her to continue. "There's a tunnel below that hooks up to a system that runs beneath the city." She narrowed her eyes at Skerth. "But you knew that."

"What I know doesn't matter. When did *you* discover it? And when did you decide to show it to the assassin?"

"If I tell you anything, you'll kill me." She paused. "*He'll* kill me. I'm not saying a word until you agree—*both* of you—to keep me safe for as long as I'm stuck in this stinkhole of a city."

"Which won't be long," Malyn growled, his eyes glittering.

She laughed. "I plan to leave this sludge on the next ship that will take me, even if I have to stow away or bargain myself to the skin traders."

"Then until you do, I'll do what I can to keep you safe," Malyn assured her. "But I can't watch you day and night, and stories scatter like dock rats for gutter scum. If I turn my back and someone with a debt to settle cuts out of the shadows—" He shrugged.

Lark paled. "If that's all you can promise—"

"We'll do it," Skerth said. "Now start talking."

She narrowed her eyes. "What'll it cost me?"

"The truth," he said. "About everything. What you know about the tunnels, who the assassin is—"

"I don't know his name."

"—and above all, I want to know *why.*"

"You know why he's killing—"

"I want to know why you betrayed us," he snapped, taking a deep breath. "Do you want the deal, or not?"

He held her gaze while she weighed her options. They all knew this was the best chance she would get. Otherwise, she was dead.

"I found the door last winter, when Taleryn and I were—" Her eyes welled. "It took me longer to find the key. Turns out one of the boys had it from way back, when Jax led the gang. Taleryn and I did some exploring down there, but we never went far." She looked at Malyn. "I didn't know, at first, why he asked so many questions about your warehouse. He must have known the tunnels let out somewhere below."

Skerth recalled the conversation he'd overheard between Dreiwend and the Caretaker. "He did."

"When I figured out he wanted inside, I told him I could let him in—for a price."

"Of course." Malyn nodded. "Though I don't recall taking my cut."

She flushed. "Things got complicated from there. He started asking what I knew about specific boys, both Skerth's and yours. At first I thought he was a skin trader, so I wouldn't tell. But then he told me he'd lost someone dear on the streets, gave me all kinds of detail, asked if I knew anyone matching his tale. I felt sorry for him, so I gave him a couple of names."

"Twelve names," Skerth said with disgust.

Lark shook her head. "Not at first. I only knew a handful who looked like his lost one and might've been about the right age. But when they turned up dead, I got scared."

Malyn frowned. "So you gave more names?"

174

Her flush deepened. "I thought about running, but I didn't know where to go, and I couldn't leave without Taleryn in any case. So I made a better plan. In exchange for my safety—and Taleryn's—and enough coin to buy my way out of this slum and into a respectable life, I gave up names."

"Then why'd he kill Taleryn?" Skerth asked.

"Yeah. I thought you bought his life by trading the rest of my boys," Malyn said. Skerth gave him credit for his restraint.

"I thought so, too." She glared accusingly at Skerth. "But then *you* got away. You lived. After you escaped into the tunnels, the assassin was certain I had betrayed him. So he went after everyone I'd tried to keep safe." She turned to Malyn, her expression earnest. "But I was only trying to save them. Especially Taleryn, but I wanted to save them all: Runner, Bedewyn, Tost. . . . I never meant for them to die."

Malyn asked the question at the forefront of all their minds: "Why did he want Skerth so badly?"

She waited a long time before answering. "I don't know." She glanced at Skerth out of the corner of her eye. "Paid near triple for him though, once I told him Skerth was the boy fool enough to drop his dagger after running smack into the assassin." She curled her lip in a mocking sneer. "If you ask me, the assassin overpaid. Taleryn was worth more than five times your value alive. And now that he's gone—"

"—you're going to help us catch the assassin," Skerth finished.

"No," she said, her voice flat and cold.

Malyn cocked his head thoughtfully. "How do you figure?"

"She's our best weapon now," Skerth explained. "She's seen the assassin and knows how he travels, how to contact him. We can use her to draw him out."

Lark shook her head. "No. I won't do it."

"Why not?" asked Malyn.

Skerth leaned closer. "Don't you want to avenge Taleryn's murder? After all, the assassin betrayed *you*. He told you he'd stay clear of Taleryn, but he lied. Don't you owe Taleryn his revenge?"

"Don't you owe it to all of my boys?" Malyn picked up the thread of Skerth's argument. "Twelve dead, Lark. Not by your hand, but by your word."

"That number doesn't even count all of those lost to the fire," added Skerth.

"The fire?" Malyn glanced from Skerth to Lark, a look of mingled horror and disbelief crossing his face.

Lark paled. "I don't know what you're talking about."

"Course you do." Skerth braced his palms on the table and leaned in until he and Lark were nearly eye to eye. "You brought the assassin and the Caretakers to my warehouse on the night of the fire. You told them I stayed there. You took their coin and fled just before they set it on fire with all of my kids inside."

Her eyes widened.

"You are the lowest of all the scats on the street, Lark, and you have only one chance left to stop all this."

Her hands trembled; she clasped them together in her lap. She looked from Skerth to Malyn and back again.

"Fine," she said at last. "I'll help you. Then I'm done with all this. Gone."

"Good choice, Lark." Malyn looked to Skerth. "So what happens next, Ghost?"

Skerth suppressed a triumphant grin. He had figured out the identity of the boy—no, *girl*—aiding the assassin and spared the lives of many more boys in the process. He'd even managed to earn Malyn's respect.

All he had left to do was stop the assassin.

He took a deep breath. "Here's what we need to do. . ."

176

Chapter Twenty-Two: The Assassin

Well before dawn the next day, Skerth leaned against the wall of an alley near the gates between the Royal Quarter and the Lower City, waiting. Maggot shifted noisily beside him; not for the first time that night, Skerth wished he'd chosen a smaller, more patient partner rather than a boy with far more bulk than brain. More than that, he wished he had brought Kiri. She knew how to stay both silent and invisible; she also knew firsthand how high the stakes were and how dangerous the assassin could be. But she was recovering and, with any luck, curled up in front of Feirwyn's fire alongside Emme, sound asleep after a hot meal.

At the mere thought of food, his stomach growled loudly. Maggot snickered, and Skerth smacked him hard on the side of his big, stupid head. Maggot grunted a protest, but did not laugh again.

Across the torchlit courtyard, a lanky shadow separated from the alley wall and crooked three fingers. Skerth returned Malyn's signal; with a nod, he slipped back into the shadows. *Good*, Skerth thought, allowing some of the tension to ease from his shoulders. *Everyone in position.* Thus far, everything had worked according to plan. Earlier that night, Lark had passed a message to the assassin that she had names, and would meet him at the crossroads of Milliner's Market and Tannery Lane at dawn. All they had left to do was wait for her to lead their quarry into the courtyard. They would have the assassin at last.

Skerth took a deep breath and shifted into a squat.

"Wish she'd move along," Maggot grumbled. "Got better things to do than fester in an alley and wait."

"Such as?"

"Sleep. Eat." As an afterthought, he added, "Piss. Anything's better than this infernal waitin'."

Skerth ground his teeth. "Told you. When I say, we're jumping a mark."

"The take better be worth this wild trick—"

"Shut it, Maggot."

Grumbling, he obeyed. They settled in for the wait, nerves twitching at every scuttling rat or passerby rushing past on their own ill-timed errands. Gradually, the shadows thinned. The sky lightened. Skerth began to worry. Lark had been gone a long time. Too long. Something was wrong.

Skerth turned to Maggot. "Get to the Swine. Ask for Feirwyn and bring him here. Now. Tell him I'm in trouble."

"But I'm supposed to stay here—"

"*Now.*"

Spitting curses, but moving quicker than Skerth expected out of a big scat like him, Maggot disappeared down the alley.

Skerth turned back to watch the square. If he would come, Feirwyn's sword might well turn a losing fight into a decent bid for survival if Lark had indeed turned against them. Taleryn's loss had destroyed her. She had as much reason for vengeance now as any of them; more if her feelings for Taleryn had indeed run as deep as she claimed, but Skerth wouldn't stake his life on her caring for anyone or anything more than she cared for herself.

Muffled footsteps echoed in the empty square. Gripping the hilt of his dagger, Skerth edged forward and tensed to spring. Directly across the square Malyn and two of his boys stood poised and ready for action. Skerth took courage that eight more scats were stationed around and over the square, prepared to strike.

The assassin moved into view—alone. He threw back the hood of his cloak, baring shaggy dark hair and a grim smile. Though he had never caught more than a glimpse of the man, Skerth knew that walk, one part stealth, two parts confidence, his height and build, the careful set of his shoulders.

Skerth's eyes met Malyn's across the square. Malyn nodded; Skerth returned a grim smile.

The two boys—one master of the Deadrun, the other the reluctant leader of outcasts and orphans, collector of the lost and forgotten—stepped from the shadows. More figures shifted to flank the entry to Milliner's Market Street, cutting off the assassin's exit. Others dropped from the roof. The assassin turned in a slow circle, assessing the situation.

"A little early for thieving, don't you think?" the assassin shouted loudly. "Come, friends, you can have my purse. But if you wait a bit, the city will wake and you will have pickings to spare."

The Staves, Skerth realized, his stomach tightening. *He intends to call on the Staves*. Their plan depended on making a quick end to the assassin, and they hadn't counted on the Staves taking his side. Or the citizen patrols, for that matter. But they would, he realized with dawning horror. The populace believed the street scats at fault for the deaths of their children, and the Staves were the well-muscled arms of the Caretakers, their eyes, ears and brawn in the Lower City. Neither would look the other way to a handful of scats ambushing a man of noble accent and bearing walking the streets of the Lower City alone. If they didn't end this—and quick—this truly would become the fight of their lives.

"We're not here for the thieving," Malyn growled.

The assassin's smile faded; his eyes narrowed on Malyn. "No, I suppose not. I had wondered why my little bird came singing so early before dawn. Apparently she no longer sings just for me." His mouth twisted into a sarcastic smile. "Pity. She was such a pretty pet."

The hollow chill of his tone sent a shiver down Skerth's spine. He gripped his dagger a little tighter.

The assassin drew his sword with one hand and unsheathed a long knife with the other. He crouched into a defensive stance, his sword waving threatening circles in the air. "Come on, then," he shouted. "I am ready!"

The boys hesitated. Their worn short knives and dulled daggers were no match for fine, royal-forged steel. Nevertheless, every one of them held his ground. Skerth tightened his grip on his own dagger and thought of Rot. Of all of them—Taleryn, Fael, Dragon. None of them deserved to die. Not like this.

Once more, Skerth's and Malyn's eyes met.

Yes, Skerth thought. *Now*.

"For the Deadrun!" Malyn cried, hurtling from the shadows, eyes wide and knife raised high to strike. Other cries followed: "For Dragon!" "Fael!" "Trick and Runner!"

"For Rot!" Skerth bellowed, his heart swollen with loss and rage and thrumming double time to the rhythm of their battle song. "For Taleryn! For Kiri!" He streaked toward the assassin, his vision narrowed to only two main focal points: the steely grey eyes that had glimmered in the shadows of the alley and the hand that had almost dealt Kiri, his best and only friend, a mortal wound.

The boys fell upon the assassin in earnest, but Malyn reached him first. The assassin swatted away his knife with the tip of his sword and spun to meet Gahn and Rock on his other side. Gahn, the smaller, quicker of the two, barely skimmed away from the long knife; Rock took a cut on the side, though he dodged in time to avoid the knife-thrust that followed.

The others closed in a tight circle, taking advantage of the assassin's engagement to swipe blows wherever they could manage—here an exposed arm, there a shoulder. But between the shielding folds of the assassin's heavy wool cloak and his quick defenses, all of the boys together proved no more useful at dealing real damage than a fly worried a mountain ox. Every time a cluster of boys would get close enough to strike, the assassin would sweep his sword in a wide arc that scattered them. Still they tried, again and again, determined to bring down the strong arm of the Caretakers before their streets ran slick with blood.

The sun crested the ocean, bringing with the first true rays of daylight the warm, heavy damp that characterized the early summer. Sweat streaked Skerth's face and stung his eyes, blood seeped from minor slashes across his arms and chest, but still he worried the assassin with his blade, longing to drive it home and end this living nightmare once and for all. The other boys held to their quarry, but with less enthusiasm. Gahn had edged into the alley, where he lay clutching a blossoming chest wound. Another scat lay unconscious where he had fallen, blood streaking his hair and face. The remaining boys moved slower, reacted less quickly—and caught more blows for their mistakes—while the assassin still seemed fresh, untouched as he whirled and dodged, slicing first with the sword, then the knife, his cloak fanning out behind him and spilling street scats in its wake.

Malyn fought his way to Skerth. "We can't hold him," he said in an urgent whisper. "He's got enough fight in him for all of us, and more."

"So you want to give up. Run back to the Deadrun and cower like beaten whelps."

Malyn hesitated. "No. But I think—"

The assassin's double-bladed thrust spared Skerth the trouble of hearing Malyn's opinion. Pain sliced hot across Skerth's abdomen as he shouldered Malyn away from the mortal blow.

While Skerth weakly parried the second blade, Malyn managed to slide a finger's worth of dagger into the assassin's ribs; the assassin roared and lashed out, but Malyn jumped clear. Skerth's dagger caught the assassin's next thrust and held it off long enough for him to duck beneath and roll free. Then he scrabbled to his feet and staggered into a run.

Enraged, the assassin pursued. His abdomen afire with pain, Skerth sprinted toward the alley, turned—

And smacked hard against the wall of flesh that was Maggot.

They hit the ground hard, the assassin close behind. Skerth tried to untangle his limbs, but the more Maggot thrashed the more difficult it became to free himself. The assassin pounded into the alley. Skerth squeezed his eyes shut, knowing this was the end. Only two steps, then one. . . .

A shout. The hum of drawn steel. Skerth looked up to see Feirwyn engaging the assassin, using his sword to push him back toward the boys who had reassembled to the assassin's rear.

Hands grabbed at Skerth, hauled him roughly to his feet. "Can't you take care of yourself?" hissed a familiar voice.

"Kiri," he breathed, his shoulders sagging with relief. He didn't know if he was angry or thrilled to see her, if he should hug her tight or shove her away and tell her to run. Before he could decide, she yanked him clear of the fight.

"You're wounded," she said, frowning. She tugged at his shirt to examine the wound, but he stopped her with a firm grasp on her wrist.

"I'm fine. But you shouldn't be here."

She looked indignant. "What, I'm supposed to just stand aside and let you get yourself killed?"

He bristled. "I can take care of myself. Besides, you're hurt—"

"You know what, Skerth? I can take care of myself, too," she snapped. "But sometimes, it's nice not to have to. Now shut it and wait." She pushed him down behind a pile of burned refuse and squatted beside him, dagger out and eyes on the animated duel between Feirwyn and the assassin.

Feirwyn had quickly gained and held the upper hand, forcing the assassin to give ground and retreat backward into the wall of boys now closing off access to the square. Malyn and a handful of scats still in the fight positioned themselves behind Skerth and Kiri,

181

blocking the only other way out. If they could hold him, the assassin was trapped. If not—

Skerth watched Feirwyn and the assassin's deadly dance with awe. He had thought the assassin skilled with a blade, but Feirwyn's tight control overshadowed the assassin's sharp, quick thrusts. Whereas the assassin had a brutal and straightforward edge to his technique, Feirwyn's was swift and nuanced, with the unconscious, easy flair of the expert training reserved for the highborn and noble. Effortless flicks of the wrist turned aside the assassin's heavy blows, blooding his opponent with quick, nimble cuts that served more to increase the assassin's ire and break his concentration rather than do any significant damage. Not for the first time, something old and familiar stirred deep within Skerth, brushing the edges of memory. . . .

At last, an elegant sweep of Feirwyn's blade sent his opponent's sword clattering to the side. Malyn lunged forward and kicked it to his scats, who immediately carried it out of reach. The assassin tossed the long knife to his right hand, but this, too Feirwyn easily knocked aside. A quick lunge forced the assassin to his knees, the tip of Feirwyn's sword pressed into the man's throat. Malyn's boys gathered closed behind him, preventing their quarry's escape.

Feirwyn's voice was as hard as his expression. "Kalen."

A slow smile spread across the assassin's face. "Well, well. So the Exile has returned. Do you ever wish I had finished the job, Feirwyn of Thalenthwynn Keep?"

Thalenthwynn Keep. The name sounded familiar. *Why?*

The assassin added, "Do you ever wish I hadn't let you run?"

Skerth never saw Feirwyn so much as twitch, but a thin line of blood issued from beneath the tip of his sword.

"All the time," Feirwyn said, his voice hard and cold. "Even more than I wish I had killed you when I had the chance." He pressed a little harder; Kalen's smile faded. "But that mistake I can easily remedy."

Kalen's eyes glinted. "Do it. You have earned the right."

Feirwyn watched him with a cool detachment that gave no hint to either his thoughts or his intentions. "While I would relish the opportunity to revenge my family and my birthright, justice and revenge belong to the rightful king, not to me."

Kalen snorted. "We have no king. And after Auberdale Eve, there will be no king, either born—or made." His gave the boys crowded into the alley a pointed look. None had escaped the assassin's blade. Blood seeped from minor gashes and lengthy cuts. Bruises blossomed on bare arms and cheekbones where fists, knife hilts or hard cobbles had battered skin. Still, they stood shoulders straight and chins high, each meeting the assassin's look of scorn with proud defiance.

His eyes rested last on Skerth. Narrowed. "Not one of you is fit to govern a crumbling ruin in the oldest slum of the city, never mind a kingdom. I would have killed every last one of you, and gladly, to keep the throne untarnished."

Feirwyn's expression did not change, but the dribble of blood at Kalen's throat thickened. "You tarnished the throne the day you aided Harrudrynn and his fellow Caretakers in murdering every last member of my family, to the child my sister bore only a fortnight before her slaughter. What you have done since only blackens your soul the more."

Kalen gave a careless shrug. "I threw my lot in with those who offered me the chance to live. And I live still, while so many others do not." His eyes glittered. "And I intend to live on, old friend, long after your ashes have scattered into the Quistand Ocean."

Feirwyn's lips tightened. "So you admit freely that you are Harrudrynn's man."

"Then and now." Kalen lifted his chin in defiance. "Always."

For a long, silent moment, Feirwyn studied the man before him, measuring the weight of his worth. Finally, he sheathed his sword.

"Rope," he said.

Kiri pulled a coil of rope from her belt and brought it to him.

"You're not going to kill me?" Kalen looked genuinely surprised.

Feirwyn tightened the bonds around his wrists. "And deprive the people of their revenge? You have far more to answer for now than eleven-year-old atrocities and treason."

Feirwyn flashed a cold smile as he bound the assassin's hands behind his back. "Take heart, *old friend*." He spat Kalen's words back at him. "Chances are excellent you will meet a swifter and more painless death than those you murdered. Nor will you ever endure the shame of exile, or the pain of knowing you live when so many others do not."

Straightening, he turned to Malyn. "Hold him in Deadrun until Auberdale Eve. But take care of our guest—we need him alive and able to confess his crimes."

"I have nothing to confess," Kalen spat. "Everything I have done was dictated by Harrudrynn's word and with the Caretakers' blessing. No man can fault a soldier for following orders."

"And no soldier loves the kill as you do, Kalen. May the Lords of the Sea bear you mercy."

With a nod to Malyn, he turned his back on the assassin and strode out of the alley.

Malyn moved to stand just behind Kalen. He braced his feet shoulder-width apart, then slowly flexed his fingers before cracking his knuckles one-by-one. His eyes met Skerth's over the assassin's head. There was anger in Malyn's eyes, but there was also a strong sense of justice. He tightened his hands into fists before returning his gaze to the assassin.

"Scats," he said quietly. "Let's get our guest back to the Deadrun."

"Come on," Kiri whispered, tugging Skerth to his feet.

Feirwyn waited just outside the alley.

"You're hurt," he said with a frown.

"I'm fine." Skerth shrugged off his assistance and hastened to keep up with Feirwyn's long stride.

The smell of hot bread and meat preceded their arrival at The Blighted Swine. Skerth's stomach rumbled. Kiri snickered. He gave her a playful shove and, despite the pain that seared his abdomen, together they tumbled up the steps to the inn.

"Come," Feirwyn said. "I'll buy you something to eat inside. Then we can talk."

Skerth blinked, his eyes adjusting to the relative dark. But he didn't need full sight to recognize that the common room was unusually full. The roar of noise quieted a bit as heads turned to the new arrivals. Most took in the nondescript traveler and the two filthy kids and went back to their business, but one man, a burly, broad fellow with a lion's mane of bushy black hair and beard, slammed his tankard on the table and rose.

Beside Skerth, Kiri stiffened.

"Kirian Viela Peltewyn!" he roared. "Where have you been?"

Skerth turned to Kiri, confused, and what he saw shocked him. She stood tensed to run, her face drained of color, her mismatched eyes wide.

"Kiri, who—"

She turned to bolt, but Feirwyn caught her by the collar and hauled her back to face the room. The stranger was already on his way over, shoving his bulk past the other patrons, mindless of the spilled ale and curses he left in his wake.

"I've had my men combing these foul streets for days, looking for you!" he bellowed. "Thought you were dead, or worse!"

Kiri struggled like a feral cat to free herself from Feirwyn's grip. "No! Let me go!" When he held fast, she turned pleading eyes on Skerth. "Skerth—I'm sorry. I will explain—"

"Yes, girl, explain away!" rumbled the stranger as he stopped before her, heavy fists set at his hips. "Well, daughter? What have you to say for yourself?"

Girl . . . daughter. . . Skerth stared, struggling to make sense of what was happening.

Kiri ceased wriggling and glared. "You're mistaken."

Feirwyn chuckled; the stranger's smile faded, replaced by thick furrowed brows and narrowed eyes. Mismatched eyes, Skerth realized with a sick feeling. One blue. One brown.

"Mistaken?" The stranger glowered at Kiri. His lowered voice only emphasized his fury. "I should've clipped your wings long ago, little bird, and I'll have them now for your defiance."

"Arran—"

He cut Feirwyn off with a look. "Did you know my daughter was running the streets Downwedge like a common gutterscut?"

Daughter. The word cut Skerth deeper than the assassin's blade. His eyes met Kiri's in disbelief. But hers told a different story—no longer stubbornly defiant, she looked resigned. Panicked. Remorseful.

"Skerth—" she whispered.

He shook his head. "No," he said aloud, unwilling to know, to believe. "No!"

Kiri had a name. A father. A *family.* Everything snapped into place: her mysterious comings and goings, her long disappearances, the food she always brought to share when the pickings were thin. The rooftop pathways upwedge, into the Royal Quarter.

The secrets she kept, even from him.

Rage flushed his skin and curdled his stomach. "It was all a caper for you," he growled. "A game."

Kiri pulled free of Feirwyn's hold, her face red. "No, Skerth," she whispered. "Listen—"

"Do you tell tales of the poor, filthy orphan boy to all your highborn friends? Have a good laugh, do you, about your adventures in the dregs of Endelas Ortanos?"

She flushed, her own anger rising to meet his. "It's not like that, not at all! After all we've been through, Skerth, you know me better than that!" She reached out, but he twitched out of her grasp.

"No—what's your name?— *Kirian*, I don't know you at all."

He turned and shoved at the door. Feirwyn tried to catch him, but Skerth dodged out of reach. Voices yelled for him to stop. He ignored them, tripping down the steps to the courtyard and sprinting into the sunlight. He didn't know who Kiri was anymore, and he no longer cared. Feirwyn could find another boy to make king. Skerth was going home to the filth and despair of the streets—where he belonged.

Chapter Twenty-Three: Into the Dark

S kerth ran. His feet flew over the broken stones, filth and mud with ease, knowing every break and rut better than he knew his own true name. He ran until the hurt, the hot pain of his wounds, the sting of his tears, the fury, everything fell away, leaving nothing left but the solid beat of his heart in his ears. He skirted rickety pushcarts full of debris and ash-dusted men and women picking through ruins. He ducked under archways newly-formed of shattered buildings and vaulted the ruined barricades that had failed to keep out the fire. His city had been ruined, remade into a blackened, broken beast, yet still he ran as fast as his legs would carry him, only a step apace of his anger, only half-seeing the devastation that his world had become.

Only when his chest threatened to burst and he could no longer breathe, Skerth slowed, then jolted to a halt. Pain rushed back—heat coursed from the slash in his abdomen, his lungs burned, his heart felt squeezed to bursting. He doubled over and dropped his hands to his knees to catch his breath. The hurt caught up with him, too; the bruises and the cuts would heal, but Kiri's betrayal had stabbed deeper than any knife.

Panting for breath, Skerth took in his whereabouts. His feet had brought him to the only place of comfort he knew: the narrow crawlspace between the dilapidated back wall of an old alehouse and the rock wall that had stood there long before the first explorers had made shore on the coast of Erados. And beyond that, his tunnel.

Skerth slumped against the wall and slid to the ground, where he lay until his limbs stopped shaking; by then the sun had long set and the rats had ventured out of their holes. With the loss of the Pleasure District, an eerie quiet settled that only reminded him of his loneliness and loss all the more. *I am all I have*, he told himself, fresh anger at Kiri surging with enough force to make him dizzy. Thoughts of Fcirwyn only made things worse. He had known something of Kiri's past all along. They had both used him. Mocked him. Made of his life a game of nobles and kingmakers, destroying what little he had in the process. *I was a fool to trust anyone else.* Unwilling to return to either the Deadrun or the Swine, Skerth half-rose, half-dragged himself the few remaining feet to the tunnel and crept inside.

As he set his hands to the walls and made his way in the darkness, the familiarity of the ancient ridges and valleys of the wall, the smell of damp stone and the tang of minerals comforted him. His hands moved by memory over rough knots of stone; his fingers slipped into narrow grooves that pointed like an arrow to his old hiding place. Finding the rock where he had once stowed his only possessions, he dug into the hollow and relaxed when his fingers brushed the scatter of objects he had left behind. This place, at least, was safe. At a time when nothing else in his life was certain, this haven remained exactly as he had left it.

Tension eased from his shoulders and back. He curled onto the ground and closed his eyes, craving sleep.

But sleep would not come. The longer he lay in the dark, willing himself to sleep, the more his mind replayed the images that would not let him rest: the assassin. Malyn. Kiri's father, rising to meet her. Her look of shock, turned to defiance, turned to defeat. Over and over he replayed the last few hours, his stomach hollow and sick, his chest aching more than he ever imagined possible. He flipped over on the hard stone, careless of the wound that tore, careless of the fresh blood oozing forth, glad for the pain that temporarily scattered his thoughts.

Memories of hours stretched into recollections of the last few days. The last few years. Her shock of white hair, falling just so over her forehead. Her smile. His heart squeezed in an entirely different way when he remembered how frightened he'd been to see her lying pale and pain-drawn in the pirates' lair. His mind shifted even farther back, shifting long-missing pieces into place at last. The sacks of food, always full, always fresh. Her fearlessness. The way she appeared and disappeared at whim, never telling where she'd gone or from where she'd come. Worry for her had led him to the discovery of the first body, had held him back from escaping the pirates on his own. And all the time, she had lied about who she was.

He had believed her his equal. Trapped on the streets together, determined to make the best life they could with the raw material that had been left to them. But she was nothing like him. She could have chosen, at any moment, to give up the game and return home to her warm hearth, clean clothes, soft bed, and a family. But he had never had a choice.

Kiri had a name. A father. And what had Skerth to call his own? A nickname given him by a vile fisherman and a broken-down warehouse—now reduced to a smoldering pile of ash—that had meant more to him than he would ever have admitted.

Tears burned his cheeks; he let them come. He had nothing to fear here, nothing to pretend. The tears came faster, his breath harder as he mourned everything: the loss of the boys whom none would ever remember, the loss of his warehouse, the loss of his only friend. Even the defeat of the assassin brought him no comfort. Nothing would ever be the same again. Nothing.

Eventually Skerth sank into a fitful sleep, full of odd images, more memory than dreams. The faces of those who died paraded before him one by one, pale and drawn, watching him through glassy, soulless eyes. He lay curled on the floor of his warehouse, listening to the rhythmic breathing and soft snores of the little ones, temporarily comforted by their contentment. In sleep he revisited his break from Malyn's gang, too: the final beating that had left him in an alley splattered with his own blood, half-dead and naked, but free of Malyn's tyranny. Farther his dreams went, farther even than the day he had bought his way into the gang—Jax had ruled the streets then, a tall, good-looking boy with a ready smile and a brutal fist. He had been kind, at first; only too late had Skerth realized the life he had bargained for was not as easy as Skerth's best friend—a younger, carefree Malyn—had told him.

Skerth shifted and murmured in his sleep, but did not wake even when dreams brought him back to the young woman who had taken him in. Nor did he stir when his mind traveled farther, returning him here to the tunnels. To the dark.

Unbidden, the face of the hag shimmered and took shape. The dream turned into a nightmare from which he could not wake: fire, swords, shouting. People running, frantic. The acrid smell of blood and over it all, hot ash showered down like black snow.

189

Farther back he reached, but only found impressions. A golden-haired woman reaching for him with a smile, a white-gold circlet on her brow. A dark-bearded nobleman, his careworn forehead furrowed deep. And a boy, of an age with Skerth, with the same bright hair and build.

And, at last, a name. *Tirith.*

As though summoned, a succession of images flashed to mind, one after the other. Rooms lavishly decorated and crowded with finely dressed people. Tapestries. Jewels. A blazing fire roared in the hearth of a grand fireplace at the end of a magnificent hall. Again, the woman, the man, the child. A handful of golden-haired boys, all of the same look and finely-dressed, listening to the drowsy monotone of an elderly tutor. The hag. Another woman, fair-faced and kind.

And at the end of it all, a sunny garden filled with early summer roses in every hue of pink, yellow and red.

He frowned into the tangle of roses. Sure enough, his new blue birthday ball lay between the thorny stems of Mother's roses, just out of reach. Tears pricked the corners of his eyes.

"Only babies cry," he muttered to himself, imagining what Tirith would say if he found him crying about the ball.

He rocked back on his heels, caught in the throes of a new idea. Tirith's arms were longer; Tirith could get the ball. But where was he? He'd not seen him since breakfast.

He stood and ran to the edge of the garden path, squinting into the bright summer sunlight. After a quick glance back at the roses to mark the pinks and yellows, he sprinted down the path into the garden courtyard.

He didn't get far before he was swept from the ground into a woman's arms. "Little one! Thank the Goddess—"

He gasped as she squeezed him tight. When she eased up enough for him to breathe again, he looked up into the tearful blue eyes of Jearney, one of the younger maids who watched him when Nurse grew tired. Nurse squeezed him too tight and frowned too much, made his stomach ache, but he liked Jearney; she always smiled.

But today was different. He touched a tear sliding down her cheek. "Why are you sad?"

"Never you mind," she soothed in a trembling voice as she held him tight and walked briskly toward the house. "We must find the queen."

"*Can you get my ball?*"

"*Later, sweeting. First there is something we must do.*"

Jearney paused just inside the door to peer into the entryway, then dodged into the main house. Normally quiet, the house bustled with activity. The men and women of the household staff rushed in every direction, some carrying clothes, books or jewels, others weapons. What were they doing? Where were they all going? He watched Jearney's face as she held him close and shoved through the crowd. He leaned into her. She was nice; she would take him to Mother and everything would be all right.

He pressed tight against her chest. Her heart pounded loud in his ear as she quickened her step. Her breath came faster. Those they passed ran now, and there was shouting, loud banging, the ring of metal against metal. Afraid, he threw his arms around her neck and squeezed his eyes shut. She caressed his hair and held him tighter, but said nothing.

"*Where are you going?*" *rasped Nurse.*

Jearney stopped.

"*I'm taking him to the queen.*"

"*Best give him to me, girl. I'm his keeper, after all.*"

Jearney's grip tightened.

"*He's no burden.*"

"*Let me take the boy. I'm old. Get out while you can.*"

No! Don't let her take me! *He bit his lip to keep the words in.*

But Jearney hesitated.

"*Come, girl, don't be stupid. You're young. Give me the boy.*"

His eyes met Jearney's in a silent plea, but it was too late. Jearney was already brushing her hand through his hair, kissing him, and prying his arms away.

"*Be a good boy,*" *she whispered as a tear slipped down her cheek. Nurse's bony hands were already clawing at his sides, pulling him away.*

"*Good girl,*" *Nurse cooed once she had him clasped tightly—too tightly— in her arms. He whimpered; Nurse pinched him. "Where are the others?"*

Jearney's eyes welled afresh. "He's the only one I've found. But I've a few more rooms to search—"

"*Never mind that now. To the East Gate with you. Go.*"

Jearney shook her head, her eyes on him. "But the children—"

"*No time for that now. Go!*" *Nurse hissed. Jearney scurried away.*

His eyes burned with tears that he would not let Nurse see. Babies cry.

Grumbling, Nurse awkwardly took to the stairs. He hoped she would find him too much trouble and set him down, but she must have known he would run. He struggled, but she only smacked his bottom and gripped him tighter. Soon I'll be with Mother, *he told himself, wishing everyone around them would stop running so much, stop the shouting and the noise. He shut his eyes and counted Nurse's heavy steps.* One. Two. Three. . .

They turned, but not in the direction he expected. His eyes shot open and he tried to lean up, to see where they were, but Nurse pushed his head into the crook of her neck. He tried not to gag at the smell of old and sweat that clung to her dress. She was taking him down now, down a stairway he had never found, through a doorway he had never seen. The way was dark, and Nurse did not have a candle. She slowed, feeling each step before taking it, periodically letting him go with one hand to touch the wall beside her. His heart pounded as the blackness swallowed them up.

"No!" he squeaked. "Not dark!"

"Hush!" she hissed.

"But Mother—"

"She cannot help you now, boy. Hush, or I'll have your tongue."

Something in her tone told him she meant it. Whimpering, he squeezed his eyes tight and pictured the pink and yellow roses where his ball lay. He didn't want to forget.

He hadn't realized he had fallen asleep until the brush of breeze against his clammy skin roused him. Nurse hurried now, moving faster than he had thought her fat legs could carry her. He opened his eyes and looked out into the shadows of a filthy street. At last, she set him down. He shivered.

She straightened, set her hands on her hips and glared down at him before drawing a small pouch and a dagger out of the folds of her apron. Grunting from the effort, she squatted before him.

"You listen to me, boy. I've brought you out safe, I have, from a terrible danger. But I'll not be caught holding you, either. I'm old, but I've a few years in me yet, and I'd like to keep them. You'll have a chance now, and a better chance than any of your kin inside." She paused and handed him the pouch. "Here's the old king's ring. He'll not be needing it, and it might do you some good in a pinch. Keep it round your neck, like this, and don't let anybody touch it." She tightened the drawstrings of the small pouch and hung it around his neck. The pouch she tucked inside his shirt. She handed him the dagger. "It's sharp, so mind your fingers. Anybody tries to harm you, stick them with this and don't think twice about it. Then run. Do you hear?"

Wide-eyed and trembling, he nodded.

"Good." Satisfied, Nurse stood. "Fine boy like you, and a little one, nobody'd think twice about taking you in. You'll have a new home, and a safe

one, in no time." He did not know if she was speaking to him or to herself. She straightened and smoothed her apron. "Mind your fingers," she reminded him coolly, and slowly turned her back.

He watched until he could no longer see her. Then, clutching the dagger hilt with both hands, he began to sob, thinking of Jearney, and his Mother, and of his blue birthday ball, trapped in the pink and yellow roses of the summer garden.

Skerth's eyes snapped open. He scrabbled to his feet and stood motionless, still held fast by the dream. "A torch," he whispered, shaking his head to clear it. "I need a torch."

The rats scampered away as Skerth worked his way back through the tunnels, through the crawlspace and the narrow passage that led out to the street. The burnt-out, vacant Pleasure District still smoldered here and there, but offered few usable materials for a decent torch. It took some doing, but he managed to find a broken shaft of board in the rubble that had escaped the blaze. He tore a strip from his now-ruined shirt and wrapped it around the top, then nurtured a hot pile of ash into a fitting spark before hurrying back to the tunnel.

At the mouth he paused and took a deep breath. He thought of the hag, the Caretakers, the dark that had terrified him once, on a sunny day long ago. Then, with grim determination, he stepped inside.

The flickering torchlight illuminated more terrors in the tunnels than Skerth had ever feared in the dark. Lost in the velvety black, he had never seen the deteriorated bones of old rats and decomposed carrion that lay scattered against the walls. Without their layer of mystery, the stone tunnels were just old rock, moist, molding, and thickened with bat guano. Above, the flame of Skerth's torch cast longer, more ominous shadows that seemed to resist the light; embedded in these were glimmers of a vast network of spider webs, intricately woven nets for dark fishermen that bolted away from the light's faintest touch. Skerth shivered and quickened his pace; while he had never before feared what he could not see, he knew now he'd never walk those tunnels again.

When Skerth reached the fork in the tunnel where he had first heard the Caretaker and Dreiwend, he veered immediately to the left. Only after he had made the choice did he realize that he would have chosen that path even if he had never heard the nobles there or seen the telltale flicker of their torches. His every instinct shouted that he had traveled this path long before.

With every step, old images, nurtured into memory by despair and birthed in his dreams, now haunted him. A woman—mother?—hair like glimmering gold silk. The king, strong and wise. Sunny-haired playmates as like in age and look as siblings. The heir and his decoys, he now knew, all bred and raised to keep the throne should the responsibility of it fall to one of them. Skerth both cherished and resented each new fragment that surfaced, evidence of a life lost to him before he had ever truly appreciated its value. His hatred and resentment for the Caretakers grew. They had stolen everything from him. His friends. A family. Peace. For that, they would pay.

At the next fork, he paused and took a deep breath to steady himself. He knew the keys to unlock his past lay at the end of this tunnel. Only a few more steps would at last lay bare the truth of who he was and prove to himself, if no one else, that he was indeed one of the last valid claimants to the throne of Erados, if not the heir himself. But did he want to know? His stomach churned; his mind whirled with possibilities. Curiosity urged him forward; dread kept him still. He feared how this new knowledge would change his life—how it would change *him*. And for the first time since her betrayal, he wished Kiri was here beside him on this last great adventure.

One step forward. Another. The tunnel curved and narrowed. The ground and cavern walls smoothed flat and glossy where carvers had brought the rough stone to heel; the torchlight highlighted intricate designs and symbols carved into their glassy face. Beneath Skerth's feet, the floor evened out into a path hewn into the rock and polished to a glimmer. Skerth thrust the torch before him, found what he had hoped—no, expected—to discover, and stopped.

The tunnel terminated in a plain wood door, rotted with age and long disuse. The only ornament was a small, black iron wyvern set over the loop handle.

Skerth's breath came harder, faster. The last time he had passed this way, his Nurse had carried him from murder only to leave him victim to the predators who worked the Lower City: the rats, the skin traders, the thieves. Whatever the cost, whatever her motive, she *had* saved his life.

But for what purpose?

Skerth stared at the door a long time. He reached out and traced the wyvern from the fangs to the curve of the forked serpent's tail. This cold iron symbol unlocked images of others that tumbled forth: the wyvern's nobler cousins silhouetted grandly in the royal crest and depicted in vibrant scarlet on the tapestry that had once hung proudly in the main hall. A standard, black beast on scarlet field, tugging in the wind against a clear blue sky. A marble statuary with ruby eyes. Twin marble beasts keeping guard over a walled gate. It was a noble beast, fit for a king.

Skerth gripped the loop handle. Closed his eyes. Took a deep breath.

Pulled.

The door didn't budge. He tugged again. After a third attempt, he realized that knowing who he was, even half-believing such a wild impossibility, was not enough to grant him access to a world that had always stood fast against him.

"No more." The words, spoken like a promise and weighted like a spell, surprised him with their strength as they rolled back at him from the tunnel walls. Something new and vital took root deep within him. He could feel a new energy coursing through him, bracing his shoulders and lifting his chin.

And Skerth knew, at last, what he must do.

He took one last look at the door, then headed back the way he had come.

Chapter Twenty-Four: Proof

All the way to the Swine, Skerth considered what he would say. What he wouldn't say. Or, whether or not he could manage to say anything at all. The truth—that he now believed he had been born and raised a decoy, if not the heir of Erados himself—felt dry and strange in his mouth. Thus far, he hadn't found the words to make sense of what he remembered, what he knew, what he felt, never mind speak them aloud.

By the time he arrived, his stomach churned. With a deep breath he shoved open the door, and felt his tension ease when a quick glance over the nearly empty room confirmed that neither Kiri nor her father were there. Grateful for at least that one small obstacle overcome, he nodded to Gil, the burly proprietor stationed behind the bar, and headed for the back stairway.

If his arrival surprised Feirwyn, the nobleman did not show it. "I had hoped you might return," he said, swinging the door wide. Feirwyn gestured for Skerth to sit and crossed the room to the sideboard. "Will you eat?"

"I'm not hungry," Skerth muttered. But the smell of warm bread, meat and cheese proved too much for his stomach, which betrayed him with a healthy growl.

Feirwyn heaped a plate with the generous leavings of his own recent meal and handed it over wordlessly.

Skerth refused to meet Feirwyn's eyes as he accepted it and settled in one of the faded armchairs near the fire. As he did so, he glimpsed a flicker of blue skirts. For a few tense breaths, his heart pounded a little harder; but he was relieved to see it was only Emme.

They studied one another in silence, his heart pounding for very different reasons this time. Washed and rosy-cheeked, loose dark curls peeking from a shining dark braid, Emme looked a very different girl from the faded, flour and fish-covered kitchen servant he had first met. Scrubbed and free of galley grime, she had her mother's look, with clear skin, eyes that curved just so at the

196

corners, and full, pink lips. She stood taller, straighter somehow, and her blue dress—faded, but clean and well-made—clung to curves he hadn't noticed before. A rush of heat colored his cheeks, and he quickly glanced away.

"Well met, Skerth." She smiled, and his heart skipped a bit. She smoothed her dress and tugged self-consciously at the end of her braid.

"How do you fare, Emme?"

"Very well. Milord and Milady treat me far better than my own kin."

"We gave her a place with us, for the time being," Feirwyn explained. "Nirue happened to require a lady's maid. A beneficial arrangement for them both, I believe."

Skerth tamped down a brief pang of jealousy that she had managed to escape the streets so easily and so well, reminding himself that he hadn't wanted that life for her. "I'm glad you are well," he told her, and realized that he meant it.

She turned to Feirwyn. "If you've finished your missive, I'll be off."

"There, on the table." Feirwyn softened his dismissal with a smile.

Emme took the sealed parchment. She curtseyed to Feirwyn, nodded to Skerth, and slipped out the front door.

No sooner did she leave than Skerth's mind refocused on more pressing matters. Still unsure of how to begin the tale he'd come to tell, he started with his easiest question.

"So. Who is she?" he asked around the chunk of bread he stuffed into his mouth.

Feirwyn raised his eyebrows. "You know that better than I, Skerth. She's the pirate queen's daughter."

He shook his head. "Not Emme. Kiri. Who is she, really? Little noble girl having a lark on the streets? One of the Caretakers' spies? Or does she work for you, too?"

Feirwyn poured himself a mug of ale and settled into the chair opposite Skerth. "Kirian's father desires, as many do, to see the kingship restored. He is oft away, which allows his daughter plenty of room to wander on errands of her own. He has only just returned. The rest you know."

Skerth picked at his dirty fingernails while he considered this information, none of which eased the hollow ache her betrayal had left behind. "Did you know who she was?"

After a long pause: "Yes."

The answer twisted in Skerth's stomach with more pain than any knife. "Why didn't you tell me?" Despite his best efforts, his voice was raw and more vulnerable than he liked.

"Kiri's tale is an intriguing one, but not mine to tell. If you would learn any more of her motives or background, you must ask her yourself."

"She can eat her secrets," he said the force of his anger surprising him. "I want nothing to do with her. She lied to me, betrayed me. I won't play a part in any more of her games."

Feirwyn kept his gaze and voice level, but his eyes were sharp as he replied, "None of this is a game, Skerth. Not to you, not to her, not to any of us. She is your friend, same as she was yesterday and the day before, and as fiercely loyal as you have ever known her. Perhaps even more than you know. Neither accident of birth nor circumstance can change that."

The rebuke stung. Caught up in his hurt, he hadn't considered that Kiri had reasons for what she'd done beyond personal amusement, despite the fact that she'd proved herself, time and again, a worthy companion and true friend. He covered his discomfort by making a show of slicing the cheese on his platter with the point of his knife. "I didn't come to talk about Kiri," he grumbled.

"I thought not," Feirwyn replied, not unkindly. "I suspect yesterday's events have left you with many questions."

And far too many answers that I don't understand. "The assassin called you—"

"Feirwyn of Thalenthwynn Keep," Feirwyn finished. "Exile of Erados."

He watched Skerth's reaction expectantly, as though Skerth would understand the significance of Feirwyn's identity. But he merely bit into a chunk of cheese and waited patiently for Feirwyn to continue.

Feirwyn sighed and ran a hand through his hair. "My father was Lord of Thalenthwynn Keep before the Purge. Kalen—" he spat the name as though it were poison—"was our steward's eldest son. He and I were close as kin until his father sent him to the city to make his fortune. After that . . . I did not see him again until the day the Caretakers' Blades ambushed Thalenthwynn in their attempt to cut off every living branch of the royal line."

Skerth didn't have to ask what happened next. *Do you ever wish I had finished the job, Feirwyn of Thalenthwynn Keep?* Kalen had mocked, *Do you ever wish I had not let you run?*

All the time.

Now burdened with the curse of memory that had blissfully eluded him all these many years, Skerth better understood Feirwyn's cryptic response. Never having a family was easier for Skerth to bear than the crushing despair of realizing that the Caretakers had brutally destroyed everyone who might have loved him, everything he had known, everything he might have become.

The full impact of Feirwyn's words sank in then, interrupting Skerth's thoughts. He looked sharply at Feirwyn. "'Every living branch of the royal line,'" he repeated slowly, his eyes widening. "The Thalenthwynns were of royal kinship. You could claim the throne."

Feirwyn laughed softly. "I could—in theory. My father was first cousin to the king, and as far as I know, I am the only surviving bearer of royal blood. But the people of Erados do not want me, the Exile who fled his burning lands to save his own skin, for their king. They do not want just any man who bleeds from royal veins." His words were bitter. "And without popular support, I cannot back a claim against the Caretakers."

Skerth pictured the Caretakers and wondered how people could prefer them to Feirwyn, who had in a short span proved himself far more worthy of respect. "What then do the people want?"

"They want a legend," he replied softly, "a symbol. A young king to rally behind, a king they have hoped for years—even against all expectation—to restore to the throne. And Erados needs such a king. We have become a fractured state since the Caretakers came to power. Weak. If we cannot unite and strengthen our people and our borders from within, we will make easy prey for our enemies."

"How can a young king with no experience, no understanding of all this—" Skerth waved a hand to encompass the politics and all possible ramifications—"take charge of a kingdom?"

"He will not rule alone. Those of us who have toiled for so many years to bring down the Caretakers and restore the heir will remain by his side, to guide and support, in the years to come."

"Just like the Pirates, should they place an heir of their own."

Feirwyn stiffened. "With one significant difference: we labor for the good of all Erados, not just our own interests."

"But you don't deny you intend to use the throne for your own purposes."

Feirwyn studied him with a mixture of irritation, amusement, and respect. "No, I do not deny the truth. That is the game we all play, Skerth, as politicians and patriots. Some of us are more adept than others. Though I do believe the motives of those I serve are more beneficial to the people of Erados than those of either the Caretakers or the pirates." He paused. "You have an even finer understanding of politics than I presumed."

Skerth shrugged. "The rules of the streets aren't much different." Skerth took another bite and considered his next question carefully. He thought of his own half-remembered past. The loss. The struggle to fit in, to scrape together a living on the streets. His warehouse and the kids he had grown to care for as his own damaged little family. And the fire that had swept everything away and once more scattered his life to the winds. "The Caretakers murdered your family. Stole your life," he said at last, realizing as he spoke them that the question was as much for him as for Feirwyn. "You could rebuild anywhere. Why bother with all of this? Why not just leave Erados and make a new life in another place?"

"Because my history, my future—all of my hopes lie here," Feirwyn answered with a crooked smile. "I will do everything in my power for the right to return to Erados, to see my name, my lands—my honor—restored. This is my home. Now and forevermore."

The simple truth of Feirwyn's declaration touched something deep inside Skerth, and he instantly recognized the final obstacle that had prevented him from confessing his identity to Feirwyn the moment he crossed the threshold: his admission would set him on a path from which he could not return. While his life on the streets was often hard and full of risks, void of any surety of basic needs, let alone comforts, laying claim to the throne meant leaving his freedom behind. Forever afterward he would belong to the people of Erados, and they to him; already that responsibility weighed heavily on his shoulders. But neither could he leave. The city of Endelas Ortanos, heart of the land of Erados, was his city. Kiri; Jemmy, Minah, the other kids in his warehouse; all the boys, cruelly murdered; even Malyn—these were his family, such as they were, and he could no more willingly turn his back and walk away from them than he could the mother he had never known. His fate was inextricably linked to the fate of his city; for better or worse, his choice now would change them both forever.

And the choice was a difficult one, perhaps the most difficult he would ever make. But the reward, Skerth suddenly realized, was not politics or birthright, revenge, or reclaiming what was lost; the reward was the choice itself. To refuse to accept the whims of fate and carve a future with one's own hands—that was Feirwyn's decision. Whatever the outcome, he was prepared to live with the consequences, satisfied that his life was his own to master.

Skerth took a deep breath. "I think—" His throat suddenly dried up like a drop of water on a hot cobble. He cleared it, then continued in a rush, "I've finally remembered something. About the dagger."

Feirwyn tensed, leaned forward. "Go on," he said, nodding. "What do you recall?"

"Everything." He exhaled the word like a sigh. The tension in his shoulders eased. The next words took less effort, and soon the story tumbled out almost faster than he could tell it. By the time Skerth ended his tale, Feirwyn had paced a path on the carpet in front of the fireplace.

"Remarkable. All this time I have searched—but to survive all those years, on your own—" He broke off, shaking his head. "I planned to create a suitable heir. I had never actually thought to find one with a legitimate claim to the throne." He paused his pacing to study Skerth. "Are you in truth my cousin, the heir of Erados?"

He looked as though he would drop to one knee and make a vow of fealty right then and there. Embarrassed, Skerth squirmed and looked away.

"I don't know that I'm the true heir," Skerth muttered. "Or even a decoy."

Feirwyn scratched at his stubbled chin as he paced. "Do you remember your name?"

Memory teased, but remained just out of reach. Skerth shook his head, fighting back a mix of disappointment and frustration that this one, basic piece—the most important to him, to his understanding of who he was and why he was brought into the world—remained beyond reach.

Feirwyn knelt before Skerth and looked intently into his eyes. "Weyth. Does that name mean anything to you?"

Skerth closed his eyes and repeated the name, concentrating, willing memory to surface, but nothing came. "No," he sighed.

Feirwyn listed more names, none of which produced even the faintest stir. "Ah, memory is a fickle thing," he said, rising. He ran a hand through his thick hair and resumed pacing.

"I do remember one name. Tirith."

"That is familiar to me." Feirwyn looked thoughtful. "He was a courtier's son. His father was Lord of Delanthwynn Keep, I believe."

Skerth's stomach tightened. "Did he—did they kill him, too?"

Feirwyn nodded. Skerth's hatred of the Caretakers flared afresh. "Your knowledge of him places you at court. Delanthwynn served as advisor to the king. That hag you mention—do you recall her name?"

Skerth shook his head. "I only thought of her as Nurse. But the other—Jearney—"

"She could have been any number of maidservants," he said with a dismissive wave. "But this Nurse. She sounds like a woman I met a time or two on rare visits to the Palace. I was only fourteen— barely of age myself—on the night of the Purge. But when I was younger, there was a nasty old woman in charge of the nursery—" he broke off, his expression thoughtful. "Do you recall anything of your mother? The other boys?"

Skerth squeezed his eyes shut. He felt a tickle just beyond his grasp, like trying to remember a word that his tongue wouldn't form, but chasing the tickle only pushed it farther out of reach. "No," he sighed at last. "Just what I've already told you."

Feirwyn squeezed his shoulder. "You have done well, Skerth. You have given me far more than I had ever expected. One thing is certain: you must come forward on Auberdale Eve," he muttered, more to himself than Skerth. "The claim must be made before witnesses . . . after the main ceremonies, I think. . . ." As Feirwyn paced and mumbled of plans and strategies, Skerth lost track of the conversation. His mind wandered to Kiri. Where was she now? Did she feel remorse for all of the lies and pretending? Was she looking for him, even now, to make amends? Or was she lying snug in her feather bed, dreaming of nobler things? *I don't care*, he told himself, but the way his heart squeezed when he pictured her smile, the crinkle of her nose when she laughed, her endless taunting of Malyn, told a different story altogether—

Feirwyn abruptly halted, jolting Skerth to attention. "There is the problem of evidence. How will we prove your claim?" He rubbed his cheek thoughtfully, sighed. "If only we had the dagger. Something solid and real to prove the truth of your tale—"

Skerth cut him off, his mind racing. "I had a ring, once." Skerth looked up at Feirwyn. "Nurse gave it to me when she left me in the alley. She said—" he swallowed hard—"She said it was the king's."

Feirwyn perched on the arm of the chair and leaned forward. "Do you remember what it looked like?"

He shrugged again. "Plain. A pure black oval stone, smooth as satin and set in gold. The surface was dull, but when I stared at it, the stone seemed to glow deep down, like warm coals in a brazier." He paused, remembering how it had come to life when he held the ring in his hands long enough, as though it borrowed the warmth from his fingers.

"Do you know what became of it?"

Skerth nodded. "When the dark-haired woman first took me in, I offered it to her. She refused, though her man didn't." He couldn't keep the disgust out of his voice as memories of the man and his cruelty resurfaced. "He wore that ring every day while he gutted fish at the docks, boasting that he won it from a young noble dicing at the Ram and Rooster." He took a deep breath, preparing to retell the more painful parts of his story. "On the night he turned me out for good, the woman sneaked it away after he'd drunk himself gone. She caught up with me around the corner—I hadn't gone far—and returned it to me. She said it would buy me a meal or two, or another family willing to take me in for a time. And it did buy me a family, of sorts."

Skerth caught Feirwyn's gaze and held it. "I met Malyn. He introduced me to his friends, and I traded it for my place in Jax's gang."

"So where is it now?" asked Feirwyn.

In his mind's eye, Malyn flexed his fingers as their eyes met over the assassin's head. Rings of all sorts glittered on every finger. But one Malyn had always wanted, from the day he had first found Skerth sobbing outside the baker's; one he had always worn, from the moment he succeeded Jax as leader of their gang.

"Skerth," Feirwyn prompted.

He looked up, met Feirwyn's eyes. "Malyn has it."

"Malyn?" Feirwyn frowned. "Are you certain?"

Skerth gave him a crooked smile. "Saw it just this morning, when he cracked his knuckles."

"I should like to see this ring." Feirwyn nodded, satisfied. "You say it *glowed* when you held it?"

"Only a little," Skerth corrected, starting to doubt the memory. "And not all over, but deep down, in the heart of the stone. Where only I could see it if I looked hard enough, long enough."

"Did you ever notice if the stone glowed when Malyn wore it? Or the other—what was his name?"

"Jax," Skerth answered. "And no, not that I noticed. Then again, if the ring was that close, it was generally because a fist was in my face."

Feirwyn grimaced; Skerth grinned. "Don't worry. I didn't give them much opportunity."

This time, Feirwyn chuckled. "No, I don't suppose you did."

"What is it?"

"There's an old rumor that the king once received a gift from a mystic of Terrenweld, a ring that . . . well, *responded* to his touch. Ordinary when held or worn by others, the ring would flare into shards of color whenever the king wore it. The Caretakers voiced their concerns that the ring was cursed, and tried to persuade him to give it into their care, but he refused. He maintained that the ring was a strange gift, one that seemed void of purpose, but an innocent bauble, not a weapon.

"After the Purge, rumors of the ring's power to identify the heir surfaced. Those who resisted the Caretakers reasoned that a ring that reacted so powerfully to the king's touch would surely respond favorably for the heir as well. Now the rumors have run so far a-field of the truth that some believe the ring possesses the power to find the heir, while others argue that it can predict who will next rule Erados. *Alairathwynn*, they call the ring. Kingmaker."

Alairathwynn. Kingmaker. What would these same people say if they found the sacred safekeeper of their future on the hand of a street gang leader with a dubious moral code and eye-teeth filed to fangs? Skerth suppressed a laugh as he imagined their reactions.

"Does it work for decoys too?"

Feirwyn shrugged. "I do not know what powers the ring possesses. What matters is what the people believe. If there is a chance this ring will seal your claim to the throne, we should get it."

Skerth slowly nodded, rising. "Then I suppose we should visit Malyn."

Skerth guided Feirwyn through short side alleys and long, curving streets until they reached the border between Skerth and Malyn's territory.

Seryn and another of Malyn's sentries leapt to their feet, abandoning the dice that lay between them.

"I'm here for Malyn," Skerth said.

Seryn gestured for them to pass. "Go on. He's expecting you."

Skerth took comfort in the knowledge that his part in ending the assassin's reign of terror had at least earned him unmolested passage through Malyn's territory, even if the privilege was only temporary. Like Malyn's sentries, none of the scats they passed gave either of them more than a passing look, even though Feirwyn hadn't concealed either his purse or his sword.

Malyn greeted them at the door of his warehouse. He swept his cool, emotionless gaze over Skerth and nodded to Feirwyn before stepping aside to admit them. Skerth hesitated only a moment, the back of his neck prickling a warning. Too many bad memories of this place—the assassin's attack only the most recent—merged into a familiar sense of unease. But the assassin was restrained and held captive in this very warehouse, Malyn an ally. Skerth shook off the ill-feelings and crossed the threshold,

Feirwyn just behind. Malyn shooed away a handful of curious onlookers with a growled "scatter!" then followed them inside.

Malyn ushered them through emptied halls—yet another sign that the oppressive layer of fear choking the streets had finally lifted—into his private quarters. He didn't speak until he'd bolted the door. "I didn't expect to see you in Deadrun again quite so soon."

"I didn't expect such easy passage."

"Don't get used to it."

"I don't intend to."

Skerth caught the barest hint of a smile at the corner of Malyn's mouth. The delicate balance of power had shifted. They would never be friends, but the future might yet allow for mutual respect.

Malyn turned to Feirwyn. "Your sword proved useful. My scats and I won't soon forget you." He held out his hand. Skerth scanned the flash of gold on his fingers and found their quarry: even dulled by a film of dirt and lack of care, Skerth knew that ring.

Feirwyn grasped Malyn's hand. "I am proud to have stood beside you against our common enemy."

Malyn nodded and turned back to Skerth. "So. You didn't just come here for my gratitude."

"No." This, he realized, would be much harder than telling Feirwyn. He took a deep breath. "I need you to return my ring."

Malyn's expression darkened. "*Your* ring? And which would that be?"

"You know which ring, Malyn."

"Ah," he said, understanding. "This." Malyn made a show of lifting his hand and wiggling his index finger. Dirt and old blood smudged the black stone, the gold band dull and thin from long wear. Some of the more intricate details, such as the king's crest, had worn smooth. Still, now that Skerth recognized the ring for what it was, he wondered how he ever could have mistaken it for an ordinary piece of jewelry. "It isn't yours anymore, Skerth," Malyn continued. "You traded it, remember? Handed it over to Jax quicker than a blink in exchange for a spot to land on in the Deadrun at night and protection from the thrashers and skin traders."

"I did," Skerth said calmly, "and now I'll have it back."

Malyn closed his hand into a fist. "We had a truce, Rat, but that doesn't give you the right to stroll into my Deadrun and claim what's rightly mine."

"Rightly *yours*?" Skerth struggled to keep his anger in check. "That ring was mine."

Malyn's hand settled on the hilt of his dagger. Skerth stiffened, his hand moving instinctively to his own weapon.

Feirwyn stepped forward. "May I see the ring?"

Malyn's eyes flicked suspiciously from Feirwyn, to Skerth, and back again. He made no move to comply.

"There is no need for discord," said Feirwyn, his palms upraised in a gesture of peace. "Perhaps we need only see the ring a moment, and we will return it to you. Skerth mentioned the ring, and I asked him to bring me to you, to make this request. Please. For my part in halting the assassin and our mutual respect, may I examine the ring?"

Malyn narrowed his eyes at Feirwyn. "What is so special about this ring?"

Feirwyn and Skerth exchanged a look. *Go ahead,* Skerth nodded. *Tell him.* Feirwyn turned back to Malyn. "If we trust you with this knowledge, you must swear never to reveal it to anyone."

Malyn straightened, looking slightly offended. "I think I've proven I can be trusted."

"Agreed. But I will have your sworn oath, all the same."

"I swear," Malyn said, looking a bit unsettled by the gravity of the moment. "By my life, the Deadrun, and all I hold dear, I swear I will take your secret to my grave." He cast Skerth a curious look. "Now what's all the fuss?"

"We have reason to believe that this ring once belonged to the King of Erados. If we could but see it a moment, we would have our answer."

Malyn laughed scornfully. "The King of Erados! Who do you think you are, Rat? The lost heir? You know, I've put up with a lot of tricks from you over the years, but this has got to be one of your best."

The laughter died out; a thick silence settled between them. "You do not jest," Malyn said at last, incredulous.

Feirwyn nodded. "We believe Skerth is either the heir himself or one of his royal decoys. Either way, he has a stronger claim to the throne than the Caretakers."

Malyn studied Skerth. "All this time, the assassin was looking for you?"

"Or someone like him," Feirwyn agreed. "Someone who could remove the Caretakers once and for all."

Skerth shifted uncomfortably under his scrutiny. "Will you just hand over the ring so we can have a look?"

Reluctantly, Malyn slid the ring from the middle finger of his right hand and held it in his palm. He studied it for a moment, his expression unreadable, before he dropped it into Feirwyn's outstretched hand.

Feirwyn cleaned it with a corner of his tattered cloak and held it in a beam of sunlight that slanted in through the window. He turned it over in his hands, rubbed at a splotch of dirt that obscured the engraved sigil of a wyvern on one side of the wide gold band, squinted at the stone. Skerth shifted closer, watched for it to flare to life, to glow, to do something extraordinary, but it remained dull and black, no more special than any of the other rings that Malyn wore.

His inspection complete, Feirwyn slid the ring onto his right ring finger and held his hand up to the light. The ring, which had seemed to fit Malyn perfectly before, fit Feirwyn's long, slender hand just as well.

"The last time I saw this ring it was on my uncle's hand," Feirwyn said, his eyes on the ring, his voice far away.

"So that's it, then? The old king's ring?" Malyn looked skeptical. "It doesn't look like much."

"Indeed," Feirwyn said, turning a thoughtful eye on Skerth, whose throat suddenly felt dry and tight. "Here. Let us see if the rumors of Alairathwynn's powers are true."

Feeling bare and awkward in front of Malyn, Skerth squirmed and shifted his feet. "I don't know—"

"Quit your fishwifing and put on the ring." Malyn crossed his arms over his chest and glared.

Feirwyn removed the ring and handed it to Skerth, who turned it over in his hand, tested its weight. Such a simple bauble, really, to carry so much responsibility. All he had to do was slide it on his finger and he would know.

Feirwyn nodded his encouragement. Malyn stared down at the ring with a mixture of anticipation and dread. Their eyes met; then he, too nodded.

Skerth took a deep breath and slid the ring onto his finger.

His body heat warmed the cold metal. Skerth held out his hand, spread his fingers wide.

"See? Nothing—"

Warm became hot—almost too hot. The band contracted until the ring had sized to fit his finger.

"What is it?" Feirwyn asked. "Speak!"

"I don't know. It's . . . hot."

The three leaned over Skerth's outstretched hand. Deep within the heart of the smooth black stone, a faint glow stirred. As it gained in intensity, the glow highlighted nuances and facets within the stone that glimmered with new color, lighting the dark, plain stone in rainbow shades of blue, red, green and violet.

Skerth's knees weakened; his hand shook. He lifted his eyes from the stone to find both Malyn and Feirwyn watching him. Malyn's eyes widened; Feirwyn's expression was a whirlwind of emotions: awe, fear, elation and a deep sadness.

"So what does this mean?" Malyn asked, eyeing Skerth warily. He looked as though he really didn't want to hear the answer.

"It means that the blood of the king runs in Skerth's veins."

"Then why didn't the ring work for you?" Skerth asked Feirwyn. "You are blood-kin to the old king."

Malyn glanced at Feirwyn in surprise. "What are you talking about? And how is this scat I've known most of my life related to the old king? Will you two please talk sense and tell me what is going on here?"

Feirwyn briefly recounted the story of his family's murder during the Purge and subsequent exile. When he had finished, Skerth told his own story.

"Skerth is right," Malyn said when they had finished. "If what you say is true, the ring should've reacted to you."

Feirwyn looked thoughtful. "Then perhaps the charm is not related to blood, but magicked to reveal the succession in some other way. Regardless, the ring validates Skerth's connection to the throne. With this proof, the Caretakers must accept him as the returned heir."

"So you're going to be King of Erados," Malyn said to Skerth.

Skerth shrugged, uncomfortable. "I guess."

Without warning, Malyn punched him in the shoulder—hard. Skerth looked up to find him grinning. "Somehow I always knew you didn't belong down here."

When he found his voice, Skerth replied, "Neither do you." And he meant it.

"What happens now?" asked Malyn, turning to Feirwyn.

"We clear the way for Skerth to claim his right to Erados and bring down the Caretakers." He studied Malyn. "We could use your help, if you are willing. Give us the ring and join us in this greater cause, Malyn. It is an honorable fight, and one that will change your life and the lives of those who follow you for the better. Forever."

"So Rat here becomes a king. What's in it for me and my boys?"

"A better life away from the streets," Feirwyn answered. "A place. A purpose. I cannot offer you treasures, but I can offer you this much: if we succeed in bringing down the Caretakers and placing Skerth on the throne, you—and anyone else who fights at our side—will never have to run the streets again."

Skerth held his breath while Malyn considered this. Finally, a slow smile spread across the older boy's face. "I'll do my part. I can bring some of the others in, too. Just tell me what you need us to do."

Feirwyn nodded; Skerth blew out the breath he hadn't realized he was holding. "Then we have much to discuss, and little time," Feirwyn said, moving to the table. "But if all goes well, by tomorrow evening Erados will have a crowned king once more."

Chapter Twenty-Five: Change in Plans

Malyn's fist banged the table in Feirwyn's quarters, nearly upsetting a full mug of ale. "There has to be another way!"

Feirwyn sighed and ran a hand through his hair. "We have tread this path a hundred times—"

"—and always it ends with my boys shouldering most of the risk! We've already lost enough to this war we didn't even know we were fighting."

Malyn pushed away from the table and stalked to the window. Skerth rose to follow, but Feirwyn stopped him with a look. Taut ropes of muscle corded Malyn's neck and shoulders; his eyes were narrowed to slits, his lips pressed thin. They waited while Malyn stared outside. Skerth followed his gaze, seeing neither the glimmer of moonlight silvering the cobbles of the back alley beneath the window, nor the string of freshly-laundered garments hanging between the Swine and its nearest neighbor, but Feirwyn's sketch of the layout of the palace courtyard on Auberdale Eve, now only scant hours away.

Sketh suppressed a weary sigh. They had worked this plan for two solid days and had come no nearer to a resolution. In truth, the more Feirwyn emphasized the necessity of using Malyn and his scats to distract the Staves and Blades outside the gates, the harder Malyn dug in his heels about participating. Rightfully, he questioned the risks to limb and life. Unfortunately, they had few options.

Malyn sighed and rubbed his eyes. "A handful of street scats against the Caretakers' own trained soldiers."

"Positioned advantageously to substantially reduce the risk of harm to any of you," Feirwyn added. He rose and joined Malyn at the window. "We need you, Malyn. The people need you."

"Fine," Malyn said at last, turning to face Skerth. "But if we live through this, I expect to never go hungry again. Whether you end up king or not."

"Done," Feirwyn said, clapping Malyn on the shoulder. "Now. You know what to do?"

He nodded. "If there's nothing else we need to discuss, I'll be off. I need to call my captains, pull together some weapons. Some kind of armor too, if we can manage." He started toward the door; then, spying a crust of leftover bread on the table, detoured to snatch it. "You'd better be worth all this fuss, Rat."

"I hope so," Skerth muttered.

A gentle knock sounded at the door before a key turned and it creaked open. Nirue peeked around the edge. "The hour grows late. May I enter?"

"Of course, my lady," Malyn said with a sweeping bow, his tone shifting instantly from harsh to honey.

Skerth covered a laugh with a loud cough. Malyn had taken a fancy to Lady Nirue. Skerth had already pointed out privately to Feirwyn that if Nirue had asked Malyn to lead his boys against the Caretakers, he would've agreed without a moment's hesitation. But Feirwyn adamantly refused to even consider bringing Nirue into his plans, believing it best to keep her innocent of all but the most basic involvement.

"If I am taken," Feirwyn had told him gravely, "I would have her live, and live long. To do so, she must deny any connection to me and say truthfully that she never knew my intentions for you." He refused to speak further on the subject of Nirue, and after she denied his requests to leave him and return to her family home, sent her away every time Malyn arrived to discuss strategy.

"Please allow me to escort you inside," Malyn said, offering his arm to Nirue.

She suppressed a smile and accepted. He led her to the couch, awkwardly settled her onto a cushion, then rose, chest puffed like a sea songbird.

"I will take my leave of you now," Malyn said with an ill-fitting formality. "Evening to you, my lady. Feirwyn. Skerth." After granting another low bow to the only person in that room who mattered, Malyn let himself out, shifting aside so Emme, only a few steps behind her mistress, could squeeze past into the room.

Emme and Skerth acknowledged one another with a nod before she made her way to Nirue and dipped into a pretty curtsy. "Have you need of me, my lady?"

"No, sweetling," Nirue said with a gentle smile. "Rest now. We must rise early on the morrow."

Emme curtsied again and removed to the far side of the room to fetch her pallet and blankets.

Feirwyn went to Nirue's side and drew her into his arms.

Feeling like an intruder into their privacy, Skerth rose and went to Emme.

"How do you fare here?" he asked.

Emme didn't look at him as she shook out one of her blankets. "Very well. Lady Nirue treats me gently. I have a warm pallet at night, food in my belly, and little to do." She gave him a wry smile. "To be honest, I'm almost bored."

Skerth suppressed a stab of jealousy that she had moved into such a soft life in so short a time. "I'm glad," he said. "What will you do after tomorrow?"

She shrugged. "Who knows what lies ahead?" She jutted her chin at Feirwyn and Nirue, who stood with heads bent close together, foreheads nearly touching, lips only a breath apart. "If all goes well, Feirwyn's name and honor will be restored. They'll marry. With any luck, I'll serve as Lady Nirue's handmaiden until I'm an old crone."

"And if all doesn't go well?"

She shrugged again. "I've looked after myself a long time. I'm more resourceful than I seem." Her eyes met his, and, just as he had in the ship's galley, he glimpsed something more behind Emme's soft expression, a glint of iron will, vanished so quickly he almost thought he'd imagined it.

"Come, Skerth. Emme," Nirue said then, disentangling from Feirwyn's embrace with flushed cheeks. She smoothed her hair and strode quickly toward them. "To bed with you both. Tomorrow rises early."

Skerth helped Emme spread both of their pallets before the hearth. While Emme went to assist Nirue behind the changing screen at the opposite end of the room, Feirwyn came over to Skerth and clapped him on the shoulder.

"The plan is sound. Tonight you sleep a boy, tomorrow a king." Skerth looked down at his feet, shifting awkwardly beneath the pride in Feirwyn's gaze and voice.

"I wish I shared your certainty," Skerth said. "I imagine I won't be the only 'heir' staking my claim tomorrow night."

"But only you have proof," Emme pointed out, turning to give Skerth a reassuring look.

"What if it doesn't work?"

"The ring is yours," Feirwyn said firmly. "It will not fail you." He squeezed Skerth's shoulder. "All will go well. Sleep well, my young, brave friend."

"And you," Skerth replied, his voice betraying his uncertainty.

Later, as he lay wide awake on his pallet listening to Emme's breathing and Feirwyn's rumbling snore, Skerth wished—as he had so many times since his revelation in the tunnels—that he could truly be sure of who and what he was.

But on the morrow, whether decoy or street scat or king, he would lay claim to a kingdom.

Hard pressure clamped against Skerth's nose and mouth, jolting him awake. He gasped, but only managed to suck in a nose full of air tainted by salt and old sweat. His eyes snapped opened, but he saw only shapes and shadows. He kicked and struggled; arms like an iron vise held him tight. Where was he? What was happening?

"Hush now, scat." The unfamiliar voice dissolved into a wet cough. The reek of sour wine and old onion permeated the barrier of warm flesh smothering Skerth's mouth; he gagged.

"Watch it there, he's gonna spew!" hissed another voice. The hand over Skerth's mouth slackened briefly, then pressed even harder.

"Then he'll eat it," warned the first voice. "Got my orders from the Captain herself, and I'll not be the one to let this little fishy off the hook."

Captain. The pirates had found him.

Skerth fought to breathe, to calm, to think. He closed his eyes and forced his other senses alert. The soft straw pallet where he'd lain the night before still cushioned his back; he flexed his hand and pushed his fingers into the blanket Feirwyn and Nirue had given him. Across the room he heard shuffling, the thrashing of feet, angry grunts and sounds of struggle. A slap—a woman's muffled cry of pain. *Nirue.* Skerth fought against a wave of fear. *Emme. But where is Feirwyn?*

214

"Keep quiet, lass!" growled a voice across the room, "and we won't have to harm none o' you."

"Get 'im out!" hissed another. "The women, too."

Skerth struggled in earnest as a sack came over his head, was bound tightly around his neck. He tried to free his arms, to kick his legs, but his efforts only earned him a hard slap across his kneecaps. He swallowed a yelp.

"Settle, you," said the pirate keeping a tight hold on his chest and arms. "Or I'll gut you like a sea lizard, orders or no!"

No you won't. Skerth redoubled his efforts to get away. He bucked and kicked, managed to wriggle free his right arm, heard a satisfying grunt of pain and surprise as his fist caught one of the pirates across the chin.

"Get 'im down!" the man roared.

Skerth's head exploded in pain. The world went dark.

Rocking. Creaking. The splash of ocean waves lapping against sea-seasoned wood.

Skerth groaned and started to roll onto his side, stopping instantly when pain splintered through his head and the contents of his stomach lurched in time to the waves crashing outside his small window. He fell back onto his pallet and took several deep, slow breaths to try and think through the pain.

He knew without cracking an eye open that he lay in the same wooden bed he had slept on when he had last enjoyed Captain Gem's hospitality. Alive, and—save the raging headache and accompanying nausea—unharmed. And to his mixed relief and dismay, his memories had not suffered from the blow to his head. He still knew both who he was and who he might have been, as well as what the dawning day meant—would mean—for not just him, but for the people of Erados.

He also remembered flashes of the night before. Waking to chaos. Nirue and Emme struggling. Losing consciousness, then drifting in and out of awareness as the three of them were forced into the back of a cart and carried off. He had feared for the women the most. He knew the pirates wouldn't harm him if they intended to use him on Auberdale Eve, but he wasn't sure about the women until he'd heard the pirates mumbling to one another about holding them as surety for his compliance. His last thought before awakening on the ship was of relief.

But dawn had brought new fears and anxieties. The pirates would hold Nirue and Emme hostage to ensure his cooperation, but what then? And what had become of Feirwyn? Not once the night before had Skerth heard either word or blade of him, and he doubted he would allow anyone to touch his beloved Nirue without laying down his own life first. Had the pirates slaughtered him as he slept?

And what of Malyn and the rest? Malyn and his scats would keep to their part of the plan and filter into the crowds amassing inside the palace courtyard for the Auberdale Eve ceremony. But what would they do when neither Feirwyn nor Skerth appeared to lay claim to the throne and oust the Caretakers? Would they assume that the plan had run afoul, or would they believe Skerth a coward who had turned aside at the last moment and fled?

Other, darker thoughts chased these, which he scarcely acknowledged before shoving them back into the dark corners of his mind, only to take them out and re-examine them one by one until his head pounded and his stomach churned so hard he could no longer think. Eventually he sank into a troubled rest, tormented by thoughts of what had happened, what would happen, and what might never come to pass.

Chapter Twenty-Six: *The Scarlet*

The door slammed open. Skerth bolted upright out of a dreamless sleep, disoriented and groping for his missing knife.

"Up, scat!" growled Xor. He tossed a pile of clothes onto the bed. "Wash. Dress. Then thump the door and we'll get some food in you and do something about that tangle of filth on your head." He shifted aside and Emme entered, shoving a heavy tub of water before her. Skerth tried to catch her eye, but she kept her gaze downcast and did not linger once she'd completed her task. His heart squeezed to see her returned to servitude. Had they punished her harshly? He didn't see any obvious marks, but sometimes the worst kind of abuse never broke the skin. And why hadn't she looked at him? Did she blame him for her recapture?

"—you listening, boy?" Xor's rising anger broke through Skerth's thoughts. "Move! Now!"

Skerth rolled onto his feet and made for the tub.

"Make it quick." He ushered Emme out, then shut the door and bolted it from the outside.

Skerth's mind raced as he washed, his thoughts sifting through every possibility for a way out of this latest predicament. But even if he could free himself from his cabin and make his way abovedeck, he had no idea where to go next. He couldn't take the same path he'd used before; the tide had come in, covering the sandbar and deepening the waters between the pirate's cove and land. He couldn't swim well enough to risk jumping ship and breaking for the shore, either. And in any case, he didn't want to leave Nirue and Emme to the pirates' whim. No doubt he could find a way to communicate with Emme, but he had no idea what had become of Nirue, and he would take no chances with her safety.

A pounding at the door. Xor's impatient shout: "Come, boy! Move!"

Skerth quickly dried and reached for the clothes. The shirt he tugged over his head was smooth—silk, he guessed, or something equally fine—and white as a summer sea-crow. He tucked it into stiff, new black breeches and pulled on a deep blue velvet tunic trimmed in gold thread around the hem, neck, and shoulders. The clothes were finely made, the best he'd ever worn, and fit perfectly. Fae, the pirates' Needle, had done fine work.

Despite his predicament, he couldn't suppress a surge of excitement upon sight of the polished black boots. He'd never owned a pair of boots—or shoes, for that matter—that hadn't pinched or squeezed or blistered his feet, and never had they come to him unworn. Most were riddled with holes, unfit for any but the most desperate. All were discarded, scavenged or stolen. More often than not, he'd never worn shoes at all.

These boots, though, had been made just for him, of supple black leather polished to a shine. They cupped his ankles and calves like a second skin. Nothing pinched or rubbed. He wiggled his toes, rocked back and forth, and felt a rush of pleasure at the feel of cushion between his feet and the hard wooden planks beneath. These were *his* boots. *His* clothes. He hadn't had to fight for them, steal them, or drag them from a rotting body. And if all went well on this important day, he would never have to go without such small comforts again.

All at once, Skerth realized the truth of his situation: he'd focused so much energy on fretting over his capture and planning escape that he'd forgotten the true key to his freedom was—himself. Feirwyn wanted an heir. The pirates wanted an heir. And, if Feirwyn was to be believed, the people wanted an heir. Their goals aligned, even if their expectations after the coronation differed. All he had to do was make it through the day, through the ceremony, and remove governance of Erados from the hands of the Caretakers. Whether he traveled in the company of pirates or Feirwyn, Malyn, and those who followed them no longer mattered. As long as he represented the hope of an heir for one faction or the other, Skerth still had a chance to make his claim. Afterward he would worry about how to free himself—and Erados—from the pirates' fist.

Xor did not need to knock again. Skerth rose, squared his shoulders, and thumped at the door.

"I'm ready!" he shouted, feeling the truth of his words at his very core. Let the day bring what fate decreed.

*　　*　　*

"Be still!" Xor growled as he tugged a comb through Skerth's hair. He snagged a tangle; Skerth bit his lip to suppress a cry of pain. He'd learned quickly enough to keep quiet. While the pirates didn't want to mar their heir, Xor wasn't above bruising a few ribs or leaving a mark where it wouldn't show.

Gem leaned back against the table in the pirates' common room, arms crossed over her chest as she supervised Skerth's grooming. Behind her sat Dark Pieroth, nursing a sturdy mug of ale.

"Perhaps you should just take a knife to it all," she suggested.

"No," Pieroth grunted. "He needs the hair. It's just the color of the old king's, and his brats besides. Every one of 'em gold as the king's coffers."

"Only one brat," Gem reminded him. "The rest were the royal decoys."

Pieroth waved dismissively. "Decoys. Heirs. All the same, now, and all of a purpose. Who knows if the true heir didn't die afore the end of his first year?" He paused for a deep draught and dragged a dirty sleeve across his mouth. "Heir's an heir, I say, and this one's likeness to the old king is uncanny."

Gem tilted her head as she studied Skerth. "You think so?"

Pieroth nodded. "Met the old king a handful o' times. Decent man. Smart. And this one—" he tilted his mug at Skerth—"looks like as kin."

"All the better for his claim," said Xor.

"*Our* claim," Gem corrected. She pushed away from the table to circle Skerth and Xor. "Isn't that right, Skerth? We'll provide you a kingdom to rule and luxury beyond your imagining. You'll have fine clothes. Jewels. Horses. Women. Whatever you like. The world that tried to crush you every day of your miserable life will become the source of your every amusement." She bent until her face was only inches away. Her voice dropped to a low caress. "And all you have to do is let us whisper in your ear. Advise you. Such a small price for such a mighty gift."

Skerth's anger and disgust swelled. "And for such a 'small price' I trade my freedom for a life of servitude."

Gem smacked him hard across the back of his head. Snagged by a particularly stubborn tangle, the comb flew from Xor's hand and skittered across the floor to land at the feet of a surprised

Emme, who had just emerged from the galley door carrying a tray laden with meat, cheeses and bread.

"Pick it up, lass, and give it here," Xor snapped.

"She's your kin," Skerth snarled, glaring at Gem. "You shouldn't treat her like a common tavern scut."

"She doesn't," Emme said. She stepped over the comb and made her way to her mother's side, where she set the tray on the table with a clatter. "Unless she's got a use for me."

Gem kissed her daughter on the forehead and ruffled her hair; Emme beamed. Skerth's stomach churned.

No.

"You've done well, love," Gem cooed to Emme before pushing away from the table to walk a tight circle around Skerth. "You're a trusting one, aren't you? And a little too quick. I knew you'd find a way to flee. You were no trouble to replace—scats like you are salt to the wind, and I've no doubt I would've found a tenfold more willing to abide my plan. But you knew too much to just set free. So I charged Emme to keep you in hand. Learn your plans. And if necessary, end you."

She stopped in front of Skerth. "But when we heard whisper that the ring of the old Regenthwynn king had surfaced, the winds changed again. And I knew Emme wouldn't fail us."

Skerth glared at Emme.

"You made my task all too easy," she gloated. "Boys are such fools for a pretty face and a skirt." She punctuated her words by batting her eyelashes and forcing her lips into a comely pout.

"You're a fool if you think she won't turn against you as soon as one of her schemes requires it," he retorted.

She flinched; her expression hardened. Looking as she did now, her blue eyes cold and her chin lifted in a mutinous stare, he wondered that he had ever thought her pretty or believed her in need of caretaking. She had the full look of her mother now: strong, stone-stubborn, and villainous. He should have known. Emme had turned so easily, had engineered their entire escape. He should have known when none of Gem's crew gave chase. He should have guessed. . . .

"The Captains' Council," Skerth said slowly, "The fighting. It was all a falsehood, wasn't it. A convenient cover for our escape."

Gem smiled. "As I said. You're smart for a gutterscut." But Skerth caught something in her expression, her voice, gone in the blink of an eye, that told him the pirates' brawl wasn't all just a show for his benefit. He recalled Janewyn trying to take them outside the ship and knew that not everything had run according to Gem's plan. The idea of Gem in full control of the heir—and their fates—didn't sit well with all in her power. The knowledge gave him hope.

"So where is it, boy?" Gem prompted, hand outstretched. "Where is that ring that's going to seal your claim and change all of our fates?"

"Ask her," he nodded to Emme, taking great satisfaction in watching her smug smile melt into doubt.

Gem turned to her. "Well?"

Emme hesitated for several heartbeats before admitting, "The Exile has it."

"What?" The Pirate Queen's smile faded.

A note of desperation crept into Emme's voice at her mother's hard stare. "I couldn't swipe it, Ma! He had it on him all the time! Wore it, slept with it—I couldn't get near the thing without waking him and setting them all off!"

"So Lord Feirwyn still has the ring."

Emme looked away. "Yes," she whispered.

Gem's eyes snapped to Xor. "Where is he?"

"Gone. I sent a handful of hounds to catch his scent, but they haven't yet returned."

Skerth's heart leapt. *He's not dead.* And he still had the ring. Which meant—

"He'll be at the ceremony," Gem said firmly, arriving at the same conclusion as Skerth. "He'll want his heir. And his woman." She stooped to pick up the comb, then tossed it to Xor without turning. "Finish with that hair. Crop it close if you have to, just be done. I'll see to the woman." To Emme she said, "Ready yourself. We leave within the hour." Without another word, she disappeared through the galley doors.

Xor resumed torturing Skerth's scalp. Emme, freed from her subservient role, sat on the table and crossed her arms over her chest to watch. Skerth attempted to look anywhere but at her—

221

which was difficult given that he was rooted to a stool and she had perched directly in front of him, less than two good strides away.

They remained thus for some time, the only sound Xor's comb ripping through Skerth's hair, until he could stand it no longer.

"What do you want, Emme? To gloat?"

"No," she said, her voice surprisingly meek. "I want to apologize."

He jerked his head up to look at her, expecting the same satisfied expression, the triumph and pleasure in her gaze. Instead, she looked contrite. Wistful, even.

"Head down!" Xor didn't wait for him to comply; he grabbed hold of Skerth's skull and aimed his face to the floor.

"I want you to know—" After a long pause, the rest came out in fits and starts. "It wasn't all fakery, Skerth. Not everything." He heard her take a deep breath. "I like you. From the night they brought you on deck, unconscious and shivering, I knew there was something right about you. And for what it's worth—my mum and her crew, the other pirates, the merchants and black traders—they could have their pick of scats. But I wanted it to be you." He heard a rustle of skirts and creak of wood as she slid from the table to the floor. "You'll make a fine king, Skerth."

Her quickly retreating footsteps spared him the necessity of a reply and left him to the mixed torment of Xor's comb and the confusion of his thoughts, neither of which promised much peace in the hours to come.

Once Xor had pronounced his hair "fit enough for the King of Scats," Pieroth bound Skerth's hands behind him with a thick coil of rope and half-led, half-dragged him abovedeck. Gem and Emme awaited them, flanking Nirue. Skerth's heart leapt to see her, despite her disheveled hair and clothes and the bruise blossoming across her right cheek. She held her hands bound before her, wrists already chafed from the night's confinement. She caught his eye and flashed him a weak smile to reassure him that she was well. He nodded and forced a smile in return, but inwardly his anger boiled to see her managed thus. At the end of the day, if Feirwyn did not kill them, Skerth surely would.

Gem swept Skerth with her gaze from head to toe and back again, then gave Xor a nod of approval. "Well done. He looks a better fit now."

Skerth held his compliments. In sharp contrast to Nirue's appearance, both Gem and Emme were beauties to behold outwardly, false as a merchant's vow on the inside. The Pirate Queen wore a fitted deep green, gold-embroidered velvet tunic-coat that flared at the hips and fell to just below her knees, highlighting her curves and concealing the black leather sword belt slung across her hips. Cream silk sleeves belled to cuffs at her wrists, where several jeweled bangles rested, and the mid-thigh high black boots she wore over black leather breeches were polished to a shine. She had worked her thick raven hair into an intricate coil that draped over her shoulder. Black kohl emphasized her green eyes. A beauty for certain, but one that held no attraction for Skerth.

Beside her, Emme seemed the light to her mother's dark, an innocent maid with fresh-scrubbed cheeks and dark hair curled into coils that piled atop her head and twisted over her shoulders. Unlike her mother, she needed no jewels in her hair and on her fingers; dressed in a pretty blue gown that brought out the color in her eyes and with white flowers pinned in her hair, she was the image of youthful beauty. His heart pinched at the sight of her, and for a moment he wondered what might have been had she not turned false. But her smile quirked into a sneer, so like her mother's, and both the thought and the feeling fled.

Gem caught his gaze and gave him a cold smile. "Do you like what you see?" She reached over and shoved Emme forward. "You can have her just after sundown. Consider her a gift for your willing participation in our scheme."

Emme's smile faded as her mother's words sank in. Gem laughed. "Did you think your part in this was done, my sweetling?" She pinched Emme's cheek hard enough to make the girl wince. "I imagine our little prince fancies he can work his way out of our web come morning. But by then he'll be king, you'll be wedded and bedded, and we'll be true kin to the crown."

The color first drained from Emme's face, then burst into a scarlet flush as her eyes moved from her mother to Skerth and the true extent of her mother's own betrayal became clear. She tried to catch Skerth's gaze, but he looked away, fearing she would see his anger and disgust. *Not her.* Once he might have fancied Emme, but now a different face came to mind—mismatched eyes, a wild crop of white-blonde hair, a mischievous smile. He shook his head to clear it, tried not to wonder what Kiri would say, what she would do if she knew what the pirates had in store.

"We will have plenty of time to discuss the wedding on the way to the Palace," Gem said lightly. "Come along, my prince. Your city awaits." She turned, beckoning, and Xor and Pieroth shoved Skerth after her down the ramp that led to the network of floating catwalks below.

The hour was still early; the morning sunlight hadn't yet pierced the thick fog that dampened the air and curled around their ankles as they walked. The poor visibility made Skerth uneasy; the catwalks were narrow and bobbed a bit with every move, forcing him to stay close to his captors and follow in their steps. Fortunately, they stopped not far down the docks, and the six of them silently loaded into a rowboat. Xor and Pieroth tied their captives' roped wrists to an iron ring on the floor of the boat before turning to the oars. When they cast off, the fog muted the heavy slap of oars against ocean and the cove retained an eerie stillness that sent a shiver down Skerth's spine.

For a long while, the rhythm of the oars on water, the creaking of wood, the cry of gulls and sea-hens were the only sounds to break the silence. Skerth took them all in, attempting to use them to orient their position, to no avail. He wondered how Xor and Pieroth found their direction in the thick fog, and guessed they must have the use of some kind of sea magic, as neither their rhythm nor their direction wavered.

It wasn't until the sky darkened, as though a shadow passed across the sun, that Skerth had some idea of their location. *The cliffs,* he realized. *Of course.* The pirates couldn't walk their prisoners through the Lower City bound as they were, and wouldn't take the chance of coming upon either Feirwyn or one of Skerth's many compatriots from the street. The royal docks farther south, beyond the wedge, were out of the pirates' reach; any one of them daring to tie up and step from their little rowboat would be killed on sight. Pirates were a necessary evil among the wealthy merchants and citizens of the Royal Quarter; all knew of their existence, relied upon their lower prices and special imports, yet none would hesitate

224

to turn them in for traitors at a moment's opportunity. So Xor and Pieroth carried them straight across the cove to the wedge itself where, presumably, tunnels like Skerth's ran down to the sea, providing easy access to both the upper and lower cities.

Once they passed through a series of choppy, gut-churning waves and the sea calmed; when the light dimmed to darkness; when the old, familiar scent of moist rock and close air enveloped them, Skerth knew: they had entered the tunnels. *His* tunnels still, yet another arm that reached far beneath the city. For a moment he tensed, recalling the rats and spiders, the bat guano, the old bones and nameless creatures he had seen when at last he brought light into this world, but the tension didn't hold. Even stronger than the presence of things unseen were his memories of how the darkness had always welcomed him when the world did not; and despite the strange irony that he found security in a place that should hold only fear and loss, he knew that this, more than anywhere else, was his home.

The knowledge empowered him. He gathered the strength of the ancient rock, closed his eyes, and allowed his other senses to dominate. The steady creak and splash of the oars intensified, in time with the men's low grunts of effort. Emme's breathing shallowed and came faster; clearly she didn't find as much solace in dark, closed spaces as he. Nirue's breathing remained even and controlled: there was fear there, but she would not give her captors the satisfaction of revealing it. Beyond them, he picked out smaller sounds—the flutter of bat wings, the whistle of wind through the small crevices that peppered the caverns, the steady drip of water. And deeper still: whispers of conversation, as though the walls themselves could not keep the silence.

"To port, men," Gem said. She spoke softly, but the sound startled Skerth nonetheless.

Pieroth steadied his oar, and the boat obediently nosed to the left. The whispers increased in volume. Words took shape, then fragments of sentences. Muffled footsteps. The rustle of cloth and scrape of wood.

The walls weren't speaking, he realized. There were people here in the dark, more than he could easily count without benefit of light. A whole network, keeping the dark, preserving the silence, carrying on activities requiring both. Strange, he had never before considered that others knew of—and used—the tunnels. For so many years they had been his secret. His safe place. But there was a whole world here he'd never imagined existed, a city beneath the city, defiant of the class and physical boundaries aboveground that separated the Royal Quarter and the Lower City so completely. He wondered who else knew of and defied the boundaries to travel freely beneath the divided city of Endelas Ortanos.

"Hood them," Gem ordered. The men pulled up the oars. Xor jostled Skerth as he fumbled for something at his belt. An instant later, a rough sack tugged over Skerth's head. He struggled instinctively at first, then forced himself to calm. They wouldn't harm him. They couldn't risk it at this late stage; they had no one else to put forward.

Just across from him, Nirue's gasp of surprise became a muffled cry as they hooded her as well. But she, too settled and quieted immediately. Skerth's respect and appreciation for her swelled. Though he didn't know Nirue well and Feirwyn had always protected her fiercely, her will and mind were strong. She would not easily break, nor would she sacrifice him to save herself. These thoughts bolstered his hope.

They resumed their journey through the tunnels, the bustle of activity around them growing in volume and number as they traveled. Skerth couldn't be sure of when exactly he noticed, but gradually light made its way through the folds of the sack. Torchlight, he guessed from the new smell of smoke and pitch mingling in with the others. Soon afterward, the boat bumped onto a gravelly shore. Hands reached to steady it. Xor and Pieroth set aside their oars, unbound Skerth from the iron ring of the boat, and dragged him ashore.

"Well met, Captain." A new voice, husky and low, as though unused to speaking above a whisper.

"Are the preparations complete?"

"As you requested. But there is one . . . complication." Skerth could almost feel the man bracing for a blow. "The Caretakers have closed the gates to the Lower City."

"What? But that's not—they've never—" After a pause she resumed, her voice calm and cold as a mountain storm. "Why?"

"Word of trouble in the Lower City reached the Caretakers' ears, and they'll have none of it on their festival day. They shut the gates to keep the streets safe, they say, but whispers are they fear a potential heir will rise from the slums to steal their throne. Either way, there's none in or out until after dawn tomorrow. They've posted guards on both sides and sentries on the Wedge."

Silence while Gem considered this. Then, "We'll shift our plan. Take the Altwynn tunnel and come out just before the Palace gates. We won't be able to pull as many men through, but it'll have to do. If our boy cooperates, it won't make a difference."

Another surge of hope. Fewer men to fight for the pirates' cause, fewer men to shield Gem when Skerth denounced her. The odds favored him with every passing moment.

His victory was short-lived, as he realized how badly the closure of the Lower City gates would impact his own half-hatched plans. Closed gates meant no Malyn and his boys. No Feirwyn. The plan the three of them had painstakingly drawn was all to scrap; and if they couldn't get through to the Auberdale Eve ceremony, then he was truly alone.

"What of the Exile and the ring?" Emme asked.

"You'd better pray to the sea-gods he made his way through before the gates closed," Gem hissed. "And if he didn't, you'll need to pray the Caretakers and the people don't need proof to accept Skerth's claim. Otherwise, you'll pay dearly for your failure to snatch that little trinket when you had the chance." To her man she said, "Send for the others. Gather as many as you can and have them follow us down the Altwynn."

"Captain." The man shuffled off to do her bidding.

"Come," Gem snapped to the rest of them. "We've a longer journey than I anticipated. We'll have to speed our pace."

"Walk," Xor grunted, shoving at Skerth's back. Having no other choice left to him, Skerth obeyed, blindly heading once more into the unknown.

Chapter Twenty-Seven: To the Palace

Skerth would never forget that long, blind walk through the tunnels. Faint shreds of torchlight filtered through the thick burlap, but the heavy cloth dampened the rest of his senses to such a degree that for the first time in memory, he felt uneasy and off-balance in the tunnels. His legs burned from the steep incline, and Gem kept the pace quick despite the uneven ground; when Skerth stumbled, Xor and Dark Pieroth merely jerked him upright and dragged him onward. Twice Skerth's heart jumped to Nirue's outcry of pain; both times he fought the urge to wrestle free of the pirates and rush to her aid. Instead, he kept his breathing even and held his anger and anxiety in check. He would call upon them later, when time and strategy would make good use of them.

One foot in front of the other. One breath. Another. A stumble, righted. One step, and so on, until the flickering light steadied, brightened, and Gem at last called a halt.

"Secure them," she ordered, her voice flat and cold.

The pirates knotted a thick rope around Skerth's waist, just under his doublet, and tugged it tight. Only then did they remove the hood, leaving Skerth blinking into the white-hot blindness of the world outside the tunnel. Pain stabbed his eyes; he blinked back sudden tears and tried to focus not on what lay beyond the tunnels, but on what he *could* see: Nirue, unhooded and blinking into the glare; Emme holding a leash of rope strung from the cord around Nirue's waist; Gem's derisive sneer.

Pieroth smacked him hard on the back. "Look here, Xor! Boy's not as tough as he'd have us all believe."

Xor chuckled and shoved Skerth's other shoulder. "All the better for our plan."

Skerth's rage boiled. His hands clenched and unclenched, tightened into fists. He opened his mouth to tell them he would never allow them to manipulate him, but Nirue caught his eye and shook her head almost imperceptibly. Once more, Skerth pushed his anger down.

Immune to his inner turmoil, the pirates unbound Skerth's hands.

"You'll look and walk natural," Xor growled.

"And what if I don't?" Skerth retorted. "You won't harm me. You need me."

"True," said Gem. She flicked her wrist and pressed the blade of a dagger against Nirue's throat. "But we don't need her. Understood?"

Skerth swallowed hard as he studied Nirue's face. He saw her fear; but he saw her anger, too. And defiance. If not for her captivity, he knew he could break away. Use the rooftops, like Kiri had shown him. Find Feirwyn, Malyn, and the others. But she was here, captive, and he would not risk her life needlessly. "I understand."

Gem dropped the dagger and turned to Nirue. "You'll look the lady out for a stroll on festival day with her companions."

"Then you must allow me a moment to make myself presentable."

Gem studied her through narrowed eyes. "Agreed." She stood aside and waited as Nirue finger-combed her long dark hair, then deftly wove it into an elaborate pattern that draped over her shoulder. Gem tugged a bit of twine free of the rope securing Nirue and handed it over; then, ignoring Emme's protest, she tugged a flower from her daughter's hair and passed that to Nirue as well.

"I am ready," Nirue said, smoothing her skirts.

"Then walk," Gem ordered with a shove. She turned back to the men flanking Skerth. "Follow apace behind. If we separate, you know what to do."

"Of course, Captain," Xor said.

Gem gave a curt nod. She gripped Nirue's arm, nodded to Emme, and the three moved out of the tunnel into the streets beyond.

The men waited until they were well out of sight before nudging Skerth forward. "Now you. And we'll have no trouble, or I'll gut you, heir or not," Dark Pieroth hissed in his ear.

Ignoring the empty threat, Skerth straightened his shoulders and obediently stepped into the sunlight, a pirate to either side.

Much like the tunnels Downwedge, this one let out in the far reaches of the Royal Quarter, nearer the sea than the city proper.

Disoriented at first, Skerth couldn't fathom where in the city they had emerged. But after they'd walked apace, heading down a rough-cut stone path worn smooth with time, sea air and the passage of many boots, he realized that they had come inland through the tunnels, then walked up through the Wedge itself, emerging onto a well-concealed path that led down to the Royal Quarter. The city spread beneath them, the blue-tiled rooftops and treasured colored glass imported from Arukin shimmering in the sun, the Palace set like a glimmering white jewel in the distance. Between them flowed a river of brightly-colored citizenry, decked in flowers and finery, all headed for the Palace gates.

Traveling the tunnels had taken them the better part of the day, and the afternoon was hot and steamy; by the time they stepped down onto the cobbled streets and slid from the narrow alley into a small, cramped avenue in the older part of the Royal Quarter, Skerth's neck and face burned and his fine vest chafed at the armpits. An unpleasant damp seeped through the crisp white sleeves of his shirt. His new boots pinched. Every step he took increased the tension in his neck and shoulders. Yet he quickened his pace, eager to meet whatever fate the day would bring.

"Slow there, scat," Xor said quietly, tugging slightly on the rope leash he'd coiled around his wrist. "Look easy."

They turned onto a main avenue, flush with activity. Townspeople of all stations—merchants, nobility, servants, sailors, and everything in between—worked their way through the city in an exodus of color and noise. Hawkers called from carts selling fruits, nuts, warm meat pies, pastries, hats, flower garlands and more, competing loudly for the attention—and the coin—of the crowds. Skerth's practiced eye scanned for thieves, pickpockets, scammers and the like—and found none. His stomach twisted painfully. The Caretakers' plan had succeeded. The gates to the Lower City held fast, keeping out all those who made a living from such festivals as this, as well as any potential heirs who might rise to make their claim.

Save one.

But without Feirwyn and the ring—both presumably also stuck behind the gates—and the ragged army Malyn had mustered, who would believe that he, a simple street scat in fine clothes with a dim likeness to the old king, was last heir to a kingdom?

They turned at last onto Regenthwynn High Street, the wide, well-kept avenue that led straight to the main gates of the Palace. The crowds here thickened, pushing people together shoulder to shoulder, rendering movement nearly impossible. The sounds of revelry reached an almost unbearable riot of shouted conversations, laughter, and squeals of delight. A sea of people crowded into every available corner of the street, from where Skerth stood at the base of the hill, snaking all the way up to the gates. Trinket and treat carts crowded both sides of the streets, blocking entry to the magnificent gated residences of the wealthiest nobles, merchants, and artisans in all of Erados. And everything—people, carts, residences and the gates themselves—were trimmed in flowers and bright ribbons to mark the day.

Skerth craned his head to search the crowd for some sign of Feirwyn, and instead found Gem, Nirue and Emme stopped just ahead. Gem, too scanned the crowd; her eye caught Skerth's and she acknowledged him with a satisfied nod. She signed to Xor, who grunted his understanding and flashed a sequence of finger signs, returning the message in a language that only they and Pieroth understood.

"This way," Xor said, pushing him toward the center of the avenue. Gem hooked Nirue's arm and pulled her in the opposite direction—back the way they had come.

Skerth locked eyes with Nirue and found his fears mirrored in her expression. He dug in his heels and tried to shrug off Xor's grip. "Where are you taking her? Why—"

"Shut, it, scat!" Pieroth punctuated his warning with a sharp dagger poke to Skerth's ribs. "Or I'll—"

Whatever he might have threatened was lost as they became aware of a subtle shift in the energy of the crowd around them. Shouts of laughter and merry greetings shifted to wondering murmurs in a ripple of quiet that began with those nearest the Palace gates and fanned downhill through the gathered crowd. Skerth, Xor and Dark Pieroth all strained to see what had caused the disturbance. Pieroth, the shortest of the three, stretched as high as he could; Skerth, taller by a head, took a perverse pleasure in thrusting his shoulder in the way of the pirate's view.

"What's happening there, boy?" Pieroth smacked him on the back.

Skerth ignored his curses and empty threats, focusing instead on the crowd rapidly parting to either side to clear passage for a score or more of riders. They drove their horses hard and fast, heedless of who or what they trampled in their path. Shouts of outrage, fear and warning heralded their advance. Not far ahead of Skerth, a tall merchant turned back to shout, "Make way for the Blades, coming fast! Make way or they'll ride us down!"

The crowd surged in every direction as the people panicked and made for both sides of the streets at once. No one seemed to know where to go or how to get there. Flowers fell like rain and smashed together into a slippery pulp. Children screamed. People fell, were yanked to their feet, fell again.

Xor and Pieroth tugged Skerth in two different directions.

"She told us to keep to this side," Pieroth shouted, dragging Skerth to the right.

"Plans changed. We need to get back to Gem." Xor pulled him to the left.

The cobbles beneath their feet vibrated to the beat of the horses' hooves, thundering closer at an unbroken pace.

"This way!" Pieroth bellowed over the din.

Just ahead, people shoved and elbowed their way to either side of the street. Skerth stared up the center of a widening gap that left him standing directly in the path of the riders. Sunlight flashed from polished silver helms plumed with blue and grey feathers. Metal scraped against metal; leather creaked and groaned. Several last, desperate townsfolk dove aside, pushing others before them, revealing the lead rider: the Caretakers' own right hand, the black-helmed Captain of the Blades. "The Fury" they called him, and Skerth finally understood why. He had never seen a man that large, either in size or stature. His chest was broad and strong beneath his plate armor, his arms bare and thick-muscled, his thighs as thick and wide as Skerth's head, at least. Thick red hair—rare as far south as Erados—streamed from beneath his helmet in wild, unruly ropes. His face was clean-shaven and made of hard lines and angles, and the eyes that peered from the helm glinted with battle-rage. He held a great broadsword aloft and shouted before him, "Make way for the Caretakers' Blades! Woe to all who stand in our path!"

Skerth pulled at the rope lead that had fallen slack in Xor's hands and grabbed the back of the man's doublet. "Move!" he shouted, dragging Xor behind as he launched himself past Pieroth and into the crowd still scrambling out of the way of the riders. Xor and Pieroth joined him in fighting to get through, drawing dagger and sword respectively to encourage the townspeople to move faster. They had scarcely managed to make it to safety when the riders, a score or more at least, thundered past.

Chaos followed in their wake. Women sobbed. The injured cried out for help. Stunned, those who had gathered to revel now searched frantically for loved ones or comforted the fallen.

"What's happening?" someone wailed, voicing what everyone else could only wonder. But no answers came.

Pieroth raised up to scan the crowd. "Where's the Captain?"

Xor turned about, squinting, then shook his head. "I don't see wind or sail of her."

"Then what?"

"We go on. Stay to the plan." He sounded more certain than he looked.

Indeed, they all felt it: something was very wrong. Guardsmen riding down citizenry on Auberdale Eve in their haste to answer some threat, the Fury himself at their lead?

Pieroth sensed Xor's hesitation. He stepped forward, an uncanny gleam in his eye. "Plans change, mate."

Xor frowned. "What's that to mean?"

The old pirate leaned in so close Skerth could smell the wine and onion on his breath. "Have you ever thought of what it might be like to slip out of her knot? Get out from behind her skirts? Raise your own flag?"

"Mutiny." Xor's voice flattened, his expression cold.

Pieroth shrugged. "Put whatever word to it you like. We have the boy, not her. He's power in our hands. With him in our control, the captains and merchant-masters won't need a high wind to change their sails. She'll be trussed and turned out before the night's over, and the cove—the city all, abovetop and below—will be ours."

Xor and Pieroth stood stone still as they considered one another, heedless of the people crashing around them like water on rocks. Hands curled around weapon hilts.

"You swore an oath to Captain Gem."

"Aye, I did. To see this scat to the throne. And I'll keep that oath."

Xor's heavy brows came down. "For your own gain."

"You might find my service more to your liking. Why don't you give it a go?" Pieroth's voice was more menace than invitation. Skerth stepped back as far as the leash would allow, glancing around for a weapon he could swipe from the crowd, but finding little more than full purses and wilted flowers. "And I've got my own whores, so that'll be one less task you'll do for me—"

Skerth barely skipped aside as Xor lunged for Pieroth. The rope leash fell to the ground. Skerth seized his opportunity and darted into the crowd.

"The boy!" Pieroth roared.

Skerth coiled the rope around his hand and pushed through the crowds toward the Palace, both pirates at his heels.

"*Scarlet!*" Xor called out. "To arms! *Scarlet!*"

Skerth ignored his pursuers, focusing on one goal: reaching the Palace gates. Already the sun was sinking. The ceremony would begin at dusk, regardless of whatever turmoil had called out the Blades. The Caretakers would be eager to secure their power. He snaked back and forth across the avenue, ducking and sliding between walls and carts and people. With no further incident, the townspeople regained a sense of order, many returning cautiously to their celebrations. Most paid him no heed as he passed; the flight of the nobly-dressed boy, while strange, caused no harm.

He didn't look back as he ran. With every step his heart pounded to the rhythm of his rising anger—at himself, the pirates, the assassin—Kalen—and above all, the Caretakers. They had all brought him to this moment, with their lust for power and blood. The Caretakers had stolen the lives of so many he knew. They had stolen Feirwyn's lands, his title, his birthright. And they had stolen Skerth's home and family—whether decoy or heir, Skerth would have known a very different life had they not chosen on that one night, eleven years earlier, to stake their claim with bloodshed.

The assassin, Feirwyn, the pirates—their influence and their machinations had all driven him to this day, to this moment, to this choice. But this fight was now his alone.

The realization gave him new strength; he felt powerful. Alive. Almost eager to face the Caretakers on their own ground. The pirates and Feirwyn both wanted him to claim the throne, and he would: for himself. For the family he had never known, and for the family locked beyond the gates to the Lower City—Malyn, Jemmy, Mina, and the rest. For all the boys who had died and all those yet to fall victim to the Caretakers' "charity." For the impoverished fishermen banned from the more abundant waters. For the men and women who struggled to feed their own children rather than turn them out to starve. For them all he would stand up at dusk and, with or without the ring, lay claim to the throne of Erados.

He reached the gates just as bells tolled the opening of the Auberdale Eve ceremony; the tide of movement behind him shifted, pushing him the last few steps into the immense courtyard. He had not expected the chaos that greeted him. Similar to the world outside the gates, the spacious courtyard was a maelstrom of noise, color, and textures. Folk garbed in their finest clothes squeezed onto the many rows of long benches placed directly before and angled to each side of the raised dais, and still more people of all ranks flowed into the courtyard. Carts lined the east wall. Blades lined the west wall and barred the main passage through to the Palace, where the eight Caretakers would enter just before the main ceremony. White and scarlet roses adorned the whole of the scene: garlands twined around every pole and balcony, bouquets spilled from vases larger than Skerth, and petals scattered across the dais.

White for remembrance. Red for blood.

The burden of his newly-remembered past soured the whole idea of Auberdale Eve. For so many years he, along with the rest of the city, had looked forward to the best festival of the year without truly understanding what it all meant. Now, the thought of celebrating such a slaughter with laughter and meat pies and flowers while those responsible sat in honored attendance fanned his anger into rage.

He scanned the crowd for familiar faces, found only strangers. Their finery, the way they carried themselves, the refined way they shaped their words only made him feel more foreign and alone. His confidence wavered. Why exactly did anyone think those brightly-colored jewels in the crown of Endelas Ortanos would ever accept him as their king? And why—

"There!" a familiar voice cried, but whatever more Emme said was lost in the blare of horns and the sudden rush of movement atop the walls.

"Blades, alert!" someone called out from one of the towers high above. The sound of armored fists striking plate silenced the courtyard. "Present arms!"

The sound of more than a hundred drawn swords rang loud as the guards spread around the courtyard and along the walls all drew steel and held their swords vertical, blade to nose.

A firm hand gripped Skerth's upper arm. "Got you!" Emme said triumphantly.

Skerth jammed his boot heel down on her toes—hard. She stifled a cry and let go. At the same time, pain exploded across his back as someone slapped him with the flat of a sword. He staggered forward, but strong hands twisted his arms behind his back, turned him to face Captain Gem.

"My mother will have a piece of you for that trick," Emme hissed rubbing her toes.

"I'll pay," Skerth promised, glaring back at her. "It was worth the price."

"Indeed?" Gem snapped her fingers and waved to someone just out of view. Two pirates appeared—neither of whom seemed familiar—Nirue held tight between them. She nodded, and one of them lifted his hand to strike her.

"No!" cried Skerth. "Don't—"

The first evening bell sounded. The ceremony had begun.

Chapter Twenty-Eight: Auberdale Eve

Spectators now pressed into every available space in the courtyard, pushing Skerth, Nirue, the pirates and Emme uncomfortably close. With every passing moment, the tension crept back into Skerth's shoulders, lodged in his stomach like a steel ball. He forced himself to bide his time. To wait.

The final bell tolled as the last rays of sunlight slipped behind the Palace. Musicians concealed behind the dais struck a melancholy chord. The crowd hushed. Another chord, then another rang out, silencing even the guards who still struggled in vain to close the gates.

A lone lute sounded, picking out a plaintive melody that resonated somewhere deep within Skerth's soul. A harp took up the counterpoint, weaving around the melody in a delicate dance, as infinitely beautiful as it was sad. Another lute joined in, and another harp, and the duet became a quartet. A quintet. And so on, until the crescendo of music washed over the courtyard, entrancing everyone within its gentle spell.

In unison, torches ensconced along the walls burst into flame of their own accord and the eight Caretakers of the city emerged from the Palace, each simply robed in a silky, silvery grey, the heavy silver medallions of their office hanging low on their chests. Their bowed heads were hooded, and each figure carried a tall white candle before him. The people rose as they mounted the dais, though those assembled shrank from them as they passed; even the nobles paid reverence out of duty and fear, not love.

The music swelled. The Caretakers spread out to stand before eight chairs set in a wide half-circle. They held their candles in arms outstretched, faceless grey stone statues made grotesque and frightening by the flickering candlelight. Skerth felt exposed; could they see him from beneath the heavy cowls that concealed their eyes? He wanted to avert his gaze, to slip away into the shadows, but held his ground. They would know him soon enough.

One by one the instruments fell away from the song. Eight, then five, then three. Soon the lute once more played solo, the tune even more heartbreaking after suffering the loss of so many companions. At last even the lute fell silent, leaving its final note to resonate across the courtyard.

The center Caretaker stepped forward and placed his candle in a tall, black iron candelabra stationed at the front of the dais. He pulled back his hood to reveal a handsome man—not young, but not old either—with thick black hair and a cold, relentless stare. Skerth recognized him as Harrudwynn, the Caretaker who had accompanied Sereia Benvedora the day Skerth had first crossed paths with Feirwyn. Skerth averted his eyes, heart hammering in his chest. When he looked back, the man held his arms wide to embrace the crowd he now held in thrall.

"Welcome, people of our fair city of Endelas Ortanos. Countrymen of Erados. Loyal subjects. Friends."

Bile burned in Skerth's throat. He swallowed. Hard.

The Caretaker lowered his arms slowly as he spoke. "We come together on Auberdale Eve, on this solemn day of remembrance, to mourn. Eleven years ago this night, our beloved king and his young family were slaughtered in their own beds, cut down while they slept, blissfully unaware that agents of our enemy had infiltrated the Palace, seeking to end the long peace of Erados. . . ."

The speech went on, but Skerth no longer heard the Caretaker's lies. *Cut down while they slept.* His anger flared, heating his skin from within. The somber scene before him dissolved in a rush of images: bright sunlight slanting onto the garden path, dappling the ground in much-welcome shade; pink and yellow roses, swaying in the breeze; Jearney coming for him; shouting, running, swords and Nurse and fear and the sharp tang of sweat and ashes, ashes burning—

"Liar," Skerth whispered, his hands tightening into fists. He hadn't realized he had spoken aloud until one of the pirates laid a warning hand on his shoulder.

Skerth's focus narrowed to Harrudrynn, whose lips still moved in rote repetition of the lies he must have told all these many years, lies Skerth couldn't hear for the rushing in his ears.

The rushing increased until Skerth realized that it was not the heat of his blood he heard, nor the violence of his memories, but a riotous clamor of shouts, screams and weaponry filtering in from outside the gates. The crowd surged. Skerth and the pirates were cast forward, pressed tight against those in front of them.

From the towers, a voice cried out, "Close the gates! Now! Blades to the gates!"

A rush of noise and outrage declared the mob's arrival at the gates, far too soon for the guards to close them. Wood and metal groaned and creaked as the guards pulled the gears into motion. Calls of "Make way!" and "Back!" and "Clear a path!" tumbled over one another. Those inside the courtyard burst into panicked debate. Men looked to wives; wives looked to children. Weapons drew. Confusion reigned as courtiers, merchants, farmers, servants, scholars, people of all stations and professions reacted to the clamor outside the gates. Those inside huddled together, hushed and confused, while those still outside continued to flood through. With so many people packing the avenue and pushing forward, the Blades' effort to close the gates stalled; Blades leapt forward, weapons drawn to beat back the crowd. Cries of pain and outrage doubled in volume and number, finally forcing Harrudrynn into silence.

"What is the meaning of this disruption?" he shouted.

"The Lower City gates have fallen!" called out a voice just outside the gates that made Skerth's heart jump. "The people rise to reclaim their city!"

A clash and clamor of steel and the speaker pushed into view: Feirwyn, with Malyn at his right hand; on his left, two scats pushing a bound and gagged Kalen between them. Behind him stood an army of scats and sailors, fishmaidens and whores, thumpers and beaters and lesser merchants, hawkers and bakers: all the lost and forgotten of the Lower City, armed with whatever they could scavenge and glaring at the Caretakers with angry faces and blood in their hearts. They pushed an open space before them, one even the Blades seemed loathe to enter.

"People of Erados!" Feirwyn shouted, "Behold the treachery of your 'Caretakers'!"

The scats shoved Kalen forward, taking care to retain a firm hold of their prisoner.

Another Caretaker—short and bloated—rose from his chair. "What is the meaning of this disruption? Blades! Seize these men! And close those blighted gates!"

Shouting a battle cry, the mob shook their makeshift weapons and surged into the courtyard. Blades rushed to meet them. Skerth saw Feirwyn and Malyn draw, saw Kalen's captors hustle him out of the fray, and then lost them all to the chaos.

At a curt nod from Gem, both of the pirates holding Skerth drew swords. To Emme she said, "Get to Feirwyn. I want that ring."

Emme looked from the full-fledged conflict at the gates to her mother, eyes wide. "But—"

"Don't fail me again, child." Gem's tone and expression closed the discussion. She tightened her hold on Nirue's arm and waved her daughter away with her free hand. With a backwards glare at Skerth, Emme adjusted the flowers in her hair and slipped into the crowd.

Nirue's guard had dropped to one, and Gem was distracted, scanning the crowd for Xor or more of her crew. Skerth's captors, intent on watching the fight, had eased their grip. It was time.

Skerth caught Nirue's eye; she nodded and sank into a false faint, nearly dragging Gem to the ground. Skerth stamped down on the instep of one of his captors and wrested an arm free. The pirates reacted swiftly, but he had already managed to wriggle free one arm.

"You scut!" spat the pirate who'd lost his hold. He lunged, but Skerth ducked and spun out of reach. The other pirate struggled to maintain his grip. Skerth twisted again and managed nearly to break free; instead his captor flung him in a wide circle and he stumbled backwards over Gem, who knelt beside a presumably unconscious Nirue.

Gem let out a string of foul curses. "Get him off me, you sea-addled ship scat!" She tried to fling the boy away and maintain her hold of Nirue, now thrashing herself free and pulling at Gem's hair. Skerth broke free and tumbled backwards to the ground. He scuttled backward on hands and feet, anxious to break for freedom, yet unwilling to leave Nirue.

Both of Skerth's captors had rushed to their Captain's side, but she batted them away. "Go! After him! I'll have your scalps for sails if you lose that boy!" Her bellow became a shriek when Nirue sank her teeth into Gem's hand. The Pirate Queen shook free and raised a hand to strike her.

"Help us!" Nirue shrieked. "Please!"

A Blade, on his way to the struggle at the gate, paused to look their way.

"Shut it, slut," Gem hissed, "or there'll be scant left to hand over to your lover when we're through."

Nirue looked her in the eye and screamed. "Pirates, by the sea gods! Murder! Help!"

The Pirate Queen backhanded her. Nirue crumpled to the ground.

"You there! Unhand the lady!" The Blade motioned to a handful of his men, who quickly gathered behind him. Together they shifted course and pushed their way toward them.

"Gods be damned," Gem hissed. She looked from the Blades to her captive. "We aren't finished," she told Nirue. "Come what may, you have my vow." To her men she said, "Leave them. We'll not tangle with the Blades today. But we aren't finished here, scat. Not today. Not ever." She turned and pushed away through the crowd, her men close behind.

Skerth rushed to Nirue's side. "Are you hurt?" She wiped at the blood dripping from her nose and shook her head.

He helped her to her feet. "Come," he said, and pulled her into the crowd.

The tension in the courtyard escalated. The ceremony forgotten, the people's attention divided between the boiling conflict at the gates and the Caretakers on the dais, who looked increasingly nervous. "Seize the Caretakers!" demanded some, while others moved to engage the mob in their defense. A tight circle had formed around the dais; Skerth's heart leapt when he recognized faces he knew mixed into that crowd, blunted street-knives at the ready. Nirue in tow, he wove through the crowds toward the Caretakers.

The sounds of battle surged as the mob gained ground. Noblewomen shrieked and cried; noblemen reached for swords they had not brought to this solemn ceremony. Some tried to flee through the garden gates behind the dais that led to the palace, or even over the walls; a few succeeded, but most were held back by

Blades no longer able to determine the difference between honored guests and angry mob. Another group pushed straight toward the dais, Feirwyn and Malyn at the head, Kalen now held fast between them.

They reached the foot of the dais at the same time. Feirwyn and Malyn pushed Kalen onto the platform like a bale of fish and climbed up behind him.

"What—" Harrudrynn spat, "You—"

"People of Erados!" Feirwyn shouted, holding up his hands for silence. "Blades! Throw down your arms and hear me!"

"Seize him! Seize the Exile!" Harrudrynn strode toward Feirwyn, hands outstretched, poised to either embrace or choke him. More of Malyn's scats, armed with staves, daggers and found swords, hopped onto the dais between them, forming a thick line between the Caretaker and the Exile. Others jumped up on the other three sides of the dais, effectively boxing the Caretakers in and cutting off their means of escape. If they wanted to leave the dais, they had to cut through the lines of weapons or leap forward into the roiling crowd.

"Stay back!" Malyn cried out to the Blades. "Leave off or we will run the Caretakers through, every one!"

"Stand down!" ordered one of the Caretakers in a tremulous voice. Behind him, Gor lunged toward him with a steel-tipped stave and a crazed grin; the Caretaker flinched and cried again, "Blades, stand down!"

"What is this madness?" Harrudrynn snapped.

"Your reckoning," Feirwyn replied. He raised his hands to the people and cried, "Hear me, people of Erados!"

"Seize this man!" Harrudrynn shouted.

"Stand down!" cried his fellow Caretakers, each of whom had acquired a weapon-wielding scat for a companion.

The Blades, not knowing what to do, pushed toward the dais, but held their weapons. Intrigued by the new scene playing out before them, the people gradually shifted their attention to Feirwyn.

"Caretakers, these men call themselves!" he shouted. "For eleven years they have held the throne in safekeeping for the lost Regenthwynn heir. For eleven years they have led us all to believe that they are just and honorable, learned men of books and wisdom. And for eleven years they have fooled us all."

Gasps and murmurs broke out, swiftly silenced by Feirwyn's next words. "I am Feirwyn of Thalenthwynn Keep, exiled for no other crime than calling myself distant cousin to the last Regenthwynn King. I witnessed the butchering of my family, the burning of my home and lands. For a decade I have wandered, seeking the truth behind those murders, searching for the missing heir, should he exist. And at last, I have my answers.

"Friends, your *Caretakers*—these noble-seeming clerics in whom you have placed your hope and your trust—have betrayed us. It was their lust for power that brought the end of the Regenthwynn family that fateful night eleven years ago. And it is that same desire to retain that power, at all costs and for all time, that has stolen the lives of countless young men over the past several years. This man—" he swept an arm wide to indicate Kalen— "the Caretakers' own assassin, has seen to the dark business of ensuring that the lost heir will never be found."

"Assassin?" Harrudrynn shouted, his face purpling with rage. "How dare you speak this treason!"

Behind him, the rest of the Caretakers echoed his cry. Some in the crowd called out their support for the Caretakers, but they were quickly drowned out by other, more insistent shouts of "Silence!" and "Let the Exile speak!"

"This is no treason!" Malyn's voice carried over the crowd. "This man's been killing off scats in the Lower City for weeks on their orders!" He pointed at the Caretakers, his eyes glittering with hate.

"Ridiculous!" Harrudrynn snapped. "Ours is an Order of peace and mercy. We have labored long to collect and care for the orphans of Endelas Ortanos, to give them food and shelter and take them from the streets."

"Take them to workhouses and the mines, more like," Malyn replied, "and leave your assassin to deal with what's left of us."

"How dare you make these unfounded accusations!" One of the Caretakers behind Harrudrynn stepped toward Malyn, pausing when a boy Skerth didn't recognize dug the tip of his dagger into the man's neck.

Feirwyn pulled the gag from Kalen's mouth and brought him to his feet. "Redeem yourself, Kalen. Restore your honor. Tell the people the truth."

243

"Reedem myself, you say. Restore my honor." Kalen studied Feirwyn with his sardonic half-smile, looked to Harrudrynn, then raised his chin and looked out over the crowd assembled there, the people still pressing in through the packed gates. "The Exile is a traitor and a liar!" he roared. "Seize him!"

The response from the crowd was deafening as shouts of support mingled with calls for Feirwyn's head and cries of treason. A flurry of activity broke out on the dais as Kalen struggled against his bonds and several scats rushed forward to help Feirwyn and Malyn restrain him. Two of the Caretakers to the rear of the dais fled to the spaces they left behind. Blades pushed forward, nearly to the platform, calling for the crowd to make way.

Skerth's mind raced. *None of this was supposed to work out this way.* Their plan hadn't accounted for the pirates' interference, the closure of the Lower City gates, the mob. The crowd was spiraling out of control, and no one would believe Feirwyn's claims without proof. And what proof did he have? The word of a handful of street scats and an assassin in the Caretakers' employ? Skerth wasn't even certain why Feirwyn had taken the risk of dragging Kalen onto the dais and denouncing the Caretakers with so little support.

"Skerth," Nirue said, squeezing his hand. "It is time."

"Time?"

She turned him to face her. Her cheeks were flushed, bruised, but her eyes shone with nervousness, excitement, and something more—

Suddenly, Skerth understood: *none of this was supposed to work out this way.* Feirwyn didn't know whether or not Skerth was alive. But if he was, and there at the ceremony, there was only one way to bring him out into the open, to reveal him to the Caretakers, to match the heir to the ring and end their reign once and for all.

"Make your claim," she said, and he could not mistake the pride in her voice. "Save Feirwyn, Skerth. Save us all."

He took a deep breath, nodded, then returned his attention to the platform. The Fury was nearly to the platform now, a handful of his men behind him. Malyn's scats looked less confident, and had a harder time managing the Caretakers and Kalen at the same time. The people closest to the platform were reaching up, grabbing at cloaks and ankles, heedless of whether or not they were attached to friend or foe. At the center of it all, Harrudrynn stood firm and tall with a slow, satisfied smile that fired the embers of Skerth's anger to full flame.

Skerth closed his eyes, took several deep breaths. *You are the heir of Erados*, he told himself, and hauled himself onto the dais.

Chapter Twenty-Nine: The Heir of Erados

Harrudrynn's eyes widened in shock. Skerth ignored him, turning instead to the crowd. His stomach lurched at the sight of so many people jammed into the square and beyond the gate, so many Blades on the walls and mingled amongst the crowd. For a fleeting moment he lost his courage; he glanced to Malyn, who nodded encouragement, and to Feirwyn, who wore an expression of mixed surprise and relief. Their support steadied him.

He took a deep breath to find his voice. Then he called out, "Feirwyn speaks the truth! This man—Kalen—is Harrudrynn's own hired assassin. And I—" another deep breath— "I am the one he sought to murder. I am Weyth Altairus Regenthwynn, heir to the throne of Erados. I stand before you tonight to rightfully reclaim what is mine."

At first, very little changed. Skerth felt the attention of those gathered on the dais shift to him as their individual struggles ceased. Gradually, the people nearest him silenced, taking in his hair, his eyes, his clothes. Their expressions shifted from surprise to awe. They turned to their neighbors, who in turn strove for a look at Skerth. Like raindrops on a puddle, whispers and speculation rippled through the crowd, leaving silence in their wake. Soon, even the noise outside the walls hushed. Harrudrynn masked his expression, straightened, and fixed Skerth with a stare that would have sent him scurrying into the shadows only weeks before.

But not now.

Skerth cleared his throat. "I am Weyth Altairus Regenthwynn, heir to the throne of Erados," he repeated, his voice ringing clear against the walls. "I stand before you on the last Auberdale Eve before the dawn of my fifteenth year to reclaim my birthright." He turned to look Harrudrynn full in the eye and recited the words Feirwyn had taught him: "I thank the Caretakers for preserving the peace of the land in my absence, and hereby relieve them of their stewardship of Erados."

The crowd burst into a mix of applause, cheers, jeers and a buzz of conversation. Harrudrynn glared at Skerth with pure hatred, his lips pressed so tightly together they nearly disappeared.

"Silence!" the Caretaker shouted, shoving past Skerth to the front of the dais and raising his arms for silence. Most people were so caught up in their own conversations that they either didn't hear or ignored him. "Silence!" he bellowed again, and again, until reluctantly the people obeyed.

"What is this?" the head Caretaker roared. "Are you so desperate for the return of your king that you will accept any young stranger who asserts a right to the throne?"

The crowd shifted and quieted; some looked shamefaced at this reprimand, some doubtful, while others wore expressions of pure hope and triumph.

Harrudrynn continued, "Eleven years we have waited for the lost heir to reveal himself and take his place as rightful King of Erados. Eleven years have passed with nary a rumor of this boy's existence." He pointed a long finger at Skerth. "And tonight, on our last night of hope before we must choose a new ruler to stand in place of those lost to the Purge, this boy appears. From whence did he come? How has he lived in secrecy for so long? And why has he never, in all these long years, come forth before this?"

The Caretaker's gaze swept the crowd, punishing their gullibility, seeding doubt with each pass. Then his expression softened, and he held his arms outstretched to embrace his audience. "Let us remove this pretender from our sight, and with him the traitors who would sully this solemn ceremony with their poisonous words." He motioned toward the Fury, poised now at the steps of the dais, and the handful of Blades nearest him. "Remove these men to the cells to await their hanging. Once we have honored the dead tonight and ushered in a new era of peace and prosperity, we will show the people of Erados how traitors shall be punished."

He dismissed them all—Feirwyn, Skerth, Malyn, and the rest—with a contemptuous wave. The Fury and his men mounted the steps slowly, sliding steel from sword-sheaths with deliberate menace.

"My Lord Harrudrynn," Kalen said in a low, urgent voice. "I have served you well, and I will serve you still if you but free my bonds—"

The head Caretaker glared down on the assassin, his expression cold, calculating. "You are a stranger to me, and if these men speak truly, a murderer. We have no dealings with such men."

"But, my lord—" Kalen broke off when the Caretaker turned and motioned to the Blades. Kalen's gaze flashed across the crowds, fear gradually pushing the confidence from his expression, neck muscles corded with tension. Spying his quarry, he called out, "Dreiwend! Stand for me!"

Skerth started at the name of the man from the tunnels. Eager to match it with a face, he followed Kalen's gaze to rest upon a round-faced, balding noble near the front of the crowd.

The Blades closed in.

"Lord Dreiwend! Keep your word! Stand and defend me!"

Dreiwend looked from Kalen to the glowering Caretakers, then slowly shook his head. He stepped back, two steps, three, then turned and elbowed his way through the crowd on a direct path to the gate.

"Take him to the cells with the others," Harrudrynn ordered.

Kalen swore under his breath and struggled afresh against his bonds. Fear hammered in Skerth's chest. He waited anxiously for the people to rise up, to cry out for them to stop, to listen, but nothing happened. The people shifted uncomfortably in their seats, at their places against the walls. They looked to one another, to their children, but no one met his eye. All the while, the Fury closed in, looking broader and more menacing the nearer he came.

His steps fell heavy on the boards; they creaked from the weight of him, his armor, perhaps even his duty.

"Get the boy," he rumbled in his deep baritone. "The Exile is mine."

Skerth straightened his shoulders and glared his defiance. This time, he would not run, nor would he cower. He would meet his fate with firm resolve.

Three steps. Two. One. . .

"Wait!" called out a voice from the rear wall. His heart pushed into his throat.

The crowd shifted and craned their necks to identify the speaker, their collective whispers like a sigh, then begrudgingly parted as someone pushed through: a girl—no, a young woman—wearing a crown of red and white roses on her short-cropped white-blonde hair.

Kiri. A mess of feelings swirled up within Skerth: happiness, anxiety, relief, anger, and so many more he couldn't name, and a few that frightened him to acknowledge.

She came panting to the foot of the platform. "The boy says he is the lost heir, the true King of Erados. Shouldn't you give him the chance to prove his claim before you put him to the noose?"

"The girl speaks sense," someone shouted. Murmurs of assent spread, wisps of conversation occasionally rising to Skerth's ears like froth from the ocean.

"—could be the king—"

"—killing innocents—"

"Let him prove it! Prove his claim!"

The Blades lowered their weapons and stood motionless and uncertain as more voices took up the call. The words became a chant, a battle cry that echoed from the courtyard to the street beyond. The force of it threatened to shake the Caretakers from the dais.

Once more, Harrudrynn held up his hands for silence. "Prove his claim," he repeated. The hint of a smirk played at the corner of his lips. "Very well, Boy. Prove your assertion that you are the missing Regenthwynn heir. If you can."

"He can prove his claim with this!" cried Feirwyn. He held his arm high, the back of his hand to the crowd. There, glittering on his forefinger, was the king's signet. "With this boy I found the missing ring of our beloved king. Alairathwynn, Kingmaker will show the truth of the last Regenthwynn's birthright!"

The crowd roared, but Skerth scarcely heard. Feirwyn shoved past the Blades and the Caretakers to Skerth's side.

"Ready?" Feirwyn asked.

Skerth nodded and turned to face the crowd. He felt a strange calm as he studied the people spread before him, an uncanny mix of nobles and poor, soldiers, merchants, bakers, tailors, pirates and everything between. He realized with a jolt that he didn't fear these people, nor did he blame them for their distrust or their doubt.

249

After all, the Caretakers had kept them well in hand, nurtured them with lies, fostered their ignorance.

Skerth took the ring from Feirwyn's outstretched hand and slid it onto his finger.

For one, terrifying moment, Skerth stared into the murky depths of the ring and feared that nothing would happen, that the ring's earlier reaction to his touch was nothing but a fluke. But only a handful of heartbeats passed before the ring tightened to fit his finger, warmed to his touch, then burst into a bright glow of color that pierced the night.

The crowd gasped and involuntarily leaned away. Skerth held up his hand and turned it out so all could see. The whispers began: "Alairathwynn." Then louder, as the crowd picked up the refrain of hope. "Alairathwynn, Alairathwynn." This new chant mingled with cheers, laughter, as the people's greatest hopes took shape before their eyes.

Feirwyn turned Skerth to face the Caretakers. "Is this enough proof for you, Harrudrynn?" he bellowed over the roar of the crowd.

The head Caretaker paled and stepped back. "This is a simple trick, Exile, nothing more. This bauble proves naught. We will not yield the throne to this found boy over a grand display of petty magic." His words were boldly spoken, but even he did not seem convinced.

"Tell that to his people," replied Feirwyn, sweeping his hand to encompass the crowd behind him.

Reluctantly the Caretaker looked out—and saw the truth of Feirwyn's words. Already the mood of the crowd had shifted. The people gathered behind Skerth, exchanging their doubt for joy, their reverence of the Caretakers for contempt. His expression unreadable, Feirwyn dropped to one knee before Skerth. And then, impossibly, the people followed, dropping weapons and bowing heads before the young heir, until only those few still loyal to the Caretakers yet remained on their feet. Tears pricked Skerth's eyes and he struggled to restrain the wash of feelings that threatened to overtake him—pride, grief, awe, and above all, relief.

The Caretakers edged close to one another, glancing nervously for a way out–and finding none.

Harrudrynn scowled down at Skerth. "This is not over. You will not have my throne."

Feirwyn rose with a bitter laugh. "*Your* throne, Harrudrynn? How quickly you shift from the role of loyal steward to king. Rule of Erados was never yours. Even stolen in blood and torment, this throne—these people—never belonged to you. Always they have awaited the return of a Regenthwynn." He laid a hand on Skerth's shoulder. "And now the Regenthwynns shall have their just revenge."

Harrudrynn's eyes burned. "You want an untried boy-king to rule your lives?" he shouted over the din. His hateful gaze settled on Skerth. "So be it."

Sweeping his robes behind him, he made for the steps.

"Do not let them go," Kalen said loudly, his menacing glare never shifting from Harrudrynn's back. "They will betray you, and everything you have gained—and more—will be lost."

"He speaks sense," said Malyn, still holding Kalen's bonds. Feirwyn nodded curtly in agreement.

Skerth took a deep breath. "Blades!"

Every Blade on the dais—the Fury first among them—turned at his call.

"See the Caretakers to their rooms and hold them there."

The Fury laid a fist across his heart and bowed his head. "As you command, my liege." Before Harrudrynn could issue a protest, the burly Blade took the Caretaker by the elbow.

"This is not over," Harrudrynn repeated, his voice a hiss of contained hatred that promised more pain than Skerth had ever known.

"Come my lord," said the Fury, and led Harrudrynn firmly down the steps to the courtyard below.

The remaining Blades had little trouble urging the Caretakers to follow suit. Some looked resigned, some curious, some angry, and one, to Skerth's surprise, caught his gaze and even flashed a weak smile. All of them descended the dais as they had mounted it: stiff and proud. Aloof. Untouchable. The crowd gave them a wide berth as they passed. None, Skerth noted, seemed particularly heartbroken to see them go. The Caretakers may have commanded the respect of the people, but they did not have their love.

Once the Blades and Caretakers cleared, only Skerth, Feirwyn, Malyn and his boys, and Kalen remained on the dais.

Feirwyn shifted to Skerth's side. "Are you ready, my prince?"

Prince. King. Skerth's stomach flipped, and for the first time in his known memory, he was grateful that he hadn't eaten.

Malyn gave over Kalen's ropes to Gor and Seryn, moved to stand at Skerth's other shoulder, and punched him lightly on the arm. "Come on, Rat. You can do this."

Skerth grinned. His nerves calmed. He nodded.

Feirwyn gripped Skerth's wrist and raised his hand high. "All hail Lord Weyth Altairus Regenthwynn, King of Erados!"

The roar from the crowd was deafening. Skerth looked out upon a sea of upturned faces, some smiling, others cheering; some even wept. They waved colored kerchiefs, scarves, weapons, house standards, flowers. Skerth's eyes filled. This Auberdale Eve ceremony was like no other. Despite the festive atmosphere that always accompanied large gatherings, despite the meat pies and cinnamon buns, despite the hawkers and garlands and finery, the people had come one last time to mourn the past. They had come to acknowledge at last, on the eve of the last Regenthywnn's coming of age, that the heir was no more. The Caretakers would officially transition from stewards to rulers, and their power would be secure for once and always.

Now, everything had changed.

The heir had resurfaced to claim his throne. A boy-king, full of promise.

A false heir, culled from the streets and shaped by desperate kingmakers, nobles and pirates alike, to fulfill an old promise by men who never intended any of the Regenthwynns—heir, decoy, or noble cousin—to survive.

Skerth suddenly felt pressure unlike any he had felt before. Between dodging the assassin, escaping the pirates, and making his way to the Auberdale Eve ceremony, he had never once considered what would happen afterward. In truth, he had never expected an after. Now, as he studied the cheering townspeople packing the courtyard and beyond, the weight of his deception suffocated him. He gasped for breath, but couldn't get any air. His vision greyed at the edges, tunneled in. His knees felt weak—

Firm hands gripped his right arm, held him upright. "Steady, Rat," Malyn said, his voice low and firm. Strong. Familiar. "Keep your feet or they'll think you weak."

Feirwyn's grip firmed, pulled, kept him stretched tall. "Almost over," said Feirwyn.

But it wasn't over, Skerth realized. It would never end, this fakery that he would have to live, day in and day out. The people wanted a king. And for better or for worse, they had accepted him. For their sake, not his own, he would give up himself and live this unending lie.

In that moment, with the people chanting his name, Feirwyn and Malyn at his side, and a platform full of street kids at his back, Skerth laid his past to rest.

After what seemed an interminable amount of time, Feirwyn lowered Skerth's arm and raised his own hands for silence. "My friends. This has been a day beyond all hope, a day that will be recorded as one of the most profound in our history. Let us now turn this memorial into a celebration!" Cheers erupted. "Musicians, sound your trumpets!" More cheers. "Let us dance!" Cheers. "Sing!" Cheers. "And rejoice!" He pumped his fist into the air and the crowd roared. The musicians, at first drowned out by the noise, launched into a merry tune. People turned to one another with smiles and laughter. Some embraced, some took up Feirwyn's call for a dance and spread into small group circles. Those nearest the dais milled about, reaching for Skerth, shouting their good wishes and blessings.

Still dizzy, Skerth waved to the crowd, occasionally kneeling to grasp hands with those jockeying for his attention below. Many of them tried to speak, gave their names and titles, but he could barely hear them, let alone sort them out. Malyn, enjoying the attention, flashed his most charming smile and waved as though he, and not Skerth, had just inherited a kingdom. Skerth swallowed against his surging stomach and forced himself to smile until his face ached.

Soon, three familiar faces pushed through the crowd to the edge of the dais: Kiri, Nirue, and the thick-bearded man Skerth recognized as Kiri's father. At the sight of Kiri grinning up at him, Skerth no longer cared who she was or what had passed between them; his heart jumped. Without thinking, he leapt off the platform and pulled her into a tight embrace. She stiffened at first, then wrapped her arms tight around his back. A calming warmth spread through him, forcing everything else out of his mind. Nothing— past, present or his intimidating, uncertain future—mattered but the comfort and sweetness of this moment between friends.

"Now I understand why you liked this scat so much," Malyn said loudly.

Skerth's face went hot; he and Kiri disentangled and hastened to put an arm's length between them.

Malyn hopped down from the dais and folded his arms across his chest. "Never cared for him myself. I always thought he—" Malyn's eyes swept Kiri from head to toe "*she*— was more trouble than a gull in a galley."

Kiri's father studied Malyn with suspicion, then frowned at his daughter. "How do you know this boy?"

"Later, Da." Flushing, she tugged him away from Malyn.

Da. Skerth stiffened, his stupid, lopsided smile fading. He suddenly found it difficult to look Kiri in the eye.

"Come," said Kiri's father, setting a broad hand on Skerth's shoulder. "We need to clear out of here. Not all the people are content with this new turn of events. Until we know everyone's loyalties and you are officially crowned, you are not safe."

"How do we know we can trust *you*?" Malyn asked.

Kiri's father reached into the neck of his doublet and pulled out a heavy gold amulet dangling from a concealed chain around his neck. The design was intricate, a shield drawn into four quarters with a symbol assigned to each: a wyvern; a thorny vine spiraling up the blade of a dagger; a ship in full sail bearing the king's standard; a rolled scroll and feather quill. Ocean waves bordered the bottom of the medallion; mountains rose at the top behind the shield.

"Fancy," Malyn said. He started to reach for it, then dropped his hand.

"What does it mean?" asked Skerth.

"It means," he said, tucking the amulet back inside his doublet, "that I am Lord Arran, the old king's spymaster. Ever since I fled the palace eleven years ago, my young daughter in tow, I have used every skill and talent I possess to find you."

Skerth looked from him to Kiri, his mind racing. "So you're—"

She shrank from his gaze. "Your Spymaster's daughter."

"Their loyalty is unparalleled, Arran's wisdom invaluable," Feirwyn said firmly, turning toward them with a flushed and smiling Nirue tucked under his arm. "If he believes we should move elsewhere, then by all means, let us follow. We have not worked this hard merely to lose you to a quiet dagger in the crowd. Which reminds me—" he drew a dagger from a sheath at his hip and handed it to Skerth hilt-first. "You might need this."

Skerth didn't need to see the well-worn designs on the hilt or test its weight to know the weapon as his own dagger. Skerth blinked back sudden tears and nodded.

Feirwyn clapped him on the shoulder, studying him with such pride that words failed him. Then he said, "You didn't tell me you recalled your name."

"My name?"

Feirwyn's expression shifted to surprise. "Your name. Weyth Altairus Regenthwynn. You declared it when you claimed the throne."

Skerth realized with a sudden jolt that he'd said the name without thinking; a name he'd never heard spoken aloud, nor called up from memory before. "I didn't know it," he told Feirwyn. "Not until I said it aloud."

"It is the name of the true heir, Skerth, a name that none have heard spoken in this courtyard for eleven years. Until tonight." Feirwyn's grip tightened. "It is your name."

Skerth nodded and swallowed against the sudden lump in his throat.

"Come," Lord Arran urged. "Let us move—"

"Stop!"

They all turned. Emme stumbled out of the crowd and reached for Skerth. The flowers in her hair had wilted and trailed loosely from her crown of braids; stray tendrils clung to her face and neck. Her face was red and blotchy, her expression schooled into a perfect mask of contrition.

"Wait!" She came to a halt in front of Skerth. "Please. Hear me out." She settled a hand in the crook of his arm.

He spared her a look of disgust before yanking his arm away.

"Skerth!" she called as he turned away. "Please, let me explain!" Despite the protests of Feirwyn, Malyn and Arran, she pushed in front of Skerth and gazed up at him, her watery blue eyes all innocence and contrition.

He stared down at her, incredulous. "What could you possibly have to say to me after all you've done?"

She opened and closed her mouth, then let out a shuddering sigh. "I know you must be so angry, but please understand—" Skerth watched as she drew in on herself, resuming her performance as the meek, unlucky daughter of pirates. "They would have killed me," she whispered. "I had no choice."

Before Skerth could answer, Kiri stepped between them. "Allow me." Before anyone could react, she curled her hand into a fist and punched Emme hard in the nose. She crumpled to the ground with a wail, both hands pressed to her nose to stop the gush of blood that spurt forth. Through tearful eyes, she glared up at Kiri with pure hatred, all pretense of innocence forgotten.

Skerth shifted to Kiri's side. "Go back to your kind, Emme. Before I charge you with treason."

Her eyes widened in shock. She shook her head once in disbelief, her gaze shifting from Skerth, to Kiri, and back again. "But—"

"We are finished here," Skerth announced firmly.

Emme's mask completely fell away. Her expression hardened and her eyes narrowed to a venomous glare. "But I and my kin are not finished with you, *Weyth*." She practically spat the name. Carefully she rose, brushed her skirts, and squared her shoulders. "I promise you that much." Without another word, she shoved past them, elbowing Kiri's ribs in the process, and slipped away into the crowd.

Skerth, Kiri and Malyn all looked at each other.

"Looks like you picked the wrong girl to cross," Malyn said with a shrug. "Come on. I bet there's food wherever her da is taking us. I plan to eat myself sick after all this bother." He clapped Skerth on the back and followed the others.

Skerth turned to Kiri, his heart full of mixed emotions, his head whirling from the day's events. His anger at her had lessened; her betrayal still stung, and he had questions, but he found himself too exhausted to care much for any of it at the moment. "You still owe me an explanation," he said.

She wrinkled her nose. "I know."

He could wait. He would have to deal with all of it soon enough—the explanations, the strategies, the Caretakers' retribution, the future. His identity tested, his claim examined over and again, perhaps until the day he died. This wasn't over yet, and wouldn't be for some time. The ramifications of what had happened this Auberdale Eve would richochet for days, weeks—even years.

But for the first time in his life, Skerth felt safe. Connected. Completely at peace with who he was and the life that stretched before him.

And that, for the moment, was enough.

Epilogue

Skerth paced the well-worn garden paths, sweltering in his finely embroidered black velvet tunic and leggings. The crisp, high white collar choked him mercilessly; he tugged at it, to no avail. The sword slung at his side seemed far too big and unwieldy for him to draw, which was a good thing, since he didn't know the first thing about using it. Not that he would have to; the sword's sole purpose was "ceremonial," designed to weigh him down and bang him on the legs if he turned too quickly. In the end, he didn't mind. The sway of the sword, the regular tap of the silver and gold-plated sheath against his hip and thigh distracted him from facing the singular truth that terrified him the most:

Within the hour, he would be crowned King of Erados.

The thought both thrilled and frightened him. Try as he might, he couldn't figure how he had gone from picking the streets and fighting for scraps to head of not only the city, but the whole of Erados. He, a king! He could barely care for himself; how would he care for all of these people? Already the weight of responsibility settled heavily on his shoulders, making him sweat all the more beneath his tunic. Then he remembered Jemmy and Minah. The little ones. Taleryn, Rot, Dragon, and all the boys who'd died because no one had looked after them. Malyn. Thinking of them lent him courage, and he knew then that he would do as he'd always done on the streets: keep a protective eye on those smaller and weaker than himself. And who better than he to look after the poor and the forgotten? *No one*, he told himself. He would do a better job than the Caretakers, that much he knew.

Skerth pulled at his collar, let out an exasperated sigh, and resumed pacing. The sun baked him in his black velvet cocoon, but he had no desire to return inside. The palace was in an uproar, with every available hand preparing for the ceremonies, and Skerth couldn't sit still. Feirwyn had finally sent him out to the garden. Skerth guessed Feirwyn's own agitation had more to do with the imminent arrival of Nirue's family than his young cousin's coronation, but Skerth decided not to point that out. After all, Feirwyn had waited a decade to restore his name and lands so he could formally request Nirue's hand in marriage. Now that his day had come, he was entitled to some anxiety of his own.

Despite the frenzy of preparations, the frazzled Palace staff, and Feirwyn's own agitation, the mood both inside the Palace and out in the streets was light and festive; it seemed no one missed the dour Caretakers, who had escaped captivity and fled the city on Auberdale Eve without so much as a spare grey robe in their possession. In fact, most people already seemed to have forgotten their existence, fully embracing the task of celebrating the coronation of their new king. Only Skerth and his loyal handful of friends worried about the Caretakers, feared that they, along with the pirates, would not simply disappear.

The call of a familiar voice stopped Skerth in mid-step. "Skerth! Where are you?"

He smiled and turned just in time to see Kiri round the corner. She picked up her step when she saw him, but he found he couldn't do any more than stare, mouth agape. Her short, flyaway white hair was unchanged, though someone had evened out the more hopeless spots. Short curls framed her face and rested against her cheeks, rosy from the sun and the heat of the day. Her eyes were as he remembered: one blue, one brown, both sparkling with mischief. But the dress transformed her. Instead of old ragged boys' clothes or a simple dress, Kiri wore a deep blue velvet gown that clung from shoulder to hip before flaring to the ground, showing her new curves to excellent advantage. Skerth caught himself staring at the soft rise of flesh at the neckline of her dress and glanced hastily away, flushing red to the roots of his hair.

She came within arm's reach, then faltered. She looked for a moment as though she would hug him, then stepped back, blushing, and clasped her hands behind her back. He tried not to notice what that small action did to draw attention to her chest.

"Kiri." He cleared his throat awkwardly. "Good to see you." *What a stupid thing to say.* He knew he should say something else, something more profound or interesting; after all, Kiri was the best of all friends. His tongue stuck to the roof of his mouth and all he could think about was how pretty she looked in that dress, with the sunlight in her hair.

"I've been looking everywhere for you. Have you been outside all morning?"

"Mostly." This he could discuss. "There's too much activity, too many people in there. And Feirwyn's no help."

"Nirue?"

He nodded and rolled his eyes.

Her answering grin eased some of his tension. They started walking, side by side, through the gardens.

"You look nice," she said at last, reaching away from him to pull a burgundy rose from the bush.

"So do you."

She shrugged. "Father insists that I'm a young woman now, and ought to dress accordingly." She wrinkled her nose in displeasure.

"Well, it suits you." He laughed at her show of disbelief. "Really."

"I'll let him know the king approves." She held the rose to her nose to hide her smile, then plucked distractedly at the petals as they walked. "You haven't asked me yet."

Skerth wracked his brain to try to figure out what she meant, but came up short. "Asked you what?"

"About . . . you know. My father. About . . . everything."

Skerth tensed. He had both dreaded and looked forward to this conversation over the past few days. Ultimately, he wasn't sure he really wanted to know her real identity, or why she'd spent so much time haunting his streets. What if he didn't care for the reason? And since he'd already forgiven her, what would the knowledge change?

Before he could respond, Kiri continued in a rush, "Running the streets with you wasn't just a lark. Well, at first it was, I suppose. Father told me never to cross Downwedge, so of course I had to do it."

Skerth suppressed a smile. "Of course."

"As time went on, I felt more at ease in the Lower City than I ever did in my own home. And when I heard about the search for an heir, I thought—" she took a deep breath. "Well, I *knew* I could help." She finally looked up. "And I was right."

His brow furrowed. "That first time I ran into Feirwyn in the Royal Quarter. That wasn't an accident."

She shook her head, flushing. "It was a trick, though, especially when you saw the Caretaker and balked. The Blades almost got me that time."

"And when Feirwyn found me in the alley—"

She nodded. "After Malyn's scats separated us, I ran for Feirwyn. By the time I found him, you were long gone. He must have searched all over for you to find you in that alley."

"Why didn't you come? Why didn't you tell me?"

She cocked an eyebrow. "Would you have listened?"

"Probably not," he admitted. "So you helped Feirwyn with all this." He swept an arm up and down to indicate his crisp new clothes, the swords, the shiny new boots. "That still doesn't explain why anyone with a roof to sleep under would prefer the streets."

She sighed. "I'm like you, Skerth, in so many ways. I don't fit here. My father's always away and my mother died a long time ago." She paused and gave him a meaningful look. "With your parents, in the Purge. She was a lady-in-waiting to the queen." The sadness in her voice squeezed his heart. "Anyway, I'm often alone. Helyn, our house servant, has the care of me whenever father's away, but she makes a terrible botch of it. She's easy to outwit, and too terrified to tell my father she loses track of me for days at a time, so as long as I come back she doesn't make a fuss." Kiri grimaced. "That was until the pirates got hold of us and father came home. Now I'm never going to be allowed out of the house again."

Skerth laughed. "Maybe he'll make an exception now and again and allow you to visit the Palace."

She gave him a wistful smile. "Do you forgive me, then?"

"'Course." Then, he grinned. "Besides, this way I don't have to worry so much about where you've run off to all the time."

"Did you worry?" she asked, watching him out of the corner of her eye.

He flushed, then shrugged. "Sometimes. But you always came back."

A comfortable silence fell between them as they walked. Kiri plucked another rose—this time white— and picked at the thorns. Skerth looked from the graveled path that lay ahead, to the rows of roses that bordered the walk, and up to the wall and the battlements above. He wondered if he would ever get used to this strange world of tight, uncomfortable clothes and walls and routine and expectations. The thought constricted his throat tighter than his collar, made him want to dart away and go up and over the wall before they could catch him. He could still disappear, and be free.

But was he ever truly free? He would miss his runs with Kiri and the others, their adventures, but he would not miss the poverty, the illness, the despair. He and Feirwyn had already found places for Malyn and any of his scats who had chosen to stay, and he would find homes for them all, if they wanted: Jemmy, Minah, Gor . . . all of them. And Kiri—she was still here. By his side. Everything had changed, yet nothing of true importance had changed at all.

"Are you nervous?" she asked at last, startling him from his thoughts.

He sighed. "Very. At least the ceremony will be over quickly."

"And then you've got the rest of your life to rule."

He looked at her with such dismay that she laughed. "Come, it's better than picking pockets."

"Is it?"

They rounded a bend in the path, leaving the blood red and white roses for a more cheerful row of pinks and yellows. He felt a rush of familiarity and stopped.

"What is it?"

"It's just—" he sighed. "What if they're wrong? What if I'm just a decoy, never meant to be king? What if—"

"Hush." She laid her fingers against his lips, then lifted his hand to show him the ring, the light of which had settled from a brilliant flare to a constant glow in shifting shades of color. "You are Weyth Altairus Regenthwynn, and in mere hours you will be King of Erados. Even the Caretakers could not challenge your claim."

The name still felt foreign, too great for him to bear, like the sword rattling against his leg. His identity, too, felt uncomfortable. Wrong. Ill-fitting. So much of his past seemed a knot he couldn't work out, no matter how he tried. And every night the whispers of his doubts grew loud and insistent. *Who are you, really?* they asked. *What if you discover that you aren't the true heir?*

One thing he knew for certain. "But to you, I'm Skerth."

"Skerth," she repeated, her voice little more than a whisper. She looked up, tears shimmering in her eyes. "I guess we won't climb many more rooftops together once you're king," she said with a wan smile.

He turned his hand to lace his fingers with hers. "When I'm king, no one can stop me from climbing all the rooftops I want," he reassured her. "But not without you."

Before he could think about it, he drew her into his arms and kissed her. He embraced her awkwardly at first—he wasn't sure where to put his hands—but gained confidence when she didn't pull away. She slid her arms around his neck and swayed close; he tightened his hold, savoring the feel of her pressed tightly against him.

After some time, they reluctantly broke apart. A bright flush colored her cheeks and neither of them knew where to look, but he kept a firm hold on her hand. She didn't seem eager to have it back; they strolled on in silence.

Halfway down the path, an overwhelming sense of familiarity overcame him. *Pink and yellow buds, bright in the summer sun. The scent of roses, and something else: the acrid tang of smoke. It was his birthday. . .*

Skerth paused and stared thoughtfully into the rosebushes.

"Skerth?" Kiri frowned. "Are you all right?"

But he didn't answer. He paced back and forth along that section of the path, peering through the tangled net of thorns and fallen petals, until at last he let out a cry of triumph, fell to his knees and reached carefully into the bushes. Along with a few choice curse words and a snagged sleeve, Skerth drew out a small round object a little larger than his fist. A simple thing, made of good rubber, dried and cracked by heat and time. It had once been a bright, shiny blue. Skerth held it out to Kiri with a look of such reverence and triumph that it might have been Harrudrynn's head.

Kiri looked interested. "What is it?"

"My ball." At her look of confusion he explained, "A gift from my mother for my fourth birthday. Just before—" he broke off, feeling the words catch in his throat. Because he suddenly knew. . . .

I am not the true heir.

The clarity and intensity of the memory surprised him. A woman with golden hair coiled and piled atop her head in an elaborate style, holding her arms out for his embrace. Her clothes were finely made, but she wore no crown. She was plump and soft,

263

always smiling. Her laugh brightened a plain face, turned her beautiful.

Beside her sat a tall, thin woman. She sat stiff and still as she passed a needle back and forth through the cloth in her lap. A silver crown sparkled in her pale hair. She didn't react as Skerth ran up to the other woman, who folded him in her arms and cooed her delight. The stiff woman didn't acknowledge either him or their unseemly show of affection. Her needle passed in and out, in and out, her expression guarded.

"Happy birthday, darling boy," said the first woman as she slipped something into his hands. He pushed away to look at it: a blue ball, so like the one the prince had received for his birthday. He held it up close, rubbed his hands along the smooth rubber. No, this was *better*, he decided.

"Pay your respects," she reminded him gently.

He hastened to disentangle from her embrace and bowed to the tall, thin woman. "My Queen," he said, just as he'd been taught, and she rewarded him with a smile of approval.

My Queen. Not *Mother.*

"Skerth?" Kiri tightened her grip on his hand.

"Skerth!" Another voice. Malyn.

I am not the heir.

He was the embodiment of a lie, placeholder for the true heir of Erados.

"We should go back," she said, squeezing his hand.

Back, indeed. But back where? To the streets? If he confessed the truth and walked away, what good would it serve? Who would look after the kids then? He was a fraud, he knew that now. But he had no other choice. Now, more than ever, the people needed a king. The Lower City needed a voice. All of them—their hopes, their livelihoods—now rested in this one, final choice.

"Yes." The words were for himself as much as they were for her. "They will need me inside."

They turned back, taking their time, enjoying their last few moments of freedom in each other's company. Some things Skerth didn't know—why he was spared, his true heritage, how he had come to this crossroads in his life. But he did know the values of honor and loyalty, and he'd keep his friends close. He would have less freedom to go where he wished and do as he pleased. His life no longer belonged to him; he belonged to Erados, and vowed to do his best to serve his people well.

But as long as he had rooftops to run and Kiri at his side, some things, he vowed, would never change.

About the Author

Author photo credit: Ginger G. Prewitt

Kim Vandervort began writing at the age of eleven as an outlet for her overactive imagination. Since then, she has published a number of short stories, and studied with Elizabeth Bear, Cory Doctorow, Debra Doyle, Steven Gould, James Macdonald, Laura J. Mixon, and Patrick and Teresa Nielsen Hayden at the 2007 Viable Paradise XI writer's workshop. Her first two novels, *The Song and the Sorceress* and *The Northern Queen*, were released to critical acclaim. She lives with her two girls, Emma and Zoe, in Southern California. When not writing, she teaches English Composition at California State University, Fullerton, where she earned a Master's degree in Medieval Literature in 1999. Please visit her blog at www.kimvandervort.com.

www.ingramcontent.com/pod-product-compliance
Lightning Source LLC
Chambersburg PA
CBHW020632260626

47157CB00008B/2709